SHINE

Read the Shade trilogy by Jeri Smith-Ready

Shade

Shift

Shine

SHINE

JERI SMITH-READY

SIMON AND SCHUSTER

A simon pulse book

First published in Great Britain in 2012 by Simon & Schuster UK Ltd
A CBS COMPANY

Published in the USA in 2012 by Simon Pulse,
an imprint of Simon & Schuster Children's Division, New York.

1 3 5 7 9 10 8 6 4 2

Simon & Schuster UK Ltd
1st Floor
222 Gray's Inn Road
London
WC1X 8HB

www.simonandschuster.co.uk

Simon & Schuster Australia, Sydney
www.simonandschuster.com.au

Simon & Schuster India, New Delhi

Simon Pulse, and colophon are registered trademarks of Simon & Schuster UK Ltd.

A CIP catalogue copy for this book is available
from the British Library.

ISBN: 978-0-85707-411-9

Printed and bound by CPI Group (UK) Ltd, Croydon, CR0 4YY

To each of you,

for bringing books to life

"A light began to glow and to pervade the cave . . . and to melt the earthen floor into itself like a fiery sun suddenly uprisen within the world, and there was everywhere a wandering ecstasy of sound: light and sound were one; light had a voice, and the music hung glittering in the air."

—George William Russell, "A Dream of Angus Oge"

Chapter One

My phone glowed bright in the dusk-drenched cemetery. But the words on its screen filled me with a dark, heavy dread.

FLIGHT 346: NO STATUS.

I reloaded the web page for my boyfriend Zachary's flight, then forced myself to look away. *Calm down, Aura.* But the black-on-white words left an afterimage floating in my vision.

NO STATUS. Blink. NO STATUS. Blink. NO STATUS.

To obliterate the image, I focused on Logan's headstone beside me. His birth and death dates were etched in granite, seventeen years and one day apart. But the stone would never mark the date and time most important to me and to everyone Logan had haunted.

June 22, nine p.m., when he'd passed on for good. Five minutes ago. After eight months as a ghost, Logan had finally found peace.

A feeling I wouldn't share until this stupid airline's flight-status page started making sense.

The silence was getting to me. On this hot, still evening, no breeze stirred the trees. The two violet-hued ghosts wandering among nearby graves didn't speak to me, maybe mired in memories of their own lost loved ones.

I plugged my earbuds into my phone, which automatically started the music player. It shuffled to a Snow Patrol song Logan and I had always adored: "Make This Go On Forever." For the year Logan was my boyfriend, and for the last three months when we were just friends, Snow Patrol was always our band.

"The final word in the final sentence you ever uttered to me was 'love.'"

My throat lumped as I realized that lyric was true.

"Don't forget me, okay?" Logan's golden-white glow expanded, erasing the violet from his ghostly form.

I laughed, because it was ridiculous. "I'll never forget you. I'll never forget your voice or your face or your dumb jokes. And I'll never forget your love."

He'd hushed me then. I'd thought it was because I'd gotten too cheesy, but now I realized it was because this song lyric had come to life.

Logan filled the silence with one last "I love you, Aura." Amid a final ethereal embrace, his light faded, then winked out.

It already seemed like hours ago. Fear was replacing the peace Logan had left behind. Staring at the phone screen that gave me no answers, I felt more alone than ever.

The bouquet of white roses I'd brought seemed to glow against his dark gray headstone. I pulled out a single bloom to keep for myself. A stray thorn scraped my palm, leaving a thin red stripe but no blood.

The song's last, quiet chord seemed to call to the handful of stars appearing above. They were a pitiful showing compared to the silver-studded sky blanket Zachary and I had lain under last night.

Hmm. Our star-gazing field was only a half hour from this cemetery north of Baltimore. I longed to return to the field, to feel close to Zachary. But first I wanted to be sure his flight had taken off.

My voice mail alert bleeped. I sighed at Aunt Gina's half-hour-old message. Why couldn't she nag me via text like everyone else's mom did?

The music stopped while her message played:

"Aura, it's eight thirty. Don't forget we're getting up at five a.m. for your DMP interview, and we still need to go over what you're going to tell them about Logan's concert. I don't want to be rehearsing in the car on the way to headquarters."

"Fine." I deleted the message and returned to the browser, which I refreshed again.

This time nothing happened. The status page for Zachary's flight was now blank.

"Damn it!" My outburst drew the attention of the nearest ghost, a boy near my age wearing an old-fashioned high-school football uniform, the kind with leather helmets. Since ghosts are captured in the happiest moment of their lives, this guy could've been older than his apparent seventeen when he died. I imagined his "best day ever"— winning the state championship while his favorite cheerleader shook her pom-poms just for him.

The song switched to the swelling opening strains of Arcade Fire's "Ready to Start." The drums slapped my brain and the guitar crunched my nerves.

Propelled by the music, my longing took on an edge. Zachary had been unofficially deported for causing trouble for the Department of Metaphysical Purity. We'd sworn to meet up in Ireland for our birthdays in December, in defiance of every obstacle. But I honestly didn't know if I'd ever see him again.

Hell, I didn't even know if his freaking plane had taken off. All I knew was that in the airport, he and Logan had met for the first and last time.

In a fresh browser window, I brought up the airline's home page again, then thumbed in 346, Zachary's flight connecting through London on his way to Glasgow, Scotland.

The site paused, searching, searching, searching. . . .

My grip on the phone grew slippery with sweat. I fidgeted with the seam of one of my worn black Skechers.

What was I worried about? Was I creeped out by the headstones' lengthening shadows and the slow pacing of the ghosts? Like everyone in the world born after me, I'd lived with ghosts my whole life. They never scared me, unless they turned into the bitter, toxic versions of themselves known as shades, which were still pretty rare.

In the corner of my eye, something moved, dark and gray. I yelped and spun around, yanking out my earbuds. A squirrel skittered away to watch me from the top of a low-set headstone.

"I gotta get out of here," I muttered. "This place is making me crazy." Clearly, since I was now talking out loud to myself.

My phone buzzed, making my heart leap. Maybe it was Zachary with news about his flight.

But then it warbled the ring tone assigned to my best friend Megan. The screen said TIFFANY. I'd replaced my contact names with code versions after the DMP had confiscated my phone last week. Last night Zachary and I'd bought new phones, both red, to communicate solely with each other.

"Hey!" I answered. "Guess who I saw at the cemetery?" Everyone, including me, had thought Logan had passed on at his farewell concert two nights ago.

"Are you still there?" she blurted.

"I was about to leave. Gina's bugging me to—"

"But you're not driving now?"

"No," I said impatiently. "Aren't you gonna guess who I saw?"

"Aura . . . you don't know, do you?"

"Know about what?" My laugh was nervous, even though Megan was known to go Maximum Drama over celebrity breakups and cafeteria gossip. "What happened?"

"You're sure you're not driving."

"Megan! What?"

She paused for the length of a shaky breath. "What was Zachary's flight number?"

The world stopped. Even the nearby ghosts seemed to halt in their tracks.

"Why?" I whispered with what felt like my last exhale.

"It just came on the news. A London flight out of BWI. It took off at eight thirty and—it went down. Flight 346."

My body went numb. My eyes fixed on a stranger's grave across the lane. A pensive angel stared back from her perch on a rose-marble headstone.

"Aura? Are you there? Was that his flight?"

I could barely feel my lips part. "Uh-huh."

"Oh my God." The last word was a squeak.

I swallowed, ready to topple. "Did they—were there any—" The word "survivors" wouldn't come.

"They're saying there was an explosion. It came down in—" Her voice broke. "Aura, I'm sorry. It came down in pieces."

Chapter Two

I couldn't breathe. I clutched the ridge of Logan's headstone to keep myself upright.

Zachary. Zachary dead. Zachary gone forever.

Not possible. Not him, too.

A low drone began inside my head, like the buzz of distant bees. I squeezed my eyes shut, remembering the last I'd felt of Zachary—his soft, dark hair threading through my fingers as we kissed good-bye. Now my fingers felt nothing but the hard granite marker of death.

"Aura, don't drive. I'll pick up your aunt and come get you."

"Unh . . ."

"Promise me!"

"I'm in the cemetery." My voice seemed to come from a mile away.

"Just stay, all right? We'll be there in fifteen."

I hung up, then stared at the phone's blank screen, where I would never again see Zachary's name.

"No." My tone was low and firm, as if this new reality was a naughty dog to be scolded. Zachary couldn't be dead. It didn't feel real.

But when Logan died eight months ago, it hadn't felt real either, even with his body in front of me—and his ghost beside me.

I slid my hand along the front of his headstone, over the quote, FOR WHAT IS SEEN IS TEMPORARY, BUT WHAT IS UNSEEN IS ETERNAL.

Wait.

His ghost.

Zachary could be a ghost, like many people who died suddenly. But he could only haunt the places he'd gone during his life.

I had to see him.

I grabbed my bag and the white rose, then stumbled toward my car, weaving among the graves.

There was no one in the cemetery to stop me, so I drove fast, tires squealing. The car careened down the narrow lanes, banging its bottom on the uneven pavement.

My mind darted through all the places Zachary and I had been together. My house. His apartment. The Inner Harbor. Our stargazing field. He had to be *somewhere*, wanting me to find him.

But if I saw his ghost, that would make it real.

I slammed on the brakes, skidding through the wide iron gates. The car came to a stop, a stone's throw from the busy four-lane road.

I shifted into park, my right arm like jelly. Tremors swept through me, building in waves until even my teeth chattered.

"No. No, no, no, no, no, no, no." My foot stomped the floor with every word. "No, no, no, no, no, no, NO!"

I pressed my forehead to the steering wheel. I couldn't see, I couldn't think, I could barely breathe. A flood of tears was dammed behind my eyes, waiting to drown me.

"Zach . . ."

My phone rang, as if in response. I grabbed it, seized by a delirious hope.

Which died when I saw the name on the screen.

I answered. "Dylan, it's not—I can't talk, I'm—"

The tears came at last, gushing like a cranked-up faucet.

Logan's younger brother spoke slowly. "Oh my God. It *was* Zachary's flight."

I heaved a sob in response.

"Where are you?" he said. "I'll come get you."

"Cemetery. Megan and Gina—coming—"

"Logan's cemetery? That's here in Hunt Valley. I'll be there in, like, ninety seconds."

"Don't hang up. Please."

"I won't." There was a shuffling noise, then the jingle of keys. "Mom, I'm taking the car!" Then Dylan spoke into the phone again. "They don't care, they're so glued to the TV news about the crash. I don't even have my full license yet. Where are my fucking shoes? Swear to God, I can never find anything after the maid people leave. It's not their fault—Mom picks up everything ahead of time. Yeah, seriously, she cleans the house before the cleaning ladies come. Is that insane or what?"

I pressed the phone against my ear. Dylan's rambling chatter felt like my last, thread-thin link to sanity.

"Here they are," he muttered. "I'll put them on in the car." A door creaked in the background. "Hey, are you sure Zachary actually got on the plane? Like, did he call you or text?"

My phone. *The red phone*, our secret connection.

Dylan kept talking as my hands dove into my bag.

" . . . my friend Rashid went to Disney World last week, and he sent me and Kyle and Jamal a brag-text when he was on the plane. Dickweed got to fly first class. Aura, are you there?"

"Hang on!"

Please, please, please, please, please. I yanked the zipper on the compartment that held my red phone. It stuck.

Shrieking, I tore the fabric. The phone tumbled out onto the floor, screen side down.

Dylan shouted from my other phone's speaker. "What happened? You okay?"

"Just wait!" I lunged to grab the red phone, jamming the emergency brake into my gut.

I turned it over.

NEW MESSAGE, it flashed.

With a whimper of hope and fear, I jabbed the screen.

MISSED PLANE THEYR TAKUNG M

My hand covered my mouth. The message was marked 9:01 p.m. Megan had said that Flight 346 took off at eight thirty.

Zachary wasn't on the plane.

"He's alive," I whispered to Dylan.

His astonishment barely registered as I used my other trembling hand to return Zachary's message:

TKING U WHWRE? WHO?

I punched send and waited.

And waited.

And waited.

I waited, speechless, while Dylan told me which street he was on, described the cars he was passing, and yelled at the stupid driver who cut him off at the intersection. He kept talking, as if knowing I needed to hear a human voice.

I was still waiting, staring at the blank screen, when a car pulled in beside me. My red phone was set on silent mode—no ring, no vibrations—so I had to watch for Zachary's reply.

It wasn't coming.

Dylan opened my car door. "If he's alive—" he said into his own phone, then realized what he was doing and hung up. "If Zachary's alive, he'll call you."

"What if he's hurt?"

"Then he'll call from the hospital, or his mom will."

His mom. "Zachary's parents!" Did they get on the plane? Had he lost them? Wherever he was, he needed me.

I rattled the red phone hard, as if I could shake Zachary's location out of the speaker. "Where is he?! What did they do to him?"

"Hey. Hey. Don't break that." Dylan crouched down and took my wrist in a soft grip. "It's gonna be okay."

I lowered my chin, dribbling tears onto the blacktop between us. I wiped my eyes and noticed Dylan still hadn't put on shoes.

His middle toe peeked out of a hole in his white sock.

Another car arrived, brakes squealing. I leaned on Dylan's arm as he helped me up.

Aunt Gina lurched out of the passenger side, her pale face pinched in sadness. She looked like she'd been crying on the ride over but had dried her eyes, thinking she had to be strong for me. Again.

The full relief of Zachary's escape hit me. I ran to her. "He's alive!" My hug knocked her back against Megan's car. "Zachary's alive!"

"What? Honey, how do you know?"

"He sent me a text." I shoved my red phone into her hands.

"He's alive?" Megan was scooting around the hood, her long auburn braid bouncing over her shoulder.

"Yes!" I hurled myself into Megan's arms.

"Ohmigod, ohmigod, ohmigod," she chanted, rocking me back and forth. "Dylan, what are you doing here?"

"Keeping me sane," I told her. "It was his idea to check for a message from Zach."

"Are you sure Zachary sent this?" Gina's voice held lawyerly suspicion.

"No one else has this number. If he'd gone down in the plane, the phone would have gone with him."

"Unless someone stole it from him before he boarded," Gina pointed out.

I leaped to correct her, needing her to believe. "My number's not on speed dial or in the contacts."

"Besides," Dylan said, putting on his sneakers, "why would someone text you that Zachary wasn't on the plane when he really was? Airlines know who's on board and who isn't."

My soaring mood plummeted at the thought of the people who had died. "What about Zachary's mom and dad? You think they—"

"No way." Gina shook her head emphatically. "No parent would leave their kid behind in the terminal."

"Let me see that." Megan snatched the phone from Gina. "Guys, it says, 'They're taking *me*.' Not 'They're taking *us*.'"

"Oh God." Gina pressed her fingertips to her eyes. "So his parents weren't with him when he sent that message."

My throat thickened with fear as I voiced the hardest questions of all. "Then who took Zachary? And where?"

Chapter Three

While Gina drove us home, zooming down the expressway, she told me who to dial from her contacts list. As a lawyer who specialized in wrongful death suits, she knew lots of people in law enforcement. Maybe one of them would know what had happened to Zachary and his parents.

But the cell phone lines were jammed. Everyone in the area must have been calling friends and family to talk about the disaster.

"Let's go to the office," Gina said. "I've got more numbers there, and maybe I'll have better luck with a landline."

She clicked on the blinker, then waved at Megan in the rearview mirror so she knew to follow. Dylan's parents had made him come home, once they realized he'd taken the car.

The radio said that more than two hundred passengers had been in the crash, with no survivors found yet. One report claimed that planes had been grounded across the country in case Flight 346 was part of a coordinated terrorist attack. But another said the crash was due to a mechanical failure.

We slowed at a stoplight. A group of girls my age were crowded around a café's outdoor table, laughing and pointing at a magazine.

Hadn't they heard? Didn't they care that the world had fallen down?

My pulse accelerated as I listened to more contradictory news reports. In one hand I clutched the white rose I'd taken from Logan's grave, and in the other, an iced-tea bottle cap Zachary had given me months ago. A spiral design adorned the cap's underside. I'd found Zachary a matching one, which he'd carried with him as obsessively as I carried mine. The spiral reminded us of the walls of Newgrange, an ancient passage tomb, which we were convinced held the secret to our very natures.

"I'll call my friend in Immigration." Gina was attempting a soothing tone. "Her home number is on my secretary's Rolodex. Maybe she can find out what happened to the Moores." She patted my shoulder. "We'll get it all worked out, I promise."

I nodded, wishing I was driving so I could get us there faster.

Dusk had turned to full dark, so ghosts were visible on the tree-lined sidewalk outside Gina's Roland Park law office. None of these half-dozen violet-hued spirits could see one another. That's why ghosts spend so much time haunting those who *can* see them—meaning, me and everyone younger.

Post-Shifters, they call us. My birth marked the moment of the Shift, though few people knew I was the first. Born a minute before me—but halfway around the world to different parents—Zachary was the last of the pre-Shifters. This was also top secret.

What no one but me and Zachary knew was *why* my birth caused the Shift and made ghosts visible to everyone born after—my own father was a ghost.

I was struck with a new, horrible thought. "The people on the plane," I said to Gina as we got out of the car. "They died suddenly, so a lot of them will be ghosts."

"Just what the world needs," Gina sighed.

Unlike most pre-Shifters, my aunt didn't hate ghosts. She pitied them, thinking it pure torture to be stuck on earth in a desperate search for peace. Many did want to pass on, but others shared Logan's most fervent wish:

To live.

Flaming wreckage, one of several pieces of what was once Flight 346, floated in a Chesapeake Bay tributary. A sheen of jet fuel lay atop the river, so it looked like the water itself was on fire.

Megan and I stared in horror at the wall-mounted television in the law office's conference room. Gina was phoning her colleagues from her secretary's desk outside the door.

The shot switched to another burning airliner piece, engulfing the low, flat roof of a discount store in Dundalk.

"I wonder if the people on the plane knew what was happening," Megan said. "And did they all die when it blew up, or did some live long enough to feel themselves fall?"

I closed my eyes and imagined it. The explosion, a sudden crack, the smell of burning metal and flesh. Then gravity having its way, the earth tugging its creatures into its hard embrace. People crying, screaming as they plummeted. Praying, as if that would break their fall.

Would lovers hold hands and kiss, or would each person be trapped in their own grief and fear? What if a mother had more than two kids—whose hands would she grasp?

Would Zachary's last thought have been of me?

My muscles went rigid, as though bracing for impact. "Zach should've been on that plane." My words were strangled by a sob. "He should be dead."

"But he's not." Megan pulled me into a hug. "The universe would totally suck if it did that to you again."

If it killed another boyfriend of mine, she meant. I clutched her back and wept for Logan, too. My grief for him and my fear for Zachary formed a double-stranded rope of misery that would surely throttle me.

My phone rang. Zero-one-one area code. United Kingdom.

I almost fumbled the phone in my excitement. "Zachary?!"

"Sorry, it's Eowyn."

My heart plunged. For a second, I'd thought a UK area code meant that somehow he'd gotten a new phone. Not that I didn't want to talk to Eowyn Harris, our friend and mentor.

"Aura, what's going on?"

"I don't know." I grabbed a tissue from the nearly empty box in front of Megan. "Zachary's plane went down, but he wasn't on it."

"Oh, what a relief!" Her usually smooth voice turned ragged, making her sound much older than her thirty-four years. "What about his parents?"

"No idea yet." I shoved back my chair to stand, though my legs shook. "And we don't know where Zachary is, just that someone took him somewhere."

"Let me know as soon as you find out." Fear filled her words. I pictured her pacing, twisting her waist-length blond hair around her fingers.

"What about you? Are you safe? Can you tell me where you are?"

"Yes, I'm safe. And no, I can't tell you."

Frustrated, I dragged the tissue over my cheeks. Professor Harris had fled to England to keep the DMP from seizing her Shift research. I assumed the agency's British counterpart, MI-X, was protecting her. Zachary's dad, Ian, had been MI-X's liaison to the DMP before he got lung cancer. Part of his job was to keep those jerks away from me and Eowyn.

Me, because I was the First, and Eowyn, because she'd been at Newgrange on the winter solstice nineteen years ago—the same morning as Ian and my mother were there. Eowyn saw the two of them light up from inside as they passed through the sunrise beam.

"Zachary called me last Friday," Eowyn continued breathlessly. "He said you two didn't get to read all of your mother's journal. I'm so thankful I made a copy."

"Me too." Eowyn had left a trail of clues to locate my dead mother's account of her Ireland trip. Desperate to know who my father was, I'd skipped to the end of the journal, skimming the middle. Then the DMP captured me and Zachary and tried to take us to a remote place in the Pennsylvania mountains called "3A." We escaped, but the journal pages had been ruined as we crossed a river to cover our tracks.

"I told Zachary I'd give him my copy of the journal when he arrived in the UK," Eowyn said, "but who knows when that'll be?"

"Can you mail it to me, or scan and e-mail it?"

"It could be intercepted. I don't trust anyone but you two. I promised your mother that even *I* wouldn't read it." She spoke more slowly. "There's only one thing I worry about more than that journal, and that's you, Aura. Please be careful."

"I will," I said, though it was the last thing I wanted to be. Zachary wouldn't settle for "careful" if I were the one who'd disappeared.

We hung up, and I turned back to the television.

The news channel was interviewing a near-hysterical woman at the airport. The caption said her sister-in-law and niece had been on Flight 346.

They switched to a picture of one of the plane crash victims, a fourteen-year-old girl with a mop of dark, wavy hair and a soccer ball under her arm. Again I was swept with relief for Zachary's survival, then guilt for being happy while so many others were heartbroken.

Gina stepped into the conference room. "Good news: Mr. and Mrs. Moore are alive."

"Yes!" I went to pump my fist, then saw that her hands were locked together, white-knuckle hard. "What's wrong?"

"Zachary and his parents have been detained."

I stared at her. Maybe that word didn't mean what I thought it meant. "Detained? Why? By who?"

"By the FBI. In case Flight 346 was bombed."

"That's insane!" I stalked toward her, almost tripping over the leg of an office chair. "They're not terrorists."

"The government doesn't think the Moores actually put a bomb on the plane, if there was a bomb. Obviously their bags were removed after they failed to board."

"But why didn't they board? Did Ian get sick?" Between his disease and the chemo treatments, the poor man rarely felt well.

"No, it's strange." Gina scratched her head, mussing her short blond waves. "Zachary wasn't at the gate on time."

"That's not like him," Megan said. "He's crazy punctual."

"The authorities suspect he may have gotten information at the last minute. Maybe he was warned about a bombing."

"If he was warned, he would've reported it!" My tongue stuttered with rage and confusion. "There's—there's lots of reasons he could've been late."

"Maybe he had the wrong gate number," Megan offered. "Or maybe he got distracted."

I pictured Zachary in the terminal, checking out the aircraft, discovering fascinating facts about—

Oh no.

Zachary had been distracted, all right. By a ghost. He'd been talking to Logan—maybe even fighting with Logan—instead of getting on the plane.

Which meant . . .

Logan had saved Zachary's life.

Chapter Four

Like most of America—and probably the United Kingdom—Gina and I stayed up late, watching our living room television, craving more news about the crash. The government remained silent regarding the cause, leaving the media to speculate.

One expert claimed that the explosion could've been due to a mechanical problem, maybe a spark in the fuel tank. Another expert argued that the pattern of debris was similar to past airliner bombings. The FBI's tip line scrolled continuously at the bottom of the screen, promising a reward for information about the incident.

Nestled in the crook of the couch's arm, I held close the red camisole shirt I'd worn last night. I'd purposely left it out of the laundry because it still smelled faintly of Zachary.

We switched to the local news, carrying live coverage of an impromptu candlelight vigil on Mount Vernon Place here in Baltimore.

Many people at the vigil held the American stars and stripes and the UK's Union Jack, I guess as a sign of solidarity.

"Can we go to the vigil?" I asked Gina.

"You should lie low tonight, in case the media gets wind of Zachary's detainment and your connection to him. Besides, I'm hoping my contact in Immigration will call me back. It's best if I'm somewhere private when I talk to her."

Under my breath, I cursed my powerlessness. I needed to do *something* other than sit here wallowing in tragedy and imagining what my government would do to suspected foreign terrorists.

I squeezed the balled-up shirt tighter to feel the spiral-adorned bottle cap tucked inside. It was a small, silly thing, but picturing the FBI confiscating Zachary's bottle cap made my fists tighten and throb.

"Aura." Gina broke through my misery. "Before you meet with the DMP tomorrow, we need to discuss what happened at the concert Friday night."

I sighed, knowing I had to come clean. Over the weekend, reports had popped up online, on TV, and in the papers about Logan's "miracle concert." Videos showed him transforming from a ghost into a living person at the moment of the solstice, then singing his new anthem, "Shade," and finally disappearing in a pyrotechnic burst simulating the glow of a ghost passing on.

I sat up, muted the television, and told Aunt Gina the truth.

First, at the moment of the spring equinox, I'd changed Logan from a bitter, dangerous shade to a benign ghost, something no one had ever done.

Second, for seventeen minutes after the beginning of spring *and* summer, including at his concert, I'd turned Logan human again.

Aunt Gina wasn't normally a drinker, but she responded to my tale by pouring herself a huge glass of wine. She seemed too stunned to be mad.

She took a long sip. "Well, I'm glad to finally know the whole story."

Or at least what she thought was the whole story.

Gina examined the glass's crimson depths. "Do you think this power has something to do with you being the first person born after the Shift?"

"Maybe," I replied. "But it probably has more to do with the connection between me and Logan." If I steered her away from my uniqueness as the First, maybe she wouldn't think to ask if Zachary had any corresponding "power" as the Last. Which he did, a secret I'd sworn to keep.

"What should I tell the DMP tomorrow?" I asked her.

"Tell them what you told me, and nothing more." She tapped her pale pink nails against her lips, contemplating. "But let's try to make them think that *Logan* is—was—the special one, not you. He's gone now, so they won't be able to use him to prove you wrong." She went to take another sip. "He *is* gone now, right? He disappeared at the concert?"

When I told her that Logan hadn't, in fact, passed on until a few hours ago, she refilled her half-empty glass.

"Why do I have to drag every detail out of you?" she snapped. "Why can't you just tell me the truth without being interrogated?"

"Maybe it's all the witness stands you've put me on." I worked as a translator for ghosts in many of Gina's wrongful-death suits. It was never boring, but often heartbreaking.

"You could be right," she said sadly. She set down her glass, went into the adjoining dining room, and returned with green votive candles and a book of matches. "We can have our own vigil here."

While Gina prayed, I stared at my candle's fragile flame, holding my breath so it wouldn't waver. The wax pooled around the wick, deep and green as Zachary's eyes. I would never forget the way those eyes had searched for me before he passed through airport security. How they'd crinkled with his smile when he saw me.

And I'd never forget our last moments together in the terminal, playing a goofy game to distract us from our impending separation.

"A'right, then." Leaning shoulder-to-shoulder with me against the wall opposite the security line, Zachary speaks in the low, smooth voice that gives me goose bumps. "Man with the gray backpack. Yank or Brit?"

We're too far to hear people's accents, but close enough to see which pass-port they produce. I suck at this game.

I check out the scuffed shoes of the guy in question. "Yank."

Zachary shakes his head, a wave of dark hair drifting over his temple. "Definitely Brit."

"He's wearing sneakers."

"Meaningless, these days. Look at the slouch of his shoulders, the way he moves forward, head down. He keeps his hand luggage close by, out of other people's way. What does that tell you?"

"That you guys have bad posture and are paranoid about your stuff?"

He chuckles. "Maybe, but it's more that we're very conscious about per-

sonal space." He tilts down his chin to gesture to himself, arms and ankles crossed, elbows splayed. "It took months for me to stand like an American. Casual, at ease in my skin, taking up more room than I need."

Sure enough, the dude with the backpack pulls out a crimson United Kingdom passport instead of the navy blue design of the United States.

"Give me an easy one," I tell Zachary.

"Blonde with the pink shorts."

I laugh and jab my elbow against him. "Figures you'd be looking at her. Definitely Yank. She has a Phillies decal on her carry-on."

"Good eye. Baseball definitely has no appeal over there." He lowers his voice, serious now. "Promise me you'll practice noticing small things about people."

"So I can beat you in Yank or Brit?"

"So you can be safe. The DMP is always watching." He takes my hand. "I wish I could show you more of the tricks I know. I wish I'd not wasted so much time."

"We both did. I'll be careful, and I'll watch everyone. I promise."

His lips tug into a hopeful smile, then he stands up straight. "There's my parents in the queue. Almost time for me to go."

I want to drag him away where his mom and dad and our governments can never find him. "Give me one more. Tiebreaker."

"What about the next couple?"

I study the two people in their late twenties approaching the head of the line, fingers entangled. No wedding rings.

The woman bounces on her toes and tugs on the guy's arm. He watches with affectionate amusement as she does a little dance, twirling her bright blue carry-on by the handle. Then he kisses her forehead and slides his arm *around her back, touching her shoulder blade. His elbow doesn't jut out, and he doesn't place a possessive weight on her.*

"Trick question," I tell Zachary. "She's a Yank, he's a Brit."

"Aye, I think so."

My heart twists as I watch them pull out their passports and prove me right. "I think it's her first time going home with him."

"Aye, perhaps." Zachary's whisper is almost hoarse.

"I think they're really, really happy."

"Aye." Zachary folds my hand between his large, strong ones, and his eyes fill with an unbearable sadness. "They should be."

Gina blew out her candle and wished me good night. I left the television on a low volume, listening to the experts expound and the families grieve.

But I watched only the candle as its green wax dripped over the edge onto the white ceramic plate. I tried to think of nothing but Zachary's eyes. Not the British guy with the sneakers, not the Phillies fan in the pink shorts, not the woman in love who'd never see London.

Somewhere out there, sleeping fitfully or staring at a bare ceiling, Zachary's eyes were still full of life.

And one day, they would rest on me again.

Chapter Five

The next morning I dressed in my hideous navy-blue suit and straightened my hair, pulling it back into a sleek ponytail—sleek until it hit the late June humidity, at least. A night of heavy crying and light sleep had left my cheeks feeling raw and my forehead, thick.

"I ordered breakfast from Donna's Café," Gina said as I slumped into the passenger seat. "Can you run in and get it if I pull up in front?"

"It's six freaking o'clock. My stomach hasn't woken up yet." I put on my sunglasses, though the sun had barely risen.

"We'll hit DC traffic getting to DMP headquarters, so we won't have time to stop later. We cannot be late."

"I know." I raised my voice to make up for its rasp. "I don't have to be happy about it."

"Neither do I," she snapped back.

"Fine."

"Fine." She clicked on the radio and pulled into the street. I slouched, fidgeting with my skirt's pinchy waistband. Bickering with Gina distracted me from my rising panic.

Inside the usually cheery café, the staff were gathered in silence, watching the disaster news on the TV above the coffee bar. I wondered if the whole city had become as paralyzed as I felt.

As the hostess rang up my order, I caught a glimpse of long blond hair streaming by on the way out. The girl stopped short.

"Aura, hi! Wow, what a suit."

"Thanks, I guess."

Amy Koeller was Ridgewood High's junior class president (and probably soon to be the senior class president). She looked her usual perky self, despite the brain-crunchingly early hour.

"Isn't it so sad about the crash?" Amy crumpled the top of her brown paper to-go bag. "One of the victims was a freshman at Ridgewood, Tammi Teller."

"I know. I never met her."

"Me neither. We should hold a memorial service. Or raise money for her little sister's college fund. Or start a circle of understanding." She spied the cardboard March of Dimes fund-raising display on the counter in front of me, and started digging in her pocket.

"A circle of huh?"

"Understanding. So people don't give in to the hate." She slid a dime into one of the charity coin slots. "If it was a terrorist attack, whoever did this must belong to some marginalized group that needs our compassion."

I blinked at her, feeling the full effects of a shitty night's sleep. "Um, the memorial sounds good. But maybe not right away. Let the family have their time."

"Ooh, I know—we'll do it after school starts. That way everyone can come. Aura, you're brilliant!" She hugged me, then gasped. "Sorry I wrinkled your suit. Good luck with your job interview."

"It's not a—okay, whatever." I backed away with my coffees and bag of food, leaving Amy to jot something on a purple sticky-note pad she'd pulled from her pocket.

Gina and I spent the next half hour rehearsing everything I was going to tell the DMP. Once we were satisfied I was ready, I reclined the seat, hoping to nap. To tune out Gina's humming along to classical music, I put in my earbuds, in desperate need of my de-stress playlist.

My eyes shut, and I drifted off.

In my dream, I was in an airliner seat across the aisle from Zachary. His parents sat on the other side of him, his mom in the middle seat and his father at the window, both asleep. All three wore dapper white clothes, like they were going yachting.

The plane began to taxi. The number 346 appeared above every window, in glaring red neon.

"No." I reached for Zachary, but my hand slipped through his arm like he was a ghost. "Get off the plane."

He didn't look my way, only watched the flight attendant as she displayed the yellow safety card, like a kids' librarian sharing a picture book. The front of the card showed a large picture of a plane cracking in half like a loaf of Italian bread.

We taxied faster. I leaped from my seat. "Stop! Get off! Stop the plane!"

The plane didn't stop. It ascended.

Zachary leaned his head back, closed his eyes, and simply said, "Bye."

The world ripped apart in fire and fear.

I jolted awake mid-scream, seizing the door handle.

"Bad dream, hon?" Gina peered at me.

"Unh." I took a sip of coffee to clear my brain, not caring that it was lukewarm. We were stuck in traffic on the Capital Beltway. Ahead, the Mormon temple's golden spire gleamed in the bright sunlight, but the dream dulled my vision with despair.

"—break in the case of Flight 346."

My hand shot out to turn up the radio's volume.

The newscaster's voice was calm and smooth, as if reading a weather report.

"Scotland Yard has uncovered an online posting from one of Flight 346's passengers, a British national. The post announced the young man's intention to suicide-bomb the flight."

My heart froze. Did they mean Zachary? Had someone framed him for this disaster?

"The suspect, aged sixteen, died in the crash."

Oh, thank God. Not that he died, but that it wasn't Zachary.

The newscaster continued, "The online announcement, which has been removed from its social networking site, indicated that the suspect had been convinced by a ghost to carry out the terrorist attack."

"What?" Gina exclaimed.

"Shh." I turned the volume up more.

"—intention was to create hundreds of new ghosts, thereby raising awareness among the living of their own potential for ghosthood. This in turn, he believed, would trigger compassion for the dead spirits among us."

"That's crazy," I whispered. Get people to like ghosts by making more of them?

"A full investigation is underway, but local authorities have reported the suspect's history of mental illness. Still no word on the name or exact origin of the suspected terrorist."

"This is bull." Gina said. "Get my phone. I need to call the office."

I picked up her purse, my stomach somersaulting. If the FBI had another suspect, maybe they'd release Zachary and his parents. On the other hand, if a ghost supposedly inspired the terrorist, and it was revealed that Zachary had talked to Logan before avoiding Flight 346, it would look really, really suspicious. People could say Logan was the bomb instigator and that he'd warned Zachary for my sake.

I found Gina's metallic-pink cell phone but held on to it. "If I tell the DMP that Logan was fully human at the concert, do you think they'll make it public? Will they say an actual ghost could've planted that bomb?"

"No," Gina said. "The last thing they want is hysteria. The DMP wants the public to be afraid of something they can protect them from."

"You mean ghosts."

"Ghosts as we've known them—harmless and incorporeal. They don't want people panicking over something the DMP *can't* protect them from—ghosts that can turn solid, even if only for a few minutes on four days out of the year."

That made sense, I thought, as I gave Gina her phone and watched her speed-dial the law office. Such a revelation would take away the DMP's illusion of power.

Still, I was more nervous than ever. It didn't matter that there was no evidence against Zachary and me. Once the media and the DMP were done with us, the world would know our biggest secret:

As a pre-Shifter, Zachary shouldn't be able to talk to ghosts. He actually *repelled* ghosts on sight, a unique power even his own father didn't know about. But for a few hours after we kissed, he took my ability to see ghosts, and in return gave me his ability to repel them.

If anyone ever found out, Zachary and I would be permanent lab rats.

By the time we arrived at the DMP's Arlington, Virginia, headquarters, Gina's paralegal had called back with a list of ghost-inspired crimes.

Most were vandalism or destruction of property, post-Shifters removing or deactivating "BlackBox" technology. These layers of charged obsidian were installed in the walls of rooms or buildings to keep ghosts in or out. By destroying the BlackBox, sympathizers felt like they were "liberating" ghosts.

Some crimes were more serious, such as assault and battery, where the ghost had a vendetta against the victim. There were even a handful of post-Shifter murderers who'd been egged on by the dead.

But were ghosts a real threat to society, or were these criminals simply wackos who would wreak havoc anyway?

As Gina and I crossed the parking lot toward the dirt-brown DMP headquarters building, I had a sudden thought. "People never become ghosts after a suicide, right? Death has to be sudden and unexpected. So if this alleged suicide bomber becomes a ghost, that'll prove it wasn't him."

"Good point. But if he didn't become a ghost, that doesn't prove it *was* him."

True. Not everyone whose death is a surprise becomes a ghost, and some who do, pass on within seconds or minutes.

In the lobby, we showed our IDs and signed in to get our visitors' badges. I noticed several names on the visitors list ahead of me, all from a company called "SecuriLab."

"Aura!" came a familiar voice across the lobby.

Oh no. I tried to hide my dismay at the sight of Nicola Hughes, DMP flack.

She hurried over, her stylish heels clicking on the polished floor. I'd last seen Nicola on Friday night when she'd fast-talked the media into believing our story that Logan's transformation had been nothing but a magic trick. As grateful as I was for her help, Nicola set me on edge.

She grabbed my elbow and squeed like we were long-lost BFFs. Nicola was maybe ten years older than I was, but sometimes acted like she was in high school. Her bubbliness felt out of place amid the tragedy and Zachary's detainment.

"I'm so glad I saw you!" She tucked her flip-curled dark-brown hair behind her ear. "I'm on my way to a press conference. Things have been insane here since we found out a ghost was behind the bombing. Can you believe it?"

"No," I said flatly.

Nicola offered Gina a wide, perfect smile. "How are you holding up? Things are going to get busy for you, I imagine."

Gina gave her a suspicious look. "How do you mean?"

"At your practice, with this wave of ghost violence. But you probably have Aura to help out full-time this summer."

Gina tensed. I'd tried to find a second job, rather than work forty hours a week at the law office. I got along with my aunt, but no way did I want to spend every day *and* night around her. In the end, my lack of a car kept me from finding nonfamily employment.

"Not quite," I told Nicola. "Just thirty hours a week."

"Oh! Well, as you probably know, the DMP has a limited number of paid summer internships for high school students. Most fill up by February. But my office will gladly open another internship under me for you. Because of your obvious value."

Because I was the First, no doubt.

"Sorry," I told her. "No car." *And no desire to be evil.*

"Our Baltimore office is on the Light Rail line. And the pay is pretty sweet." She delivered the last word in a singsong manner.

"Aura's not interested," Gina said firmly.

"Consider it and call me. About anything. I'm here to help." Nicola gave me her business card as her grin faded into a more genuine expression. "Aura, I know you think the DMP is the enemy, and I admit, a lot of agents are pretty heavy-handed. But we're not the bad guys. Our mission is the same as yours: to understand ghosts. If we work together, we'll find the answers."

I hesitated. The DMP's theories about the Shift would always be imprecise, because they didn't know my father was a ghost. But the knowledge they did have could be useful.

I tucked Nicola's business card into my suit pocket. "I'll think about it."

Chapter Six

Though your interview was previously scheduled," Agent Ritter said, closing the door of our sparse, claustrophobic interrogation room, "obviously there have been significant developments. Last night's tragedy was a game changer."

I tried not to show my disgust at his word choice. This wasn't a game to me, or to the families who'd lost loved ones.

"Of course," he continued, "with this morning's news about the ghost-provoked terrorist act, we can no longer afford to take chances with the dead. The country is feeling a new urgency to protect the living."

The DMP agent sat across the scratched-up linoleum table from me and Gina, heaving the kind of sigh that seems reserved for adults over forty. As he scanned my file, he tapped his ballpoint pen against his temple, where his sandy hair was thinning.

"So." Agent Ritter set a small black digital recorder on the table. "Your aunt says you're ready to discuss what happened at Friday night's concert. We appreciate your cooperation, and we understand it's not easy for you to reveal things about those you love."

I resisted the urge to roll my eyes. *Pander much?*

He clicked on the recorder, and I cut to the chase:

"Logan got his body back during the concert. At the moment of the solstice."

Ritter nodded—he'd obviously seen the online videos. "Did you anticipate this?"

"No."

"Then why was the concert held at that date and time?" He checked his records. "Ten thirty p.m. is very late. Was it a coincidence that the concert began just before the ten fifty-one solstice?"

"Not at all." I kept my focus on the agent, feeling my confidence grow. "We scheduled the concert for that time in case something bad happened and Logan freaked out. We thought if he shaded near the solstice, he could turn right back to a ghost."

"Why did you think that?"

I pressed my lips together to seem like I was revealing a big secret, though the DMP had probably figured it out. They were annoying, but they weren't stupid.

"It happened before. Logan became a shade in January and was gone for months. But then just after midnight on March twenty-first, he came to me."

"As a shade or as a ghost?"

"A shade, but then suddenly he was a ghost again. The next day I realized he'd changed at the moment of the spring equinox. It couldn't have been a coincidence."

I still got a pang of longing at the thought of that night. Logan had taken on human flesh for seventeen short minutes. His skin had been warm and sweet, and his eyes shone blue as they gazed into mine.

Ritter leaned back in his chair, which squeaked at the shift in weight. "Interesting."

"Logan and I hoped he could make this change on the summer solstice, too."

"Were you worried about him shading again?"

"A little. He thought you guys might end the show early." I softened my voice. "His music and his band meant everything to him. Taking that away might've made him mad enough to turn shade."

The agent sounded genuinely sympathetic. "Miss Salvatore, what were—"

"You can call me Aura." I gave Ritter a slight smile. This interview was going so smoothly, it was making me nervous.

"Aura, what were the plans for the end of the concert?"

"The plan was for Logan to go backstage before the finale. His older brother, Mickey, would come out dressed like Logan, with his hair bleached and a fake tattoo of my name on his chest. We thought it would be fun to pretend Logan had come back to life. He said it would make people remember him after he passed on."

"Which he planned to do when?"

"That night, after the concert, with his family and close friends."

Ritter nudged the recorder an inch nearer to me. "And did he?"

"You know he didn't. Your agents were there. Nicola Hughes

helped us come up with a cover story for the media. She said the most important thing was to keep people from believing that ghosts could come back from the dead."

"Yes, our public affairs folks are very experienced at calming the public." His smirk faded. "Aura, when did Logan pass on?"

I squirmed, pretending it killed me to reveal the truth. If they thought I was making a huge sacrifice, they might be less suspicious of what I was still hiding.

"He passed on last night with me, alone in the cemetery near his grave."

"What time exactly?"

"About nine o'clock."

"And you're certain he's gone?"

"He's gone for good." Even though I was happy for Logan, it hurt to say it aloud.

"Hmm." Ritter hoisted a briefcase from the floor beside his chair. "Let's confirm that, shall we?" He lifted the lid with a flourish, then pulled out a small disc of clear quartz.

Gina pointed at it. "Who's the summoner for?"

He set it on the table and tapped its shiny surface. "Logan Keeley was tagged before last week's concert, so he could be retrieved in the event of a disruptive incident."

I was 90 percent sure that Ritter was bluffing. Logan would've told me if he'd been tagged, the way he'd been before testifying at his wrongful death trial. The summoner devices allow ghosts to be called to a place they never traveled in life, such as a courtroom.

Ritter watched my face. He didn't believe my claim that Logan was gone. Even now, I wondered: If Logan could cross the boundary between shade and ghost—and between the dead and the living—maybe he could also cross the boundary between dimensions, or whatever it was that separated this world from the true afterlife.

Ritter slid his thumb under the disc and clicked it on. The clear quartz glowed with a pure white light.

My pulse pounded, waiting for Logan to manifest in the room the way he had at his trial, looking around with a bewildered grin. My breath quickened at the warring fear and hope of seeing him again.

Then the crystal's light dimmed, its signal unreturned. Logan was truly gone.

"Did you think I was lying?" I asked Ritter, my voice hard with emotion.

"I was curious." He placed the summoner back in the briefcase and snapped the lid shut. "Logan Keeley seems—seemed, rather—to be able to do a number of extraordinary things." Ritter counted off on his sunburned fingers, his fake sympathy dwindling. "First, Logan turned shade temporarily on the winter solstice. Yes, we knew about that, though you didn't bother to mention it today. Second, after being a shade for weeks, he turned back into a ghost on the spring equinox. Before Logan, no one had ever un-shaded, so to speak."

I gave the slightest of nods.

"Third, last Friday night, on the summer solstice, he had a solid body for an unknown period of time."

I knew how long: seventeen minutes. The same amount of time it takes the winter solstice sunrise light to trace the floor of the chamber at Newgrange. I hoped the DMP hadn't made that connection yet.

"And finally, last night, Logan Keeley appeared to a pre-Shifter." The agent placed his palms on the table. "To your new boyfriend, Zachary Moore."

My heart stopped, then lurched forward, as if making up for lost beats. I could feel the blood drain from my face.

"That's impossible," Gina said. "Zachary can't see ghosts. No one born before the Shift can."

Ritter answered her, but kept his eyes trained on mine. "We have a witness, a fourteen-year-old post-Shifter, who saw them speaking in the airport."

My mouth was too dry to release the words of protest piling in my throat.

"Impossible," Gina repeated. "The witness is lying."

"I'm afraid the witness cannot lie. She's a ghost."

"Ghosts can't see other ghosts," she scoffed.

"The witness was not a ghost before the flight took off."

Gina's face froze. "This girl died in the plane crash?"

"Yes. Along with two hundred and fourteen other people." Ritter aimed a sharp gaze at me. "So you'd better start talking."

"Absolutely not," Gina said. "My client has been completely forth-coming about the incidents of last Friday night. She knows nothing of this alleged meeting between the two boys."

He ignored her. "Aura, when Logan passed on in the cemetery, did he mention his conversation with Zachary Moore?"

I didn't need Gina's advice to know what to do: shut the hell up.

"The more information you give us," Ritter said, "the less we'll have to extract from Zachary."

A chill zipped among my internal organs. "What do you mean?"

"The FBI has transferred him into our custody."

No. I wanted to beg and scream, but could only emit a feeble "For how long?"

"Aura." Gina's voice held a warning.

"As long as it takes to get answers." Ritter looked at Gina. "His parents are being released today, and they'll be home tomorrow."

"They'll leave their son behind?" Gina asked.

"They have no choice."

My mind whirled. What would the DMP do to Zachary? I'd heard of people being detained for weeks. How would he feel knowing his parents had been forced to abandon him?

"Can I see him?" I asked. "Please?"

"Aura, do not speak. Agent Ritter, let me get this straight." Gina was in full-on lawyer mode. "You're detaining a minor based on the claim of one fourteen-year-old ghost? Even if Zachary could talk to ghosts—which he can't—since when is it a crime to do so?"

"It's not a crime, it's a curiosity. Zachary Moore is a pre-Shifter. We want to know how it happened."

Aunt Gina slammed her hand on the table. "It *didn't* happen. This ghost witness can't lie, but she can be mistaken. I demand you set Zachary free."

"Sorry." Ritter peeled open another folder. "He didn't help his case by threatening the officers who searched him at the airport."

"Threaten how?" I reached for the file, which Ritter snatched away.

"Apparently he said, quote, 'If you touch my mum or dad, I'll punch you so hard you'll have eyes at the back of your head.'"

I would've laughed if I weren't so close to throwing up.

"Charming fellow." Ritter shut the file and pushed it aside. "You certainly know how to pick 'em."

Right then I could've punched someone myself.

"We began to speculate," Ritter continued. "Perhaps it wasn't Logan who was special. Perhaps it's Zachary. As the last person born before the Shift, maybe he's some sort of pre-Shifter/post-Shifter hybrid. Do you know?"

I folded my hands and straightened my back, then put on a blank look that said, *I can keep my mouth shut all day.*

"Know this, Miss Salvatore," Ritter growled. "We'll find out if Zachary Moore is extraordinary. One way or another."

"Did Logan tell you about meeting Zachary?" Gina asked once we were in the car with the doors shut.

I'd used the long walk out of the DMP headquarters and across the visitors' parking lot to decide how to answer. It was an easy choice—I'd promised Zachary I'd never reveal *his* power, much less the fact that we could exchange powers with a kiss.

"Logan couldn't tell me about something that didn't happen. Ghosts can't lie." I jerked the seat belt across my chest.

"But the DMP has a witness."

"You're the one who said their witness was bull." I checked my phone for messages so I could avoid her eyes. "The DMP is making stuff up."

"I wouldn't put it past them." She turned the ignition with a quick wrist snap. "But if this post-Shifter witness could be real, you need to tell me."

"There's nothing to tell." I started answering a text from my friend Jenna. She'd known Zachary was leaving last night and was wondering if he'd been on Flight 346.

HIS FLIGHT WAS EARLIER, I replied. HE'S FINE, THX!

Gina kept talking as she drove out of the complex and onto the tree-lined parkway. "This is a whole new can of worms. If Zachary can talk to ghosts, they'll want to know why. They'll want to know if it has to do with him being the Last. Which leads back to you, as the First." She plucked the phone from my hand. "Listen to me when I'm talking."

I swallowed my anger, though it burned my gut. If Gina got too annoyed, maybe she wouldn't take me to see Zachary's parents at the deportation center. I needed to see the Moores myself. If they'd survived questioning unharmed, maybe Zachary had, too.

"I don't know anything about a meeting between Logan and Zachary," I told Gina in a calm, firm voice. "But Logan is definitely gone now, and I'm really, really scared for Zach." The second sentence was the absolute truth.

Gina's shoulders sagged. "I'm sorry, hon. This must be hard, and I've made it worse by riding you all morning. I'm just trying to protect you."

"I don't know if you can anymore." I turned toward the window so I couldn't see her pain when she realized I was right. "I don't know if anyone can."

* * *

- 44 -

Aunt Gina's lawyer friend Cheryl, who specialized in immigration cases, met us in the lobby of the deportation center in downtown Baltimore.

"You're just in time," she said. "We're leaving for Dulles in fifteen minutes." Cheryl led us to a nearby hallway, which smelled faintly of floor wax. "As their attorney, I have to make sure they catch their flight without further detainments."

"How are the Moores?" Gina asked her.

"Ian's a fighter. So's his son, I hear."

"You haven't seen Zachary?" I tried not to shout. "How do we know he's alive?"

"I've seen the surveillance tape of his arrest. If you ask me, his detention is extremely suspicious."

"Suspicious how?" Gina asked.

"Usually when a minor doesn't board a flight, the airline sends a security officer to search for them, not the FBI. And Zachary was arrested mere minutes after the explosion, before they officially suspected a bombing."

I could barely believe my ears. "So he never should've been detained in the first place? Will they let him go now that that kid confessed to the suicide bombing?"

"I'm afraid it's not that simple, hon." Cheryl touched my shoulder briefly. "Now that he's in DMP custody, I have to go through a whole different process. They claim they have cause to hold him, and I have to prove they don't."

A ball of rage began to form in my core. Zachary had been set up. The plane crash was just an excuse to get him back in DMP hands.

"They can't make Zachary disappear," Gina said, "even if he is a foreigner. We'll get him out, Aura."

"When?"

"Hard to say." Cheryl sighed. "The DMP keeps putting up roadblocks in the court system. It's like they planned this."

They probably had, before grabbing us last week. It could be him *and* me stuck in there.

We entered a warmly decorated office, with plants and a sofa and a calendar with photos of dogs—those gray bird dogs, whatever they're called. Not the harsh, prisonlike atmosphere I was expecting.

Ian and Fiona sat across a desk from a heavyset immigration officer in a yellow shirt and blue tie, who gave me a welcoming smile.

"Aura." Fiona swept me into her slender arms and clung tight. "I'm happy you came."

Happy. It was so like her—so like Zachary—to gloss over the worst hurt. Though he'd acquired his dad's Scottish accent, charm, and bluster, his mother had bestowed her endless English patience.

"Are you guys okay?" I realized my question's stupidity. "I mean, are you hurt?"

"We're fine, Aura." Ian stood unsteadily, gripping the back of his chair and looking much older than his fifty-eight years. It seemed like he'd aged since I'd seen him yesterday. "It's no' us you should be worrying about."

"Have you seen Zachary?" I asked him.

"Aye, too briefly." He looked past me at his wife. "I dunno how we walked out of there. How could we leave our son behind to be—" Ian coughed twice, lowering his head and putting out a hand to stop us from helping him. "He's a brave boy, Aura. A very brave boy."

"I know." Zachary had stood up for me after we first met, when I was harassed by my classmates about Logan's death. He'd stepped between me and an armed DMP agent when we were detained last week. And he'd caught me when I almost fell off a cliff racing to escape, though I could've easily knocked him off with me.

It was my turn to be brave for him.

"What can I do?" I glanced at the immigration officer, wondering how much we could say in front of him.

"Just keep yourself safe." Ian pressed his hand on my shoulder to emphasize the last word.

The sadness in his eyes made my own feel full and hot. "I can't believe they're making you leave him behind."

"Don't worry about us. Here." He pulled me close and patted my back. I put my arms around him, gasping at how frail he felt.

Then Ian whispered, "Someone will be contacting you shortly."

I hoped he meant someone from MI-X who would not only help me, but also get Zachary released.

"We'll call you the moment we arrive," Fiona said.

"Can't MI-X do something?" Gina asked. "They're DMP's counterpart. You'd think there'd be a mutual respect or agreement that—"

"Respect?" Ian's rough voice rose again as he let go of me. "The DMP thinks we're their servants, not their partners. But they're frightened bairns shrieking at every bump in the night. I should know, I—"

He grimaced, then erupted into a hacking cough, longer and

stronger than before. Fiona helped him sit while he fumbled in his pocket for a handkerchief. The immigration officer drew one from the pocket of his own jacket slung over his chair.

"I'm sorry." The officer held out the handkerchief.

"Sorry?" Ian's green eyes filled with fire. "'Sorry' doesn't give us our fuckin' son, now, does it?"

"Darling . . ." Fiona touched his shoulder.

"Ach." He bent over, elbows on his knees, hands clasped at his forehead. Slowly he dragged his thumbs over his salt-and-pepper brows to calm himself.

My heart crumpled. I'd seen Zachary make that exact gesture a hundred times since his dad had been diagnosed with lung cancer. Sometimes in history class I'd catch him doing it and have the worst desire to stroke the angles of his face, smooth every worry line until his eyes filled with peace.

I knew it destroyed Ian to not be able to provide for his family— and worse, to be the one who needed caretaking. Despite the power he once wielded in MI-X, he was helpless to protect his own son.

If Zachary wasn't released soon, this ordeal would surely hasten Ian's death. And if Zachary couldn't be at his father's side at the end, my kindhearted boyfriend would be consumed by misery and rage. Like a living shade.

I'd do anything to stop that from happening. Anything.

Chapter Seven

"A ura." On the phone, Megan sounded like she'd been crying. "Sorry I'm running late."

"What's wrong?" I took a seat on the city bus headed down Charles Street. "Is it Mickey?" Megan's morose boyfriend, Logan's older brother, was the usual cause of her tears.

"It's everything else." She sniffled. "We're doing three viewings tonight for Flight 346 victims. That's why I can't meet you on time."

"Did you have to talk to their ghosts?" At her family's funeral home, Megan translated dead people's wishes for their services.

"One of them, this fourteen-year-old girl. She said she won't pass on until her little sister stops crying. Sometimes I hate this job."

Megan rarely complained to me about work. She couldn't wait to take over the business one day and make it more ghost-friendly, catering to goths and punks or anyone who wanted drama with their final exit.

"I never cry when strangers die," she told me as my bus rumbled past row homes in various states of repair—some boarded up and falling apart, some with full flower gardens and painted porches. "But I can't stop thinking about this crash. On TV it's nothing but Flight 346, Flight 346. I feel like I know every person on that plane, even the ones who aren't our clients."

"Yeah," I said sympathetically, though I'd tried to avoid OD'ing on disaster coverage. Maybe it was callous, but I was too worried about the living to mourn the dead.

I thought about the fourteen-year-old girl Megan had mentioned. Could she be the DMP witness who saw Logan and Zachary talking in the airport?

"How was your interrogation?" Megan asked.

I was relieved to hear she knew nothing about Zachary from watching the news. Gina said the DMP wouldn't release his name to the press, supposedly because he was a minor. But I wondered if it was really because they didn't want the public scrutiny.

An old guy in a floppy hat got on the bus and sat in front of me. I looked around, but didn't see any seats away from people who might hear. "I can't talk about it."

"Then I'll come to your house tonight—with mochas."

After hanging up, I frowned at my phone. If the DMP had bugged it, I couldn't have a private conversation with anyone, no matter who was around.

A sudden thought slapped me so hard, I almost yelped.

Eowyn Harris called me last night. On this *phone.* The one the DMP had probably bugged. That meant they could trace the call and track her down. Steal my mom's journal. . . .

And find out my dad was a ghost.

I stood at the Flight 346 vigil site at Mount Vernon Place, inhaling the scent of fresh-cut flowers and trying to calm my fears.

Photo posters of the deceased were taped to the gilded wrought-iron fence encircling the Washington Monument. The pillar was about a third the height of the more famous monument in DC, but topped with a statue of George Washington. Every December, Baltimore decorated it with white holiday lights, then purple lights when the Ravens made the playoffs. Now, it was draped in black.

Traffic rumbled over the plaza's cobblestones, but I could hear the prayer group gathered on the north side of the monument. They were singing both national anthems, though most were merely humming "God Save the Queen," which had the same tune as "My Country 'Tis of Thee." Baltimore and London would be forever linked in mourning.

A college-age African-American guy wandered closer to where I stood. The piles of flowers and teddy bears created a wide moat, so he had to bend forward to read the posters' captions. He adjusted his glasses and squinted at a heart-shaped piece of pink construction paper that read in a child's scrawl, *We Love You, Miss Korman.*

The guy pulled out a small white flag with a red cross. He crouched down and inserted it next to an American flag, between two gilded whorls in the wrought-iron fence.

"What kind of flag is that?" I asked him.

He looked up at me, startled. "Hmm?"

"Which country? Switzerland?"

His face broke into a warm smile. "It's England, love."

Okay, so he wasn't African-American, he was, uh, African-English? Or maybe just English.

"Sorry," I said, "I didn't know England had its own flag. I figured they used the Union Jack."

"That's for the United Kingdom, which England is part of, along with Wales, Scotland, and Northern Ireland."

"Well, I knew *that*. And I knew Scotland had its own flag. The Saint Andrew's Cross."

He gestured to the English flag. "Ours is Saint George's Cross. How do you know so much about Scotland?"

"My—" I stopped, not wanting to reveal too much. "My English class. We studied Robert Burns."

"Ah." He started reciting one of Burns's poems, in an even worse Scottish accent than mine. I couldn't help wonder what Zachary and his dad would—

Wait. Thinking of Ian reminded me what he'd said today. *Someone will be contacting you shortly.* Maybe this was that "someone."

But as much as I liked the direct approach, it seemed dumb to blurt, "Hey, are you a secret agent?" So I checked out his clothes to see if anything screamed "spy." Which of course it wouldn't, if he were a good one.

"What did you think of Wee Robbie?" he asked.

His question jolted me out of my thoughts. "Who?"

"The poet?"

"Oh. I couldn't understand a single word on the page, but when the teacher had—" I stopped myself from mentioning Zachary. "When she had a, um, recording of an actual Scotsman reading it, it made sense. Except the words that weren't in English."

Zachary had hammered home the point that Scots wasn't a dialect but a language sprung from others like French and Norwegian, in the same way that English mostly evolved from Latin and German. I longed to hear one of his patient, pedantic explanations right now.

The Englishman stepped closer, avoiding a bouquet of red and white daisies leaning over into the sidewalk.

"Did you lose someone in the crash?" he asked softly.

Hmm, if he's MI-X, this could be a test. See how much I'll give away about myself.

"No. Did you?"

"I'm here in the name of international solidarity." He shifted his feet. "Talking of which, fancy a cup of coffee?"

I followed his gesture to see a violet-and-black NEW LOCATION! banner over the Free Spirit Café, a local coffee shop where ghosts took people's orders and live humans delivered the food and drink. It was popular with pre-Shifters and their little kids, but no one I knew hung out there.

"We just met." I was not going to make this easy for Spy Boy. Not until I knew that's what he was, and not some random college dude chatting me up.

"True, but by the time we have coffee, that 'just met' will be a bit further behind us."

"I can't. I have—" *No, don't say "boyfriend."* "Work in the morning."

"It's only quarter past eight."

"And in an hour, you'll still be too old for me."

"I'm only seventeen," he said.

"More like twenty-two, I'm guessing."

His mouth opened, then closed. "I thought I was getting it right."

"Getting what right?"

His tone turned pure business. "Have coffee with me, and we'll discuss how we can help Zachary Moore."

"Is this decaf?" the thirty-whatever mom asked the human waitress as I took a window table with the English stranger.

The waitress checked the ticket. "It doesn't say decaf."

"I can't have caffeine." The customer slammed the mug onto the waitress's tray, almost spilling it onto her young daughter's head. "It makes me tense."

I grimaced across the table at my companion. "I hate these places."

"I know," he said. "Er, that is, it seemed best for us to chat somewhere we wouldn't be seen by any of your usual acquaintances."

I wanted to ask him a million questions, starting with, "How'd you know I never come to this coffee shop?" but more important, "How do we help Zachary?"

"Hello!" A ghost with short hair and straight-cut bangs appeared beside our table. "I'm Tracy! Welcome to the Free Spirit Café." She beamed at me. "Can he see me or just you?"

"Just me." Maybe Mystery Dude looked younger than I thought. The woman in the corner was still berating the human waitress.

"Tell that stupid ghost I'll have her fired if she doesn't shape up."

Ex-Tracy clicked her tongue. "God, her again. She's one of those pre-Shifters who comes in here all the time for the sole purpose of mocking ghosts. So what can I get you?"

I placed our orders quickly to make her go away.

When she vanished, I said, "We're alone."

"Right, then." The English guy opened a crimson three-ring binder. "You're probably wondering who I am and who I work for."

"From your accent, I'm guessing you work for MI-X, and your name is something über-British like Nigel."

"Close. Simon." He reached across to shake my hand while sliding a folded black leather badge holder across the table. I opened it, noting his full name, Simon Wheeler, then examined the MI-X logo. A three-headed serpent with the body of a dragon reared fiercely in the center of a circle topped by a crown. The Latin motto, *Verum ex arcanum*, curled beneath the hydra's talons.

"What's that mean in English?"

"Roughly? 'Truth from secrets.'"

I found the translation comforting but creepy.

"Please tell me good news on Zachary." I gave back the badge. "You're cracking skulls to set him free?"

"MI-X is doing all it can, at every level." His dark eyes softened. "It could take a while."

"What's a while? Days? Weeks?" When Simon glanced away, I nearly shouted. "Months?"

"I'm so sorry."

My hands tightened on the polished table edge. "You asked me to have coffee so we could talk about how to help him. So how do I help him?"

"In the immediate future, the best way to help him—or to not make things worse, at least—is to keep yourself safe. Don't do anything foolish."

"What's that mean? Don't do anything at all?"

"Yes, for now, during this chaos. Remember, it's only twenty-four hours since the crash. Your role is more long-term."

"Here you go!" The waitress delivered our cappuccinos and biscotti. Simon drew four sugar packets from the dispenser and gave me two.

How did he know I took two sugars? How long had he been watching me?

He pulled a padded envelope from his backpack. "Your new phone. Use it only to call us in MI-X. No one else has the number."

I peeked inside the envelope—the phone was red, which gave me a pang of longing for Zachary. It also reminded me:

"You guys should check on Eowyn Harris. She called me on a phone the DMP might have bugged."

He grimaced. "Oh, that's not good. I'll alert my supervisor so MI-X can remove her to a safe house. Do not attempt further contact with her."

I seethed in silence as he placed a hushed, hurried phone call. Eowyn had been my and Zachary's best source of information about the Shift, and now she'd be out of reach.

"Who is your supervisor?" I asked after he hung up.

"Minerva Wolcott. She's MI-X's new DMP liaison."

"So your boss is Ian Moore's replacement, which is why you're following me."

"Precisely. I'll be enrolling in your high school as an exchange student."

"How old are you?"

"Twenty-two. As you guessed."

His face could pass for eighteen, but his demeanor was way too mature for a high school student. Then again, people might think he was just being English.

Simon swirled his spoon through the cappuccino. "It's probably best if we avoid each other at school, lest the other students wonder why you always hang out with foreigners."

"Let me get this straight. I have to (a) shut up, and (b) ignore you. Then Zachary will magically be released? This is bullshit, Simon."

"There is something else you can do." He let the spoon drip into his cup before setting it on the saucer. "Should you encounter information that would damage the DMP, please let us know. It could give us the leverage we need to gain Zachary's freedom."

My pulse jumped with hope. "What kind of information? Where do I get it?"

"That's up to you." He dunked his biscotti with a calm, elegant maneuver, again stretching out the tension. "The key is to ensure that they see you sympathetically. If you continue to piss them off, all avenues of information could close." He bit the biscotti, then wiped his mouth with the violet paper napkin. "Things could get dangerous."

My spine chilled. "Dangerous for me?"

"Some elements within the DMP are looking for any excuse to, well—disincentivize you, as we say in the business."

My mind replayed his words in a rapid panic.

"Disincent—what, kill me? Why?"

"Your birth coincided with the Shift. Both agencies know it. What we don't know yet is whether your birth *caused* the Shift."

Yes, it did. "No, it's a coincidence."

He angled his head in an *oh please* posture. "Point being, if your birth did cause the Shift, perhaps only your death can end it."

I'd never heard anyone but me say that out loud.

Simon continued, "The DMP's unstated mission is to rid the world of ghosts, or at least make it so they can't communicate with the living."

"Why are they so afraid?"

"Their fear isn't entirely irrational. Almost any sensitive government information—weapons development, diplomatic strategies, troop movements—could be revealed by a ghost who was in the right place at the right time."

"No, it couldn't. Military bases and government buildings have BlackBox to keep that stuff safe from ghosts."

"But what happens when a person with a top secret security clearance dies and becomes a ghost? He won't forget everything he knew in life, will he?"

Simon had a point. Because ghosts were almost everywhere, and since they couldn't lie, post-Shifters had to live painfully honest lives. A few weeks ago the Ridgewood prom prince broke up with the prom princess because a bratty eleven-year-old ghost saw her making out with a guy from Gilman (our archrival).

But the honesty wasn't all bad, and it affected more than post-Shifters. In the four years since ghosts had started testifying at murder trials (some of which I'd translated for), the homicide rate had plummeted. Organized crime rings were disintegrating, since bosses could no longer use the fear of "getting whacked" against their own members. Murders that did occur were either complete stealth jobs or crimes of passion.

So in our future world of ghosts and post-Shifter adults, governments would have to be as honest as their citizens. No wonder they were scared.

"But if they wanted to kill me"—I tried not to stutter—"they could've done it last week when they captured me and Zach." I glanced at the window, painted black to keep the restaurant dark enough to see ghosts. "Heck, they could do it any minute."

"True. I honestly don't know why they haven't taken you out." He picked up his cappuccino. "But I can only assume you're more useful to them alive than dead."

"For now, you mean."

Simon's cup stopped halfway to his lips. "Yeah. For now."

Chapter Eight

I couldn't sleep that night, waiting for Zachary's parents to call me. Their plane would land in Glasgow in early morning, which meant two or three a.m. here. Would they call me right away, or wait until they thought I was awake? Wouldn't they know I'd stay awake until they called?

The first thing I'd ask Ian was whether I should trust Simon, and whether the young agent's warning could be true. I still had trouble believing that the Department of Metaphysical Purity—or at least some part of it—wanted to kill me. But maybe MI-X knew worse things about the DMP than I did.

Giving up on sleep, I slipped out of bed and put on an old pair of jeans and a long-sleeved T-shirt. It was warm out, but where I was going, there'd probably be mosquitoes.

Carrying my shoes, I tiptoed down the hall past Gina's room. As

I reached the stairs, she gave an extra-loud, snorty snore, the kind that made me wonder if she had sleep apnea and would have a heart attack one night and never wake up. Not that I'm morbid much.

I stood on the top step, toes hanging over and twitching in the air as I decided what to do. Finally, I went to her door and pushed it open.

She came instantly alert, mom-style. "Yeah! What's wrong?"

"I can't sleep."

"Aw, hon. Did you want to sleep in here with me?"

"No, thanks. I'm not tired." *I'm also not four years old.* "I need to take the car."

She squinted at the red digits of her nightstand clock. "It's midnight. Where are you going?" When I told her, she shook her head. "That's ridiculous."

"It's safe up there."

"Maybe. But driving between here and the highway is definitely not safe for a girl on her own."

"I could've snuck out."

"You think I don't keep track of the odometer? That's the first thing they teach in Surviving a Teenager 101."

I sighed at her patronizing joke. "Gina, I need to go. Can't you understand why?"

"Of course I can." She threw back the sheet. "Which is why I'm coming with you."

On our way to Farmer Frank's wheat field, where Zachary and I had spent one night a month mapping stars for Eowyn, I found the nerve to ask Aunt Gina about my dad.

Indirectly.

"Why did my mom want to go to Ireland so bad? And why Newgrange at the solstice? Did she hear about it and think, 'Wow, that sounds cool'?"

"Sort of." The blue dashboard light cast shadows on Gina's smile lines. "You remember that guy Anthony I told you about? The one who—"

"Took care of Mom the first time she had cancer." *And who you had an affair with.*

"Right. He used to teach European history at Saint Joe's. He'd been to Newgrange—not for the solstice like your mom, but on a summer tour of Ireland the school did with some students. By the way, put that on your list of colleges. With your grades, it'll be a solid safety school."

"Uh-huh." I hadn't yet told Gina that if by some miracle I could afford a college I couldn't commute to, it would be a lot farther away than Saint Joseph's University in Philadelphia. More like University of Hawaii or Arizona. Somewhere the stars were even brighter than where we were going tonight.

After marveling at the clear, dark sky above the field, then breaking into a sneezing fit from the pollen, Gina retreated back inside our car to read a book.

I spread a blanket on the grass next to the field, in the exact spot Zachary had laid it Saturday night, then sat on it off-center, as though he would join me.

Which he did, but only in my memory.

* * *

We lie on our backs, staring up at the stars. Zachary grips my left hand firmly inside his right, as if I'll float away into the sky.

"See that there?" *With his free hand, he points to the far right stars of the Big Dipper, then traces through Draco up to Cepheus.* "I declare a new constellation—Principal Hirsch's head."

"Wow, yeah, it's got his hairline and comb-over and everything. Okay, starting with Deneb, going over to Andromeda's butt, and then all of Pegasus? That is now officially Guy Getting Parking Ticket."

"Brilliant," *he said.* "I see it, I do. But sadly, that overlaps with my signature constellation, Cinnamon-Raisin Bagel."

"You have your mythology, I'll have mine."

"It's best we agree, so when I'm far away, we can see the same things in the sky. It'll be like now, only without the snogging."

Like now, only without the happiness.

"The snogging's important." *I roll on my side and tug on the tail of his dark green polo shirt, wanting to slip my hand under but stopped by a lingering, inexplicable shyness.* "It's the part we didn't have for so long."

"It was torture." *He turns his head to face me but stays on his back.* "And if it's all we think about for six months, we'll die of frustration."

The huskiness of his voice makes me want to risk frustration-death just to kiss him right now. I'm already regretting our decision to wait until December to make love. Out here, under the stars, it'd be perfect.

Perfect, except for the rampant mosquitoes and the fact that if a car drove by on the nearby lane, we'd have about ten seconds' warning to get dressed.

He looks at the sky again, long lashes silhouetted against the wheat's pale background. "That's why we need the distraction of Cinnamon-Raisin Bagel."

"You mean Guy Getting Parking Ticket."

Zachary laughs. "A'right, then. Whatever you want."

"Whatever I want?" I snuggle against his shoulder. "Anything?"

He curls his arm around me. "Anything. When we've finished our sky."

But he's not watching the sky anymore. He rolls on his side and presses his forehead to mine. Our bodies meld together, head to toe.

"We can't see the sky now," I whisper.

"Yes, we can." He kisses the spot between my brows. "Close your eyes."

I do, and imagine the darkness above us. Lying here with Zachary, I've never felt so connected to the sky and the earth.

"Now, then. The beauty of my bagel constellation is that the Milky Way runs through it, making the streaks of cinnamon."

I see it in my mind, the lacy arm of our galaxy stretching in a north-south arc over the sky. "I can't see the Milky Way from the city. Too much light pollution."

"Then you'll have to come out here to look at it." He slides the backs of his fingers down my arm, creating a tingling path. "I'll go out to the countryside when I can. If it's late, I'll phone you so we can see it together."

The idea warms me almost as much as his touch. "Do you know where you'll be living?"

"I hope we can stay in Glasgow for Dad's treatments. It's been years since we lived there. I miss it." He sighs, fluttering the hair at my temple. "But not as much as I'll miss America."

His words make the air seem heavy. It'll be hard for him to get a visa to come back, after the trouble he made for the DMP last night, diverting them so that Logan's concert could continue.

Despair settles into my stomach. If I want to see Zachary, I'll have to *go overseas, maybe even stay there. I'm dying to travel, but this is my home.*

I trace Zachary's thumb with my own, trying to memorize the lines of his knuckles and correspond them to the lines of the constellations. "You win. I'll give you Cinnamon-Raisin Bagel, as a going-away gift."

He chuckles, his chest vibrating against mine. "Thanks."

"As a bonus, I'll give a special companion constellation." I shift half onto my back, let go of his hand, and point to a random group of stars. "A toaster."

"Ah, brilliant." His fingertips glide slowly up my raised arm. "Can I tell you a wee secret?"

"Ooh." His secrets were rarely shared and always juicy. "What is it?"

"I prefer my bagels untoasted."

I bring my arm down, jabbing an elbow into his ribs. Zachary cries out, half laugh, half oof.

We start to wrestle, and he lets me win. Then we start to kiss, and we let each other win.

For tonight, we are finished with the sky, and the earth, and everything but each other.

I stretched my arms above me, feeling strength return. Hearing Zachary's voice in my memory was like food for my mind and soul. In the same way I couldn't take an exam on an empty stomach, I hadn't been able to think straight all day. But now my head was starting to clear, and for the first time since the crash, my thoughts weren't drowned in panic.

I spoke to the stars. "What do I do, Zach? How do I save you?"

No one answered, of course. No one could, but me.

If Zachary were in my shoes, he'd work the problem logically, eliminating the implausible choices until the right one remained. (If he couldn't fight his way to get to me.)

Simon had told me not to do anything foolish. He'd also said to learn new information. But what could I discover that highly trained special agents couldn't?

Then it hit me. *I can talk to ghosts.* From my work at the law firm translating for the dead—not to mention having had a ghost boyfriend for months—I could calm almost any spirit long enough to find out what I needed.

I didn't yet know exactly how to end Zachary's misery. But I had an idea where to start.

Chapter Nine

Zachary's parents called me on my "private" red phone the following morning while I was working at my aunt's office. Ian confirmed that Simon had been assigned to protect and assist me, but I couldn't get far enough away from my coworkers to ask about the DMP's death wish for me.

Knowing that the Moores were safe, and that Ian was linked into MI-X enough to know about Simon, made me feel less alone, and more confident for what I was trying next.

That night I arrived at the McConnell Funeral Home to find the front door locked, with a paper sign taped to it.

TONIGHT'S VIEWINGS ARE PRIVATE. PLEASE RESPECT THE WISHES OF THE VICTIMS' FAMILIES.

Under the plea were details for the Flight 346 public memorial service, to be held at the World Trade Center Plaza at the Inner Harbor the following night.

Despite the announcement, dozens had gathered in the funeral home parking lot holding candles and laying flowers. As I peered through the glass door, I heard the first strains of "Amazing Grace" begin behind me.

Mrs. McConnell was hurrying through the lobby, looking harried but still dressed to perfection in a tailored gray suit. I tapped the glass, and she trotted over to unlock the door.

"Aura, thanks for coming to help." She ushered me in, giving a polite wave to the mourners. "Megan's in the office assembling programs. Our folding machine broke, and we can't have them done at the copy shop, in case details of the funerals are leaked to the public."

"Makes sense. I'm glad I could help." I felt a little guilty, since that wasn't the main reason I was here.

She sped off, and I headed for the office, passing through the lush foyer, where even the walls were upholstered in silk. Down the hallway lined by viewing rooms, pastoral paintings with gilded frames loomed over tables accented with lifelike decorative plants.

There'd been a time when I would often drop by the funeral home to visit Megan at work. Death hadn't bothered me much back then, and since the building was almost totally BlackBoxed, it had felt like a ghost-free sanctuary.

Then Logan died. He'd appeared as a ghost right after his death, but then disappeared. Everyone thought he'd passed on. So the night of his viewing here, looking at his dead body, I thought I'd never see him again.

Now Logan really was gone. Videos and photos were all I had left. And the memories, which stabbed at me as I veered away from the room where he'd lain on display.

I knocked on the office door. It opened a crack to reveal the darkness inside.

"Is she here?" I whispered.

Megan placed a finger to her lips, then stepped back and swung the door wide.

"Oh my God," said the fourteen-year-old girl on the sofa. "You weren't kidding. It's Aura freaking Salvatore."

Through her violet glow, a clear quartz summoner disc shone on the sofa's center cushion. The funeral home used it so that their ghost clients could relate their final wishes.

I stepped closer to see her better. The design on her shirt came into focus: the skull-and-shamrock logo of Logan's punk band, the Keeley Brothers. "Tammi Teller."

"Yeah," she sneered at me. "How'd you know?"

My boyfriend is in DMP custody, thanks to your big mouth. "You've been on TV a lot."

"I'm famous now. All I had to do was get on a plane that landed, like, seven hours too soon." She crossed her ethereal arms. "I can't believe I'm in the same room with Logan Keeley's slutty ex-girlfriend."

I gaped at her. Out of all the people who could've held Zachary's fate in her hands, it had to be one of Logan's most fervent fangirls?

I had more important business with ex-Tammi than arguing about my relationship with her idol. I needed to know what she'd seen at the airport between Zachary and Logan—and what she'd told the DMP. I needed to know how bad it could be for Zachary.

"We all loved Logan," Megan said sweetly.

"Ooh, guess what?" Ex-Tammi beamed at her, then pointed to her own T-shirt. "I was in the front row Friday night. Logan touched my hand." She gazed at her palm. "He looked into my eyes and told me to meet him—" She stopped, then scowled, realizing she literally couldn't tell a lie. "No, he didn't."

"Did you see him after that?" I asked her.

Ex-Tammi's mouth twisted, like she didn't want to answer. But I'd asked a direct question, and she was too new at the ghost thing to realize she could simply say nothing.

"In the airport," she said, "talking to Zachary, that Scottish guy from our school. By the way, I can't believe you went with Zach after he hooked up with Becca Goldman on prom night. Logan never would've done that to you."

My cheeks flared. "Zachary wasn't my boyfriend at the time, and anyway, it's none of your—"

"So, Tammi," Megan broke in, "did you go to the police?"

"No, I told my best friend, Carla, when I haunted her. She told the police for the reward money. Then Carla tricked me into coming back to her house. That's where the DMP tagged me."

"Nice friend," Megan said.

"Seriously. They told Carla they'd take back the reward money if she told anyone I'd seen those guys."

So the DMP definitely didn't want the public to know they were holding Zachary. Interesting.

"Have you told anyone else?" I asked her.

"No, I wouldn't rat out Logan." She watched her sneaker soundlessly scuff the carpet. "I shouldn't have told Carla, but when she saw me as a ghost, she started crying. I wanted to tell her something happy. And I was sooooo excited to see Logan, like, in the wild. He's incredible."

"He sure was." Megan sat beside her on the sofa. "So what exactly did Logan and Zachary do in the airport? Did they argue?"

"Not really. They seemed nervous, but basically cool with each other."

I ached with envy to have seen Logan and Zachary together, forging a peace at last. But that would've been impossible, since Zachary and I couldn't see the dead at the same time. One of us always wielded that ghost-repelling power.

Ex-Tammi examined her chipped black nail polish as she told the story. "My mom and I were eating in that bar-type restaurant, where it was dark enough to see ghosts. Logan came up to Zachary there, which totally weirded him out—Zach, I mean. Anyway, then after his parents went to the gate, he ditched them to go talk to Logan."

"Where?" Megan asked.

"That was the weird thing. They went all the way back out into the main part of the airport, past the security line. So I had to stop following them."

Apparently there was no private place to talk in the international terminal. It explained why no one could find Zachary in time for the flight. But it must've made him look even more suspicious to the authorities.

"Were they talking while you were following?" I asked her.

"Yeah, but they shut up when I got close. I guess they could tell I was a post-Shifter. And Logan didn't recognize me." Her pierced lower lip jutted out in a pout. "I wish I'd been like Zachary and made me and my mom miss the flight."

"Aww, it must've been really scary," Megan said.

Ex-Tammi hunched her shoulders, squeezing her hands between her knees. "All I remember is a huge noise, then it was really hot, and then nothing. I guess I was one of those people who got ripped apart." She gave Megan a nervous glance. "I heard there's not much of us to bury."

Megan seemed like she was about to cry again, so I spoke up. "We're really sorry you died, Tammi. And your mom."

She ignored me and spoke to Megan. "Is my mother a ghost, too? No one I know has seen her."

"She didn't come when I called her," Megan said gently. "About the funeral plans."

Ex-Tammi looked relieved. "I hope she's not a ghost. It sucks. Logan made it seem so fun."

"It wasn't always fun for him," I said. "Most of the time he felt pretty bitter."

"Then why did he stay for two hundred forty-seven days?"

It creeped me out that she knew *that* bit of Logan Keeley trivia. "He had unfinished business."

"Yeah, like a girlfriend who didn't appreciate how awesome he was."

"I appreciated him," I said in a steady voice. "I loved him."

"*Loved.* I still love him. I'll always love him."

"You didn't even know him."

"Aura." Megan tilted her head. "Remember Rule One?"

I gritted my teeth and cooled my temper. Rule One of being a rock star's girlfriend: no catfights with groupies. It was beneath us, especially since Logan and Mickey weren't the type to sleep around.

I changed the subject. "What about you, Tammi? Do you have unfinished business?"

"I thought I wanted to see my funeral. But I can't watch my dad and sister cry anymore."

Sympathy thawed my anger a little, and I wished this girl could find peace. But if ex-Tammi passed on, there'd be no witness to Logan and Zachary's meeting. Would the DMP then let Zachary go, or would they test him themselves?

"I'm gonna turn off the summoner now," Megan said. "So you can leave, go visit your friends or family, or whatever you want to do."

Ex-Tammi seemed to be in deep-thought mode, peering inward more than outward.

"Thanks a ton, Tammi." I hoped my words and lively tone would distract her from thoughts of passing on. "Have fun doing ghost stuff."

She extended a slim middle finger in my direction. "Glad I finally got to tell you what I think of you. Bitch."

"Hey, guess what?" Megan asked her before I could respond. "Ridgewood is having a memorial vigil for you after school starts. You should totally come."

"Maybe. That's a long time from now." The dead girl pressed her palms to her knees, elbows splayed. "Okay, I'm ready. Turn off the glowy thing."

"Bye, Tammi." Megan reached through the ghost and slid her thumb under the summoner. With a click, the device started to dim.

Ex-Tammi looked up suddenly. "You know what, I think I'm ready—" She disappeared.

"Ready to what?" I asked the empty space, my heart pounding. "Megan, can you call her back?"

She picked up the summoner. "Not without my dad noticing I used this. I might get in trouble as it is."

"But what if she passes on? What would they do with Zachary?"

"Maybe it'd be a good thing," Megan said. "They can't prove Zach can see ghosts, right? No witness, no evidence."

"Zachary *is* evidence. If they put him in a room with a ghost, and the ghost freaks—" I couldn't finish the sentence. I could only imagine the DMP's reaction: shock, then fear, and finally greed. They'd hook him up to machines for the rest of his life, trying to reproduce his power. They'd use him to make anti-ghost weapons.

"This isn't gonna help," Megan said, "but won't they test Zachary whether they have a witness or not?"

"Probably." I slapped the cushion where the ghost had sat. "But without Tammi, they'll do it sooner. One day could make a huge difference."

"True. I'm sure MI-X'll get him out soon."

I hadn't told her Simon's pessimistic estimate. I hadn't told her about Simon, period. "If they don't get him out, I will."

"What are you gonna do, hold up DMP headquarters like that

crazy guy last month? They'd shoot you to death like they did him."

"I can't just do nothing!" I stomped over to the piles of funeral programs and picked up two sheets. "Look at all these holes in people's lives. I don't want to *mourn* Zachary, I want to save him."

"I know, I know." She dug in her bag, which was sitting on the floor. "Hey, I know this won't help you in that department, but it might make you feel better."

"What is it?"

"A new band: Frightened Rabbit." She gave me a CD with a rough brown jacket. "They're a little folky-indie for me, but they do say 'fuck' a lot."

"What's this got to do with Zachary?"

"They're from Glasgow, so they sound like him. The accent. It's not the same as hearing *his* voice, but—"

I cut her off, throwing my arms around her. No one, not even Zachary, got me the way Megan did.

She hugged me back. "It's only a dumb CD."

But it wasn't. It might not help me save Zachary, but it was a lifeline, a way to connect to the person I loved most through the *thing* I loved most: music.

Maybe it would keep me sane long enough to save him.

Chapter Ten

I woke to an aching Scottish voice and a tear-dampened pillow.

The Frightened Rabbit CD played beside my bed, left on repeat the night before. The music wasn't morose—in fact, it was filled with hope and humor. But the singer's inflection, so like Zachary's, pierced my heart. The syllables rolled from the back of his throat and over his tongue, cracking with emotion. And the way he sang the word "love" like "luv," made me feel like Zachary was here in my room, ready to take me in his arms.

The night had felt like one long dream, where I'd wandered in a fog, searching for Zachary, hearing his call, but never knowing which direction it came from.

Gina knocked, then spoke through my door. "I'll be home for lunch, hon. Then you can drive me back to the office so you can have the car for errands." That was our bargain—she'd give me one day off a week, and I'd use half of it to get our groceries and dry cleaning.

I mumbled a thanks and flipped my pillow to the dry side, hoping to catch up on sleep. But I was haunted by the thought of ex-Tammi. Did she know she could hurt me, her imagined nemesis, by passing on right away? Had I accidentally given her peace by letting her vent her jealousy over Logan?

Outside, rain pattered on the porch roof. The sound of water made me notice my throat was parched. I'd cried so much last night I'd dehydrated myself.

I slumped down the stairs, passing a series of photos of my mother on the wall. One was taken a month before she died, holding me as a toddler in her lap. I wondered how often she had thought of my father in those last days.

I stopped so fast, I almost stumbled.

My father. Anthony. Gina had been in love with him. He'd been a friend of the family, a friend of my mother's.

There must be pictures.

I didn't hesitate. This was the first time I'd been alone in the house since I knew my father's name.

My aunt's bedroom wasn't locked, even though she knew I occasionally snooped. If I hadn't poked around in her closet last summer out of sheer boredom, I never would've found the box with my mother's journal and photos from Ireland. I never would've studied Newgrange. I never would've tracked down Eowyn and learned about my parents.

The closet held nothing but clothes—Gina had gotten wise to me. I burrowed through her drawers, careful to replace each item the way I'd found it.

I went slowly, to cover my tracks, so it was almost ten o'clock by the time I swept aside the pale pink bed skirt.

Sweater boxes, sweater boxes, and more sweater boxes. No way Gina had this many sweaters.

The first two containers actually did contain sweaters. But the third slid out heavy and slow. I lifted the lid.

I'd never seen this scrapbook. Its pristine red leather cover held no label, dates, or decoration.

I frowned at the interior. The plastic photo sleeves left no spaces for notes and captions that could've identified my dad.

I pried the pages apart, skimming photos from Gina and her ex-husband Danny's honeymoon on Capri. They looked so happy back then, before she met and fell in love with the man who would one day die in a car accident, haunt her and my mom, then become my father.

More pictures, from blurred-together family events—baptisms, weddings, graduations. I studied the group shots, scanning past uncles and cousins, hoping I would somehow *know* my father on sight.

Empty spaces appeared in the album pages, like missing puzzle pieces. I saw through the plastic sleeves to the white photo backs dated two years before my birth.

I turned the final page. A funeral program was tucked into the album's back pocket.

In Loving Memory,
Anthony Pasquale Liberati

With shaky fingers, I opened the program. A photo dropped into my lap.

Gina and my mother stood on either side of a dark-haired man.

My grandmother was in the picture, too, on the other side of my mom.

They'd all known him. I never would. Those dark brown eyes would never watch me graduate high school or college, and those tanned arms would never encircle me on the dance floor at my wedding.

Stupid, stupid. I'd thought I wanted to know and see my father. But now all I knew was the void he'd left behind. All I saw were pictures of me he would never be in.

Keys rattled in the front door downstairs. Gina was home early.

Blinking back tears, I shoved the album into the sweater box and slid it under the bed. Then I hurried to my room, sliding with my back to the hallway wall like a ninja.

"Aura?" my aunt called from the living room. "I have news."

I froze, then sprinted down the stairs, clutching the banister to keep from tumbling. *Please, please, please let this be good.* "Are they letting Zachary go?"

"Sit." She gestured to the dining room chair with a formality that reminded me of her courtroom demeanor. "They've moved him."

My knees felt like rubber as I sank into the chair. "Where?"

"Remember that young girl who died in the plane crash, the one who allegedly saw Zachary and Logan meeting? Apparently she has passed on."

Oh God, oh God, oh God. "That's good for her, right?"

"Yes, bless her soul, she's at peace. But that leaves the DMP with no witness." She set her purse on the table and held on like someone would steal it. "They're transporting Zachary to Area 3A for testing immediately."

"3A?" I leaped out of the chair. "That's where they tried to take me and Zach after they kidnapped us. Nicola made it sound like a horrible place! What will they do to him there?"

"I don't know." Aunt Gina rubbed the bridge of her nose. "I don't know," she repeated in a whisper.

I *did* know that if they tested Zachary to determine whether he could see ghosts, it would take one second to discover that he was a walking BlackBox.

They'd split him open to find his secret, then use it to "protect" the rest of us from ghosts. And they'd never let him go. He'd either be too useful or too dangerous.

Or too broken.

Anger and fear coiled in my gut. It was no longer enough to merely free Zachary. Now, I would wage a one-girl vendetta against the DMP for what they were doing to him. For what they'd tried to do to Logan. For what they wanted to do to me.

I would destroy them.

Chapter Eleven

I know how I can help you."

"I'm splendid, thanks," Simon said over the phone. "How are you?"

I parked around the block from my aunt's office, where I'd just dropped her off. "Are you being sarcastic or is someone there?"

"Sarcastic. Continue."

"Okay, so Nicola Hughes at the DMP offered me an internship. I told her no, but what if I took it? Then I'd be on the inside and could get you dirt so you can have . . . what did you call it? Leverage? To set Zachary free." When he didn't respond, I shouted, "They moved him to 3A!"

"I know. Agent Wolcott is incensed, as am I. But Aura, you can't work for the DMP now. After what they've done, you have every reason to hate them. If you try to cozy up to the agency, they'll be more suspicious of you than ever."

He was right. By keeping Zachary, the DMP had all but declared itself my enemy.

"I'm sorry," Simon said quietly. "I do appreciate your willingness to take such extreme measures."

"Extreme?"

"What you're describing is espionage. You could go to prison, perhaps forever. Since you're not of age yet, they probably wouldn't execute you."

My stomach flipped. *Execute?*

"This Nicola Hughes," Simon said. "Can you get closer to her? Maybe she'll tell you something useful. Then any transgression would be hers, not yours."

"Perfect." I hung up, not caring that I'd been rude at both the beginning and end of our call. Then I dialed Nicola, using the business card she'd given me.

While I waited for her to pick up, I glanced around, wondering if I was being watched. Maybe by that guy in the backward baseball cap lounging against the side of the bus station. Or the gray-haired lady with the stroller who'd stopped on the sidewalk to adjust the blue sunshade over what may or may not be a real baby.

The line picked up. "Hughes, Public Affairs, how can I—"

"Nicola!" I choked out her name. Sympathy was my only weapon. "What the hell's going on?"

"Oh, Aura. I heard what they did with Zachary."

"Not 'they'—you. You're part of them. You said you'd always help me. How could you let this happen?"

"Sweetie, I'm sorry. There's nothing I can do. The Investigations Division has its own agenda."

"It's your job to explain that agenda to the public. So start explaining." From the center console, I grabbed a pen and an old gas station receipt. "Please."

"Aura, I can't tell you what I don't know."

"Then find out. Did Zachary do something wrong? Did *I* do something wrong?"

Nicola's voice went low and soothing. "Neither of you did anything wrong. It's not about that."

"When you thought they were taking me and Zach to 3A last week, you almost had a heart attack. Why? What'll they do to him there?"

There was a long pause. Then her voice came hushed and echoed, like she was cupping her hand near the receiver. "Let's not discuss this over the phone."

Nicola met me at an indie record store in Fell's Point. We both thought it'd be a secure, anonymous place to rendezvous, better than her coming to my house or me going to her office. Plus, now that I was officially obsessed with Frightened Rabbit, I had to pick up their exclusive, as-yet-unavailable-for-download EP.

Nicola chattered about music, a topic I normally enjoyed. But I was dying to shake some answers out of her.

I ran my fingertips over the foot-long selection of Rancid releases. "This was one of Logan's favorite bands."

Nicola came over with a small stack of alt-metal CDs. "I've heard of them. I think." She flipped through the rack, her silver thumb ring clacking against the plastic CD holders.

"We saw them in concert when we first started going out. Logan bought me a T-shirt." My throat tightened. "I was wearing it the night he died."

"That must still hurt so much." She gave me an awkward one-armed hug, then smoothed a wrinkle in my white cotton shirt.

"He died eight months ago, but to me, he's only been gone a few days."

"I bet you haven't had time to mourn him, with all that's happened to Zachary."

I started to deny it, then realized she was right. Logan had left a void no one could fill. But it comforted me to know he was at peace—not to mention safe from the DMP.

"Nicola . . ." I held my CD in both hands, its corners digging into my palms. "What do they do to people at 3A?"

"It's a ghost-research facility, so I don't know what they'd do to a living person there. All I know is that sometimes a truck shows up to headquarters, collects a few ARGs, and ships them up to 3A."

ARGs. At-risk ghosts: those that the DMP captures and puts into tiny obsidian-lined boxes so they won't become dangerous shades. They'd tried to do it to Logan, but he'd turned into a shade in time to escape.

"What do they do with the ARGs there?"

"No idea. Since 3A isn't known to the public, they don't need to tell us flacks in Public Affairs."

"Can you give Zach a message from me? I want him to know I love him and that I'm thinking about him."

Her face softened. "Oh, sweetie, I'll try. It might have to go through a few intermediaries, but I'll make sure he knows."

I believed her, or at least I believed that she believed they'd pass on the message.

"Aura, I know you're mad at the DMP, but we're doing the best we can. We're not—" She cut herself off, rubbing her pressed lips.

"You're not what?"

Nicola fingered the lapel of her black pin-striped blazer. "We're not the ones calling the shots." She went back to flipping through the row of Rise Against CDs, though she didn't look like she was actually seeing them.

"Who's calling the shots?" I reviewed my basic civics knowledge. "Congress? The president?"

"I wish. The president is temporary. This has been going on since way before—" Nicola stopped and scanned the ceiling. Her gaze rested on a security camera in the corner. "You ready to check out?" She held up her stack of CDs. "I should stop before I break my bank account."

We headed for the cashier, my mind spinning. I had to tug more information out of her.

Nicola turned down the offer of a plastic shopping bag and stuffed her CDs into a black canvas tote. I angled my head to see the bag's logo, which looked like red prison bars. The company name made me pause.

SecuriLab. The same firm with ten of its employees on the DMP visitors registry the day I was there. The day after the bombing of Flight 346.

"Cool bag," I said. "What's SecuriLab?"

Nicola looked embarrassed. "They're the people who make Black-Box. They come into headquarters for meetings, and always bearing gifts. Usually it's pens or pencils, but last Christmas they gave us these sweet tote bags. Look, it has a pocket that'll fit my phone."

I tuned out her babbling about the tote bag's marvels and wondered: Why would BlackBox manufacturers visit DMP headquarters the morning after a major disaster?

I pondered this puzzle while we walked down the hot sidewalk toward Nicola's car. I had to make our last few minutes together count.

"So why did you want to work for the DMP?" I asked her.

"I lost my mother ten years ago, when I was almost your age."

"I'm so sorry." I felt bad for Nicola. I missed my mom, and I'd never even known her. "Was it sudden?" The polite way of asking, *Did she become a ghost?*

"It was a car accident. My little cousin could see my mother's ghost, but I couldn't. It took Mom almost a year to pass on."

"Yeesh. That must have sucked."

"Totally. So I decided to help ghosts. Or at least help us understand them. That is the department's mission, though I know it doesn't always seem like it."

No, it really doesn't.

"We need post-Shifters' help," she added. "But I get why you don't want to work for us, especially now."

I shrugged, not wanting the conversation to turn back to me. I was still trying to understand her motivations. "What about before your mom died? What'd you want to do for a job?"

"I was always a government geek. But back then it was for the environment. I'm from Wyoming, so my big passion was protecting the wilderness. Problem is, there's a lot of money to be made there."

"Like tourism?"

She laughed. "That's pennies. I mean like drilling, timber, ranches. Businesses pay lots of money to make sure the government lets them do what they want."

"So these companies pretty much own the agencies that are supposed to tell them what to do?"

"Maybe not own them, but they have a lot of influence." She stopped next to a silver Prius. "Send me a written message for Zachary, and I'll do what I can to get it through."

After she drove off, I trudged through the thick summer air to my own car, thinking of what she'd said about companies influencing government agencies.

Could it be the same way with SecuriLab and the DMP? Life with ghosts was a lot easier since BlackBox was invented. Without it, the dead would be everywhere, even in bathrooms and military bases.

And without BlackBox, the DMP would be powerless.

My phone rang as I got in my car. I checked the screen. "Hey, Dylan." I rolled down the windows, expecting to be here a while, since Dylan tended to talk in circles and take forever to get to the point. "What's up?"

"Aura. I need to see you."

Chapter Twelve

This. Was weird.

Dylan hadn't been in my room since we were kids. The last time we were alone together (other than in the cemetery) we'd made out like crazy on his bedroom floor, driven by our grief for Logan and my confusion over Zachary.

I wondered if Dylan was thinking of that now. Or maybe he was only thinking of the pizza he was shoveling into his mouth.

"So what did you want to tell me?" I asked once we'd inhaled half of our first pieces.

Sitting on the floor across from me, Dylan wiped his mouth with a Fourth of July–themed paper towel. "Logan came to see me on Sunday. Before he went to find you."

"I'm glad you guys got to say good-bye."

"Yeah, it was cool." Dylan was almost whispering now, though my door was closed and Gina was downstairs, eating her own pizza before going out to meet clients. "He told me something he didn't want you to know until after he passed on."

I tensed. Had Logan withheld some hurtful secret from me? He hated having anyone be mad at him.

"It's not about you." Dylan chomped the last bite of crust. "It's about shades."

The word alone made me nervous. "What about them?"

"He said, and I quote, 'Shades can do whatever the fuck they want.'"

My entire body turned to ice. "What does that mean?"

"They can't change into ghosts on their own. But other than that they go where they want and do what they want."

"What about BlackBox?"

"He said for shades, BlackBox is like red is for regular ghosts—it hurts, but they can ignore it if they want to be somewhere bad enough."

"Wow." This was new. Shades weren't common enough yet to be thoroughly studied. Pre-Shifters couldn't detect them, and post-Shifters couldn't be around them without passing out or throwing up. "That's pretty scary."

"I know, right? But there's a good side, too, Logan says—I mean, he *said*. Shades aren't just mindless, crazy-ass monsters. They're people, like ghosts are. Shades can think." He popped a piece of pepperoni into his mouth. "Shades can choose."

I looked at my window, where dark violet curtains blocked the evening sun's glare. Logan had streaked through that window as a shade before turning back into a ghost. "He told me he stayed away from post-Shifters once he realized he made them sick."

"It wasn't easy, though. You know how he was. Attention was like food. Plus, he said that when he first turned into a shade, he thought being around people would help him feel human. But watching them puke or pass out just made it worse. He got more and more pissed." Dylan hung his head, and a lock of straight brown hair flopped over one eye. "He said, 'The more I hurt people, the more I *wanted* to hurt people.'"

My stomach grew heavy with sorrow for Logan's suffering. "Why didn't he tell me this before? Why didn't he trust me?"

"Cuz he knew you'd get upset. It was hard enough for him to tell me. But we gotta deal with shades, Aura. This is like inside info on the enemy. Logan was helping us protect ourselves."

True. I'd only encountered a few shades in my life, and hoped to never see another. But if they could be reasoned with . . .

"Should we tell the DMP?" I asked Dylan. "I don't trust them."

"Neither did Logan. He knew if the DMP found out the truth, they'd lock up every ghost that was even a little bit shady. Logan would've been the first."

"So he waited to tell us so he could save himself."

"Can you blame him?"

"No. The thought of Logan in one of those little boxes makes me sick." I blotted the pizza sauce stain on my white shirt. "I'm glad he's free."

"Me too. I think he's okay." He started a second slice of pizza. "So what's up with Zachary? Did they let him go? Is he back home now?"

I hadn't planned to tell anyone but Megan that my boyfriend was in DMP detention. Between Logan's jealousy and his own, Dylan had never been a fan of Zachary.

"It was a misunderstanding. He and his parents went home Monday."

"Back to Scotland?"

I didn't meet his eyes. "Yep."

"Good." He looked around my room, maybe searching for pictures of Zachary. I had none up yet, since we'd been going out for less than a week, a period that included a plane crash and a harrowing escape through the mountains.

Mountains that contained Area 3A, where Zachary was now trapped, maybe in pain, maybe unconscious. Maybe dead.

"No," I said, trying to talk myself back to sanity. They wouldn't take him all the way up there just to kill him. Would they?

"No what?" Dylan asked. "Oh, you mean, no, it's not good that he's gone back to Scotland." He shrugged and looked away. "I get it."

I switched my mind from boy issues and pondered what Logan had said about shades. If they could choose their actions, then they could be reasoned with. They could be persuaded.

They could be used as weapons.

"Oh God," I said. "We can't ever tell the DMP. They'll try to use shades against post-Shifters. They could make the shades attack us if we don't do what they want."

"But they'd need other post-Shifters to *tell* the shades to attack." He stopped chewing. "Shit, they keep talking about a DMP draft. They might make us work for them, starting with you."

His words rang odd. "What do you mean, starting with me?" I'd never told Dylan I was the First.

He froze. "Whoops."

"What did Logan tell you?"

"Just that you were the first person born after the Shift and Zachary was the last person born before. And that you both had special powers to go with it." He folded the edge of his paper plate. "And that you switch powers when you hook up."

My head felt like it would burst into flames. "Why would he tell you all this?"

"I guess he thought I could look out for you after he was gone. Since Zachary's all the way in Scotland."

Elbows on my knees, I pressed my fists to my temples, my anger at Logan battling my need for honesty. Now that Dylan knew everything Megan knew, why not tell him the truth? Maybe he could help, or at least listen to me.

"Zachary's not in Scotland," I whispered. "The DMP has him at some hellhole called 3A, where they tried to take us last week."

Dylan let out a low whistle. "They took him after the plane crash? Why?"

"Because they found out he met with Logan at the airport. By now they know he's a walking BlackBox. I'm scared I'll never see him again. Just like—" My voice broke, and it felt like the rest of me would break, too, if someone didn't hold me together.

Dylan crawled around the pizza box. "Come here."

"No."

"I swear to God I won't try anything."

"I can't."

"I swear on Logan's grave."

I gave up and let him pull me against him, realizing only now that he smelled sort of like Logan.

Gone was the grasping touch that had marked our encounter on Dylan's bedroom floor. Now his grip was solid, his hands motionless on my back, just as I needed them. My skin felt bristly, like it was made of thousands of shards of glass, connected by a weak glue. One stroke would send me flying apart.

"I'm sorry, Dylan." My tears dampened his T-shirt collar. "This isn't fair to you."

"What are you talking about?"

"Letting you comfort me when we're not—when I don't—"

"Jesus, Aura, with all the shit you've had to deal with, I'd be a dick if I got mad at you for wanting a hug." He shifted his chin against my hair. "I used to think, maybe when Zachary left, I'd have a shot with you. But then in the cemetery, when I saw how destroyed you were about the plane crash, I decided no way I'd even think about it."

"Why not?"

"Because if Zachary had died, I didn't want to be what he was for you after Logan died. I couldn't deal with the waiting. Zachary was like a freaking superhero. Captain Patience or something."

I laughed and wiped away a tear. "I wish I had his patience. All I want to do is pull a commando raid and bust him out."

"That would be awesome." Dylan went still. "Wait. That *would* be awesome."

"What?"

"Commando raid." He let go and sat cross-legged facing me. "Maybe not bust him out, because we'd need some serious weapons for that. But we could go there and see what kinda security they've got." He bounced his palms off his bare knees like a kid. "And then maybe you could send him a coded message that tells him how and when to break out. Then we go pick him up and bring him here. Or no—to the embassy, right? That's where people in the movies go when they get in trouble in other countries."

It did sound like the plot of an action movie—a bad one. Or a good action movie with a bad ending. "There's no way that would work."

"How do you know? Maybe there's hardly any security because they're way the hell out in the woods."

"I don't even know where it is. Zach and I escaped before we got there."

"But you drove back from that area with Becca. I bet if we looked at a map we could figure it out. Then we tool around the back roads until we find it. Or not. But at least we try."

I remembered the general store/gas station/pizza place where we'd waited for Becca to pick us up, and the name of a nearby town. Maybe that would be enough.

"Come on, Aura. We could all go—Mickey and Megan, Siobhan and Connor. They'd love it." He tapped his fist against the bed frame, chanting, "Road. Trip. Road. Trip. Road. Trip."

It sounded ridiculous, but it made my heart glow with hope. Besides, I craved my friends' support now more than ever.

"Let's do it," I said.

"Yes! We should go Fourth of July weekend—I bet there won't be as many guards working on a holiday. We'll tell my parents we're going to our house at Deep Creek Lake instead of Ocean City like we planned."

I'd completely forgotten about my beach trip with the Keeleys. Two weeks ago one of my biggest dilemmas had been whether to pack the Cute Bikini or the Hot Bikini.

"3A might be just a couple hours from Deep Creek Lake. So we could do recon, then stay at your family's house to plan our next move."

"Now you're talking." He gave me a high five.

I felt giddy with the possibilities. "This is insane."

"Not as insane as sitting here freaking out. And we won't do anything illegal." He shrugged. "Unless we have to, to save the day."

I pulled the pizza box closer to snag a second piece. "Why do you want to do this? You don't even know Zachary."

"I know you. And . . ." He dragged the word out into several syllables. "I want to stop seeing you so bummed. Megan and all them do, too."

I smiled at him around the pizza, the first food I'd been able to taste in days. For the first time since the crash, I felt something besides rage and despair.

Gina and Ian and even Simon would explode if they knew what Dylan and I were plotting. But their caution and prudence had produced zero results so far. Zachary was alone in a sea of DMP agents who cared nothing for his kind heart or his brave soul. When he finally was released (I made myself think *when*, not *if*), he might never be the same.

After Dylan left, I went to my bookshelf and pulled everything from the top level—my SAT prep books, my assigned summer-reading novels, my pom-pom-waving Johns Hopkins stuffed jaybird.

In their place I lined up the mix CDs Logan had made for me, then the scrapbook full of photos and ticket stubs for concerts and movies we'd gone to together, then the bootleg DVDs of Keeley Brothers concerts.

I went to my dresser to pull out the final item—my worn green Keeley Brothers T-shirt. I refolded it so that the skull-and-crossbones-and-shamrock logo faced up, then placed it at the front of the shelf, as the shrine's centerpiece.

I remembered the day the first shipment of Keeley Brothers T-shirts arrived at Logan's house. He was so eager, he accidentally sliced open his hand with the box cutter. The wound needed stitches, but Logan insisted on seeing the shirts before going to the emergency room. He even used one to stanch the bleeding.

Now, atop my own Keeley Brothers shirt, I laid the limp white rose from his grave.

"I miss you, Logan." I touched my fingers to my lips, then the forehead of the Keeley Brothers skull. "I miss you so much."

Missing Logan was an emptiness, an ache so dull and deep, it was a permanent part of me. I would never truly get over his death, but someday I would find peace.

Missing Zachary, on the other hand, was a searing knife in the gut. I burned to save him from the horrible fates I imagined, and the need to be in his arms again set my skin ablaze.

One boy was gone forever. The other was gone now.

Chapter Thirteen

The following night, Ian called to tell me that Eowyn was in a new safe house, but he wouldn't give me her phone number. I decided not to push it, knowing how stressed out he was, but I vowed not to give up. I couldn't wait forever to read the rest of my mother's journal.

I put on my favorite Irish folk music and sat on the bed with my laptop to record the parts of the journal I remembered. Maybe I could pursue a clue buried in those details.

My mother wrote that she'd gone to Newgrange at the winter solstice to feel close to my father, a friend of the family who'd taken care of her the first time she had cancer. Her disease was in remission, so her motto was "Life is short." Plus, she apparently had a massive crush on Anthony, even as he was having an affair with my (married) aunt Gina. Though the Newgrange solstice itself was a mystical, uplifting experience, afterward she felt depressed and bitter over Anthony's death.

A few nights later, he appeared to her in Ireland as a ghost. They fell in love, and on the night of the spring equinox, he regained his body long enough for them to conceive me. Then he passed on for good. When Mom found out she was pregnant, she was understandably freaked.

I hit save, sat back against my headboard, and pondered what Gina had told me a few days ago, about my dad being a history professor at Saint Joseph's University.

"Duh!" I smacked my forehead, then opened a web browser and typed his name and the college into a search engine.

Bingo. He was no longer listed on the university's faculty page—having been dead for almost twenty years—but he was listed as author of several academic papers. I scrolled down the list. His area of study seemed to be the Moroccan Crisis and the First World War.

"Hmm. That's random."

So why had he gone on that summer tour with students to Ireland? I thought of Ridgewood teachers begging our parents to chaperone school field trips. Maybe one of my father's colleagues had asked him to go along to Ireland as a favor.

The current faculty directory showed when each member had started teaching at Saint Joe's. I made a list of history professors who would've been there at the same time as my father. Then, using the academic journal database my aunt's law firm paid big bucks for, I ran a search on each of them.

One name came up as an ancient Ireland scholar: Daniel McClellan.

"Doesn't get any more Irish than that," I murmured as I printed a list of McClellan's papers. They weren't online, but the Johns Hopkins University library carried the academic journals that contained them.

I considered calling Professor McClellan. If he'd traveled with my father, he probably knew him well. I was hungry for everyday details: Did the students like my dad? Was he always on time for class? Did he drink coffee, tea, or gallons of Diet Coke?

But how would I explain my interest? "Hi, I'm the daughter of a guy you used to work with. I was born two years after he died. Is that weird?"

With a sigh, I shut my laptop and set it aside. Instinctively my hand reached for the photo of Zachary on my nightstand, one I'd just framed today.

It was from last Saturday, our big date day. He'd been crouching by the Lincoln Memorial Reflecting Pool, looking pensive as he watched the ducks. I'd sneaked away to the opposite side of the pool so I could take his photo.

Realizing I was no longer next to him, Zachary had peered from side to side with amusement. The picture had captured his eyes lighting up at the sight of me.

I traced his silhouettes, both real and reflected, grateful to have this one perfect image.

I hit play on the Frightened Rabbit EP I'd bought at the record store with Nicola. These three songs were raw sadness and strength—an exact mirror of my feelings.

I hugged the photo and closed my eyes. My belly warmed as I imagined Zachary crooning these lyrics so full of longing. I'd never had the guts to ask him to sing to me. He would've thought I was comparing him to Logan.

But I wouldn't have. Zachary wasn't a replacement for my first love. He was my third half, as odd as that sounded. With him gone, I felt—not *incomplete*, exactly. More like *unfinished*. Like there was something I was meant to be and do and discover. Without Zachary, that something would always be out of reach.

This thing between him and me had become Us, an entity to be kept alive at all costs. Tonight all I could do was shut out the world and imagine his arms around me.

But tomorrow, I would find another key to saving Us.

I sat in the JHU library, knees pulled to my chest to keep warm in the overly air-conditioned reading room. Four empty cubicles lined one side of the tiny space, but instead I sat at a table where I could see the sole entrance. Paranoid? Maybe.

Copies of Daniel McClellan's journal articles were spread before me. I'd highlighted his thoughts and scribbled my own notes in the margins of several pages.

One article speculated on the dual purpose of the Irish megaliths and cairns that marked the solstices and equinoxes. The Stone Age people who'd built them wanted to measure time for practical reasons. Obviously they needed to know when to plant and harvest crops. But the timing might have also had spiritual meaning, McClellan said.

It is significant that these megaliths capture the light at sunrise or sunset. Among the Celtic peoples, and indeed

among many cultures, dawn and twilight are considered
magical times of in-between, when anything is possible.

The solstices and equinoxes also embody that "in-between-
ness." For one moment, it's neither autumn nor winter,
spring nor summer. It's the borderlands.

I gnawed the end of my blue ballpoint pen, contemplating.

The borderlands. Kind of like me and Zachary, on either side of
the Shift. Together, we became the In-Between. With just a kiss, I
took on his "red power" to repel ghosts, and in exchange, he became
like a post-Shifter, able to see ghosts.

But why? Because we were born at the winter solstice? What did
Newgrange have to do with it? We hadn't been born *at* Newgrange
during the sunrise. In fact, my birth took place in the middle of the
night—3:50 a.m. With the five-hour time difference between here
and Scotland, Zachary would've been born at . . .

Oh my God.

8:49 a.m.

My finger trembled as it slid down the article, confirming what
I already knew as well as my own name: the time of the Newgrange
solstice sunrise.

8:50 a.m.

And the year Zachary and I were born, the solstice took place at
8:50 a.m., too.

I did a quick calculation in my notebook. The winter solstice usually took place within a twenty-four-hour period between December 21

and December 22. "Twenty-four hours times sixty minutes an hour is . . . whoa." In any given year there was only a 1-in-1,440 chance of the winter solstice taking place *exactly* at sunrise.

Was this why my mingling with Zachary had such weird results? Because our births were on a double borderland of night-and-day, autumn-and-winter?

Dizzy with discovery, out of habit I reached for my phone. *Wait'll I tell Zachary.*

My hand halted halfway, then curled into a limp fist. There would be no calling Zachary. Not today.

"Hello there."

I jumped at the interruption. Simon strode toward my table in a casual manner, as if we'd had a study date. He wore a pale-blue Hopkins Lacrosse hoodie, with a backpack slung loosely over his shoulder. Now he could definitely pass for eighteen.

"You almost gave me a heart attack," I whispered, glancing at the door. "Why didn't you call first?"

"Spies don't call first." He sat down, letting his backpack slide to the floor. "Any news for me?"

I told Simon what Nicola had said about the ARGs being shipped up to Area 3A. He scribbled in his Johns Hopkins notebook, and I was relieved to see him using some kind of shorthand or code. If anyone found those notes, hopefully they wouldn't lead to me or Nicola.

"Also," I said, "the company that makes BlackBox—"

He looked up quickly. "SecuriLab?"

"Right. A bunch of them came to visit DMP headquarters that morning after the crash."

Simon slid the tip of his pen back and forth over the notebook's spiral spine. "Fascinating."

I told him about Nicola's bag. "SecuriLab seems really buddy-buddy with DMP. Is that normal?"

"Unfortunately, yes, and not only in America. Corporations everywhere buy as much power as they can. But since the DMP is of interest to us, anyone with influence on them is obviously a target for further investigation."

He went back to scribbling in his notebook. I tapped my heel against the floor impatiently.

When his pen stopped, I asked, "Are you any closer to getting Zachary out?"

"I swear to you, MI-X is doing everything it can. But I'm told there are . . . other interests involved."

"What other interests?"

"Dunno. I'm only a field officer, I haven't got the full picture."

I frowned. Who would want to hurt Zachary, besides the DMP? Not MI-X, I assumed, since his father was still connected to them. Someone from a third country altogether?

Or maybe someone who thought Zachary and I were getting too close to the big truths.

"Simon, you said I was more useful to the DMP alive than dead for now. Would they study me, like they're doing to Zachary?" I hoped that was all they were doing to him.

"Perhaps, but if they were determined to do that, they would've taken you against your will, like they did him. Unlike Zachary, you're American. You can work for them."

"No way. Never."

"I didn't say it would be voluntary."

I glanced past him at the door. "You mean a DMP draft? It's never come close to passing."

"It could be very popular with pre-Shifters, the only Americans at the moment who can vote."

"But it's wrong. That's why they got rid of the military draft, like, a million years ago."

"Dealing with ghosts isn't like going to war. No lives would be in danger. And given the right circumstances, wouldn't your country be eager—nay, desperate—to do something about the influence of ghosts?"

"First of all, never use the word 'nay' at high school, or you'll get beaten up. Second, what do you mean by 'right circumstances'?"

"Such as the Flight 346 disaster. Its timing was convenient, no?"

A sour taste formed at the back of my throat. "You think the DMP caused the crash? I'm not a big fan, but I don't think they'd kill two hundred and fifteen innocent people."

"There were supposed to be two hundred eighteen people on that flight. Maybe not all of them innocent in certain eyes."

"The Moores," I whispered. "Someone wanted them dead?"

"The DMP was not pleased with Ian Moore's performance as MI-X liaison." Simon's eyes narrowed behind his glasses. "American agencies think their British counterparts should be at their beck and call. But Ian Moore was no servant boy. When the DMP asked him to jump, he didn't say, 'How high?' He said, 'No, I think I'll punch you in the throat, thanks very much.'"

"But he was already leaving. He was sick."

"And he'd handpicked his successor—my boss. The DMP might have wanted to send her a signal." He folded his arms. "Play by our rules, or you and your family will end up dead."

Chapter Fourteen

On July third, I gave Nicola a handwritten message for Zachary. It was a simple note that wouldn't raise suspicions: *I love you. Be strong.* I hoped he would receive it, and that the DMP would find it so boring that they wouldn't suspect any subsequent messages. Messages that might help set him free.

On July fourth, I set out to rescue my boyfriend.

Dylan and I sat in the middle seat of the Keeleys' black Escalade, reviewing the map I'd made from memory. Based on the direction Zachary and I had fled from the DMP and the location of the gas station where Becca had picked us up, I was able to figure out within a hundred square miles where Area 3A might be.

Megan rode up front next to her boyfriend, Mickey, while Mickey's twin sister, Siobhan, and her boyfriend, Connor, sat behind us. No one seemed bummed about going to the mountains instead of the beach. In fact, they were all pretty psyched to be part of what Dylan had dubbed Operation Scot Free.

Dylan fell asleep an hour into the four-hour drive, so I practiced playing memory trainer games on my phone. If I wanted to gather dirt on the DMP, I had to be able to recall small details. Having a better grip on my surroundings would also help me know whether I was being followed.

Ironically, I was so busy learning to be observant that I didn't notice the rising tension a few feet away.

"I don't get why I can't come with you," Megan whined to Mickey. "I wanna see what your college town looks like, and your new apartment."

"You'll see the place once it's set up," he replied with an edge. "I'll only be gone for a weekend. Relax."

Mickey, the other brother in the Keeley Brothers Irish-flavored punk band, had been Logan's dark, scowling antithesis. Onstage, their contrast had created an irresistible dynamic, but in real life, it had meant a constant, exhausting tug-of-war. Logan's happy-go-lucky, über-ambitious nature had clashed with Mickey and his desire to keep the music pure and serious.

But when Logan had died, Mickey had blamed himself and sank into despair. His demeanor and outlook had improved when he saw Logan one last time at the concert, but his happiness hadn't lasted. Megan's attempts to "fix" him only made him more miserable.

Connor and Siobhan continued their quiet conversation over a bag of corn chips. "So you're just gonna be undeclared?" he asked.

"I have no idea what I want to major in," she replied, crunching. "I'll try a little of everything, like a buffet."

"Cool. I wish I could do that."

"You can," she said. "Just don't be an engineer."

"But I want to be an engineer. A really relaxed engineer."

Witnessing the agonizing college choices by Siobhan and Connor had made me dread facing the same decision myself that year. Mickey's choice, on the other hand, had been easy. He'd only ever wanted to study music, so he was going to Shenandoah Conservatory in Virginia.

"Oh, guess what, you guys?" Siobhan finished chewing, then swallowed. "Connor and I have an announcement."

Megan whipped around in her seat. "Oh my God. You're getting engaged."

The two of them laughed. "No," Connor said.

She gasped. "You're pregnant?"

"God, no." Siobhan took Connor's hand and smiled at him. "We're breaking up."

What? The car fell into a stunned silence. Only the sleeping Dylan hadn't reacted.

Connor gazed at Siobhan so serenely, I wondered if we'd heard wrong.

"You're breaking up?" Mickey exclaimed. "As in, the two of you, not going out anymore?"

Connor nodded. "Yeah, but not until we start school next month."

"This way we can enjoy the time we have," Siobhan said, "without angsting over whether it's going to end."

"We'll still be friends," Connor added.

"Totally. The alternative was trying to do that whole long-distance thing two hundred miles apart." She unwrapped the plastic from the sandwich she'd packed. "We've seen too many friends go through that, and someone always ends up crushed."

"Usually by the end of September," Connor said. "It's inevitable."

Megan looked mortified. "It is?"

"Not for everyone," Siobhan blurted. "I'm sure you and Mickey will be fine."

Dylan gave a quiet snort, his eyes still closed. "Nice save, Siobhan." Apparently he wasn't asleep after all.

"You guys are equally cool with this?" I asked Connor and Siobhan.

"Uh-huh." She studied her bread crust. "I hate flaxseeds. They look like deer ticks."

Connor reached for her sandwich. "Let me exterminate them for you."

"No, I'll deal." She went to bite the sandwich, then handed it to him. "On second thought, thanks."

I watched their familiar, easy exchange. They were the best-matched couple I'd ever known, and now they were throwing it all away.

Meanwhile, up front, Mickey gripped the steering wheel, and Megan sat with her arms crossed over her chest, her face turned away from him. Siobhan and Connor's discussion had thrown gasoline onto the flames of Mickey and Megan's own long-distance-relationship tension.

Though my stomach was knotting up from nerves, the smell of Siobhan's ham sandwich made me hungry. I opened a bag of cheese puffs, the crackle of plastic sounding as loud as a shotgun in the strained silence.

"We shouldn't have said anything," Connor murmured to Siobhan behind me. "It was stupid timing."

"You're saying I'm stupid?" Siobhan snapped.

"We both are. We should've thought how they'd react, is all. Now we're stuck with them all weekend."

Dylan and I exchanged a worried look. If this operation failed because of relationship drama, I was going to scream.

In the front seat Megan wheedled, "I just don't see why I can't come with you next weekend."

"I don't see why you'd *want* to." Mickey dragged a tense, freckled hand through his wavy brown hair. "I'll be sitting around waiting for furniture to be delivered. There won't even be electricity yet."

The heat of embarrassment crept over my cheeks. I hated when they fought in front of us.

"It'll be romantic," Megan said to Mickey.

"It'll be hot as hell without air-conditioning. You'd complain the whole time."

"No, I wouldn't!" Her whine gained an edge of rage, then softened. "I swear I won't."

"See what I mean?" Connor said to Siobhan.

"Okay, fine. It was stupid to tell them at the beginning of the trip. Happy?"

From the corner of my eye, I saw Connor kiss the top ridge of Siobhan's multi-pierced ear. "I got you to admit you were wrong. I rock."

She laughed, leaning into him and wrapping her hand around his thigh. "Shut up."

"It's not worth you getting in trouble," Mickey told Megan. "Your mom would kill us if she caught you going away overnight with me."

"I'm going away with you now."

"As part of a group. Your mom can tell herself you'll be sleeping in Aura's room."

"Maybe I will." Megan clicked her seat-belt latch and snapped the strap away from her shoulder.

"What are you doing? Watch it!" Mickey said as she clambered over the center console.

"I'm taking a break." Megan plopped into the seat between me and Dylan. Her tone was angry, but there were tears behind it, and her ruddy skin was even more flushed than usual. She needed a distraction.

I took out the small green memo pad I'd started carrying since Simon told me to get information from Nicola. I wrote, *I want to try to change a shade to a ghost on the fall equinox.* I wiped off the cheese puffs' orange powder and passed the pad and pen to Megan, pointing at Dylan so she'd show him, too.

Megan read the note, then shoved the pad into Dylan's chest. "Are you crazy?" she whispered, though Mickey had cranked the music back up.

Dylan wrote on the paper. *You'll be a total puke machine.*

Me: *If I could do it for Logan, maybe I can do it for anyone. SHOULD do it for anyone.*

"Why?" Megan asked out loud.

Dylan proceeded to scribble on the pad without taking it off her leg. She tensed at his almost-touch, but didn't brush him off.

Dylan: *Because being a shade sucks. Logan said so.*

Me: *Will you guys come with me in case I pass out?*

They nodded without hesitation.

Megan: *How will you find a shade?*

Me: *The DMP started a list on their website last week.* It was like the FBI's Most Wanted list, except these poor souls usually hadn't committed any crimes. *I'll call their names and tell them to fly through me like Logan did. If it works, they'll be ghosts again.*

Megan flipped the page and wrote, *THIS IS CRAZY!*

I gestured to the SUV around us, as if to say, *We're heading into Nowheresville, Pennsylvania, to find the hidden laboratory of a government agency, so we can rescue my boyfriend and send him on the first plane back to Scotland.*

She snatched the bag of cheese puffs from my lap. "Good point."

Around two o'clock we reached the area in the mountain forest where the DMP had taken me and Zachary. Connor was driving now, since he was the least likely to be recognized if we were stopped.

"You'd think there'd be a sign." I twisted the end of my ponytail around my fingertip as I scanned the endless, thick forest. "Even the National Security Agency has a sign at the start of the highway exit."

"And armed guards at the end of it," Mickey grumbled behind us.

"That's the thing." Dylan peered through the windshield between Connor and Siobhan. "No DMP sign, probably not much security. If we do find it, maybe it'll be easy to get in."

"Or out," Megan added, now in a better mood. Mickey's doubts aside, the atmosphere in the car buzzed with anticipation.

Little by little, that anticipation turned to frustration, as we proceeded to find, as Dylan put it, "precisely dick." Siobhan marked off each part as we explored it thoroughly, but three hours later, we'd covered only a small portion of the county's pothole-punched roads.

"We're destroying the shocks on this thing," Mickey murmured to Megan. "And for what?"

"It's an SUV. Yeah, a froufrou one, but it's still built for this. And how can you ask, 'for what?'"

"I don't even know this Zachary guy. Logan hated him."

"No, he didn't." Dylan glared at his brother. "Not at the end."

Mickey gave a sullen sigh. My shoulders tingled with tension at his hostility. Also, I wondered what Dylan knew about Logan and Zachary that I didn't.

I was about to ask when Siobhan shouted, "Is that it?"

Connor hit the brakes, jolting us against our seat belts. Behind us, someone honked.

Ahead on our right, a heavy-duty, pale-green steel box sat next to a narrow driveway. It showed no name or number.

"Let me get closer." Connor steered the SUV toward the shoulder.

"Watch it!" Mickey said. "Don't put us in the ditch."

"Calm down." Connor glanced in the side-view mirror. "I'm gonna let this jerkwad behind me pass. He's been riding our bumper for miles."

A big white box van zoomed by. The logo on the back tossed my heart into my throat.

SECURILAB.

Chapter Fifteen

Follow him!" I pointed at the truck. "He's going where we're going."

Connor jerked the steering wheel to the left to put the Escalade back on the road.

I explained. "SecuriLab is the company that makes BlackBox. They're tied up tight with the DMP. If they're out here in the middle of nowhere, they're going to 3A."

"Good eye, Aura!" Megan leaned forward for a high five.

We followed the SecuriLab van down ten miles of winding, nauseating highway, until it pulled onto a rough-paved, heavily wooded road to our left.

"Follow from farther back," Dylan said, then noticed I'd twisted the seat belt strap around my wrist in my anxiety.

"Hey." He unwrapped my hand. "We got it, okay?"

I stretched my fingers, which tingled with the return of blood. Our lucky streak would have to continue for me to share Dylan's confidence.

We rounded a curve in time to see the SecuriLab van turn into a driveway, passing under an unmanned security gate.

"Now what?" Connor asked. "There's no guard. Maybe we could lift the gate."

"That guy used an ID card," Mickey pointed out. "No way we can drive in."

"Maybe we can walk in." I tapped the back of the driver's seat. "Let's go back and see if there's a fence."

"Wait a few minutes," Dylan warned. "There might be a camera at that security station. If they see us drive by again so soon, they'll know we followed the van. They might run our license plate."

I got the feeling Dylan was forming his plan of attack based on TV shows, movies, and video games. Still, what he said made sense.

Connor eventually turned the SUV around, and we proceeded back to the gate at 3A.

No fence. No armed guards. No plaque with the DMP insignia or even PROPERTY OF THE FEDERAL GOVERNMENT. Just a dark road plunging into an even darker forest.

"Guys," Siobhan said, "the GPS says we're an hour away from our lake house. We could go there, change, maybe take a nap, then come back in the middle of the night."

We all agreed—out loud at least. I longed to smash the SUV through the gate, drive up to Area 3A's front door, and demand Zachary's freedom.

But Siobhan was right. Stealth was our best bet. The moment I showed my cards to the DMP, the moment they knew I was doing something other than sitting around crying, or getting over Zachary by hanging out with Dylan, I'd lose the upper hand.

Assuming I had it in the first place.

"How do you spell SecuriLab?" Megan asked me, opening Mickey's laptop.

I sat down next to her at the long dining table in the lake house's rustic great room. "I've already done searches on them." Using the library computers (I assumed the DMP was tracking my own laptop), I'd learned that SecuriLab was a multinational corporation charged with bribery in four different countries.

Megan ran a search, thumbing her sun-chapped bottom lip as she scrolled through the results.

"That's interesting," she said. "Their patent on BlackBox is running out in a few years."

"What does that mean?"

"It means other companies can start making it. At the funeral home, there's this new machine that takes the body's—" She cut herself off. "Never mind."

"Thanks." I didn't need an image of any machine doing stuff to Logan.

"Anyway, my dad always complains how expensive it is, because the company that invented it still has the patent. Their obnoxious salesmen are pushing it big-time right now. That way when other companies can start making it, all the funeral homes will have already bought one from the inventor company. They're greedy bastards, but smart greedy bastards."

Because of her job, Megan was even more jaded than most post-Shifters. Death was big business.

"Let's go lower in the search results," she said. "The weird stuff is always on pages ten and up."

We kept scanning, and finally on the twenty-sixth page of results, a rumor-mill website contained the heading: "BlackBox maker hiring private spies?"

"Uh-oh." Megan clicked.

According to the article, SecuriLab was paying a group called Nighthawk to perform corporate espionage. Nighthawk employed ex-spooks from intelligence agencies all over the world—CIA, KGB, MI6, Israel's Mossad—along with ex-special forces operatives.

Megan read a quote aloud. "'Everyone does it,' said an anonymous source. 'Corporations have to get the edge on their competitors.'" She slanted a blue-eyed gaze at me. "By hiring ex-assassins? I'm definitely majoring in business now. It's a lot more exciting than I thought."

"And this is more dangerous than we thought." Mickey read the screen over her shoulder. "What if Nighthawk is at Area 3A? We could be going up against professional badasses tonight."

The rest of them were milling nervously around the table. Instinctively my eyes went to Dylan, Operation Scot Free's co-mastermind. He turned away and stared out the floor-to-ceiling window overlooking the sun-spattered lake. From here the boaters, Jet Skiers, and swimmers looked so carefree. Their biggest concern was avoiding sunburn, or where to find good, cheap barbecue.

"I still say secrecy *is* their security," Dylan said finally. "You don't need a thousand guards when you're hard to find. You only need a few."

"We could be supercareful." Siobhan stirred the ice cubes in her lemonade with her straw. "Go up there, see what we can see, then leave. No unnecessary risks. It's better than driving all this way for nothing."

Mickey groaned and pressed the heels of his hands to his eyes. "Not getting killed isn't 'nothing.' I don't wanna have to tell Mom and Dad that I lost another one of you."

My gut froze as we all stared at him. Mickey still felt responsible for Logan's death, despite his claims that he'd made peace with it.

Megan went to him. "Logan would've wanted us to do this. Hell, if he were here, he'd be leading us."

"She's right," I said. "If he hadn't turned into a shade back in January, he'd be in a little box at Area 3A right now. If you won't do this for Zachary, do it for ghosts like Logan. Do it for their families."

Mickey backed away. "Look, I know someone has to do something about the DMP. I just don't see why it has to be us."

"Why not us?" Siobhan shrugged and crunched a piece of ice. "Seriously. Why not us?"

Mickey did a slow pace, half the length of the table, rumpling his dark hair until I thought he'd pull it out.

Finally he stopped and turned to us. "I'm outnumbered, so okay. But I have a really bad feeling about this."

While waiting for pizza delivery, we watched online videos about how to avoid the authorities—or escape them.

Dylan made us all practice slipping out of zip ties, which he said a lot of law enforcement types used now instead of handcuffs. They were based on the plastic-and-nylon ties used for household jobs like bunching up video cables, or hanging Christmas garland, so the Keeleys had a package of them in the lake house basement.

"This is kinda fun," Siobhan admitted, watching Connor try to Houdini his hands out of the bindings.

A grin dimpled his lean cheeks. "You would like me like this, wouldn't you?"

"It's easier for girls," Dylan said quickly, probably to change the subject. "They have smaller hands."

"I will not even comment on that," Megan grunted. "Oh! I got it." She waved the white tie triumphantly, then rubbed the red marks on her pale wrists.

"Are you sure this is what they'll be using?" Mickey seemed more reluctant to escape now that it was a matter of hand size.

"Cops in New York were using them on ghost-rights protesters last month." Dylan watched me struggle with my restraint. "Aura, it's easier if you relax."

"I'm trying," I said through gritted teeth. "Funny how we haven't heard anything about ghost rights since Flight 346."

"Guess it's not cool to like ghosts anymore." Megan came over, bopping to the music on the stereo. "Aura, twist one wrist at a time. Once your thumb is loose, the rest is easy."

"Why am I the only one still bound?" Even huge-handed Mickey and Connor were tossing their zip-tie loops up and over the great room's high wooden beams like glow sticks at a concert.

"You weren't listening to the video." Dylan gave me a stern look, taking this more seriously than the rest of them put together. "The most important part comes before you're tied up. You gotta be passive. Don't let them think you're a threat."

"Right." I was supposed to present my hands, thumbs together and wrists flexed. This would make slack in the tie, so I could slip out easily. "Would a DMP agent really fall for that?"

"Maybe not." He patted my shoulder. "But if you ever get kidnapped, this'll come in handy."

The pizza arrived then, and everyone started eating without me. Mickey offered to cut me free, but I refused. Eventually I tried a new tactic: shifting the zip-tie's plastic lock so I could use my thumbnail as a shim, separating the tie from the teeth that held it tight.

"Finally." I slapped the plastic-and-nylon nightmare on the table and took a slice of pizza. My friends cheered and toasted me with raised sodas.

We went to bed at nine, setting alarms for a midnight departure. Between the midsummer sky's lingering light and my mind's restless worry, I couldn't even doze.

Hearing the television on in the main room downstairs, I got dressed and went out to the hallway, which overlooked the dark lower floor. Dylan was sitting on the love seat by the giant stone fireplace, bare feet propped on the edge of the coffee table.

"What are you watching?"

He waved the remote control, his face blue-white from the TV light. "Everything."

I went down and sat in the overstuffed armchair while Dylan flipped through the channels faster than I could follow.

"Are you looking for something in particular?" I asked.

"I keep forgetting you don't live with guys. You never watched TV with Logan?"

"Not like this. He couldn't sit still long enough."

Heated voices leaked from an upstairs bedroom. "Megan, why are you doing this?" Mickey yelled.

"Doing what? Asking to spend time alone with you for once?"

"We went out last Saturday."

"Yeah, out. In public. Not alone. Ever!"

Dylan turned up the TV volume so we couldn't hear.

"You think Mickey and Megan'll stay together?" I asked him.

He snorted. "Shyeah, right. Long-distance relationships always crash and burn."

"You're an expert?"

"I watch TV. People go to college and meet hotter people."

"Mickey won't leave Megan for a hot college girl," I said.

"You wanna bet?"

"I'm not betting on my best friend's happiness."

"If they break up, can I at least say, 'I told you so'?"

"Whatever." I wondered if his point about long-distance relationships was meant for me and Zachary, or if it was only my doubts and fears that made me interpret it that way.

"I remember when we were kids." Dylan tugged on the hem of his gray sweatshorts. "We'd come here with our cousins. Our parents and aunts and uncles and Nana would take the bedrooms, and all of us kids would camp out here in the living room."

"It must have been jammed."

"Yeah, it looked kinda like a hurricane shelter with all the sleeping bags lined up. But it was awesome. We hardly slept the whole week."

Something he said awakened a memory in me, and I sat forward in shock. "Oh my God, in the cemetery, Logan asked me to convince your grandmom to pass on. It was like a last request." I put a hand to my head, hot with shame. "I can't believe I forgot."

"That was right before the plane crash. I can totally believe you forgot."

"We could call her at your old house on Calvert Street. I've seen her ghost there in the front yard, complaining about the flowers."

"Okay, we'll do it for Logan." Still flipping channels, Dylan slouched to recline against the love seat arm, smushing a wave of brown hair against the side of his face. He paused at the twenty-four-hour concert station. It showed an old Nirvana gig from what looked like their pre-*Nevermind* days. Before I could say, "Ooh, let's watch this," Dylan kept clicking. Soon the channels were no longer in English.

"I miss Logan," he said suddenly. "Back when he was a ghost, Mickey and Siobhan were jealous I could talk to him and they couldn't. But now that he's passed on, they seem so normal, and I feel so abnormal."

It was good to hear someone else say it. "It feels like I just started missing him."

"Because he just left."

"The worst is when I listen to the radio," I said. "I hear a new song, and it hits me that he'll never hear it. He'll never say something sucks or something rocks. We'll never argue over whether a band is so last month."

"It was really bad last weekend at the beach. I kept expecting his ghost to show up at the arcade or in our cousins' apartment where we stay, like he did Memorial Day weekend. I couldn't even eat a stupid funnel cake without remembering how he liked them."

"With powdered sugar and apple pie filling." I tried to laugh, but it came out like a cough. "So gross."

"I know, I *hate* the pie stuff. They're better with just sugar."

"That way you can taste the dough."

"Seriously. And our parents always used to make us share one, because a whole funnel cake would get us too wired. But last Saturday I had one all to myself, just the way I like it, and I couldn't—" His jaw worked, like he was trying to swallow. "It tasted like nothing."

To my left, the TV suddenly went silent. I looked at the screen to see that Dylan had reached the top of the listings, where everything was pay-per-view.

"Four hundred channels of shit," he said. "How is that *possible?*" He hurled the remote control at the couch across from me. It bounced off the back cushion and onto the floor.

A heaviness filled my chest at the sight of his grief. Dylan understood more than anyone how much pain remained. But getting closer to him felt as dangerous as stepping into a bonfire.

Still, Dylan had comforted me when I'd needed him. I could do no less.

I stepped around the coffee table, sat on the edge of the love seat beside him, and took his hand.

It felt strange, like it was a different hand than the one that had groped me back in May. Maybe that was a good thing.

Dylan gave my hand a quick squeeze, then a longer one. He fidgeted with the seam of the green throw pillow, his face tight with tension.

Uh-oh. Was our new lack of attraction mutual or something only I felt? Would he be relieved or hurt if I let go?

"You shouldn't do that." His knee jittered, making his heel tap the floor. "It makes me want to—"

"Oh my goodness!" a woman shouted. "Am I interrupting something?"

We jerked our hands apart, and I almost slipped off the love seat. A trim, elderly lady sat in the chair with her legs crossed primly and her entire form shimmering in violet.

Dylan touched his chest like he'd had a near heart attack. "Nana, what are you doing here?"

Chapter Sixteen

W hat do you mean, what am I doing here? You called me, so I came."

"We didn't call, we just mentioned you." Dylan stood and stepped forward. "Hi."

"I'm so sorry I haven't been around. I was afraid the men with the black uniforms and little boxes would try to grab me again."

I gaped at her. "The Obsidian Corps tried to get you?" The Obsidians were the DMP special forces unit that protected the country from shades and at-risk ghosts.

"I saw them at your old house," she said to Dylan, "and on my street in Ellicott City. I don't go there anymore."

"Why would the Obsidians want to capture you?" he asked her. "Were you shady?"

"Oh goodness, no. I don't know why they'd find someone like me interesting."

I knew why. She was a ghost related to Logan. If the DMP thought he had special qualities, they might wonder if it was genetic.

Ex–Nana Keeley turned to me. "I'm ready now."

"To pass on?"

"No, to play roulette at the Bellagio. Of course, to pass on." She looked between us, maybe trying to read the nature of our relationship. "Are you two alone?"

"Nana Keeley!" Megan straightened her nut-brown Sleater-Kinney T-shirt and beckoned Mickey to follow her down the stairs. "She's in the chair."

"Great." Mickey sounded skeptical. "So what, uh . . ."

"Brings her here?" Dylan was still on the love seat, knees drawn to his chest. "She wants to tell us good-bye."

Mickey stopped on the landing. "Oh," he whispered. Then he moved forward reverently, as if down the aisle of a cathedral, stopping to kneel beside his grandmom's chair.

"Nana? Is that really you?" Upstairs, Siobhan clutched the wooden railing. "Aura, ask her why she's passing on now after all these years."

"If Logan can do it," their grandmother answered, "so can I. He loved this world more than anyone I know, but he left it behind. And after less than a year of being a ghost." She scrunched up her eyes. "It was less than a year, right? I lose track of time."

"Two hundred forty-seven days," I confirmed, thinking of ex–Tammi Teller's obsessive count.

"So how do we do this?" she asked me. "Is there a light I'm supposed to walk toward?"

"I think it's more like, you become the light." I looked at the Keeley siblings. "Did you guys want to tell her anything before she goes?"

"I'll start." Dylan gripped his knees, knocking them together. "I'll miss you, Nana. But I'm glad you're going. I think you'll be glad, too." His lips folded under for a moment. "I love you."

Ex–Nana Keeley wiped a tear from her right eye. I made a mental note to call my own grandmom when I got home.

Siobhan sat on the arm of the love seat. "Nana, I wish I could see you one more time, but I want to say, thanks. Thanks for buying me that fiddle when I was seven and for not letting me quit when I sucked at it. And thanks for all the banana bread. No one makes it like you." She scrunched the material of her green pajama pants and looked at Connor, who stood near the stairs. "That's my boyfriend, Connor. He puts up with me. You'd like him."

Her grandmother laughed. "Silly, I already like him. I've been watching you two for over a year."

I decided not to translate the second sentence.

"Anyway," Siobhan concluded, "I love you, Nana. Say hi to Granddad for me, okay?"

"Ugh, Lord, spare me the sight of him. But I love you, too." As I translated the last bit for Siobhan, their grandmother turned to Mickey, kneeling on the floor beside her. "Look at you. I always knew you'd grow up to be so handsome."

Behind me, Megan sniffled. Mickey blushed when I told him

what his grandmother had said. He shifted closer to her and started to whisper words I couldn't hear.

Ex–Nana Keeley leaned in, her eyes growing distant. Finally she nodded slowly. "I guarantee it."

Then she sat back in the chair and looked straight ahead, as if settling in to watch TV. A golden light began to glow in her stomach.

Megan slipped her arm through mine. "Mickey, it's starting."

As the glow expanded outward into her limbs, their grandmother's smile widened. The only sound was Siobhan's soft sniffles.

With a burst of light that made me shade my eyes, the ghost of Nana Keeley vanished.

"Wow." Dylan's feet slid from the edge of the couch, thumping the floor. "I wish there was a way to let Logan know."

Siobhan reached for the floral tissue box on the end table. "Maybe she can tell him herself."

We sat in silence, thinking of departed Keeleys, then Dylan said, "The DMP was following Nana."

Mickey lifted his head. "They were *what*?" he snarled. "Why?"

"Because of Logan?" I said. "Maybe they wanted to figure stuff out about him by studying her."

Dylan gave his brother a level look. "They would've stuck our grandmother in a little box. Forever."

Mickey drew in a deep shaky breath through his nose, then blew it out. "Let's go destroy them."

We parked the SUV half a mile from the DMP entrance and far enough from the road that it couldn't be seen.

Dressed head-to-toe in black, including ski masks—in case of security cameras—the six of us trudged through the woods. Luckily, this terrain had a gentler slope than the mountains Zachary and I had fled down a couple of weeks before. The night was new-moon dark, so we used flashlights to keep from breaking our ankles.

Thinking of the black Escalade we'd left behind reminded me of my last day with Zachary.

"Those movies get it all wrong." He frowns at the tricked-out Aston Martin on exhibit at the International Spy Museum. "This car's too flashy. The whole idea of spying is not to be noticed."

I raise my voice over the music and gunfire. "What do real spies drive?"

"In my country, mostly black Range Rovers." He checks out the line of James Bond posters. "None of these lads would blend in. Too good-looking."

"That disqualifies you, then."

Zachary laughs, then under his breath does a spot-on Austin Powers impression, telling me to "behave." Spots of red appear on his cheeks in perfect symmetry. Wow, he even blushes gorgeous.

We enter the next corridor, a replica of the hidden tunnel the CIA built under Berlin during the Cold War. I wait patiently while Zachary reads every informational plaque, as he did at the Air and Space Museum earlier.

"Incredible." Zachary gestures to the walls. "The Soviets knew about this tunnel for years, and they didn't do anything. They let their East German allies be spied on."

"Why?"

"Because they found out through a British agent of theirs, and they didn't want to blow his cover. He was too valuable an asset." His face turns pensive. "Pays to be a traitor. You never get left out in the cold."

A metallic clamor comes from overhead, the thump of feet and taunting laughter of what sounds like middle-school boys.

"What's that?" Zachary asks.

"There's a tour that'll let you explore secret corridors and stuff on your own. So you can play spy."

"Secret corridors?" He sidles closer, near enough so I can inhale him. "Away from the crowds?"

"It costs extra."

"I don't care." He nuzzles the corner of my jaw, making me shiver. "I'd pay anything to get you alone."

I shook myself back to the present. Now was not the time to get caught up in memories of Zachary's hotness.

I thought about what he'd said in the museum, before the boys had distracted us: that spies took care of their agents, the people they'd paid to betray their own countries. Would MI-X have my back if I got caught? Probably not, since I wasn't officially working for them, which made me feel both less guilty and less protected.

I felt in the pocket of my hoodie, where I'd sewn a secure pouch for the red phone Simon had given me. Its presence was a comfort, and if anyone found it, it held no evidence, since I'd already memorized his phone number, as well as the Moores'. In my other pocket I carried my bottle cap with the spiral, for luck and strength.

Ahead, the undergrowth thinned and the land between the trees flattened and cleared. Gone were the rocks and vines and clumps of brush we'd been battling.

"Thank God," Megan muttered. "If I trip over one more rock, I'll—aaugh!"

Her shriek echoed in the breezeless woods. She flailed at the ground in front of her, where a thick black snake slithered away through the fallen leaves.

"Jesus, Megan!" Dylan hissed. "Why don't you wake up the whole—"

There was a flash as bright as lightning, then a sickening *zap!* My heartbeat spiked like I'd taken an electric surge myself.

I shielded my eyes and tried to blink away the blindness. Had someone attacked us? I couldn't run or fight if I couldn't see.

"Holy shit," Connor said. "What was that?"

Slowly my vision returned. The black snake was writhing on the ground, shifting leaves and soil in its agony. Then it lay still.

At the smell of burnt flesh, I covered my nose and mouth with my sleeve.

"Electric fence," Mickey said. "But where?" He waved his flashlight beam over the terrain. Nothing appeared except two thin poles about twenty feet apart.

No wires, no bars. No warning.

"An invisible electric fence?" Siobhan asked. "Like what people use for dogs?"

"Invisible dog fences don't work that way," Connor said. "They only give a shock to whatever's wearing the collar."

"Uh-oh, check this out." Dylan's flashlight beam swept an arc across the ground. What it illuminated made my blood run cold.

An array of dead animals—mice, squirrels, rabbits—marked where the invisible fence ran to our left and right.

"Poor babies," Megan said. "Except for the snake. I'm glad it's dead."

I snorted. "Yeah, because if it weren't, we'd all be zapped."

Everyone fell silent, contemplating the fate the snake had saved us from. Then Dylan spoke.

"The fence might not have killed us. All these crispy critters are little. No deer or coyotes or bears."

"Bears?" Megan took a step back. "There are *bears* in these woods?"

"They're probably not the kind that eat people," Mickey said. "Those are out west, right?"

"Actually, I read an article—" Connor cut himself off at a look from Mickey. "Um, an article that said, yeah, bears around here are safe. Totally afraid of people."

"You guys!" I whisper-shouted. "We have bigger problems than bears. We can't go any farther, which means we can't help Zachary." I shoved my hands in my pockets before I threw my flashlight in frustration.

My fingers hit the red phone. *Maybe there* is *a way to help Zachary.*

"I think we should leave," Siobhan stated firmly. "Like, yesterday."

Everyone agreed, some more eagerly than others. I pulled out my red phone and activated the camera feature.

"Good idea," Dylan said. "Evidence. But who can you give it to who won't rip you a new one for being here?"

"I'll worry about that later." I took three zoomed-in photos of the sad display of animal carcasses, then three wide shots of the poles where I assumed the fence's electrical current originated.

We trekked back toward the car as rapidly as we could without tripping. I lingered behind so I could text the pictures to Simon.

PLS REPLY WHEN U GET THES. I'M @3A.

As I trotted to catch up to the others, Simon texted back:

RECEIVED 6 PHOTOS, ALL CLEAR. PLEASE TELL ME YOU'RE JOKING.

I deleted the photos and repocketed my phone without answering.

Suddenly Connor stopped. He was the only one not breathing hard, probably because he was half a foot taller and therefore had to take fewer steps to cover the same distance. "Do you guys hear that?" he asked.

I held my breath and tilted my head. An engine whined far behind us. Then another, and another. It sounded like the DMP was having a motorcycle rally.

"ATVs," Dylan said. "Run!"

We ran. My legs screamed, and I could barely pull air into my lungs through the woolen ski mask, but fear propelled me forward.

The engines grew louder. Closer. No way we could outrun them. I grabbed Dylan's arm and pulled him to a stop.

"You guys—go on"—I panted—"without me."

"No way!" He tugged me forward, but I dug in my heels.

"I'm the one they want. I'll tell them"—I gulped air, my thoughts frantic—"I went with you to Deep Creek then hitchhiked. I'm the only person with a reason to be here. Better one of us gets in trouble than all."

Dylan nodded solemnly. "Very logical, Mr. Spock." He bent to scoop me up. "But you're coming with us."

I held back a yelp as he swept my legs out from under me. Dylan took one step, then collapsed.

Suddenly Megan was beside us. "Connor's running for the car alone. We'll meet him on the road 'cause it's more direct, and he's faster, so—oh, screw the explanation." She jerked us to our feet. "Come on!"

We headed straight up the hill until we reached the road. Then we ran along the shoulder toward the pull-off spot, which was almost half a mile away.

No sign of Connor. Had he gotten lost? Hurt? Had he taken off without us?

The ATVs hummed ever closer.

"Come on," Siobhan huffed as we sprinted. "Connor, baby, don't leave us."

A flood of light burst through the trees behind us. "Freeze!" said a rattling voice from a megaphone.

An ATV's engine whined with effort as it tried to climb the steep hill near the road.

"Keep running!" I shouted.

"This is your last warning," the voice came again. "Stop immediately, lie on your stomachs, and put your hands behind your heads. Or we will be forced to—"

Another engine roared, cutting him off. The Keeleys' Escalade careened toward us, fishtailing around the bend in the road.

The brakes screeched as the SUV came to a stop. We piled in, clambering over the seats and each other to reach safety. Connor gunned it before the doors were even shut.

Keeping my ski mask on, I looked out the window as we drove away. Several men in dark blue uniforms stood on the side of the road. Another ten seconds and Connor would've been too late.

"They might've seen our plates!" Mickey said.

"Nope." Connor tossed two flat white pieces of metal into the seat behind him. The license plates were bent nearly in half where they'd been pried off, probably with the crowbar lying at my feet. "We might wanna stop by the DMV on the way home."

We spent the rest of the weekend at the lake house, jumping at the sound of every car driving past. After several urgent texts from Simon, I found a moment alone to let him know that yes, I was okay, and no, I wasn't coming back that instant so he could ream me out.

Mickey and Megan's tensions rose over the next two days, until finally, on the drive home . . .

"I love this song!" Megan cranked up the satellite radio station. "We should put it on our road trip mix for next weekend."

Mickey said nothing, but his shoulders rose an inch or two. Normally when Megan had her mind set on something, he eventually gave in out of exhaustion. I wished Megan could sense that this time was different.

"It's a great song," I said, before they started another argument. "But I heard it's the only track worth getting off the new release. The rest supposedly suck." I'd actually heard the opposite, but I wanted to distract her.

"Hmm." Her tone, and the way she stared at Mickey's clenched jaw, told me my tactic hadn't worked.

I looked over at Dylan, who was mesmerized by a handheld video game. Behind me, Siobhan and Connor appeared to be napping.

"So I can come with you next weekend, then?" Megan asked Mickey. "You've changed your mind?"

He remained silent for a full ten seconds, then slapped on his turn signal. "Guys, we're making a pit stop. Siobhan, can you fill the tank?"

"What?" His sister yawned. "Where are we? Didn't we just stop?" I shook my head at her in warning.

Mickey pulled off at the exit, then into a gas station across from the on-ramp. We were in the mountains west of Hagerstown, more than an hour from home.

While Siobhan was filling the tank, Mickey stalked around the back of the station, Megan on his heels. I got out of the SUV and considered going to the bathroom, but it was one of those gas stations with the restrooms on the outside of the building. Those were always gross, and you usually had to ask some skeevy dude for the key, which always had something huge like a carburetor attached so you wouldn't walk off with it in your pocket.

Dylan and Connor and I went to the rust-rimmed vending machines for chips and sodas. The clank of our change and the thunk of the cans couldn't cover the shouting behind the station.

"This has nothing to do with you," Mickey said. "I want two days to set up my apartment on my own. With no one's help or advice or interference. Can't you understand that?"

"I can't understand why you'd turn down a chance for us to get away together alone. Why does spending time with me not sound like more fun than buying a toaster?"

"It's not about fun. It's about getting the fuck away."

"From me? You want to get away from me?"

Mickey groaned. "Could you try just once speaking a sentence that doesn't use the word 'me'? Just *once*, Logan?"

My stomach flipped. I raised my gaze to meet Dylan's, then Connor's. They shook their heads sadly and walked back toward the SUV. Dylan kicked an empty soda can, bouncing it off the station's dingy concrete base.

Megan whimpered. "Did you—Mickey, what did you call me? Am I really that much like him? Is that why you—" Her next words were muffled, like she was covering her mouth. "You do need to get away from me, don't you?"

"No." His soft protest sounded halfhearted. "Megan, no." Shoes scraped loose gravel. "Come here."

"Uh-uh." Megan sniffled hard. "I get it now. I finally get it." Her voice turned calm and hollow. "I have to let you go."

I stepped away quietly, but instead of returning to the car, I waited by the front of the gas station. Connor started wiping the Escalade's windshield with the station's squeegee.

The salt-and-vinegar chips had no taste. My tongue felt numb and my fingers cold as I contemplated our collective future. No more me & Logan, no more Siobhan & Connor, and now no more Megan & Mickey.

After paying for the gas, Siobhan came over to me. "What's happening now?"

"I think she's breaking up with him."

"Whoa. I always thought it'd be the other way around."

"Me too." I offered her my chips.

"Thanks." She took the bag and leaned against the building next to me. "This is gonna sound weird, but it makes me hopeful."

"You want them to be miserable?"

"We've all been miserable since Logan died. We thought we had to be, to honor him. But that's the last thing he'd want."

She was right. Logan always wanted everyone he loved to be happy, and thought it was his own personal failure if they weren't.

"I'm sorry we couldn't help Zachary," Siobhan said. "Don't give up fighting for him. Let me know if there's anything else I can do for you, like bitch-slap some dumpers." She spat out the last word, our favorite term for DMP agents.

Mickey and Megan appeared then, shuffling like zombies toward the car. Their eyes were red and their faces, pink.

Siobhan pushed away from the wall. "I'll drive."

Mickey gave a shaky nod and kept moving. The rest of the way home, he sat with Dylan in the middle seat while I sat in back with Megan.

No one said anything. Mickey and Megan stared straight ahead, frozen, as if one movement would shatter them. I reached for her hand to comfort her, but she moved it, patted mine quickly, then crossed her arms so I couldn't try again.

When we dropped her off at home, I climbed out to help get her bags. "I'll call you," I said.

"No. Let me call you." She picked up her bag and gave me a limp half hug.

"Okay," I said, but didn't mean it. I'd let her have half an hour, tops, before I showed up at her door.

But I doubted a tub of rocky road ice cream and a stack of cheesy-movie DVDs would be enough to comfort her. Maybe that old cliché was right, and time could one day heal all the wounds Logan's death had dealt.

Now that he'd found his peace, we each had to search for our own.

Chapter Seventeen

"*What* were you thinking?" Simon stalked past the Poe House's antique dining room table. His usual calm demeanor had dissolved into full-fledged twitchiness.

"I was thinking that Zachary was in a horrible place while you guys were doing nothing. Turns out I was right. Have you shown your boss the pictures I sent?"

"You think we didn't already know about 3A's security features? You really believe that you lot were able to accomplish what trained agents of Her Majesty's Secret Service were not?"

"Were we?"

Simon didn't answer.

I sat with my back to the narrow staircase, which I'd climbed with Zachary on our last birthday, up to the attic bedroom, where he'd held my hand and told me he was determined to possess my heart. The memory both saddened and comforted me.

Decades ago MI-X had helped the Edgar Allan Poe Society keep this small brick home from being torn down, and in return, the society let MI-X use it as a short-term safe house. Ian had brought me and Zachary here that night to explain our sensitive security situation in private.

In other words, to yell at us, like Simon was doing now.

"In the future," Simon said, "do nothing. No more investigating. No more spying."

"But I thought—"

"No more thinking. Be a normal teenager."

I scowled. Had he forgotten he'd been a teen himself three years ago? "What about Nicola? You told me to get information out of her."

"Stop meeting with her for now, until we're sure the DMP doesn't suspect you were one of the trespassers." Simon took off his glasses and squinted through them at the flickering wall sconce.

I thought of the men in midnight-blue uniforms who'd chased us. "Have you ever heard of a group called 'Nighthawk'?"

Simon froze, staring at me, looking suddenly younger. "Of course I have. Why?"

"SecuriLab may have hired them. They might've been there Friday night, but I'm not sure."

He said nothing as he cleaned his glasses with the tail of his brick-red polo shirt.

"You didn't know that, did you?" I asked him.

"Not personally." He examined his glasses, then put them back on. "I'm sure my superiors know."

"It would've been nice if they'd told you, so you could tell me what I'm up against."

"Aura, listen!" He jerked out the chair across from me and sat down. "Isn't it enough to know we're up against something big? Why must you question?"

"Because I'm not paid to take orders like you are. How big is this 'something'?"

"Big enough to scare both our governments."

"Shit." I remembered something he'd said a couple of weeks ago when I'd asked why MI-X couldn't demand Zachary's release. "Does this have to do with those 'other interests' you mentioned?" I dug my nails against the rough wooden tabletop. "Is SecuriLab the 'other interest'? If they make BlackBox, they must be superrich."

"True." He drew his bottom lip between his thumb and forefinger. "A company that size would have both our countries by the bollocks." He glanced at me. "Sorry."

My nose wrinkled at the gross but convincing image. "So it's SecuriLab we should be worried about? Not the DMP? Or do they want the same thing?"

"They both have an interest in the dead. But the DMP would like to end the Shift and get rid of ghosts."

"Which would mean no more need for BlackBox."

"And no more money for SecuriLab."

I looked out into the Poe House living room, filled with the author's possessions from his early twenties, when he fell in love with the girl he would someday marry. The museum's caretaker had told me and Zachary that Poe had never gotten over her early death. At the time, I'd wondered if I would ever recover from losing Logan.

Poe came back to Baltimore years later, but not to this house. He was found wandering the streets, incoherent or maybe drunk, and died a few days later. No one knew the cause of death, but some conspiracy theories said he'd been murdered because he'd pissed off someone powerful.

I sat up straight, glimpsing a new possibility, like someone had ripped aside a curtain to let in the afternoon sun.

"Simon, that's why the DMP hasn't killed me yet."

"Sorry?"

"Because my death might end the Shift. No more ghosts, no more BlackBox, no more humongous profits." I forced out the ugliest truth. "SecuriLab might be all that's keeping me alive."

Simon had told me to stay away from Nicola, but of course he didn't tell *her* to stay away from *me*.

"Aura!"

I looked up from my desk to see Nicola parading across my aunt's law office toward me. At a nearby file cabinet, our paralegal, Terrence, gave me a "Should I get rid of her?" look.

I shook my head and tried to smile. "Hey, Nicola."

"Told you I'd come through for you!" She held out a blank, white, letter-size envelope at either end with her fingertips, displaying it like a game-show hostess with the grand prize.

I leaped out of my chair to grab the envelope. I tore it open, glad it wasn't sealed, or I would've gotten a nasty paper cut.

I unfolded the single sheet of notebook paper. The handwriting was definitely Zachary's, though shakier than usual.

> July 10
> Dear Aura,
> I needed you to know that I
> am alive, and that I love you.
> Don't give up hope.
> Zachary

My knees wobbled as I sat slowly, brushing my fingers over the words.

Which were way too few. I flipped the page over. "This is all they'd let him write?"

She peered over my shoulder. "Ooh, that is brief. Is he usually more verbose than that?"

I shook the paper at her. "Does this sound like a letter from a boyfriend or a letter from a hostage?"

Nicola crossed her arms and tapped her French-manicured nails against her biceps. "Hmm. They probably told him what he could and couldn't say, for security reasons. So do you have a response for him?"

"I do." Still holding the letter Zachary had sent, I pulled my memo pad from my bag. I tore out the back page and handed it to Nicola.

I hoped the DMP would think my message was harmless enough to give to Zachary unedited. Even if he couldn't guess my exact meaning, maybe he'd take the hint that he shouldn't try to escape. The thought of him running full speed into that invisible electric fence made me shudder as if my own body had been shocked.

Dear Zachary,
I love you and miss you so much. I'd give anything to bust down your door and be in your arms again. But the world doesn't work that way right now. Please stay strong, stay safe, and stay there.
Love, Aura

"What's going on?"

Gina's sharp voice made me and Nicola jump.

"Aura was—"

"Give me that." Gina snatched the note from Nicola and held it at arm's length so she could read it without her glasses. "Aura, why didn't you tell me about this?"

I crammed the letter from Zachary between my skirt and the chair I was sitting in. "I was about to do that when you walked up and stole it."

"Is there a problem?" Nicola asked her. "I don't want to cause trouble."

"You're with the DMP, so by definition, you *are* trouble. Please leave my office."

Nicola reached for the letter. "Of course, but can I—"

"No!" Gina put her hands on her hips and took a step toward her. Though Nicola had five inches of height on my aunt, she backed away quickly, her face crumpling.

"I'm so sorry. I wanted to help." She hurried out, her steps unsteady, like she couldn't quite see where she was going.

"Can I please have my note back?" I asked Gina.

Her face softened. "Hon, I know it's hard not be able to communicate with him. But your letters won't get through, and they'll only expose you to the DMP." Though we usually didn't hug at the office, she put her arm around my shoulders and squeezed me tight. "We'll get through this together."

When she went back to her office, I rewrote my letter to Zachary and slipped it into the blank envelope. Hiding it in my lap, I copied the address off Nicola's business card.

My cell phone buzzed with a text message:

Nicola: MAIL IT TO ME.

I smiled. ALREADY DONE. :)

Nicola: MEANT TO TELL YOU, THERE WAS A SECURITY BREACH @3A LAST WKD.

I was glad she couldn't see my face, only my words: OMG! WHO WAS IT?

Nicola: THEY DIDN'T CATCH THEM. ANYWAY, TALK SOON, I HOPE! *WAVES*

I folded the letter from Zachary into a tiny square, then clutched it inside my fist. "I hope so, too."

Chapter Eighteen

As the heat wave intensified, so did my fear and frustration. Every rescue scheme I devised came unraveled in the face of reality. I began to feel like a ghost, wandering through my own life like it no longer belonged to me, like I could no longer change even one small corner of the world.

Cheryl, Gina's immigration-lawyer friend, was finally allowed to visit Zachary. She took with her a man from the British consulate, and afterward reported that Zachary was "fine, but a little thin." I knew that couldn't be the full truth, but I clung to that proof of his survival like a life jacket in a stormy sea.

A hundred times I picked up the phone to call a newspaper or TV station, hoping media attention to Zachary's case might set him free. A hundred times I put the phone back down.

Gina had warned that now that the DMP were seen as heroes

protecting us from ghosts, revealing Zachary's whereabouts would only make him look suspicious. People would ask, "Why would they detain him if he'd done nothing wrong?" When it came to ghost-crimes these days, guilty before proven innocent was becoming the rule. And if the person was a foreigner like the alleged suicide bomber teen? Doubly suspicious. Doubly condemned.

Tammi Teller had become the symbol of the Flight 346 tragedy, and her Keeley Brothers' fandom kept people talking about Logan. Since I was connected to him, the spotlight was always searching for me. If people found out my new boyfriend was some kind of anti-ghost freak, that spotlight would find and destroy my life.

And if it became known that I was the First, soon everyone would draw the same conclusion the DMP had: If my birth had caused the Shift, then maybe my death would end it. Killing me would be one quick solution to the "ghost problem."

The media fed the country's rising hysteria about the dead. Every week brought a new prime-time TV program about "radical influential ghosts." These always got huge ratings in the pre-Shifter target audience.

Post-Shifters felt like we were under a microscope. I'd walk down the street with Megan and our friend Jenna, and the other pedestrians would examine us to determine (a) whether we were pre- or post-Shifters (one of "them" or one of "us"), and (b) whether we were talking to one another or talking to ghosts. It was like when we were little kids and the world had just started believing us. But now we were old enough to understand: *We* were the enemy within.

I kept myself sane by researching university astronomy programs to narrow down my list of colleges. In a moment of extreme hope, I put the University of Glasgow on my list. It helped to pretend that my future could one day be my own.

And lastly, to feed my hope, I got up at sunrise every morning, rain or shine. I lit the green candle Gina had used for our vigil on the night of the Flight 346 crash. For exactly one minute, I closed my eyes and thought of Zachary. Then I blew it out and went back to sleep, hoping to dream of him—and that somehow, somewhere, he'd dream of me, too.

"How did you get these amazing seats?" I asked Nicola.

She shrugged. "From work, of course."

Nicola Hughes had called me out of the blue and asked if I wanted to see an Orioles game with her at Camden Yards. I didn't follow baseball much, since the only thing that changed from year to year was the degree of the Orioles' suckitude, and by August the season was long past hope. But I couldn't pass up the chance to get more information.

I set my soda in the cup holder and examined my surroundings. We were so close to home plate, I swore I could feel the breeze from the batters' swings.

No way a government agency could afford Camden Yards box seats. I'd seen the DMP offices—their decor was vintage early '90s. These seats belonged to SecuriLab.

Eating my crab cake sandwich, I thought wistfully of the times I'd been here with Logan and his family, and resolved to call Dylan the next day. Megan and I hadn't spent much time with the Keeleys since our failed Fourth of July "commando raid." It was too painful after her breakup with Mickey.

Nicola elbowed me. "You should put your hat back on so you don't get sunburned."

"But it's seven o'clock in the—"

"Put your hat on." Nicola peeked over her shoulder up the stairs. "Now."

I didn't question. I pulled my battered black Orioles cap out of my bag and placed it firmly on my head, pulling my ponytail through the hole.

In a low voice, Nicola said, "Two places women are most invisible in this world? Boardrooms and sporting events. When I go golfing with my coworkers, I learn a lot by just shutting up. They forget I'm there, and they discuss things I'm not supposed to hear."

I tugged down the brim of my hat, sat back in my seat, and watched from the corner of my eye as two late-middle-aged guys in expensive polo shirts and khaki slacks sat behind us.

They turned out to be Yankees fans, so they spent the first hour dissing the Orioles. I wanted to throw them a dirty look, but couldn't risk them recognizing me. For all I knew, my face was on a Most Annoying poster in the SecuriLab offices.

"Did you see those July numbers?" asked the guy on the right, the one with the deep voice and the heavier New York accent.

"Did I *see* 'em? I'm thinking of getting them tattooed on my ass. Biggest sales growth since the first two months of release. Can't wait to see those quarterly figures."

"Tell me about it. Gonna be a good Christmas."

I tried to chew softly so I could hear.

"I'm taking the family to Tahiti. Hang on." He let out a forceful sneeze that made me want to go buy an umbrella. "Damn hay fever. Happens every time I leave Manhattan."

"Tahiti, huh?"

"Yep." The sneezer blew his nose. "Tax-deductible, of course, since it's a market we've been trying to reach. I'll make a few initial contacts, feel them out. Don't want to lay on the hard sell yet."

"Don't need to anymore—346 speaks for itself."

My spine jolted. Did they mean *Flight* 346? It sounded like they were talking about the increased sales of BlackBox since the disaster. It made sense—with the rising paranoia, people would be clamoring for a way to make their homes and businesses off-limits to ghosts.

I glanced at Nicola, who had been unusually quiet, especially for her. She paged absentmindedly through her ball-game program as she sipped her soda.

Deep-Voice Guy added, "Of course, part of the profit increase is the unit price, not just number of units moved. Demand went up, so we raised the price, because we could. Nice, huh?"

The sneezer gave a heavy sigh. "Nah, Joe, it's not nice. This whole business . . ."

I stopped chewing. Beside me, Nicola had gone totally still. Their next words could hold the key to—

A crack sounded, then the crowd roared, rising to its feet. *Damn it.*

"No, no, no, no, no, no!" Joe whined as the ball soared over the center-field fence. His next words were lost in the crescendo of cheers and blare of music.

While I clapped and danced, I checked out the men from the corner of my eye. They wore and carried nothing that gave me a clue. Not that I thought they'd bring a briefcase of classified documents to a baseball game, or wear badges that read: I BOMBED FLIGHT 346. ASK ME HOW!

The men sat back down while the home crowd savored this rare crushing of the Evil Empire. I strained to hear the guys' next words, which were louder than I think they knew:

"The lengths we gotta go to sometimes," said the sneezer. "The slime buckets we gotta deal with. Sometimes I think I'd rather, I don't know, retire to a farm somewhere and forget them all."

"I take it you mean Nighthawk?" Joe asked.

I sat down, partly to hear better and partly because my legs had gone rubbery from the shock and thrill.

"Yeah," the sneezer said. "If those pit bulls did what I think they did, and did it for us—"

"Don't think about it. When the cards are all counted, we're protecting the public. Never forget that."

I sipped my soda to ease my nerves and look natural.

"I know, I know, I tell myself that all the time. But whenever I see Tammi Teller's face on the news, I wonder, did we put her there?"

I bit the straw so hard it cracked.

There was a long silence, then Joe spoke. "Did we?"

They stopped talking for several minutes. I got a headache from straining my ears to hear them. Eventually they started discussing the Yankees' playoff chances.

When Nicola went to the restroom, I jotted everything I could remember of the guys' conversation into my phone, looking like any other bored girl at a baseball game, texting her friends. I held it low in my lap so they couldn't see.

I felt a tap on my shoulder. "Excuse me, miss."

Instinctively I shoved my sunglasses up the bridge of my nose to better cover my eyes. "What?" I snapped.

"Your friend. What's her name?"

I kept my mouth shut. I didn't want to tell them a fake name for Nicola, in case they actually knew her.

"It's not what you think," he said. "I'm not trying to hit on you guys. I just thought I knew her from work."

"Then you can ask her when she comes back."

But they didn't.

Nicola and I walked to the parking lot amid the jubilant Oriole fans and morose Yankee fans. My stomach was twisted in a knot, and not just from all the junk food. I sensed that if I asked the perfect question, Nicola would confirm my suspicions about SecuriLab and Flight 346. She must have brought me to the ball game tonight hoping I'd hear what I needed to know.

"Um, Nicola?"

She spoke quickly. "Those guys behind us were obnoxious, weren't they? When I go to Nationals games, the Phillies fans are the same way. They come in from out of town and take over the stadium. It ends up being like a Phillies home game, with all the noise they make."

She kept chattering, which gave me my answer. We weren't to

remotely acknowledge why we'd really been at the game.

That night I typed up the rest of my notes, which now totaled nearly a hundred pages' worth of conversations, conjectures, and search results. None of it was hard evidence, but it all pointed in one direction:

MI-X was wrong when they thought the DMP sent that plane down. It was SecuriLab—or rather, it was Nighthawk, SecuriLab's "pit bulls."

Or was it? The guys at the game had only implied that Nighthawk was responsible. Maybe they weren't high up enough in the company to know that kind of dirt for sure.

But they'd had their suspicions, and my goal wasn't to convict them in a court of law. I just needed the DMP to know that someone on the outside suspected, too.

Someone who needed "leverage" to set Zachary free.

"I got you a present," I told Simon as I slid into the seat across from him at the Free Spirit Café.

He eyed my office-supply store shopping bag. "Huzzah?"

"School supplies. They were on massive sale, and I figured you might not know what to get." I set the bag on the shiny black-tile floor next to his feet.

"You realize we have schools in England. I went to one, in fact. They let each of us have our own notebook and everything."

"Three-ring binders are really big here. They're the best for organizing information." I emphasized the last word. "For projects. Especially."

Simon tilted up his chin, a barely perceptible gesture of understanding. "Brilliant. Thanks very much."

I tapped my heel against the floor, bobbing my knee. Inside that binder were my notes—the activities of the DMP and their BlackBox-making buddies. Which I was now giving to a foreign agent.

This information wasn't stolen, and I didn't work for the government myself, but this act probably made me a traitor. It could've fallen into the category of "whatever it takes" to get Zachary free.

But I didn't just want my boyfriend back. I wanted revenge. I wanted to destroy the DMP forever.

Chapter Nineteen

I nsomnia usually plagued me the night before the first day of school. I'd be worried I'd forgotten everything about math, or that I'd get a teacher in love with pop quizzes, or that my lunch schedule wouldn't match any of my friends' and I'd have to eat alone.

But the night before my senior year began, I lost sleep for another reason: It had been a week since I'd delivered to MI-X what seemed like killer dirt on the DMP, and Zachary was still in custody. Maybe they would never let him go. Or maybe he was already dead. His parents hadn't heard directly from him since early July, when he'd sent them a brief letter like the one he sent me. The man from the British consulate hadn't seen him since the beginning of August.

When I finally drifted off to sleep, I wished I hadn't.

In my dream, I walked through the woods alone, and though

it was dark, I didn't stumble. In fact, I could barely feel the ground beneath my feet.

Just ahead over a slight rise, a brilliant white light coaxed me forward, flashing like the strobe lights at a concert. I clapped my hands in a quickening rhythm, as if to call out the band for one more encore.

I crested the hill and stopped short. This light heralded no music or any other kind of fun. And rather than one light, it was hundreds, arcing back and forth to create a wall.

The DMP's invisible electric fence. A small animal was caught in it, triggering the continuous zaps. I picked up a crooked branch and hurried forward. Maybe I could safely pull it away from the fence and end its flailing struggle.

But as I reached the fence, I realized that the foot-long creature was on the other side, facing me. I couldn't touch it without hurting or maybe even killing myself.

The electric flashes blinded me. I could barely see the little paws clinging to the fence's invisible wires. Was it a squirrel? A rabbit? Its form was so familiar. . . .

The light flashed above its face, and I screamed.

It wasn't an animal. It was Zachary. Tiny, terrified, helpless. His eyes rolled back in his head, and his mouth opened in silent agony.

Knees shaking, I took a step back. But then my hands reached out, as if of their own accord. I lunged through the fence to save him.

The world turned white.

A knocking sound jarred me out of sleep. "Zach?" I half sat up, reaching for the sliver of light at my door.

"It's me," Gina said. "There's news."

Darkness lay outside the window. Middle-of-the-night news was always bad.

Zachary was dead.

"Immigration called. The DMP is releasing Zachary. He's going home."

I sank back onto my pillow, still seeing his twisted body on the flashing fence. Maybe *this* was the dream.

"It's five thirty a.m. now." Gina stepped closer. "They said you can see him briefly before you go to school." She paused. "Aura, did you hear me?"

I ran my hand over my blanket. It was frayed in all the right places. The Band-Aid from a day-old paper cut snagged a stray thread. "This is real."

"Of course, hon." She switched on my nightstand lamp and sat on the bed. "He's free."

I blinked at her in the sudden light. The tension in her smile made my chest tighten, like I was trying to breathe sand instead of air.

Zachary was leaving Area 3A, but I feared he would carry a part of it with him, tucked deep inside his soul. That he would never truly be "free."

My palms were pumping cold sweat as I waited with Gina and Cheryl for Zachary to be released. We sat on a row of blue vinyl chairs, their seat edges contoured to keep people from lying down to nap. Though it was the same building where we'd met Ian and Fiona, this room held no ferns, no soft-rock radio, no cute-dog calendars.

This room felt like a prison.

Behind us sat pairs of cubicles separated by a floor-to-ceiling glass partition. The cubicles each had a beige phone, one on either side of the glass. A smaller room, as bare as this one, lay on the other side of the divider.

I smoothed my hair, which I hadn't had time to wash or barely even comb before we'd left. But my ragged appearance on the first day of school was the least of my worries.

If Zachary looked damaged, could I be brave and strong for him, or would pity fill my eyes and hurt his fierce pride? And what would I say to him? "How's your summer been?" "Read any good books lately?"

As if hearing my thoughts, Gina put her hand on my jittery knee. "Don't worry, hon. You'll know what to say."

I could hear every sound in the echoing hallway outside, each squeak of shoes on polished linoleum. I checked the clock for the fourth time in the last minute. "It's almost seven. Maybe they took him already."

"They would've called to tell me," Cheryl said, shifting her weight on the chair. "Remember, you can't hug or kiss him."

"But we can hold hands, right?"

"Briefly. Then you can sit here and talk, but no touching."

I seethed, remembering a reality show about a prison, where the visitors had similar restrictions. Zachary wasn't a murderer or bank robber. He was a pawn. We both were.

But not for long.

A group of footsteps slowed, approaching our room. I leaped to my feet as the door opened.

Zachary entered, a large agent at each elbow. His hair had grown shaggier, almost to his shoulders, and his green eyes were bloodshot, with the wariness of a wild animal. My mind flashed back to the dream of the fence.

Maybe it was the hulking size of his guards, but he looked so, so thin.

Hands unbound, he reached for me. "Aura . . ."

On pure instinct, I launched myself at him.

A body met mine, too soon. Not Zachary's.

"Let me go!" I struggled in the guard's grip. I had to touch Zachary with more than hands, bury my face in his chest and feel his arms around me. I had to know he was real.

"Sorry, miss." The guard held me firmly. "Full physical contact is against the rules."

"But he didn't do anything! I didn't do anything! It's not fair!"

"Aura!" Zachary's ragged voice receded into the hallway. "Let me go! I just want to see her."

Were they taking him away? Had I blown my only chance to talk to him?

I went limp. "I'm sorry. I promise I won't touch him. Just please let me see Zachary." I whispered through my tears. "Please."

"At least let them speak through the glass," Cheryl said.

The guard holding me turned to his partner. "Put him on the other side." As soon as the door closed, he released me. I lunged to sit at the center cubicle.

The door in the other room opened. This time they let Zachary go, and he walked slowly, glancing to each side, as if expecting to be tackled. Then he sat across from me and lifted his gaze to the window between us.

My eyes devoured the sight of him. Zachary was here in front of me, not in a dream or a memory. *Here.*

He wore a loose shirt, so it was hard to tell exactly how much weight he'd lost. His dark brown hair was unkempt but clean and shiny. His face was so freshly shaven, the skin glowed pink, with tiny bumps and scrapes, the way my legs get when I shave them after several days of neglect.

They'd just now polished him up. Who knew what he'd looked like an hour ago?

I pressed my hand to the thick glass. Zachary spread his palm in the same place, his long fingers extending past mine. His cuff slipped back, revealing a wrist so thin, it made my heart crack in two.

"Are you okay?" I asked him.

He tilted his head quizzically.

"Pick up the phone," Gina said gently.

"Oh." I lifted the beige receiver on my side, and Zachary did the same. "Are you okay?"

"I'm tired. Homesick. Otherwise, can't complain." He threw a fleeting look behind him.

I wondered what would happen if he did complain. "I missed you. I still miss you."

"I miss you, too." He cleared his throat. "How was your summer?"

"Better than yours."

"Likely." His mouth opened and closed, as though he was trying to remember how to form a full sentence. "What did you do?"

"I worked. I went to the mountains." *I sold out my country to set you free, and I'm not sorry.*

I squirmed in the hard plastic seat with the desire to tell him everything I'd learned about the DMP, SecuriLab, and the Shift itself. But nothing we said now was between us.

He leaned closer, a wave of hair brushing the glass. "I love you."

I closed my eyes, bathing in his words and the intimate way he said them, as if we were alone. I pretended for one long moment that nothing stood between us but air.

Then I opened my eyes and said, "I love you, too."

His face melted into a sad smile, then he let the receiver drop onto his shoulder and gazed at me. I did the same. No words could follow those we'd just uttered.

We sat, each pressing a hand to the glass, letting the world around us dissolve, for the rest of our five measly minutes. It reminded me of moments with Logan's ghost, when we'd touch-but-not-touch for hours.

But in the depth of Zachary's weary, determined eyes, I saw more than a desperate longing. I saw a future.

When the guards moved forward to lead him away, Zachary and I put the receivers back to our ears.

"I'll see you," he said, stating it like the promise it was.

"You better." I hung up, then pressed my other palm to the glass. He mirrored my move.

The guard touched Zachary's shoulder. Zachary's eyes flashed cold. I yanked my hands back.

He started, then gave me a pleading look, fingers curled against the window. *I'm sorry*, he mouthed.

I shook my head and touched the glass again. "It's okay." Then I signaled him to call me, thumb to my ear and pinkie to my mouth.

He nodded, then said one word I could easily read on his lips. *Promise*.

Chapter Twenty

"Y ou completely failed to warn me about American girls."

I smiled into my locker at the sound of Simon's voice, then closed the door to find him leaning against the wall about ten feet away. The hallway was otherwise empty—I'd stayed late on the first day of school to meet with my guidance counselor about college financial aid applications.

"The accent?" I asked him.

"Astounding." He shook his head as he shuffled closer. "How will I ever engage in a covert operation when half the student body is staring?"

"Do you think anyone suspects you're not really one of us?"

"They're more curious than suspicious. A few seemed surprised that England had black people."

I laughed. "It makes you doubly intriguing. Remember, anyone under eighteen is jailbait."

He mock shuddered. "Not tempted. High school girls don't provide much intellectual stimulation."

"Hey."

"Present company excepted, of course."

"Right." I moved near him, double-checking that the hall was still empty. "Simon, was Zachary released because of the information I gave you?"

"It was a combination of factors."

"And?"

"One of which was you."

"Yes!" I gave a fist pump and a twirl of victory.

Simon frowned. "It's not a game, Aura. Never forget that. There are no winners." He walked away down the hall, books under his arm. "Only losers."

My phone rang just after midnight. Wide awake, I lunged across my bed to grab the phone from where it was charging on my nightstand.

Gina shouted from her room, "Is it him?"

"UK area code!" I bounced on my knees.

"Answer it!"

I did, my hand shaking.

"It's me," Zachary said.

I dug my fingers into the sheets as Gina appeared at my door. "Are you there?" I asked him. "Are you safe?"

"I'm in London. My mum met me." His voice was flat and dull. "We're flying to Glasgow together."

"That's great. How are you?"

"Tired. They gave me something to help me sleep on the flight."

"Did it work?"

"No. But I'm here. I'll be walking on Scottish soil in two hours." He gave a hollow chuckle. "Probably kissing it, too, when no one's looking."

I laughed with relief at the humor that had come back into his words, if not his voice. "I wish you were kissing me instead." I winced at Gina's "Awww" from the door. "Sorry, that's cheesy. Except I really, really mean it." I squeezed my bare toes. "Oh my God, it's so good to talk to you. I missed you and wanted so bad to call you and just tell you about stupid stuff, but mostly I wanted to know you were okay." I stopped babbling. "Zach?"

There was only silence.

"Zach, are you there? Did we get cut—"

"I'm here." He spoke barely above a whisper. "You've no need to worry about me. I'm fine."

He sounded the opposite of fine. "How is that possible?"

"It—it must be. It is. Possible." His voice seemed to rattle, or maybe it was the connection. "Can we video-chat later?"

"Of course." I clutched the phone, trying not to break it.

"I have to go. Mum is frowning."

"Okay." I started to add, "I love you," but he quickly said, "Bye" and hung up.

I set my phone carefully on the nightstand, as if Zachary lay fragile inside it. "He's in London."

Gina let out a heavy breath and sank onto my bed. "Thank God he's finally safe."

Nowhere in the world seemed safe anymore. "And three thousand miles away."

Then it all spilled forth—an entire summer of fear and grief and rage. My tears came so fast and so fat, I thought they'd bruise my eyes on their way out.

Gina scooted over and wrapped her arms around me.

I clung to her as I cried. "I miss him even more now."

"I know. It was hard seeing him like that today. But he'll recover."

What if he doesn't? "All this time your lawyer friend was lying. Zachary wasn't 'fine, but a little thin.' I could see it in his eyes."

"I saw it, too," she said. "I swear we don't know what he's been through. He wouldn't tell Cheryl or the man from the consulate. I'm sorry I didn't tell you how bad she said he looked. I knew it would upset you."

I wanted to be pissed at Gina. But was it any different from me keeping my father's identity from her, to avoid breaking her heart?

Thinking of my father reminded me of something else I needed to tell her.

"I'm going to see Zachary again."

She smoothed a wrinkle in my nightshirt. "Sweetheart, I don't know if they'll ever let him back in the country."

"I know." I crossed my legs so that I could sit up straight. "Aunt Gina, I'm meeting Zachary in Ireland on December twentieth. We're going to Newgrange for our birthdays."

Her face froze. "This coming December?"

I deflected her arguments before she could present them. "I promise I'll be back for Christmas. And yeah, I know my mom said that and then didn't come home until April. But I swear that won't happen, and I won't get pregnant, either."

"Where are you staying?"

"At a B and B that used to be a castle."

"With Zachary and his parents?"

"No. Just the two of us."

Aunt Gina's mouth dropped open. "You want to go on an overnight trip with a boy, across the ocean."

"I'll be eighteen the day after I get there."

"But not the day you leave." Her firm tone said, *Which means I can stop you.*

"I thought you liked Zachary."

"This isn't about liking him. Trouble always follows the two of you, and if it follows you across the Atlantic—" Her neck muscles twitched as she swallowed. "I won't be able to save you."

"You'll have to trust me to save myself."

"This isn't about trust. This is about you being too young and inexperienced to deal with the potential dangers you'll face."

"I've lived in Baltimore my whole life. I'm not some innocent bumpkin. Zachary's got street smarts, too. Plus, he knows Gaelic." That last part sounded feeble. "I'll use my Italian passport. They say it's safer to travel as a non-American." My mom's father was born in Italy, which automatically gave her dual citizenship. When I was a baby, she did the paperwork so we could both get Italian passports. I cherished this connection to her—a connection I needed to strengthen by walking in her footsteps in Ireland.

Gina shook her head. "I just don't like it."

My eyes heated, and I clenched the blanket. "So you won't let me go?"

"Once you're eighteen and—"

"I'll *be* eighteen, almost."

She raised her voice above mine. "Once you're eighteen and living under your own roof, then you can make the rules. You can gallivant off to anywhere you want."

"I'm not gallivanting, I'm doing research!" I was yelling now, helpless in the face of my rage. "I'm trying to solve a huge mystery here, and you're making it sound like I'm going to Cancún to drink beer and get laid."

Gina put a hand to her stomach. "Let's not talk about—"

"I knew it! This isn't about safety, it's about sex. Guess what, Gina? I'm almost eighteen and still a virgin. Zachary and I could've done it before he left. But we decided to wait. Just like Logan and I waited and waited until it was too late, and then he was dead."

My voice cracked. I had to get ahold of myself before I went full tantrum.

Gina spread her fingertips over her eyebrows, like she was wiping away a mental image. "Aura, there's no shame in being an eighteen-year-old virgin. Plenty of people wait until college, or even after."

"I have to do what's right for me. You always taught me that."

"Don't use my life lessons to argue for a sleepover with your boyfriend."

My pulse raced with fury. How dare she make it sound sleazy and childish? "If you were so concerned about my virginity, why'd you let me go to Deep Creek Lake with the Keeleys? I could've done it with Dylan, or someone I met at a party."

"You're not that type."

"So you'd rather I hang out with guys I don't love, just so I'll keep my clothes on?"

Gina turned away, probably counting to ten to rein in her temper.

I spoke again while I had the chance. "You said he might never be allowed to come back. If I don't go over there, I might never see him again."

"You will. And if you don't, you'll survive."

No. Maybe my heart would keep pushing blood through my arteries and veins, maybe my brain would still send signals to my nerves. But if I truly lost Zachary, to distance or madness or both, I was certain I'd become a living ghost.

"I'm going to Ireland, Gina," I said in a strong, steady voice. "I'll be careful, in every single way, and I'll call you every day to check in. But I'm going."

"No." She stood and put a firm hand on my shoulder, as if she could physically hold me in this country. "You're not."

Gina walked out, shutting the door behind her. I wanted to hurl my pillow at it, or better yet, hurl something loud and breakable.

Instead I went to my computer and logged into my bank account. Had I saved enough money to move out of the house? What about college? Maybe I could get a free ride with a work/study program somewhere. I was pretty sure my Ridgewood tuition was paid a year in advance, so that took care of high school.

Maybe the McConnells would let me have Megan's older brother John's room, since he hardly ever came home from North Dakota. I could pay them rent, or help out around the funeral home. It would be sad and sometimes gross, but I'd do anything.

Just as I finished a despair-inducing monthly budget plan, Gina swung open my door. "Twice a day," she snapped.

I stared at her. "What?"

"When you're in Ireland. Call me twice a day."

Before sunrise the next morning, my phone bleeped with a text from Fiona Moore's phone.

IT'S Z. YOU READY?

I'M HERE. VIDEO CHAT OPEN. My stomach fluttered at the thought of seeing him again, even after only twenty-four hours.

START WITH IM. I'LL EXPLAIN.

I went to my desk and activated the instant message window. A link appeared from Zachary, with the words GO HERE.

I clicked on the site, which automatically e-mailed me an ultra-strong password with approximately a million letters, numbers, and symbols. I had to type them in individually—the site's security was so hard-core it wouldn't let me copy and paste.

Zachary was waiting, his username sitting alone in the blue box to the right.

Me: HEY. WHERE ARE WE?

Him: ENCRYPTED PRIVATE CHAT ROOM. IT'LL APPEAR IN
YOUR BROWSING HISTORY AS "PERIODIC TABLE FOR
DUMMIES."

Me: HA!

Him: WE'LL SWITCH TO VIDEO IN A MINUTE.

Me: HOW DO I KNOW YOU'RE REALLY ZACHARY?

Him: HOW DO I KNOW YOU'RE REALLY AURA?

Me: WHAT SONG DID WE DANCE TO AT PROM?

Him: "WHEN YOU SAY NOTHING AT ALL" BY ALISON KRAUSS.

Me: HUH. I ALWAYS THOUGHT IT WAS TAYLOR SWIFT.

Him: YOU NEED TO STUDY YOUR COUNTRY MUSIC.

Me: NO THANKS. HEY, WE CAN USE VIDEO CHATS TO
    PLANT DISINFORMATION FOR THE DMP.

Him: I WAS THINKING THAT TOO. <GRIN> ALSO, WE
    NEED A CODE WE CAN SAY ON VIDEO TO SIGNAL
    WHEN WE WANT TO COME HERE TO TALK IN
    PRIVATE. SOMETHING THAT SEEMS NATURAL.

Me: HOW ABOUT "I HAVE A HISTORY PAPER TO WRITE"?

Him: MINE'LL BE, "MUM NEEDS HELP WITH DAD."
    READY?

I hesitated before asking the question that burned fiercest inside me, knowing I might not want the answer.

Me: SO IF THIS CHAT IS JUST BETWEEN US . . .

Him: *INTRIGUED*

I imagined him imagining me wanting to have a serious sexting session. But his body wasn't the first thing on my mind—at least not that aspect of his body.

Me: CAN YOU TELL ME WHAT HAPPENED WHILE YOU
    WERE DETAINED?

No response, not even the little "so-and-so is typing" icon.

Me: ZACH, YOU THERE?

Him: YES.

Me: WE CAN TALK ABOUT IT SOME OTHER TIME.

Him: YES.

Me: THE IMPORTANT THING IS THAT YOU'RE

OKAY NOW.

No response.

Me: YOU ARE OKAY NOW, RIGHT?

Him: CAN WE GO TO VIDEO? I WANT TO SEE YOU.

In the video chat program, a black square with a generic silhouette appeared while it retrieved his feed. I noticed the live shot of me down in the corner of the screen. Was my hair really that frizzy? Was it shadows or did I have major bags under my eyes?

I sprang out of my chair to turn off the extra lamp, hoping that would help. In my hurry, I knocked it over. "Crap!"

"Aura?"

I flew back to my desk to see Zachary's face on the screen. "Hi. Wow. Hi."

"Everything all right?"

"Now it is."

He looked straight into the camera. Straight at me. "Hi," he said, almost breathlessly.

"Hi." I wanted to throw my arms around my computer. "It's great to see you."

"Aye. You look beautiful."

"No, I don't. I mean, thanks. But no, I don't." I gave what I hoped was a coy shrug. "Not this early in the morning, anyway."

Gazing at him, I could almost forget that we might not be alone. If we were going to give disinformation, the DMP needed to hear us talking like we thought we had privacy.

"I miss you so much," I told him.

"I miss you, too." He rested his chin on his fist. "I dunno what else to say. I can't stop looking at you."

Heat rose into my cheeks. "Can you show me your room?"

"No' yet. Looks like a thirteen-year-old boy's room."

"It's been that long since you've lived in Glasgow?"

"We've come back between trips abroad, but only for a few days at a time." He sat back in his chair and looked to his right, at the gray glow of a window. "I didn't know how much I missed it until I saw the city lights from the plane. I'd forgotten how beautiful it was."

"What will you do first?"

"Ring up some of my old mates. Pick up where we left off, terrorizing the streets with useless patter." He almost smiled.

"Hitting the pubs? Getting your Scottish on?"

"Maybe, now that most of us are old enough. But don't worry, I won't drink. I can't, anyway, until I'm eighteen. Unless I buy a meal, and that gets expensive on a pub crawl. Besides, I know it'd bother you if I became a drinker, after what happened."

I wasn't sure if he meant Logan's death or Zachary's own hookup with Becca, neither of which would've occurred without booze. But I wondered if the DMP had left Zachary with memories he wanted to obliterate with a bottle.

"I bet you're happy to see your parents again."

"I am." His eyes turned sad.

"How's your father?"

Zachary's mouth opened as he stared past the camera, but it was several moments before he spoke. "We've an electric tin opener now."

"Sorry, what?"

"Dad always said they were a waste of money and electricity, and they clutter up the counter. No sense in it when there's a perfectly good—" He mimed twisting a handheld can opener. "But his hands, they're too weak now."

"I'm sorry," I whispered.

"When I walked into the kitchen and saw that machine . . ." Zachary swallowed hard. "I should be happy he didn't die while I was—" He swept a hand back and forth over his head, finally tugging on the dark waves that flopped in front. "I need a haircut."

He remained that way, eyes fixed on the table below the screen, rubbing the ends of his hair between his fingertips and thumb.

My throat ached at the sight of his anguish. I only knew the pain of losing a father I'd never had. I couldn't imagine watching the slow decline of one I'd been close to.

"Should I let you go?"

Zachary looked up suddenly. "What? No! Don't. Please."

"I thought maybe you wanted to be with your parents."

"I do, but—I don't want you to let me go." His left eye twitched. "Ach, that sounded pathetic."

"I don't care."

"I do." He stared hard at the camera. "Aura, don't pity me. I can't take that. This summer wasn't easy, but it's over, and I'm fine." He stressed the last word so hard, it cracked. "Except for missing you, and that's a pain I want to cure in only one way."

My pulse pounded at the thought of being with him again, but we couldn't discuss details when the DMP could be listening. "Do you know what made them decide to let you go?"

"Not sure. I was told the Foreign Office leaned on the State Department, who leaned on the DMP, but why they changed their mind, I dunno."

That was exactly what I'd expected to hear Zachary say on video.

I checked my watch. "Would you believe I have a history paper due on the second day of school? I need to go proofread it before I hand it in."

He nodded understanding. We said our good-byes, then joined each other in the encrypted chat room.

Me: I KNOW WHY THEY LET YOU GO. IT WAS THE STATE
DEPT AND WHATEVER, BUT ALSO MI-X.

Him: I FIGURED. BUT WHAT TOOK THEM SO LONG?

Me: THEY NEEDED LEVERAGE AGAINST THE DMP.

Him: LIKE WHAT?

Me: LIKE THE FACT THAT THE COMPANY THAT MAKES
BLACKBOX HIRED PRIVATE SPIES TO BOMB FLIGHT 346.

Him: WHAT?!!! HOW DO THEY KNOW THIS?

My fingers paused over the keyboard.

Me: BECAUSE I TOLD THEM.

Zachary didn't respond for several moments, then the chat window showed that he was typing, then stopping, then typing, then stopping again. Finally he simply said, SORRY?

Me: I DID RESEARCH. AND I GOT INFO FROM NICOLA.
Him: NICOLA FROM DMP? YOU WERE SPYING?
Me: NOT SPYING. INVESTIGATING.
Him: YOU COULD GO TO JAIL!
Me: I DID THIS FOR YOU.

After a long, excruciating wait, while my heart seemed to stop, he typed: I'M NOT WORTH THAT.

I felt like crying, but tried to hold it together. CAN I SEE YOU?

Him: I HAVE TO GO NOW.

And he was gone. I let the tears pour forth. Maybe I shouldn't have told Zachary what I'd done, but it would've felt like lying. I'd always been honest with him, even when it hurt.

My vision blurry, I started packing my book bag. Normally the smell of new school supplies filled me with anticipation. Now I felt nothing but dread.

My phone buzzed with a text message from Zachary.

AURA, I'M SORRY. I LOVE YOU.

I LOVE YOU TOO. ARE YOU MAD?

NOT AT YOU. NEVER AT YOU.

IF YOU NEED TO TALK . . .

I CAN'T. NOT YET.

WHEN YOU'RE READY.

His reply took so long, I double-checked that my phone was receiving a signal. Finally . . .

I WILL.

Chapter Twenty-One

S houldn't we feel different?" Megan asked as we worked our way through our first lab experiment in AP Chemistry. "Now that we're seniors?"

"What did you want, a red carpet when we walked into school yesterday morning? Trumpets? Confetti?"

"Something like that. We worked and suffered all these years." She carefully measured the liquid in the test tube. "They should honor us."

"I think the honor comes in June. A little thing called graduation?"

"We don't need a reward at graduation. Leaving this place is reward enough." She glanced up at Mrs. Oswald, who was hovering around our side of the room, checking on students' progress. When she drifted away, Megan added, "Did you see the new exchange student over there?"

I adjusted my goggles and peered across the room at Simon, pretending I was hearing about him for the first time. "Cute. Where's he from?"

"England. His mom's a diplomat or something."

It felt like Simon was the only person in school *not* watching me. I heard the whispers in the hallway as I passed, the conversations that mysteriously stopped when I approached. Two-and-a-half months after Logan's concert, people were still speculating that I'd somehow brought him back to life.

In my junior year, I'd been the girl with the dead druggie boyfriend, someone to pity. In my senior year, I was destined to be a freak. Someone to fear.

It bothered me, though it shouldn't have. I had way more important concerns, like bringing down the DMP.

Megan continued to hog the hands-on portions of the experiment—she planned to learn every aspect of the funeral home business. Bored, I snuck another glance at yesterday's text message from Nicola:

GLAD TO HEAR ZACHARY'S FREE! :) THIS IS THE LAST YOU'LL HEAR FROM ME, FOR YOUR SAKE. I HAVE SOME STUFF I NEED TO DO ON MY OWN.

What did she mean by "stuff"? If she had more dirt on the DMP, I wanted to know. But she hadn't replied to my texts or phone calls.

I brought up the most recent message sent from Zachary late this morning. Since no signals would reach inside our school's BlackBoxed walls, I hadn't received it until Megan, Jenna, Christopher, and I had gone outside to the senior courtyard for lunch.

Zachary: CAN'T CHAT TONIGHT. GOING OUT OF TOWN FOR A GOOD CAUSE. WISH ME LUCK.

At least he sounded like he was in a better mood. But where was he going? Who was he seeing? Was he pulling away from me already?

"Siobhan called me last night," Megan said, interrupting my gloom. "She said College Park is crazy fun."

"So she's not missing Connor?"

"You know her." Megan made air quotes. "That 'whole long-distance thing' never works."

"She better be wrong."

"I'm sure you and Zach will be fine. You're way different."

Right. Because before he left, we'd been boyfriend-girlfriend all of three days. If Siobhan and Connor—who'd been together for more than a year—couldn't make it, how could we?

And after what Zachary had been through this summer—which he wouldn't even tell me about—he might decide it'd be easier to forget the entire continent. He could start up with a girl from his hometown, someone who never had to ask him to repeat himself or explain a phrase or a joke. Someone who could help him forget.

"Ready?" Megan held up the beaker. "If we did it right, it'll be so cool." She poured the fluid into the test tube. The mixture bubbled, steamed, then changed from white to black.

"Whoa." I jotted our observations in our lab notebook, then glanced around the room to confirm that others' experiments showed the same results.

I began to write the explanation for the reaction, then stopped and stared at the test tube. The two chemicals on their own had certain original properties. But when they mingled, they took on a new life with new qualities. New powers.

In my own notebook, I doodled in the margin, using chemical equation notation:

$$me + zachary \rightarrow weirdness + happiness$$

As much as I'd loved Logan, and as much as I cared for Dylan, neither of them had ever changed who I was, turned me into a new person like Zachary had. And as much as it scared me, these changes seemed like a sign that we shouldn't walk away. We were each other's way forward in life.

Zachary and I had done many so-called impossible things together. But only one thing was truly impossible: leaving each other for good.

The following night Zachary was waiting in our encrypted chat room when I logged on with my excruciatingly long password.

Him: I HAVE GOOD NEWS AND BETTER NEWS. WHICH ONE
DO YOU WANT FIRST?
Me: OOH! THE GOOD NEWS. SAVE THE BEST FOR LAST.
Him: THAT'S MY GIRL. THE GOOD NEWS IS, I'VE FOUND AN
APP THAT'LL LET US ENCRYPT VIDEO CHATS.

"Yes!" I shouted. Then I held down the shift and 1 keys to rattle off a hundred exclamation points.

Him: I'M GLAD, TOO. MY HANDS ARE GETTING TIRED.

Me: I MISS YOUR HANDS.

Him: HAH! CHEEKY MONKEY. I'VE UPLOADED THE VIDEO
PROGRAM HERE.

He posted a link to a secure file transfer site. It took forever to install, but ten minutes later, there he was on my screen.

I dropped my pen. "Your hair! That's where you went yesterday for a good cause?"

"What?" He passed a hand over his head, where the dark strands were shorter now and nearly straight. "No. I got it cut today here. It was hideously long."

"I liked it."

"I needed a change, and this is more the style here. Does it look bad?"

His face was more visible without the wavy bangs tumbling down his forehead. I'd never noticed how high and defined his cheekbones were, and his eyes now seemed twice as green.

"It looks hot."

He gave me a crooked grin. "So, I went overnight to the Black Isle, up in the Highlands." He slid a large white box in front of the camera. "I got this."

"A case of copy paper. Congrats."

He lifted the lid, spinning it in his hands, then withdrew a manila envelope with a red wax seal, like the seal on—

"Oh my God! My mom's journal?"

"Aye. I saw Eowyn. She's up north in a new safe house."

"Open it! Open it!" I bounced in my chair, then dove under my desk for the pen I'd dropped. "Start after January twentieth. That was the last date I read. After that I skimmed until the equinox." When my mom had described her seventeen minutes of passion with my dad. Blech.

Zachary scanned the sheets, hands trembling from fatigue or excitement or both. "I don't remember this bit.

"January 24

Haven't had time to write lately—out wandering with Anthony, down the streets of medieval towns like Slane and Kells and Trim. Since I pretend I'm walking alone, he does most of the talking.

But I had to journal tonight. Anthony told me something odd, something he said he's been holding back until he could figure it all out. He didn't want to worry me."

Hmm. I was getting a better picture of my dad—a little protective, a little secretive.

Zachary kept reading.

"We were walking down the sidewalk in Kells, near the famous church and tower. Anthony said that the night of the solstice—after I'd been to Newgrange—he was haunting one of the local pubs. He overheard a middle-aged woman speaking with a young couple about something that had happened that morning at Newgrange. Not tourist-talk—this was serious.

The older lady was speaking in Gaelic, and the young man (her son, apparently) was translating for his wife. The mother said, 'The good god has done his work. The day will rise again, with the next return of the light.'

I had no clue what that meant, but Anthony (ye olde mythology buff) said that 'the good god' was a name for the Dagda, one of the Tuatha Dé Danann. The TDD weren't creator-gods, more like superhero wizard types that lived in Ireland way, way back.

"Remember the Tuatha Dé Danann from our thesis?" Zachary pronounced the Gaelic, *TOO-ah jay DAN-an*.

I nodded. According to legend, after the Celts invaded, the Tuatha Dé Danann literally went underground and now lived in the "Otherworld" in hills or mounds called *sidhe* ("*shee*"). Over time, *sidhe* came to mean faeries themselves. The Dagda has supposedly lived inside Newgrange all this time, which is why the locals were too scared to disturb it for thousands of years.

Zachary flipped the page.

"I asked Anthony what she meant about Dagda's work. He had no idea, except that it had something to do with the solstice.

Because of that, he started following this older woman. He found out her name was Brigit Murphy, and she lived in Rathcairn, a nearby Gaelic-speaking town, one of the few in eastern Ireland.

Anthony said that after he left me around midnight last night, he went to Brigit Murphy's house and found a group of people gathered there. It was like a cult meeting of the TDD worshippers. He said they wore robes like Druids, but weren't real Druids. They call themselves Children of the Sun."

"Creepy," I commented.

"Aye, but how would your father haunt Brigit's house if he'd never been there during his life?"

"Before the Shift, ghosts could go anywhere they wanted." I tried to avoid a "well, duh" tone.

"Oh. Right." Zachary scratched his forehead, looking embarrassed. "I forgot.

"Their rituals—all in Gaelic—seemed to be about the light and the sun and the cycles of nature. But the translating son said that the cycle of the TDD was so old, no one had seen the real ending, which was now 'imminent.'

So Brigit got up in front of them and declared in Gaelic, 'I have succeeded where my ancestors failed. The one who was filled with light will bring forth a new day.'"

I covered my mouth. "Whoa. The one filled with light. That was my mom."

"And my dad." Zachary kept reading, faster now.

"When Anthony told me this, I stopped right there on the sidewalk. Thank God the street was pretty empty so no one saw me wigging out at thin air.

I took him into the St. Columba's churchyard, where the famous crosses are, so we could be alone. Then I told him how Eowyn had said she'd seen *me* filled with light inside Newgrange."

I held up a hand. "Zach, can you go back and read that part from the day of the solstice?"

"Let me find it." He shuffled through the pages. "Here we are. This is from twenty-first of December.

"An American teenager with long blond curls told me the strangest thing—when I'd passed through the solstice sunbeam, she saw me lit up from the inside, like my skin was a lampshade."

"I remember now," I said. "The tour guide told them they could step through the light."

"Eowyn said something about people making wishes, aye?"

"Or hoping it could heal them." Maybe it had. Neither my mom nor his dad were able to have children before they went to Newgrange. We were both kind of miracle babies.

Zachary found the January 24 entry again and repeated the last line.

"Then I told him how Eowyn had said she'd seen *me* filled with light inside Newgrange. He thought there's no way that could be a coincidence, and if it'd really happened, then these crazy cult people might want something from me. He said to come back to the B and B and keep watch until he could find out more.

I feel vulnerable as hell. Beating cancer made me feel invincible, but now, lying here in my room alone, it seems like something new has me in its sights, something more dangerous than any disease."

He set down the pages. "That's the end of the entry."

"Part of that's not right. Brigit Murphy said, 'the *one* filled with light.' But Eowyn told us that your father was filled with light, too. She called it the Shine."

"So either Brigit didn't know that the light went into two people, or she knew and didn't tell her followers."

"You mean, that she'd screwed up."

"They were probably expecting one person to walk through the light at the moment of the solstice, but both my father and your mother were there."

"What did she mean, '*I* have succeeded'?" I wished I had the journal in my own hands. "How did she make it happen?"

"Some sort of ritual? Hold on." He flipped the page back. "It says that 'the one who was filled with light will bring forth a new day.' Is that the Shift?"

I slapped my palms on the edge of my desk. "Zachary, it was us.

'Bring forth,' like give birth or conceive. Like a mother or a father."

"So *we're* the new day? What the bloody hell's that mean?"

"Read that other part again. About the good god, the Dagda."

While he shuffled the pages, I thrilled that we were solving mysteries again. Some things, it seemed, we could only figure out together, as if we shared a brain, one that would malfunction without its other half.

"It says, 'The good god has done his work. The day will rise again, with the next return of the light.'"

"Was something supposed to happen the next day?"

Zachary shook the papers. "No, you were right! It's about us. The 'next return of the light'—the winter solstice the year after."

I gasped. "The day we were born!"

"It's got to be. 'The day will rise again.'" He lurched out of his seat. "Be right back."

Luckily, Zachary only took about five seconds, or I would've exploded with anticipation. He sat down hard, already paging through a dog-eared book on the ancient Celts.

As he flattened the book on the desk and ran his finger over the page, I saw that intensity back in his eyes. I had planned to press him again about what had happened in DMP custody, but now decided to save it for another time. He looked too happy, too alive.

"Here it is. Óengus, the son of the Dagda. He was the personification of the day."

"Cool." I rewound his words. "So these cult people wanted to raise a god out of Newgrange?"

"Where else? It's the gods' legendary place of rest."

"That's freaking crazy."

"Aura, they may have created the Shine and the Shift. That's no less crazy."

I squeezed my head, as if to keep my brains from scrambling. "Keep reading the journal."

"Right." He laid the journal pages atop the open book.

"January 26

Weirder and weirder! Anthony tracked down Brigit Murphy and her son, Padraig, at her house. Hoo boy, Brigit was tearing Padraig a new one. But it was all in Gaelic, so Anthony couldn't make out much. He knows basic greetings and how to ask directions. And of course numbers, so he can ask how much things cost.

Brigit kept shouting the words for 'one' and 'two,' and from what Anthony could tell, 'two' was really, really bad."

"Oh my God," I interrupted Zachary. "You think they're talking about the Shine? They knew the light went into two people instead of one."

He nodded but kept reading.

"Padraig kept saying the Gaelic phrase for 'sorry.' Eventually he left. Anthony stuck around Brigit's house to see if anyone else would come, but she just turned on the radio and ate dinner by herself. And I'll never forget how he described this next part: Brigit began to weep quietly, letting her tears fall into her stew."

Zachary turned the page. "That's it for that day."

I pondered the power of what we'd learned, how much the day of the Shine had meant to this Children of the Sun cult. If they'd only imagined what they would unleash.

"It sounds like it was Patrick's fault the light went into two people instead of one. But why?"

"Maybe he was there at Newgrange on the solstice. And it's Padraig, not Patrick." He spelled the Irish version of the name for me.

"Everything's prettier in Gaelic," I said with a sigh. "Go on."

"January 27

No more word on Brigit—relief! I keep looking over my shoulder to see if someone's following me.

Tomorrow I'm going to ask Anthony why he haunted Gina after he died, to the point she was so grief-stricken she dumped her husband. Why did he let her ruin her life over him? If we're going to 'be' together, whatever that means, I need to know. No matter how much it hurts."

I braced myself. Like most ghosts, including Logan, my dad must have had trouble letting go of his loved ones—even the ones who belonged to other people.

"'January twenty-eighth. I didn't know ghosts could cry.'" Zachary lifted his head. "I'm sorry, Aura."

I rested my elbows on the desk and cradled my face in my hands. "What's next?"

Zachary went to the following page. "We've seen that." He flipped through every sheet, front and back. "I've read all the parts we didn't read in June. I'll type up everything and paste it into our chat window tomorrow."

"Thank you." I squirmed, wishing he would do it now, but at the same time I just wanted to talk to him. "What else is in that white box?"

"Ah." He slid it closer. "Eowyn's research. As much as she could boil it down, anyway."

"Why did she give it to you?"

Zachary ran his finger over the box's top corner. "Remember I said she was in a safe house? That's because when she rang you the day of my flight, the DMP traced the call."

"Damn it!" I pounded the side of my fist on the desk. "I was afraid of that."

"She's done with the Shift, she says." He looked sad. "Eowyn's turning it all over to us."

"Now? When we're getting close?"

"She was offered a job teaching and doing research in Western Australia. It starts next week. That's why I had to hurry up north to get the material. Much of her time she'll be in the desert with no communication."

Australia. It felt like another planet. "She's abandoning us?"

"She left all this." He patted the side of the box. "Together with what we know—what no one else knows—maybe it'll give us the answers."

"Give *you* the answers." My fingers itched to pore over the box of mysteries. "I'm stuck here, doing stupid schoolwork." Zachary was finished with high school—in Scotland, they could start university a year earlier than in England and the United States. But since he would've had to apply to a Scottish university last fall, he was taking a "gap year." In other words, a year without homework.

"There'll be plenty for you to do," he said. "After I sort through this box, I'll make a list of things for you to look up."

"So I'm your research assistant now?"

He smiled. "Something like tha'." Then he grew serious again. "Aura, mind your grades. If you keep them up, you can go to university anywhere you want, even—" He cut himself off, as if afraid to hope.

I finished his sentence, but only in my mind. *Even in the UK.* I wanted it more than anything, yet it still seemed like a long shot. And what if we didn't get accepted to the same colleges? We could still end up several hours apart.

I caught sight of my chem notebook and remembered the equation I'd doodled in the margin: *Me + Zachary → weirdness + happiness.*

Whether it was ancient destiny or simple chemistry, we would find a way to be together.

Chapter Twenty-Two

Tammi Teller's memorial service at Ridgewood High took place the following night, on what would've been her fifteenth birthday. They'd decided to hold the ceremony on the front courtyard—partly out of respect to ghosts, who couldn't get inside our BlackBoxed school, and partly because Principal Hirsch worried the candles might burn down the building.

As I walked from the parking lot with Megan, Jenna, and Christopher, we saw four of the more familiar ghosts milling near the fountain behind the rows of seats.

"I wonder if somewhere out there," Jenna said, "another school's having a vigil for the suicide bomber kid."

"They never did give out his name," Megan said, "so his friends are probably mourning him, thinking he's innocent."

"I heard they weren't even sure anymore that it *was* that kid,"

Christopher said. "Some people say that post online was faked, or that he doesn't even exist."

"You and your conspiracy theories," Jenna said. "Why else would they announce the day after the crash that it was a post-Shifter suicide bomber?"

I snorted. "Because they wanted to blame somebody."

"Hi, guys!" Amy Koeller stood near the fountain handing out white candles, the kind with paper circles to catch the wax. "Thanks so much for coming. Principal Hirsch wants to start in a couple minutes." With each candle, she gave out a VOTE KOELLER 4 SENIOR CLASS PRESIDENT button.

Christopher pocketed the button and said to Jenna, "Pre-Shifters were primed for something like Flight 346, something that would tell them that ghosts suck."

"But with so many new ghosts coming out of that flight," I said, moving toward the fountain, "you'd think people would feel more compassion. They'd be reminded that they could be ghosts one day."

"Nope." Christopher adjusted the stub of his candle's wick. "Pre-Shifters see Flight 346 and maybe for a second think, 'That could be me,' but it freaks them out so bad that then they're like, 'No way, never. I hate ghosts.'"

"That doesn't make sense," I told him.

He shrugged. "People don't make sense."

"Still." Jenna flipped her candle end over end and caught it. "No reason to join the bastards."

I turned to her quickly. "Who's joining which bastards?"

She nodded to Christopher. "Can't resist free tuition."

Megan clucked her tongue. "Aww, Chris, no."

"What choice do I have?" he asked her. "Besides, they're probably going to pass a DMP draft. Might as well sign up early and get placed where I want."

It had been all over the news—Congress members' summer town-hall meetings had been jam-packed with panicky pre-Shifters and their ghost paranoia. People wanted something done, especially after Flight 346. The DMP was happy to suggest mandatory service for all post-Shifters. I wondered if studying abroad would make me a draft dodger, and if I cared. After a claustrophobic summer, I was dying to live somewhere else for a while—and to be closer to Zachary.

Thinking of the way he'd looked after his captivity made me feel heavy with the weight of worry. I sat on the flat slate edge of the fountain, though it meant not being able to see the podium. Megan and Jenna flanked me, the latter linking hands with Christopher.

A microphone thumped, then made a feedback squeal. Our principal's deep voice came from the speaker to our left.

"Good evening. I'm Albert Hirsch, principal of Ridgewood High School. Welcome, students and families. Thank you for coming tonight to honor Tammi Teller and all the victims of this unthinkable tragedy."

It was hard to hear his speech over the splash of water in the fountain behind us. The cool mist soothed the heat at the base of my neck, exposed by my ponytail.

Principal Hirsch's voice rose slightly. "As you probably know, our outgoing senior class president, Nikki Fowler, is already studying at Harvard. So filling in to give the main memorial address is our—well, our prom queen, who's leaving for UCLA bright and early tomorrow morning. Ladies and gentlemen, Becca Goldman."

Great. I'd thought I'd never have to see her again in my life.

Jenna and Christopher climbed up to stand on the edge of the fountain so they could see over the crowd to the podium.

"Wow," he said. Jenna elbowed him, a jealous scowl on her face.

Megan scrambled to her feet to join them on the fountain edge, balancing herself with a hand on my head. "Yuck. How can someone so rich dress so tacky?"

I stayed seated, having no desire to set eyes on my arch-nemesis, who'd chased Zachary all last year and come *this* close to catching him on prom night.

Becca's voice rang out from the speaker—unlike Principal Hirsch, she'd make sure every word was heard.

"My fellow Americans, good evening. My name is Becca Goldman, and I weep with all of you."

I texted one word to Megan:

GAG.

She wrote back: MY NAME IS BECCA GOLDMAN, AND I SLEEP WITH ALL OF YOU.

I turned my croak of laughter into a fake coughing fit.

"What happened on June twenty-second was more than a tragedy," Becca said. "It was an outrage. Ghosts may not have planted that bomb, but one of them inspired a post-Shifter to do it. Who knows what they're whispering in the ears of our children? 'Hate the living'? 'Hate your own life'? They must be stopped before more innocent people die."

A lot of older heads nodded, and a few pre-Shifters even clapped. A man whose giant video camera displayed the local news channel logo moved closer to the podium, along with a woman holding a microphone.

Becca continued, "I know that post-Shifters, like us pre-Shifters, dream of making the world a better place. Maybe some, like me, want to follow in their parents' footsteps and become doctors or lawyers."

Becca's dad made the world a better place by performing "cosmetic enhancement" surgery on aging rich ladies.

"But it's post-Shifters' duty as Americans to devote their talents to protecting all of us. Only they can stop this plague of undead."

A gasp rippled through the crowd at her last word. Three of the ghosts disappeared instantly, and the last one—ex-Jared, a former student who'd died in the war—started to back away toward the road.

"Undead?!" I jumped up on the edge of the fountain to let my voice carry. "They're not undead, Becca, they're dead!"

"Excuse me?" Becca said in a NutraSweet voice. "Aura, did you have a response?"

My stomach twisted as everyone stared at me. Drawing attention to myself was a dumb thing to do, but I didn't care. I wasn't going to let her, of all people, get away with this.

"I said, ghosts are dead. Like we'll all be someday." *The way I wish you were right now.*

"Oh my." She let loose a gleaming, prom-queen smile and tossed her perfect sable hair behind her shoulder. "You sound like a ghost sympathizer."

"And you sound like an idiot."

"Ooh," Megan said.

I kept going. "Becca, you have no clue what you're talking about. How many people have you loved who died just like that?" I snapped my fingers. "If the answer is zero, then you're luckier than most of us. If it's more than zero, then I hope their ghosts have never heard you compare them to zombies."

"Ladies." Principal Hirsch stepped up and angled the microphone to his mouth. "This is not the proper venue for a political discussion. Becca, please wrap up now so we can move on to the candle lighting."

"But I have this whole speech to—"

"I said, wrap it up." Their angry gazes clashed for a long moment, then Becca collected herself and flipped to the last page of her speech.

Principal Hirsch pushed the microphone in her direction, then took one small step back, maybe ready to grab the mic again.

"In conclusion," she said rapidly and without inflection, "please keep Tammi Teller, her mom, Iris, and the other Flight 346 victims in your thoughts. Thank you."

Becca sent me a cold, hard stare before turning away from the podium. It took every scrap of self-control not to give her the finger.

Jenna and Megan leaned in to me and said, in stereo, "You rock."

Amy Koeller led the gathering in a moment of silence. Then Tammi's dad lit the first candle—a sky-blue one, for Tammi's favorite color—and began to spread the light. One by one, the small white candles came to life, until it looked like a field of yellow fireflies.

A girl of about nine years old came over to the fountain to light our candles. As I bent to touch my wick to her flame, she beamed up at me.

"Thank you," she whispered. "For what you said to that mean girl."

I returned her smile, then thought about Becca's fake-sweet demeanor at the podium. "How do you know she's mean?"

The girl's eyes shadowed. "I can tell."

"You have a Becca at your school."

She looked at the flagstones beneath her feet. "A bunch of Beccas."

I touched her shoulder. "It gets better."

Her face contorted with skepticism as she lit Jenna's candle. "Tammi was my sister."

Megan said, "Oh," maybe just realizing where she'd seen the girl before. Jenna cooed sympathetically.

"I'm sorry," I said. She didn't seem to recognize me as the girl her sister hated for loving Logan. "About your mom, too. That must be hard."

"Yeah." The girl scratched the back of her neck. "If Tammi had stayed around as long as she said she was going to, she could've been here tonight."

"How long was that?" Jenna asked her.

"Two hundred forty-seven days."

I closed my eyes. As long as Logan had stayed. I hoped that no other follower would pattern their ghostly existence after Logan's. He was so full of life, the last thing he would've wanted was to create some kind of death cult.

"I'm glad she left, though," the girl said, "and that my mom wasn't a ghost at all. It was bad enough."

A low, mournful bleat sounded on the other side of the crowd. Bagpipes. I hadn't noticed the piper when we'd come in from the parking lot.

Megan took my hand and squeezed just hard enough to give me the strength not to sob. I let the tears spill quietly, for Tammi and Logan, who'd lost their lives; and for Zachary, who'd lost a part of himself he might never regain.

Chapter Twenty-Three

After what felt like a thousand-hour day at school, I reunited with Zachary on video chat to discuss the results of our research. Not most girls' idea of a fun Friday night, but it was all I wanted to do.

"You go first," I told him. "What'd Eowyn discover?"

He looked more fatigued than when we'd last spoken, his eyes red-rimmed and drooping at the corners. From late-night reading, I wanted to assume, but feared it was something more.

"She seems obsessed with the number three," he said. "The three recesses, the triple spiral, three megaliths in the Boyne Valley—"

"But there used to be more than three megaliths there."

"The three big ones, then, the ones that are still around." He rubbed his forehead. "And there's a great lot of material on this philosopher, Hegel."

"Never heard of him." Then again, my knowledge of philosophy consisted of Plato's Cave and Descartes's "I think, therefore I am."

"German fellow, so I can't read it in the original language." He spread out the pages. "The part Eowyn seems fascinated with is what people call his dialectic."

"Is that the stuff in diet pills?" *I said that out loud, didn't I?* "Sorry, that's diuretic."

"Right. Anyway, there's this process: thesis, antithesis, synthesis."

I nodded, not wanting Zachary to think I was an idiot after my last remark.

"You have one thing: *A*." He held out his left hand, then his right. "And its opposite: non-*A*." He laced his fingers together. "Ideally you want to get to *B*."

"A synthesis, you said. So like a combination?"

"Or something in between. A third thing."

"Eowyn's magic number three again." I thought of our chemistry experiments, where two substances formed a third that had completely different properties. "What's that got to do with Newgrange?"

"Ah." Zachary looked around his desk. "Bugger it, where'd I put that part? Just a second."

He pawed through papers I couldn't see. I studied his face, noting the contrast between his exhaustion and his intensity. It reminded me of mad scientists in old movies, working obsessively to solve a problem while they slowly lost touch with reality.

"Here it is!" He lifted a blue spiral notebook with an orange sticky note poking out. "She says there's evidence that Newgrange may have been built for two purposes." He found the page. "'To serve the dead, but also to separate them from the living.' Then there's a note on the side asking, 'How to do both at once?'"

"The synthesis, right? The third thing?" My temples throbbed. "Do you actually know what she's talking about and want me to guess?"

He put on a hurt look. "Naw, I wouldn't play wi' you like that."

"What else is there?"

"That's as far as I've read. The Hegel put me to sleep a few times. What about you?"

"My research wasn't so much in the clouds." I lifted a printout of an *Irish Times* article. "I did a web search on one of the school computers, in case mine is being monitored. Padraig Murphy and his mom, Brigit, died in a car accident in February."

"How horrible."

"Get this. Padraig's daughter was driving. A post-Shifter, obviously, because she supposedly saw a ghost in the road. She panicked and swerved, then boom! Hit a tree. Killed her father and her grandmother."

"Christ, that poor lass."

"The article doesn't give the driver's name. Padraig's obituary says he was survived by a wife and five kids. He was apparently employed by the Office of Public Works—they run national parks and stuff."

"What did he do for them?"

"It doesn't say. I'll keep searching. Also, I need to check out this Children of the Sun cult, see if they're still around."

"Good." His eyelids drooped, then he straightened up quickly. "Sorry."

I wanted to ask him about his dad, but didn't want Zachary to think that all this obituary talk had reminded me of Ian. Even though it had.

"Are you okay?" I asked. "You look, you know."

"Like pure shite? Aye, I do know." He slouched in his chair. "Tell me something good."

"Like what?"

His gaze rose above the computer screen, searching the wall near the ceiling.

He can't think of anything good.

"Guess what?" I blurted out the first thing I could think of. "On the equinox, I'm going to try to turn a shade back into a ghost."

Zachary sat up. "Really? That's fantastic."

I felt warm inside. He was the first person not to tell me I was crazy for wanting to try.

"You'll have someone with you, aye?"

"Megan and Dylan will be there."

His jaw shifted. "Dylan? Is there another option?"

"We're just friends."

"Snogging friends at one point."

"That was only once."

"Twice."

"Okay, twice. You hooked up with Becca," I reminded him. Seeing her last night had torn open that old wound.

Zachary spread his hands. "And Becca's not here. I'm no' hanging out with Becca, like you are with Dylan."

"I don't know who you're hanging out with. You'll probably meet tons of girls in bars and clubs, and your friends who're in college will know college girls."

"I don't care. I don't want them."

"And I don't want Dylan!" I stopped. "Why are we arguing?"

"Aura, maybe it needs saying." He planted his hands on either side of the keyboard, resting some of his weight on the desk. "This is real, aye? We're going to do this?"

My heart pounded. "Do what?"

"Be together," he whispered. "Officially. Because right now, and for all time, I only want you."

"And I only want you," I said softly. "For all time."

Zachary had to sign off soon after to help his dad. I considered seeing if Megan wanted to go to a club, but it was raining, and we had Saturday night plans, so I decided to tackle my homework.

I started with AP Chemistry first, but the structure of the equations kept bringing me back to what Zachary had said about Eowyn's research. Newgrange was built to "serve the dead" but also to keep the living and dead apart. Eowyn thought there was a way to do both at once.

I turned the page of my notebook and drew a set of mingling stick figures—purple for ghosts, black for people. Ghosts were always badgering post-Shifters for help, which we often gave them, even if only by listening to their stories. So clearly we were "serving the dead."

Next I drew a heavy red line separating the ghosts and the living. It made me think of BlackBox. But how could this separation *serve* the dead? As far as I could tell, BlackBox helped only the living.

I stared at the red line until my eyes crossed, making it blur and waver. Then I blinked, and it hit me.

Zachary was a walking BlackBox, the ultimate red. I was the ultimate violet, able to save shades (at least Logan, and maybe others). I helped ghosts, Zachary repelled them.

We were the two faces of Newgrange. The power of the Shine split between his father and my mother.

But when we kissed, we changed. Was that the synthesis? Did we make something new in those moments when we were together, soul *and* body?

It was almost nine thirty—two thirty a.m. in Scotland. Zachary should've been asleep, but I had a feeling he wasn't.

I switched on my computer, opened the video chat program, and saw that Zachary's status was still set to "online." I called him.

Less than ten seconds later, his face appeared on my screen.

"I think I've got it," I told him. He listened carefully, taking notes while I rattled off my theory as coherently as I could, given my excitement.

When I was finished, he dropped his pen on his notepad. "You're brilliant. And I'm no' just saying that because I love you. You're—" He smoothed his page of notes, gazing at it like it was a rare document. "Just brilliant," he finished in a whisper.

My whole body heated. "Thanks."

"But what is it that we make? This thing that isn't you or me. In those moments when we . . ." He drew in a deep breath. "Ah, I really want to kiss you right now."

I grinned. "For science, right?"

"Aye, purely in the name of research." He put his chin on his hand, his head obviously heavy. "Did I just change the subject?"

"I think you did."

"Sorry, I'm—" He waved his other hand beside his head, then dropped it back to the table with a thud.

"Not sleeping?"

"Aye."

"Why not?"

He tensed. "I don't want to."

We were inching closer to what he couldn't tell me before. "Bad dreams?"

He pulled back from the screen, elbows sliding near the edge of the desk. "Sometimes."

By "sometimes," I could tell he meant "always."

I pressed on, despite his sudden wariness. "Are they about what happened this summer, when you were—"

"Look!" He sat back in his chair so hard it squeaked. "I know you want to help, but stop asking about that time. I can't talk about it."

"I'm sorry, I—"

"Can you please be the one person in my life who isn't trying to fix me?"

I stared at him, my jaw frozen open. He'd never spoken to me like that before.

He cringed at my expression, then covered his face. "I'm so sorry. I don't want to hurt you."

"Zach." I touched the screen with a trembling hand. "What if I stay with you until you fall asleep? You could lie down, put your laptop on the bed so we could still talk."

"No. No. It'd be too much like—like you're my psychiatrist."

He spit out the last word. I wondered if he resented psychiatrists in general, or someone specific.

"Not if I lie down with you."

Zachary opened his mouth to protest, then shut it. "You'd do that?"

"For you, anything."

He curled his arms around his waist, as if he had a stomachache. "Just this once. I'll ring you back in a half hour."

I brushed my teeth and hair, then changed into a sleep shirt— nothing too revealing, since I did want him to actually sleep. Then I got into bed and set my laptop next to me.

I turned on the video chat but still had ten minutes left, so I opened a browser and ran a search on the Children of the Sun. I had to click through several pages of results that referred to a comic book by the same name. Annoying.

Finally I came to an archived post on a blog called Druid Daily, entitled "Wannabe's." The blogger, according to the sidebar, was a "real Druid in the spirit of the ancients," and the post spoke of the dangers of misconceptions about Druids.

The third paragraph cited the Children of the Sun, making my heart race. The blogger claimed that a group of teenagers call-ing themselves by that name were running around County Meath, Ireland, committing acts of trespassing and simulated violence. They would perform "Druid rituals" (the quotes were the writer's), using stage knives and fake blood to pretend-sacrifice one another to the gods. According to the blogger, real Druids had never done human sacrifices—those horror stories were rumors started by the conquering Romans.

The video chat room dinged. I closed the browser and clicked answer.

Zachary's face appeared, this time horizontal. His room was dim, so I barely saw the contours of his head and shoulders. But the light of the laptop screen reflected off bare skin. He wasn't wearing a shirt.

"Hey," I breathed. "Is that how you're going to keep me awake for homework?"

"Sorry?"

"Being half-naked."

"Oh." He chuckled. "What do you mean, 'half'?"

A wave of fire swept over me, and joy that his cheeky side was reappearing. "Are you kidding?"

"Well." He gave an agonizing pause. "Aye, I'll not lie t'ya. I'm wearing boxers."

"What do they look like?"

"You'll see in less than four months."

"I wanna see now. Show me."

"I can't," he said.

"Because you're not really wearing any?"

"I am, I swear."

"Prove it."

His hand snaked out from under the blanket, but only to tug it up over his bare shoulder. "Not yet. I've gone all . . . scrawny over the summer."

My smile faded as I realized that he felt self-conscious. Anger replaced my desire, a boiling fury toward those who had diminished his seductive swagger.

"No pressure," I said, "but you should know, I love your body, all of it. Skinny, fat, anywhere in between."

His fingers twitched. "You don't make anything easy, do you?"

"Nope." I licked my lips. "I try to make everything hard."

Zachary groaned and rolled on his back. "Now I absolutely can't show you, because it would be pornographic."

Every cell in my body wanted to urge him to show me everything, and let me do the same for him. But I sensed that what he truly needed was a place to feel safe.

"Maybe tomorrow," I said.

"Aye." He turned his head to face me, but stayed on his back. "You look beautiful."

I glanced at my live shot in the corner. My features were as dim as his. "You can barely see me in the dark."

"I don't need to see you to know that you're beautiful."

It was my turn to emit a whimper and twist the sheets. He could still slay me with the simplest statements.

"Why don't you try seeing the backs of your eyelids?" I said. "I'll stay until you fall asleep, and then I'll sign off. I promise."

"All right." He closed his eyes. "Keep talking."

"About what?"

"Something good, but boring."

The stuff I'd learned about the Children of the Sun wasn't good *or* boring. "I went to an Orioles game a couple weeks ago."

"Baseball," he murmured. "Nothing's more boring than that."

I told him every play I could remember, and made up what I couldn't. I explained the designated hitter rule and the intricacies of the unassisted triple play.

Within minutes, Zachary's hand went slack on the blanket, and he was asleep. Just to be sure, I kept talking until my mouth was dry and my throat was rough.

My finger reached out to the laptop's touch pad, guiding the cursor over the red hang-up button. Then I hesitated.

It was wrong, but I wanted to watch Zachary sleep. I wanted to see if he thrashed and moaned, wanted to see evidence of the nightmares he denied. If he wouldn't tell me what had happened, maybe I could steal the truth from his sleep. Only then could I help him heal.

No sooner had I thought this than Zachary's shoulder started to jerk. Then his jaw clenched, clacking his teeth together and grinding them hard. One fist clutched the edge of his sheet, and a low growl began in his throat.

No. I'd promised to hang up once he dozed off. The DMP had taken so much from him—all Zachary had left was his pride. If I took that, too, he'd have nothing.

I had to have faith that someday, he'd find the strength to speak.

"I love you," I whispered, and hung up.

Chapter Twenty-Four

On the night of the fall equinox, Dylan, Megan, and I went to a wooded area bordering Loch Raven Reservoir, where no one would see us calling the shades.

When we climbed out of the Keeleys' car, I realized Dylan was wearing a dark-gray suit and blue striped tie.

I waved my flashlight beam over his tall, lean frame. "What's with the dress-up?"

"I told my parents I was going to Career Night at school." He took off the jacket and laid it carefully on the backseat. "Otherwise they'd never let me out this late on a weeknight."

I understood why Logan's death had made Mr. and Mrs. Keeley overprotective of Dylan, but it sucked for him.

He adjusted his tie. "Does it look that bad?"

"Dylan, you dumb-ass." Megan faced away from us, using her

own flashlight to scan the trees around the small parking lot. "You have no clue that you can actually be cute. No wonder you've never gotten laid."

I waited for him to correct her delusion that he was a virgin. But he just tugged his collar, as if it had suddenly constricted. It reminded me of prom night and his discomfort with his stunning tuxedo.

We took a short trail down to the reservoir shoreline, where we found a flat, dry area beside the water. The waning crescent moon, just past third quarter, shone silver on the placid man-made lake.

I pulled the folded list of shades from my back jeans pocket. "Which should I call first?" I had to almost shout to be heard over the cacophony of crickets.

"Start at the top of the alphabet," Megan said.

"Or the end of the alphabet," Dylan argued. "Those people never get to go first."

"We'll do random." I counted the names. "Pick a number between one and twelve."

"Seven," Dylan and Megan said together, then looked at each other.

Huh. "Tell me when it's eight forty-six."

We turned off our flashlights and went silent, listening to the plop and rustle of night creatures in the water and woods. The *whoosh* of cars on the Baltimore Beltway seemed both too close and too far away.

"Okay." Dylan watched his cell phone screen, fingers outstretched. "When it's time, I'll count down from five, silently."

"You don't have to be quiet, it's not—"

"Shh." Dylan waved his hand frantically, then folded down his five fingers. When he got to one, he pointed at me, like I was on camera at a news station.

I took a deep breath. "Randall Madison! I can help you." *At least, I think I can.* "This might be your only chance to be a ghost again. Your only chance to pass on."

Silence.

Dylan's voice startled me. "Logan said it was really loud being a shade. It's probably hard for them to hear."

"Logan could hear me just fine at the spring equinox." I tried again, louder. "Randall Madison! If you want to stop suffering, please find me." That sounded weird, but honest.

Still nothing.

"Try another name," Dylan said.

I shouted the four names after Randall, but no shades appeared. The woods had fallen silent—my yelling had probably scared away the animals. "Maybe Logan only came because *I* called him. Maybe it has to be someone the shades know."

"But shades show up all the time around strangers," Dylan said.

"I'll try again. Randall Madison—"

"Oh, for God's sake, these are shades we're dealing with." Megan snatched the list and flashlight from my hands. "Hey, Randall, Paula, Sloan, Gavin, and Latisha! We know you dickweeds can hear us, so get your shady asses over here. Now!"

Dylan cackled. "Awesome, but do you really think that'll—"

A screech shattered the night. It was joined by another, then another. The shades swarmed us from all sides, buzzing like crushed locusts. Megan and Dylan collapsed, hands to their ears.

My head spun like it would twist off my neck. I knelt down on the reservoir bank so I wouldn't stumble into the water, then forced my mouth open to speak, despite my nausea.

"I can help you! You can be a ghost again." I reached for the closest shade, remembering what Logan had told Dylan about their ability to choose. "It's your decision."

Three shades hovered near the branches above me, making a gnashing noise that gnawed my brain. The other two floated in front, over the water.

"Aura, hurry!" Megan gagged. Dylan lay on his side in the mud, every muscle spasming.

In the middle of the maelstrom, I thought of Logan, and suddenly I knew what to say. I spoke softly into the whirlwind. "You don't have to be alone anymore."

The shades screamed louder—in protest or assent, I couldn't tell.

I lifted my arms, opening my body to them. "Now!"

Two shades zoomed forward. Their dark energy entered my gut, then left through the small of my back, fast as a bullet.

My muscles turned to jelly. I fell forward, raising my hands too late to break my fall. My cheekbone hit a rock, sending a gong of pain ricocheting through my head. The other shades gave squealing laughs and swooped closer. It felt like they would devour me.

"Aura!" Dylan and Megan shouted from the ground nearby. The shades filled me with dark vibrations, until I felt ripped apart atom by atom. I couldn't see through the blackness as I started to vomit.

Someone grabbed my shoulders and propped me up, while another pair of hands held my hair back. My body shuddered and spasmed, trying to rid itself of the shades' bitter rage.

"Unhhh." I pushed myself back from the water's edge. My throat burned, liked I'd puked a mix of grapefruit juice and hot pepper sauce.

"Here." Breathing hard, Dylan held out his tie, which he'd removed. When I gave him an odd look, he said, "It's either this or my undershirt."

"Thanks, this is fine." I wiped my clammy forehead, then my mouth, with the soft silk. "Is there a 'Kill me, I'm stupid' sign taped to my back?"

"You were trying to help them." Megan was sitting beside me, holding her stomach. "You know what's weird? As soon as they went through you, I started feeling better."

I looked around, though turning my head made it feel like it would split open. "Does that mean it worked? Did the shades turn into ghosts?"

"They disappeared," Dylan said. "Flew through you and came out the other side. They were violet for, like, a millisecond, and then they were gone."

"That's what I saw, too," Megan added. "I remember seeing violet reflected in the water."

My heart leaped. Whatever happened with Logan wasn't just a Logan thing. Shading didn't have to be a one-way trip to hell. Unless . . .

"Why'd they disappear? Did they turn back into shades and go somewhere else?"

"Oh." Dylan looked at Megan. "Maybe."

I groaned at the uncertainty, then saw the mess I'd made of myself. "Ugh, I can't go home like this. Gina will think I got drunk."

Jeri Smith-Ready

"I brought a change of clothes, because of this stupid suit." Dylan knelt beside me and draped one of my arms over his shoulder. "Megan, get her other side."

We wobbled up the trail to the car, where Dylan gave me a T-shirt and a pair of jeans that were about a foot too long. The back of Dylan's dress shirt was muddy, but he put on his jacket to cover the stains. Megan had managed to fall down on the driest part of the reservoir bank, so she'd suffered only a scraped elbow.

The closest bathroom was at a Dairy Queen on York Road. I changed and washed up while Megan and Dylan ordered food we probably couldn't stomach.

I staggered out into the fluorescent light, holding up Dylan's jeans at my waist, the cuffs rolled to my knees. His Spiderman T-shirt fell halfway down my thighs. Dylan and Megan sat hunched side by side at a table next to the condiment stand.

Megan's eyes glinted at me as I approached. "Aura, guess what? We—oh, wow, you look, um. Really, not too bad."

"No worse than a refugee camp reject." I sat across from them and rested my head against the back of the booth. "What's up?"

"We were thinking," Dylan said, chowing down on a burger despite having nearly had a seizure half an hour ago.

"*I* was thinking," Megan corrected. "Shades can go anywhere, but ghosts can only go where they went during their lives, right? Remember that time Logan disappeared from the car when we drove down a street where he'd never been?"

I'd never forget that. He'd stood there in the intersection, forlorn and violet, while the car behind us drove right through him.

"Those shades tonight," Dylan added. "When they were alive, I bet they never went to that reservoir."

"So if they'd turned back into ghosts," Megan blurted, "they would've disappeared."

"Gone back to someplace they'd been before," Dylan finished.

Megan reached across the table and grabbed my wrist. "Aura, you can cure shades," she hissed. "Not just Logan. *Any* shade."

I pulled my soda closer, desperate for sugar and caffeine. "We can't know for sure unless someone sees one of those ex-shades as a ghost again." My mind fought the lingering dizziness. "Wait—could we try to call them as ghosts?"

"Yes!" Megan pulled out the list of shade names. "I bet some of their obituaries are online, and if they died here in Maryland, they'll be in the state medical examiner's database." She shimmied her shoulders in a triumphant dance. "Which I have access to at the funeral home."

"Awesome." Dylan picked up my burger. "Are you gonna eat this?"

I shook my head and sipped my soda, my stomach roiling.

Did I want to be the Secret Savior of Shades? After hearing first-hand of Logan's hellish ordeal, how could I not help them?

Besides, this experiment wasn't just charity work. Tonight had given me a big piece of the "Who Am I?" puzzle. One I planned to finally solve in Ireland, with Zachary.

Chapter Twenty-Five

Early the next evening, Megan got the scoop on one of our hopefully ex-shades, the ghost of a woman who'd lived in Baltimore and worked in Annapolis. We decided to try to reach her in the capital city next Friday night instead of screaming her name outside her old house.

I told Zachary all about it in that night's video chat.

"If this worked," I said in conclusion, "if I did change a shade to a ghost, I want to try it again on the winter solstice when we're in Ireland. Is that okay? I know we're supposed to be on vacation."

"It's not just a vacation." He typed on his keyboard, his eyes searching the screen beside me. "This year the solstice is at two fifteen a.m. Ireland time on the twenty-second. We'll find somewhere private for you to call the shades."

I grinned, relieved I hadn't had to convince him. "So how are you?"

Zachary waved his hand without answering, as always. "Thanks very much for the biscuits." He reached to the side, then lifted a cardboard box so I could see it. "From your grandmother's bakery, right? My mum loves them. She doesn't have as much time to bake, what with taking care of Dad."

"I like your parents. They seem to really love each other."

"Aye." He took a bite of almond cookie and chewed while he pondered. "They come from such different backgrounds. He's working-class Glasgow, and she's boarding-school south England. They're like, em, what's that Disney movie about the dogs?"

"101 Dalmatians?"

"No, the one with the cocker spaniel and the spaghetti. At the Italian restaurant, where the waiter sings 'Bella Notte.'"

"Lady and the Tramp?"

"That's it. They're Lady and the Tramp."

I laughed. "When they had puppies, some of them were little Ladys and some were little Tramps. Which are you?"

"Well, I'm no' a lady, that's for sure."

The way Zachary looked at me made me wish we were sharing a single strand of spaghetti, like the dogs in the movie. Not that we would need that as an excuse to kiss.

"Did you see a lot of Disney movies growing up?"

"I loved them." His eyes grew as animated as the films he was talking about. "I thought that's what America must be like. Bright colors, singing and dancing. Heroes and villains easy to tell apart."

I smiled, both at his words and at my realization that his face looked less gaunt than before. "Was America like you imagined?"

"It was almost as colorful. And God knows, people sing and dance on television constantly. But the good guys and bad guys weren't as clear as I thought they'd be."

His gaze shadowed, and I waited for him to tell me what the DMP had done to him.

Instead he brightened and dusted the sugar off his hands. "We've had a bit of drama, too. Martin, my best mate from round here—" He cut himself off and spoke bitterly. "My only mate now. He's moved in with us."

"'Only mate now'? I thought you were hanging out with all your old friends."

"Not after what they did to Martin last week. After he came out to them."

"What happened? Did they hurt him?"

"Naw, it wasn't as if he was doing something truly shocking, like supporting the wrong football club. But the bastards said stupid things. He got angry, rightfully so, and I was caught in the middle. It was an easy choice." Zachary frowned and drew a thumb over one dark brow. "No, not easy. But simple."

"That sucks."

"It does, because on any other day, any of us lads'd take a punch— or a bullet—for any o' the others."

"So why's Martin living with you? Did his parents kick him out?"

"No' officially. But they decided that now he's seventeen and not at university, he should start paying rent. My parents said he could stay here for free." Zachary adjusted the collar of his light-brown T-shirt, looking embarrassed. "On the condition that he cheers me up."

"Is he?"

He nodded. "I can't wait for you to come and meet him."

My belly warmed at the idea of visiting Zachary in Glasgow. That wasn't part of our December itinerary, so it meant he was thinking beyond.

"Is he home?"

"He just got back from work at the pub, so he'll pop round in a minute."

A knock came from behind him. Zachary turned his head. "Aye!"

"A'right, mate?" A moment later a redheaded boy appeared behind Zachary's chair. "You must be Aura."

His bright grin provoked one of my own, and of course the accent made my eyes glaze over. "Martin?"

"Martin Connelly, pleased to meet ya." He said to Zachary, "If tha's what she looks like on a wee screen, I cannae wait tae see her in 3-D."

Zachary kept his eyes on me. "Not as much as I can't wait."

Another knock came at the door, and I heard Fiona's voice.

"It's a whole crowd," Zachary muttered. "Come in."

"Oh, are you speaking with Aura?" She peeked over his other shoulder, wisps of dark hair in disarray around her face. "Hello, love. How are you?"

"I'm great." I tried not to show my dismay at her obvious exhaustion, and wondered why she was up at two a.m. "How are you and Mr. Moore?"

"Ah, well." She touched Zachary's arm. "Can I have your help with your father for just one minute?"

"Of course."

Zachary stood up, and Martin slipped into his chair. "I'll keep Aura occupied till ya get back." His gaze went past the camera as he watched them leave. Then his face turned suddenly serious, which didn't seem like its natural state. "How is he, wi' you?"

It took a moment to understand not only Martin's meaning, but his words. His accent was ten times stronger than Zachary's—not surprising, since Zachary had spent the last four years in England and America.

"Sometimes he's normal," I said. "Other times, he seems really distant. Is he mad at me?"

"Aw, no, no. Never think tha'." He put his cheek on his tightly balled fist as he leaned closer to the camera, hazel eyes burning. "It's that fuckin' DMP. They fuckin' did something to him. How could anyone stand two fuckin' months of that?"

I stammered at the barrage of profanity. Zachary had said that the word was a verbal tic among Glasgow boys. *Like a comma,* he'd said.

"Two months of what?" I asked Martin. "Do you know what they did to him?"

"No, he willnae talk about i'. But he's different. Fuckin'... damaged, know wha' I mean?"

"I can tell. But you live with him, you must see more of it."

"True. I notice he—" Martin broke off and looked away. "I shouldnae be sayin' it. It makes him look mental, and weak."

"I don't care. He doesn't have to be strong with me."

"Aye, he does. Wi' everyone. It's a Zachary thing."

"So what did you notice?"

"Well, here's the scene, right?" Martin spread his hands like Ls to form a frame. "We're in the living room, watching the fitba. I get up for a beer, and let's say I get distracted in the kitchen. Tryin' tae sort out if I want some crisps, too, or maybe a sandwich."

"Okay." I wondered where this was going.

"If I'm gone more than a few minutes, he comes and finds me. Like a—" Martin wiped his mouth. "Like my dog used tae do."

My stomach went cold. "What's he worried about?"

"Dunno. That I left out the back door, maybe."

"Why would you leave?"

"I wouldnae. He does the same to his parents. And at night before he goes to bed, he walks around the whole fuckin' house, makes sure we're all where we're meant tae be." Martin folded his arms on the desk and leaned in. "When I asked him what he was doing, he called it a 'perimeter check.'"

"What's that mean?"

"I looked it up. It's what soldiers do at a camp. Make sure there's no security breaches."

I glanced at my dark window. Though our Charles Village neighborhood bordered on some rough areas, I'd never felt unsafe in my own home. "You think Zach's just being protective? Or is he pretending to be protective because it's better than being scared?"

"Dunno." Martin looked away, his lips forming a tight line. "But he never used tae be like this. With me and our mates, we'd be out and suddenly he'd just be like, eh, I'm fucking off home to read or whatever. Like he had to have X amount of hours on his own every day or he'd go mental."

"He was independent."

"Right! Now, he wants nae time alone. Ever. I think if it wouldn't piss off his da, he'd sleep in my fuckin' bed wi' me." His eyes widened, and he thrust out his palms. "Oh, dinnae worry, that lad is heartbreakingly dead straight. Not that there's anything wrong wi' that."

I laughed, though my amusement was weakened by the thought of Zachary's restless fear. "I don't know how to help him."

"Me neither. His ma said he goes to MI-X for counseling, fuckin' post-traumatic stress."

"Good. He didn't tell me that."

"Of course not. That'd make him imperfect, aye?"

I'd learned more about Zachary's true state of mind in the last minute than in a month of video chats. "Will you let me know how he's doing? I hate to go behind his back, but could you e-mail me?"

"Good idea. It's for the best." He wrote down my address and stuffed it in his front jeans pocket.

"Sorry to hear about you and your friends."

"Ach, cretinous bawbags." He rubbed his freckled cheek, just under his left eye. "I've new mates now, who don't think a night of culture means watching Spanish football instead of English."

"New friends are great, but old ones are the best."

"Hmm. Sometimes old ones suck."

"Yeah, they can screw up pretty bad. And because they're your friends, they think they can be mean to you without breaking up the whole gang."

"Right," he said uncertainly.

"But it's usually worth it to give them a chance to make it up to you." I shrugged. "Or maybe it's better to trade them in for shiny new friends."

He crossed his arms and looked at me with a raised eyebrow. "You and Zach talk about me when I'm no' here, and you and I talk about him behind his back. Time for him and me tae talk about you."

"Like you don't already."

His mouth quirked up at the corner. "Maybe a wee bit."

"If you won't make peace with those, um, bawbags for your own sake, then do it for Zach. He needs all the friends he can get."

"I'll think about it. Just one question." He gave a full, bright grin. "Does Zachary know how cute you are when you say 'bawbags'?"

Chapter Twenty-Six

I tugged my hood to keep my face drizzle-free as Dylan, Megan, and I walked up a steep, silent Annapolis street. The state capital was a mere half-hour drive from Baltimore, but we'd never visited any sections other than the busy waterfront.

Out of all the shades I'd maybe turned back into ghosts, Latisha McKenzie was the only one who had lived nearby. In life she'd worked for a state senator, and while we couldn't sneak into the legislature buildings, research told us there was one place the political types loved to lunch.

Lawyers' Mall was a small brick courtyard across from the State House. A bronze, benevolent-looking statue of Thurgood Marshall dominated the plaza, which was framed by a low brick wall, the perfect height for sitting.

Hopefully we wouldn't need to sit, or even stand, for very long.

"This better be quick," Megan said, huddled in her black hoodie. "I'm freezing."

Dylan checked his watch. "Oh my God, McConnell, we were here almost thirty seconds before you started bitching. You feeling okay?"

She flipped him off, but he just smirked and pulled down the sleeve of his orange St. John's College sweatshirt. We figured if at least one of us was wearing swag from the Annapolis institution, it'd look less suspicious for us to wander away from the touristy areas.

I held my palm faceup—the rain had stopped. So I pulled back my hood. "Latisha McKenzie, come and—"

"There you are, girl!"

The thin, middle-aged woman opened her arms, long fingers waving toward herself, beckoning me. The orange streetlights couldn't dampen her violet glory.

I just stood there for a moment, stunned. I'd really done it. I'd cured a shade.

Then I dashed forward into her ethereal arms, overcome with joy. She was the only ghost I'd ever "embraced" besides Logan.

"Wow," Dylan and Megan said together behind me.

Ex-Latisha stepped back to look at me. "I wanted to thank you before I passed on, but I wasn't gonna wait much longer."

"Already? Are you sure?" I thought of Logan's first, unsuccessful attempt to leave this world.

"Oh, I'm ready." She counted off on her fingers. "Said good-bye to my grandkids, my great-niece and -nephew, and had them talk to my son and daughters for me."

"But today when I checked the DMP website, it said you were still a shade. Your family didn't tell anyone you were a ghost again?"

"Uh-uh! They know those men'd put me in one of those little boxes like that." She snapped her fingers without sound. "But I don't wanna push my luck. You know how little children are at keeping secrets."

"Excuse me."

I jumped, startled, and turned to see a patrolling police officer. "What are you kids doing?" he boomed.

"Standing," Dylan said.

I glared at Dylan. "Sorry, officer. Are we breaking any laws?"

"Not that I know of." The policeman was young, blond, and well built. "From where I was standing, it looked like you were talking to a ghost."

Beyond him, ex-Latisha closed her eyes, and a glow ignited in the center of her body. I was glad she wasn't bothered by the police officer.

"We were talking to a ghost," I told the cop. "I know it seems weird, but it's perfectly legal."

"For now." He propped his hands on his hips, as if showing off the gun in his holster. Meanwhile, ex-Latisha's form became a gorgeous, shimmering golden-white. I pitied the cop, that he couldn't see what was taking place just a few feet away.

"Why don't you run along now," he said, "before I have to take your names and charge you with loitering?"

"Loitering?" Megan exclaimed. "This is a public place."

I gestured my friends toward the road. "Guys, let's just go." The last thing I wanted was a report filed with my name on it, even though we were innocent. Aunt Gina would want to know why in the world we were all the way down in Annapolis.

After crossing the street, we looked back to see the young patrol officer peering around the plaza, oblivious to the spectacle in front of him. Ex-Latisha's glow filled the courtyard, shining off the Marshall statue and glinting even in the officer's badge.

We waved as she disappeared.

Like those in a spaceship approaching light speed (according to general relativity), I felt time slow down as the autumn wore on and my trip to Ireland got closer. I took the SATs again, and scored well enough to give me courage to apply to Johns Hopkins and a couple of Ivy League schools, and of course the University of Glasgow.

Zachary and I video-chatted at least every other night, making sure not to let our schedule lapse. He'd lost his previous girlfriend Suzanne after she moved to another country, so I wanted to reassure him I wouldn't drift away. I sensed that beyond his inexplicable insecurity lay a deeper fear of being alone.

Martin and I e-mailed a few times, though it felt like a betrayal. But I craved more knowledge of Zachary's life than he was offering himself. Martin said Zachary had been having nightmares and sometimes wouldn't fall asleep until six a.m., and then wouldn't wake until noon.

On October 18, which would've been Logan's eighteenth birthday, I joined the Keeleys at the cemetery for a memorial service. I'd visited Logan's grave every few weeks since he'd passed on. Sometimes I'd drop off flowers and leave quickly. Other times I'd stay for an hour and talk to Logan or listen to music or just sit, remembering.

But on this brisk sunny day, standing here with his friends and family, I realized something: I'd spent the last year mourning Logan—sometimes with him right by my side—but I'd spent very little time reliving the night of his death. Now it all came crashing back at once, like a movie played at double-speed.

Logan onstage, full of life and energy as he commanded the spotlight, the audience, and what seemed like every note from every instrument.

Logan at his birthday party, draining that life out of himself with each drink he took.

Logan in his bedroom, displaying his tattoo of my name over his heart, promising to love me no matter how famous he got, touching me as we started to undress.

But never finished.

Logan on the floor outside the bathroom, his ghost standing beside me, body and spirit forever parted.

I wanted to be strong for his family on this anniversary, wanted to be the friend they needed. But tears drenched my face, and sobs racked my chest so hard, I thought my ribs would crack.

Finally I fled to my car, parked in the same place as the night Logan had passed on. I didn't want anyone to see me through the windows, so I sat behind it, leaning against the tire.

That's where Mickey found me.

He said nothing, just reached down and offered me a hand. I stared up at him, confused. Did he want me to come back to the grave? Did he want me to leave?

Then I saw what he held: Logan's acoustic guitar.

I grasped his hand, realizing too late that mine was wet with tears. Mickey didn't flinch, though, as he pulled me to my feet.

We walked down the cemetery lane without looking back, until we arrived at a shady arbor. A circle of crimson-leaf maples surrounded a small fountain, which was dry. Two curved marble benches flanked the empty concrete basin.

Mickey and I sat at either end of a bench, only a few feet apart.

"Siobhan and I finally wrote . . . this," he said. "It'll sound better at the reception tonight, when she adds her fiddle part. But I thought maybe you'd want . . ." Running his hand over the guitar's curves, Mickey stared at the trumpeting cherub atop the dry fountain.

"Thank you," I whispered.

Mickey tuned the guitar, then silenced the strings with his palm. "I'm sorry it took so long."

"What was stopping you before?" I worried he was going to say "being with Megan."

"I kept reimagining that night—not the way it was, but the way it should've been. And the way everything would have been on any given day if he hadn't died."

"Like a parallel universe, where Logan made different choices."

"Yeah. Right now he should be applying to colleges and maybe thinking about signing a record contract."

He should be celebrating his eighteenth birthday. In our universe, Logan would remain forever seventeen.

"You can drive yourself crazy thinking like that. Believe me, I know."

"And that's the thing." Mickey raised his blue eyes, deep like Dylan's, not bright like Logan's. "Once I stopped imagining that better world, I was left with nothing but this one."

My heart folded in on itself to see his hurt. But it was a clear, sharp pain now, not the dull sheen of despair I'd seen in his eyes for so long.

"Anyway," he said, "that's when this came."

Mickey began to play Logan's song, a raw, haunting tune of farewell. My tears, falling in time with the rhythm, felt as if they were squeezed out by my heartbeat.

Wherever Logan was now, he was at peace. Our own journeys to peace would last us the rest of our lives. But I felt one certainty as surely as I felt the earth beneath my feet: This song was one of that journey's largest steps.

The ceremony at Logan's grave site was followed by a reception at a local Irish pub. Mickey and Siobhan played a set of mostly traditional music on their guitar and fiddle. As the night went on, they mixed in acoustic versions of Keeley Brothers songs, which had us all cheering and weeping, sometimes simultaneously.

Then, a few minutes before midnight, they played Logan's song.

Even the second time around, the lyrics and melody reached through my ears, bypassed my brain, and went straight to my heart, where they wriggled around, causing a hundred different pains.

When the song was over, the crowd let out a deep sigh before exploding into applause. Tears were wiped and glasses were raised, and then midnight arrived.

It was no longer Logan's birthday, but his death day. Our minute of silence seemed to stretch into an hour as we remembered the life that had been stolen from us.

Afterward, Mickey and Megan disappeared outside for almost half an hour. When they returned, they were smiling but not holding hands, to my surprise.

"What's up with you and Mickey?" I asked her when we met at the bar for a soda refill.

"We're friends." She gave a serene sigh and a little laugh. "Wow, I didn't think that word could ever not hurt when applied to us."

I hugged her hard. "As long as you're happy."

"We are." Her arms tightened. "Holy crap. Look!"

Connor and Siobhan were kissing in a corner booth, their bodies melded together as they ended their six-week breakup—or at least interrupted it.

"I didn't think that'd last," said a voice behind us. We turned to see Dylan, who looked down at Megan. "Wanna dance?" he asked her in a flat tone, like he didn't care.

She scrunched up her face. "Um, you hate me."

"Yeah, come on." He took her hand and led her away.

I watched, amazed, as their begrudging affection slowly emerged from under their armor of bickering.

Then I raised my glass to the final photo taken of Logan during his life, poster-size on the wall. He stood in the center of the stage, his blue eyes turned to the lights above, one hand holding the mic to his lips and the other reaching out to the crowd. Out to the world that loved him.

I wondered what Logan had seen in that moment. A future as a rock star? A future with me? Or just a blinding white spotlight obliterating every thought? I wished I'd asked him.

Logan could no longer fill in those blanks. From now on, we'd have to imagine what he would say if he were here. And imagine how he felt, wherever he was. There was no way to know for sure.

But I thought of ex-Latisha's face as she'd glowed, then faded on Lawyers' Mall. The memory of her smile—and Logan's, too—told me the only answer that still mattered: They were happy.

Megan and I were in AP Chemistry one day early in December when the ax finally fell on our lives.

Mrs. Oswald had just told us we had to cover two sections per class between now and midterms or risk not having studied everything we needed for the Advanced Placement test. We were all trying to keep our grumbles to a sub-riot level when a crackle and whine came over the PA.

"Everyone," Principal Hirsch said. "May I please have your immediate attention."

My heart rate quickened from the tone of his voice and the timing. Routine announcements always came during homeroom. I glanced across the room at Simon, who looked as perplexed as everyone else. Then again, he could be faking confusion.

The principal continued, "There will be an emergency assembly in the auditorium immediately. All students, staff, and faculty are required to attend. No exceptions."

* * *

The entire student body—seven hundred people, more or less—filed into the auditorium by grade.

"Feels weird to finally sit in the front," I told Megan as we took our seats. I saw Simon at the end of our row, as usual keeping me in sight without *looking* like he was keeping me in sight.

Principal Hirsch stood at the podium, appearing unusually somber. I wondered if someone had died.

"Silence, please." Our principal's voice was so serious, people actually listened. Something was very wrong. "This morning, the U.S. House of Representatives passed the Defense of the Living Act."

"Oh no," I whispered. The girl on my left gave me a quizzical look.

"The Senate is expected to pass its version later this week, and the president has vowed to sign the law." Principal Hirsch took off his glasses. "Henceforth, all post-Shifters, upon turning eighteen, will be required to register for selective service to the Department of Metaphysical Purity. In other words, a DMP draft."

The auditorium erupted in cries of confusion and protest. "This is bullshit!" some guy in the junior class behind me shouted. "Yeah, bullshit!" someone echoed from the sophomore section.

The crowd took up the chant: "Bull-SHIT! Bull-SHIT! Bull-SHIT!"

I didn't join in. My throat had closed up so that I could barely breathe. The DMP had always wanted to use us, had tried so hard to recruit us, and now we had no choice.

Principal Hirsch folded his glasses and put them in his sport-coat pocket. He made no attempt to quiet the chants, but let them die down on their own.

"I sympathize," he said, clearing his throat. "I myself had to face a very different kind of draft during the Vietnam War."

"When does it start?" asked Amy Koeller.

"Once the bill has been signed, the DMP is expected to move quickly to put the system into place. They cite the need to protect the public." Principal Hirsch's tone oozed skepticism. "It will begin with the first post-Shifters, those born December twenty-first at three fifty a.m. and later."

In other words, with me.

"What about college?" Megan asked without raising her hand.

"You can file for a deferment, which they may or may not approve. But the moment you graduate from university or stop attending full-time, your name will go back into the lottery. You may also sign up voluntarily, which will presumably give you a better position with higher pay. Either way, by your eighteenth birthday, you must register."

I sat there, steaming. I'd done everything I could to hurt the DMP, but it wasn't enough. They were using Flight 346 to make the public, and therefore politicians, so scared of ghosts that they'd take the freedoms of post-Shifters.

"For some of you, it will no doubt be an adventure," Principal Hirsch said. "If you can pretend you have a choice."

Megan nudged me. "Won't you be in Ireland on your eighteenth birthday?"

"I guess I'll have to register before I go."

Or not register, and never come home again. I felt Simon's eyes. What did MI-X plan for me now?

A murmur started in the back of the auditorium. Megan and I

turned to see several male DMP agents in white uniforms taking up stations near the exits. Two more flanked a blond woman in a suit, striding down the aisle toward the stage. I recognized her as one of the recruiters who'd visited our school last year.

The two agents mounted the stage and moved to stand by Principal Hirsch. As he sputtered a protest, they led him away from the podium. The blonde took his place and addressed us.

"Ladies and gentlemen," she said, "forgive the interruption. The DMP hoped to introduce its new policy directly to post-Shifters, without the filter of pre-Shifter experience."

"Like she's not a pre-Shifter herself," Megan growled.

I tapped her arm. "I bet Hirsch called the emergency assembly because he knew the DMP was coming."

The two dumpers led our principal offstage and toward the back of the auditorium. He began to struggle in their grip. "This is an outrage. This is *my* school!"

I looked to the side of the auditorium, where some of the teachers were conferring. Why weren't they stepping forward to stop this? Was every pre-Shifter now crazy enough to believe the DMP knew best?

I stood up. "Where are they taking him?" I shouted at the woman in the suit.

"Everyone calm down," she said. "Or we'll be forced to take harsher measures."

Three huge sophomore guys got up and stood in the aisle in front of Principal Hirsch and the dumpers. I recognized the boys from last year—they'd been recruited with lacrosse scholarships. They were intimidating even without sticks in their hands.

"Stand back, kids," said the one of the agents who held Principal Hirsch.

Calling us "kids"? The fastest way to get on our bad side. In response, the giant sophomores widened their stances, blocking the aisle.

I hurried up after the agents, Megan on my heels. "Do you have a warrant for Principal Hirsch's arrest?" I asked them.

The lead agent laughed at me. "Why do you think we need a warrant?"

"We're not stupid," our goalkeeper said. "We watch police shows."

"My aunt's a lawyer." I gestured to the auditorium. "Half of us here have lawyers for parents. And thanks to our American-history teachers, we know our rights." It couldn't hurt to suck up to the faculty— maybe it would get them to actually do something besides fret.

"They don't need a warrant, Aura." Principal Hirsch jerked his elbows out of their grip. "Because I'm not under arrest. Isn't that right, sirs?"

The lead agent grimaced. "Of course. We just want to question him."

"What's he done wrong?" I asked them.

The recruiter woman tapped the microphone. "We requested that your school administration allow us to announce the legislation directly and simultaneously to every student body, so that we might put it in the proper context."

So they could "control the message," as Nicola would say. "Principal Hirsch ignored a 'request.' He didn't break a law."

"Free speech!" someone in the middle of the auditorium shouted.

I pointed to the recruiter. "Yeah, ever heard of the First Amendment? Or does your stupid law repeal that, too?" The woman's lips tightened, and my chest went cold. "It does?"

"Of course it doesn't repeal it," she said, as if talking to a five-year-old. "But it does make provisions regarding public criticism of the selective service program. For security purposes."

"That's unconstitutional!"

She shrugged. "The courts will decide. In the meantime, people need to watch what they say."

If I could've shot lasers from my eyes, the woman's pretty face would've had two burning holes in it. I looked at our principal. Did he want us to rise up and defend him? Or sit down and take it, plan to fight another day?

But what if there wasn't another day? What if they locked him up and replaced him, and we never saw him again? What if we were next?

"We won't let you take him," I said, hoping I was right, that it wouldn't be just me and three sophomores against half a dozen armed federal agents.

"Who's 'we'?" the lead dumper snarled.

With a shuffle of book bags and creak of fold-down seats, the student body rose as one. A moment later, the faculty joined them, moving to block the exits.

The freshman students left the rows first, filing between the agents at the door and the agents who had Principal Hirsch. Then came the sophomores, then the juniors, and finally the seniors.

Jenna and Christopher joined Megan at my side. Even my old enemy Brian Knox stood by me.

We didn't shake our fists or wave so much as pencils at them. Our numbers and our rightness were enough.

Finally I said, "That's we."

Chapter Twenty-Seven

That night I told Zachary about the assembly and the DMP's attempt to detain our principal. In the face of the student and faculty solidarity—and our threat to call in our lawyer parents—they'd abandoned their efforts, giving Hirsch an official warning. Which probably meant they'd had no legal basis to detain him in the first place.

"That's pure bollocks." Zachary looked as if he'd like to punch a few dumpers himself. "What'll you do now?"

"I'll register before my birthday. If I don't, they'll think I'm dodging and stop me in the airport on my way to see you."

"We definitely don't want that."

"I know. But it's so scary, feeling like we can't speak out."

His face hardened. "You've no idea." Then he looked away and rubbed the back of his neck, which his hair was beginning to cover again. The memory of its end-of-summer shagginess, combined with his present troubled demeanor, made me want to hug him and beg him to finally tell me what the DMP had done.

"Let's switch to unencrypted now," he said. "We'll start over and discuss all our lovely false plans."

I nodded, hiding my disappointment. We logged off, then back on with the signal unscrambled. At least I never had to pretend to be happy to see him.

After we chatted aimlessly for a few minutes, Zachary said, "Just two more weeks until you come to Glasgow. It's all arranged—the rental car, our ferry to Orkney, the bed and breakfast. I've even made birthday dinner reservations."

"Where?"

Zachary hesitated. He hadn't invented that part yet. "It's a surprise."

I struggled to keep my smile from turning into a laugh. It was fun pretending I was going to Scotland instead of meeting him in Ireland. For extra serendipity, there was a megalith similar to Newgrange in Scotland's Orkney Islands, called Maeshowe. Its inner chamber marked the winter solstice sunset instead of sunrise. So there was a plausible reason why we'd be going there.

Just to be sure the DMP believed our conversation, I turned it to a personal subject—one I needed to discuss, anyway.

"Zach, I have a slight packing issue. What do you like girls to, you know, wear?"

He angled his head, clearly confused. "Whatever they want."

"I mean"—my face heated—"in bed."

"Oh!" He blinked rapidly, probably imagining government guys in bad suits listening in. "Dunno. Never spent the night with anyone."

At least our nervousness wasn't being faked. "But what do you think is attractive?"

He paused. "Nakedness?"

"Besides that! You must have some preference."

"Are you getting this from a magazine?"

"Of course not." I pushed the latest issue of *Cosmo* farther back on my desk.

"Because honestly, I don't care." Fully himself again, he held out his hands, palms together. "I promise, it willnae matter what you wear. I willnae see it. I want you now, and I'll want you then, more than anyone ever wanted anyone."

I waited, unsatisfied.

"You need an answer, don't you?" he said.

I nodded.

He glanced away, then back again. "I like red."

I grinned. I looked hot in red.

"Listen," he said. "Don't think I expect us to—just because we have a room together doesn't mean we need to—"

"Yes, we do." Forgetting the rest of the world, I reached out to the screen to touch his lips. "*I* need to. With you."

"Oh." His eyelids went heavy. "Me too."

My pulse pounded with a sudden craving. "I wish you were here right now."

Zachary's eyelashes flashed as he leaned in. "I am there now." He lifted his hand to a spot below the camera. "Guess where I'm touching you."

I gave him a wicked smile. "Here?" I fingered the top button of my green silk pajama shirt.

He clicked his tongue. "What do you take me for, lass? I'll no' be groping you long-distance. Guess again."

I swept my hand over my neck. "Here?"

"You're getting warmer."

It was true—literally. I hoped he couldn't see me sweat at the thought of his hands on me. I touched my cheek. "Here?"

"A bit warmer."

I smushed the tip of my nose. "Here."

"Boiling hot."

I let my fingers drift down an inch, brushing my parted lips. "Here?"

"Aye." He pressed his fingers to his own lips, then reached for the camera. I did the same, and for a moment, our virtual touch-kiss blotted out our views of each other.

Then he whispered, "You'd best let me sleep now. Not that I'll be able to." For once I thought he meant for a good reason.

"I'll see you soon."

He nodded once. "And then 'good night' won't be just another word for 'good-bye.'"

Monday morning I found a note slipped into my locker, in Simon's handwriting:

EARLY CHRISTMAS GIFTS FOR YOU. BACKSTAGE AFTER SCHOOL.

The drama class had just done five performances of *Antigone* (a holiday classic!) and was taking the day off before this week's shows. I found Simon sitting on Creon's throne, legs crossed and arms resting on the sides in a lordly posture.

"You look a little too comfortable there." I glanced at the closed curtain, which blocked us from the auditorium.

"You and Zachary have done well. Our source tells us the DMP thinks you're meeting in Scotland."

"Thanks for buying me the extra fake ticket. Must've been expensive."

"That's not all we've done." Simon pulled his backpack onto his lap and withdrew a large manila envelope. "We want you and your boyfriend to make it to Ireland and back safely. To that end, once you board your respective international flights—from Atlanta, in your case—Aura Salvatore and Zachary Moore will disappear."

I opened the envelope. Inside was a stack of papers and what looked like a brick-red UK passport.

Simon continued, "We've arranged it so that your plane tickets, your rental car, and your bed-and-breakfast are now under the names Laura and John MacLean. John goes by Jack, by the way. It rhymes with Zach, so if you make a mistake, people might think they've misheard."

The passport showed my photo beside LAURA REESE MACLEAN. "Are we supposed to be brother and sister?"

"No." Simon opened his other hand to reveal a small, blue, velvet jewelry box. He popped it open with his thumb. "More like husband and wife."

Inside was a gold wedding band, sitting next to a pear-cut diamond engagement ring. "Whoa."

"Forgive me for not getting down on one knee to present them." He held the box out to me. "Go on, see if they fit. We can have them adjusted before you leave if necessary."

The rings fit perfectly. I quickly removed them and stuffed them back in the box.

Simon zipped up his backpack. "Put them on when you board in Atlanta. MI-X can protect you in the United States. We can protect you in the United Kingdom." He met my gaze. "We cannot protect you in Ireland."

"Why not?"

"We have no agreement with Irish authorities to conduct covert operations within the boundaries of the Republic. In fact, we're expressly forbidden, as is the DMP." His mouth twisted. "The Irish love their ghosts."

"You let that stop you?"

His lips quirked. "Officially, yes. If we were caught, heads would roll. By the way, there's no BlackBox in Ireland. Enjoy having a piss with ghosts watching."

Great, I thought, remembering a ghost surprising me in the woods in just such a situation.

I lifted the passport. "If we're on our own in Ireland, how does a fake identity protect us?"

"Because no one wants to kidnap Jack and Laura MacLean. Or kill them." Simon cocked an eyebrow and sat back in the throne. "Do you feel more comfortable wearing those rings now?"

My silence was enough of an answer.

He pointed to the envelope. "That contains your legend—your

false background. The white papers are copies of your university records and marriage certificate. Keep them with you when you travel. The blue papers form your cover story. Memorize every detail, then destroy the blue sheets. Confer with Zachary to invent stories about how you met and fell in love, et cetera, et cetera. The more detail, the better, but only if you can both remember. And of course, let me know what they are so I can find people to corroborate if necessary."

"Can you at least tell me who might be trying to kill us?"

He sighed. "If we knew that, we'd go and get them, now, wouldn't we?"

I didn't answer, because I honestly didn't know if MI-X would or not. I had a feeling they were only letting me and Zachary go to Ireland because they thought the real bad guys would follow us. Maybe MI-X was using us as bait.

We could be more valuable dead than alive.

I stared at my bedroom mirror that night, teaching myself who I was.

"My name is Laura MacLean. I'm twenty-one years old. I was born July nineteenth as Laura Reese in Liverpool, England. My parents got divorced when I was six. My mom moved to Baltimore, where I grew up but never became a citizen because I visited my father every summer and wanted to move back to my native country one day. I majored in communications at Johns Hopkins University."

I jotted a note to study up on Liverpool, as well as the curriculum for Hopkins's communications majors. On my packing list, I wrote *JHU swag for me and Zach*.

I turned back to the mirror. "That's where I met John MacLean from Glasgow. We fell in love, and when I visited the UK last summer"—I checked the latest stamp on my fake passport—"in July, Jack and I got married. I came home to settle my affairs, and now I'm returning to the UK to live with him. We're honeymooning in Ireland for a few days, then going back to Glasgow for Christmas."

I went to my bed, where the papers were spread across the comforter, and double-checked my information. My finger traced my college transcript, including my fake 3.97 grade point average.

If only it was the truth. If only I were finished with school and moving to another country to begin an exciting life of adventure with Zachary.

Maybe not married to him. Yet.

My million-and-one memory exercises had paid off. I knew Laura's personal history as well as I knew my own. Zachary and I just had to flesh out our pasts.

Time to destroy the evidence.

Unfortunately, my smoke detector would go off if I burned the papers. When I'd started going out with Logan, Gina had installed the supersensitive detectors in our house. She knew he'd been kind of a stoner back in middle school.

Instead, I pulled out what must have been the world's quietest and most expensive shredder from my bottom desk drawer. In less than a minute, Laura MacLean's cover story was reduced to a handful of blue dust, which I flushed down the toilet.

At eight o'clock, my phone buzzed with a text message from Zachary.

HIYA LAURA, IT'S JACK. READY TO TELL SOME STORIES? ;-)

Chapter Twenty-Eight

With the help of an airline seat that folded out into a bed, a pair of shortbread cookies, and the perfect cup of chamomile tea—MI-X had sprung for a first-class plane ticket—I got a decent night's sleep on my way to Ireland.

The sun rose as we passed over the center of the country. Glimpses of landscape through low clouds showed a patchwork of green fields, set off from one another by crooked rows of fuzzy brown objects I assumed were trees.

The sky cleared when we neared Dublin, and my throat lumped at the thought of my mother making this journey nineteen years ago. Had she wept at the sight of it?

My second thought was of Logan and how much he'd loved it here. As a ghost, he'd probably spent more time in Dublin than in

Baltimore. I wondered if any post-Shifters in his adopted city missed him as much as we did.

But by the time we touched down, my only thought was of Zachary. His flight from Glasgow had been scheduled to arrive three hours before mine. There was a message from him on my MI-X-issued red phone, sent just a few minutes before:

WAITING FOR YOU AT MEETING POINT.

I sent back a quick OK!, then called Gina to let her know I'd landed. She sounded sniffly.

"I promise I'll check in after I get to the B and B." Maybe not *immediately* after. "Before dinner, at least."

The Dublin Airport's shiny hallways seemed to stretch for miles. I waited at baggage claim for over half an hour, and started to regret checking a suitcase. But part of me had thought that maybe I wouldn't be going back home.

Then Immigration, where I calmed my pulse enough to recite my story. I hoped the officer would interpret my jitters as excitement to see "my husband, Jack" for the first time in months.

I got my stamp, and then it was just one more gate to get to Zachary. I glimpsed the MEETING POINT sign in the airport's bright outer terminal. But only for a moment, as a swell of tall passengers got in my way—Norwegians, based on their accents and blond hair.

Crap. I'd craved this moment for six months, and I couldn't see through the crowd of Scandinavians. Along the railing, people waved and jumped, some flashing signs with names. A woman held a toddler with a fake holly wreath on its head. A ragged chorus of "Happy Christmas" rang out in the delightful Dublin accent.

But no Zachary. He'd said he was waiting. Had someone taken him in the last half hour?

I stepped out past the gate, into the open area, then turned a slow circle to look behind me. And there he was.

Zachary stood with his back to a cylindrical silver column, still facing the gate. He hadn't seen me pass.

I lingered a moment, watching him watch for me. He shifted his weight, hands stuffed deep in the pockets of his black leather jacket—apparently he'd replaced the brown one, or the DMP had kept it.

No, only one hand was in a pocket. The other held a bouquet of red and yellow roses.

More people passed, and Zachary's eyes turned vulnerable. He pressed back against the column as if to keep himself from leaping forward to find me.

I couldn't wait another second. I pushed against the stream of disembarking passengers, tripping over feet and suitcases and umbrellas to get to Zachary's side.

My hand brushed his soft leather sleeve. Zachary jerked his arm away instinctively. Then he saw me.

"Au—" was all he got out before our mouths met. I clung to him with everything I had, letting the hunger and joy in his lips consume six months of fear in a single moment. My knees buckled, but he lifted me up and pulled me against him. He was as strong and solid as the Zachary I'd always known.

I felt the floor beneath my feet again, but he didn't let go. "You're here," he whispered, then kissed me. "You're really." Another kiss. "Truly." Another kiss. "Here."

I couldn't speak, so I wrapped my arms around his back and pressed my face to his chest. Through his earth-red rugby shirt, he smelled just as I'd remembered.

"Aura, I thought this day would never . . . ach, I'll just shut up."

We held each other, still as a mountain in a hurricane, while people rushed by, laughing and chatting.

I finally opened my eyes and saw the roses that had tumbled to the floor. "You dropped something."

"Oh!" Without letting go of me, Zachary reached down and snatched the flowers. "You take these, I'll take your bags. I've got the rental car all sorted, we just have to fetch it from the car park." He took the handle of my suitcase, then stopped. "You're really here."

Though our hands were full, we kissed again, testing this new, miraculous reality.

Finally Zachary pulled away a few inches. "The sooner we start walking—"

"Yeah," I said with the little breath he'd left me.

As we made our way down yet another endless corridor toward the car park, he kept looking at me, as if to confirm I was still there.

I buried my nose in one of the red roses. "These are just like the ones you brought me last year in the hospital." The morning after we'd first kissed, to be exact.

"These are a wee bit different."

I examined them. They looked the same—half red, half yellow. Yellow for friendship and red for much more.

Ah, no. Now there were seven red roses and only five yellow. He'd tipped the balance.

In the parking garage, Zachary opened the trunk and placed my bags next to his. He shut the lid slowly, letting his hands rest on it. "Did you want to visit Dublin now?"

"As opposed to . . ."

"Going straight to the bed and breakfast. Checking in. To our room." He adjusted the car's rear wiper blade, though it wasn't crooked. "You must be tired."

I wasn't, not with him so close after so long. "I would like to see Dublin." Or rather, I felt like I *should* like to see Dublin. "Is it on the way?"

"No, Dublin is south. County Meath is north. A half-hour drive, if we don't get lost."

"Oh." I examined the oil-stained concrete at my feet. In less than an hour we could be alone in a room together for the first time in six months.

When I looked up again, our eyes met.

"North," we said.

On the way out of the parking garage—I mean, "car park"—Zachary handed me the road map. "You'll have to navigate. I marked the spot, so just tell me when to get off the M1 and everything after that."

I blinked the blurriness out of my contacts, wishing I'd worn my glasses on the overnight flight. There was a star and a question mark near the village of Slane. "You don't know where it is?"

"Not precisely, but I'm sure there'll be a sign. If not, we'll ring them."

I looked up from the map as we entered the motorway, which

had two lanes in our direction and two in the other—but on our right instead of the left.

"Everything's backward." Sitting in the left seat, I put my hands into thin air where the steering wheel should have been.

"Confession: This is only my second day driving on the left side of the road. The first was when I somehow acquired a driving license back home." He tapped the brakes too hard, jolting us. "The examiner was very forgiving."

"You don't drive in Scotland?"

"I've no need for a car in the city. I walk or take the bus or subway." He carefully shifted gears. "I'm a wee bit out of practice." His arms tensed as we entered heavier traffic. "I have to stop talking now or we'll die."

We didn't die, but we did want to kill whoever built the back roads and made the signs and maps that supposedly went with them.

"It's like they know," Zachary muttered, after we made the third wrong turn down a mismarked country road.

"Like who knows what?"

"The Irish, that our marriage is a sham." The car lurched as he shifted down into second gear instead of up into fourth. "This is their way of keeping us frustrated and pure."

I focused on the map with renewed determination. The hedgerows blocked the sight of landmarks and gave the road a claustrophobic feel.

Suddenly a gap appeared, with a small brown sign. "Slow down," I said. "Stop!"

Zachary jammed the brakes. We skidded across the damp road.

The car fishtailed, but stopped at the edge of a ditch on the opposite shoulder.

"Sorry," he said. The engine coughed and stalled.

I pointed out the windshield at the break in the hedgerow. "I think that's it."

Zachary started the car, then eased us out of the path of potential oncoming traffic. The tiny brown sign came into view.

BALLYROCK CASTLE B & B.

Chapter Twenty-Nine

The brass key trembled in Zachary's hand as he inserted it into our door. My heart felt jammed between my tonsils, I was so nervous myself.

Before turning the knob, he lifted a finger to his lips as a silent warning to *Shhh*.

The moment we were inside with the door shut, Zachary whipped out his phone. Tapping the screen, he activated an innocent-looking icon marked "Files." The words "Sweep activating" appeared.

He was looking for bugs. I wasn't sure if this made me more or less jumpy.

The suite's walls were gray castle-stone, and the floors a warm, dark wood covered in thick earth-toned rugs. Near the door where I stood, a love seat and coffee table sat facing a fireplace, flanked by armchairs. Straight ahead, double doors opened onto the balcony, where I could see the dim afternoon light through translucent white curtains.

But I barely registered all this, because of the bed. Tucked back into the right side of the room, it dominated the space with its king-size hugeness and what looked like the world's fluffiest quilt. The carved dark wood frame reached four posts up toward the low ceiling.

I needed air.

I went to the balcony doors, leaving Zachary sweeping the phone in slow arcs at arm's length, watching the screen carefully. He nodded to me when I put my hand on the latch, so I opened the doors and went outside.

"Whoa." I stepped out into the mist and rested my elbows on the stone railing. Below, the hills and trees sloped down toward the stately River Boyne, whose northern shore I could just glimpse through the fog. I wondered how many ghosts I would see peppering the distant fields and streets if I hadn't been so recently—and so thoroughly—kissed.

A few minutes later, the balcony door creaked open behind me. "We're alone," Zachary said softly.

"Great." I cleared my throat and repeated the word, but kept my eyes on the river, wishing I could borrow its silent, silver serenity. "Did MI-X give you the bug sweeper?"

"My dad did, as long as I promised not to tell Mum. She doesn't want me following in his footsteps." He gripped the railing. "But I'll do whatever it takes to protect you."

I began to tremble, from his proximity and the strength in his voice. Desire and fear were playing tug-of-war with my thoughts.

"I bet when it's clear," I said quickly, "you can see the whole valley."

Am I really talking about the weather to hide how nervous I am about sex? Seriously?

"I hope it's clear for sunrise tomorrow at Newgrange."

And now he's doing it, too. "It will be, I just know it."

"Aye, this weather's no match for that beautiful Yank optimism."

"No way." My voice was a bare whisper now.

Our hands lay inches apart on the balcony's stone railing, but the distance might have been miles. That's how much courage it would take to join them, because once we touched, here in our room alone . . .

I spread my fingers, and he did the same, until the tip of my right pinkie and the tip of his left pinkie almost brushed. Almost.

The thick Irish mist seemed to fill my lungs, drowning me in fear and anticipation. I wasn't sure what would kill me faster—touching Zachary or *not* touching him.

"Are y'hungry?" he finally asked in a low voice.

"No," I whispered, not looking up.

"Thirsty?"

"Uh, yeah. No. I don't know." I risked a glance at him. "What's there to drink?"

"Water from the tap?" He uttered a short, hoarse laugh. "I dunno why I'm acting like a waiter. I suppose, now that you're in my part of the world, it feels like you're my guest, and I want to make you, em . . ."

"Comfortable?"

"Happy."

I summoned every scrap of courage and turned to face him straight on. "You do."

"Aura." Zachary drew his top lip between his teeth, then spoke to the stone surface just beyond my feet. "I tried tae think of the perfect things to say and do right now." With each quickening blink, his eyes shifted, never leaving the ground. "But then, I thought maybe this would never happen, that I'd never even see you again. And then every time I turned my mind to this moment, it went blank." His lashes lifted to let his gaze meet mine. "I couldn't imagine a future that would be so kind."

My eyes burned with tears—of anger as much as sorrow or love. Whatever those bastards had done to him, the one thing I'd never forgive was the haunted look they'd put in his eyes.

"So I'm sorry," he continued, "if I'm no' quite the most, em, smooth person when it comes to these things. I never did sort out what to say and do, how to get from here"—he pointed to the space between our feet—"to there." He gestured behind him, toward the door. Toward the bed.

I took a shaky step forward, so that we almost touched. "You're not the only one who can sort stuff out." I twined my fingers with his, feeling his hands tremble as hard as mine. "Let's go inside."

Sitting on the edge of the love seat, I watched Zachary start the fire. His face set in concentration as he reached up the chimney to open the flue, which settled into position with a heavy iron thunk. "There." Then he pulled a long match from a green cardboard canister on the hearth. Our hosts had arranged the wood for us ahead of time, with kindling and paper underneath.

"Wait." I went to kneel beside him. "Let me do it."

With a faint smile, he handed me the red-tipped match, then held out the rough bottom edge of the canister for me to strike.

I hadn't realized how dark the room had grown until the flame burst white-yellow from the match head, searing my vision. Zachary pulled back the fireplace's webbed-steel curtain so I could touch the match to the paper beneath the kindling.

The fire crackled and curled the paper, then snapped at the dry wood. I sat back on my heels, offering the lit end of the match to Zachary. "Make a wish."

His green eyes, dark with desire, met mine as he blew out the match. Then he leaned forward, and without touching me, brought his lips to mine.

We'd had perfect kisses before. Our first one, a year ago on that ship. Our last one at the airport in June was pretty amazing, too. And then there was the time in the woods, when we finally decided to be together.

But this . . .

It was as if with one kiss—one long, deep, shivery kiss—he'd turned me naked beneath him, and I was feeling his lips and tongue on every inch of my skin. In that moment, I lost all fear and nerves. I became pure want.

He finally reached for me, but instead of giving me the caresses I craved, he slowly unbuttoned my top, his fingers not even grazing my skin. I moaned, relishing this delicious torture, realizing that he meant to touch me only when he could press hands to flesh.

Zachary peeled back my shirt, one shoulder at a time. Even as my skin met the chilly air, it was warmed by the swelling fire and this never-ending kiss.

He finally broke away, long enough to pull off his own shirt, the collar sweeping his hair forward over his temples, almost to the ridge of his brows. Unable to resist, I brushed the dark waves off his forehead, then traced his hairline down to the curve of his jaw.

Zachary closed his eyes and turned his head to kiss my palm. In its soft, tender center, I felt the touch of his tongue. I gasped as the electric sensation seemed to skip my arm and go straight to my core.

My pulse skyrocketed until I could hear nothing but its pounding in my ears. I wanted to grab him and drag him to the bed, but obviously he wanted to take this slow. I'd let him do whatever he wanted, *how*ever he wanted, as long as he didn't stop.

But to encourage him to move a little faster, I pulled my hand from his face and unhooked my bra. Zachary swallowed hard, Adam's apple rising and falling, as he watched me remove it. Then I lay on my back on the thick rug in front of the fire.

He moved forward, lithe as a cat, to plant his hands beside my shoulders, his knees astride my thighs. For one long moment, we just stared, drinking in the sight of each other.

Then all at once, he brought his body to mine. Our flesh collided, hot and smooth, as we kissed with a new ferocity. We grasped and clung and stroked every inch of skin we could find, rocking our hips in a frantic simulation of what was to come.

When I reached between us to find his belt buckle, he took my hand and threaded his fingers with mine. "Come." We somehow got to our feet, and he led me to the bed.

Which might as well have been another world.

Maybe it was the distance from the fire, or maybe it was the sudden realization that This Was It. But as we finished undressing and found ourselves together on the bed, with him doing all the things I used to love, my fear froze me right out of the moment.

Zachary noticed immediately. Lying on his side facing me, he ran his hand down my goose-bumped arm, his brow creasing with concern. "Are ye cold?"

"Yeah."

He drew the red flannel sheet and the white quilt up to our shoulders, creating a warm cave. "Better?"

"A little." I pulled my arms to my chest, feeling small and vulnerable.

He took my right hand and kissed my knuckles. "What's wrong?"

"I don't know. I'm just, I don't know."

"Nervous? Me too."

"More than nervous."

Zachary stroked my hair. "I'll do all I can not to hurt you."

I closed my eyes, wishing that now of all times I wasn't thinking of Logan. Of that afternoon a week before he died when we'd tried to do this and I'd stopped us because of the pain.

"We can wait if you want," Zachary said. "You're tired."

"I'm not tired, and I don't want to wait." I bit my lip at the sound of my whine. "Sorry I'm being crazy."

"We're both crazy." His broad, strong hand stroked my lower back. "Crazy and naked."

I gave a shaky laugh, clearing my head. I let my limbs relax, muscle by muscle, until my toes stopped pointing and my fists unfurled.

My fingertips splayed over Zachary's chest, at first only resting.

Then, slowly, they began to trace the top contour of his pectoral muscle. They continued down, over the bumps of his breastbone, pausing to feel his heart thump five times fast before moving on, lower.

When I touched him under his last rib, his breath caught so suddenly, I realized he'd been holding it. My hand slid around his waist and into the valley of his spine. I traced each vertebra, halfway up his back, before stopping, then descending.

This was what I needed to feel safe. Not him touching *me*, demanding my body to respond. Me touching *him*, making him warm and familiar again, yet new enough to fascinate. Hearing Zachary respond with quickening breath and needful groans.

The need in my own voice when I touched him *there* seemed to be the signal he was waiting for.

"Stay a moment," he whispered against my cheek. "Just like tha'." Zachary moved to the edge of the bed and unzipped his bag. Clearly he'd put the condoms in an easy-to-find pocket—figures, since he was the plan-ahead type—because it was barely half a minute before he turned back to me.

I didn't know how to ask about the logistics of positioning. "Where should I—"

"This is best for you, for the first time." He moved close, to where he needed to be. "Side by side, so gravity won't rush us."

I smiled at his mention of one of the fundamental forces. It reminded me that he was the same randomly geeky scientist I'd known for over a year. It reminded me that he was my friend.

"Thanks," I said. "And sorry for being scared. I don't really know what I'm doing."

Zachary went still, hand on my hip, for so long I wondered if I'd upset him. Then he spoke.

"Aura, I dunno what I'm doing either."

"At least you've done this before." My remark was met with silence. "Wait . . . what?"

He hesitated. "I've never done this before."

My mind swirled. All this time I'd had horrible images of him shagging Suzanne on a twice-daily basis for the eight months of their relationship, and he was actually a virgin? "Never? As in never ever?"

"Never ever," he said. "I'm sorry."

"Why are you sorry?" Relief flooded my veins. "And why didn't you tell me?"

"I figured if you thought I had experience, you'd be less nervous."

I suddenly loved him so much, I almost cried. But I wanted to savor this sweet, light moment. "Anything else I should know about you?"

"Hmm. Besides my real name?"

Mind, further blown. "What?!"

"A'right, legally, my real name is Zachary. But in Gaelic it's Sgàire." He spelled it for me.

"Sgàire." I tried to replicate his pronunciation, *SKAR-uh*, balanced between my throat and tongue. "Did I say it right?"

"Aye." He moved against me, kissing the hollow of my throat and tightening his grip on my back. "Beautiful."

I whispered it again, thrilling at his reaction, and at my own giddiness that we would discover this new world together.

When we were both ready, he gently took my elbow and guided

my arm around him. "Just hold on to me, and don't forget tae breathe."

I drew a deep inhale, and as I let it out, he moved up and in. My eyes flew open at the sudden pain, and I couldn't suppress a faint cry.

Zachary stilled. "I'm sorry," he whispered. "Should we stop?"

"No." I inhaled again, even deeper, and eased my grip on his shoulder. "I'm okay." As I uttered the words, I realized they were true—I wasn't just trying to make him feel better. "I'm really okay." My relief and amazement bubbled into soft laughter.

"You're no' okay, you're perfect," he murmured against my cheek. *"Mo anam caraid."*

At the sound of this phrase that only my heart understood, I felt a wave of joy wipe away my last bit of fear. We'd waited so long and fought so hard for this, and now it was happening.

I'd always thought we'd be in two separate worlds in these moments—his of pleasure, mine of pain. But we took it slow, lingering over each touch, even the fumbling motions that made us laugh. And when my ache faded and we found our rhythm, the boundary between us dissolved, then formed again far outside our bodies, creating a new space and time in the universe just for Us.

Even as Zachary's breath shortened and his voice sharpened, and the muscles beneath my hands tensed into taut wires, I could imagine he was taking me with him.

We were linked, for the endless now that felt every bit like forever.

Chapter Thirty

We held each other tight in the awed silence that followed. Finally Zachary stirred and said, "Are y'all right, then?"

I sniffled, only now realizing that my eyes had watered. "Great. You?"

He offered a soft laugh. "Aye. Great."

I gazed at Zachary's face. The worry lines between his brows were gone, and his lips, flushed from kissing, were curved slightly up instead of down. I wanted to take a picture of him in this moment, make a permanent image of his serenity.

"So, if you'd never done this before," I said, "how did you know how to make it, um, easier on me?"

"Something this important, you think I'd not do my homework?"

"Of course you would," I said with a laugh. "And of course you'd figure it out using gravitational forces."

"Sorry."

"No, it's why I love you."

"Oh." He brushed a lock of hair off my cheek, smoothing it back over my pillow. "Of course, technically gravity's not a force."

"I know, Big Brain—I've read Einstein. Gravity is what bends space-time."

"Aye." His fingertips drifted forward, over my shoulder. "Keep talking."

"So everything, including light, travels in a curved path."

"Curves are good." He traced my collarbone to the center, then slid his hand downward as he spoke. "Everything in the universe is always falling through space-time."

I pressed my hand over his and tilted up my chin. "Always."

"But sometimes, like right now"—he kissed my neck, caressing me—"I think I can feel it."

I could feel it, too. It was like we were falling faster or slower than the rest of the universe, but at the same speed as each other, and that was all that mattered.

As his hand passed over my belly, my stomach responded with an insistent growl.

"Oh my God." I covered my face, embarrassed.

Zachary laughed. "So you're hungry now, aye?"

"Starving. But I want to shower first."

"Go on. Take with you whatever clothes you want to wear to dinner."

"Why?"

"You'll see." He kissed my cheek. "There's something I need to do, to make us safe."

When I got out of the shower, Zachary was unpacking, wearing nothing but a pair of light flannel pants slung low on his waist. Which somehow made him look even hotter than when he was naked.

I padded over to the bed, passing the coffee table where my roses sat in a china vase, which Zachary must have gotten from the B and B lady.

On the bed, my suitcase lay open. And empty.

"You unpacked for me?"

"Just your clothes." He bent low over the top dresser drawer. "Everything else, I set with your hand luggage."

I joined him at the dresser, where he'd laid out his shirts, socks, and boxers in a neat row in the top drawer. My own clothes had been arranged in the right-hand set of drawers. So much for my red lingerie "surprise."

Zachary murmured to himself, then bent over to write a number on a scrap of paper. A ruler lay atop the wooden dresser.

"Are you measuring the distance between your socks?"

"Aye." He scribbled another number.

"Are you OCD or something? Not that there's anything wrong—"

"Ha, hardly." He beamed up at me. "You've seen bits of my room at home on our video chats. It's a disaster."

Zachary shut the drawer and took a step back from the dresser, guiding me to do the same. Then he picked up a white plastic bottle of talcum powder. Holding his breath, he twisted open the top, held the bottle over the dresser, and gave it a hard squeeze.

A cloud of powder erupted from the bottle. Zachary stepped out of the way and let the powder settle on the edge of the dresser. He repeated the action another step back. The snow-white substance drifted onto the polished dark wooden floor.

"Right, then. Don't go over there." He picked up a black shaving kit and strode off to the bathroom.

What the hell was he up to?

It was too quiet, so I switched on the radio, finding a Dublin alternative-rock station. As I dressed and put on my makeup, I pondered the puzzle Zachary had left me. Through the bathroom door, I heard him singing in the shower, sounding smug.

The water turned off. Determined to solve this mystery before he returned, I opened the wardrobe door. He'd twined the arm of his shirt around the arm of mine, but loosely enough that they'd separate if they were moved.

Oh . . .

I slowly examined the room again. My gaze landed on the wooden balcony doors. The crack between them was straight and dark—except for one sliver near the top. I walked over, giving the dresser a wide berth, then stood on tiptoes to examine the door.

A piece of tape, half the width of my pinkie nail, stretched across the gap. It would break at the slightest pressure.

Now I saw the careful arrangement everywhere—the tape across the master light switch by the door, Zachary's extra pair of shoes set perpendicular to each other at the foot of the bed. Even the bedsheets were mussed in a discernible pattern, the wrinkles forming a Z.

The bathroom door opened, revealing his silhouette. "What's your guess?"

I crossed my arms in triumph. "Counterespionage tricks."

"Brilliant." He brushed his hand over my shoulder as he passed. "If anyone comes in while we're out, we'll know."

"And then what?"

"I haven't thought that far ahead yet."

"Liar. You so have."

Stepping into his shoes, he tugged his sweater over his head. "If things get dodgy in the Republic, we'll drive north."

"We can't leave before solstice tomorrow."

"No, not unless our lives are in danger."

"You think they could be?"

"After what I've been through—" Zachary withdrew a slim object from his shaving kit. With a click, a blade flicked out of the handle. He folded it back in, then tucked the contraption into his jacket pocket. "Can't be too careful."

"Do you know how to use that?"

"Of course I do." He grinned as he helped me into my coat. "The sharp end goes into the bad guy."

It took almost an hour of driving in the rain to find the pub, but the place was worth the search. Rather than the tiny, dark drinking hole I'd imagined, it had a full, wide restaurant with cozy, plush embroidered booths. Zachary and I grabbed one in the far corner, inside an almost gazebo-like structure. I was glad for the semiprivacy, and glad that we could sit side by side, looking out on our surroundings.

In the center of the large octagonal room, a huge iron chandelier cast overlapping patterns of light. Shadows from candle sconces danced on the walls, flickering in time to the holiday pop tunes piping over the speaker. On a small stage at the other side of the room, a three-man band was setting up their equipment.

"I hope they play something other than Christmas carols," I said to Zachary. "You think they'll take requests, or—"

I stopped when I saw his face. He'd closed his menu and was staring through it, flipping the cardboard coaster over and over.

Uh-oh. Megan had warned me that guys changed after sex. They got distant, or possessive, or clingy—or all three on infinite repeat.

"What is it?" I asked.

He looked up quickly, and I expected him to say, "Nothing," then retreat into one of the many corners of his mind.

Instead his eyes held mine for a long, silent moment. "You'll think I'm crazy. Maybe you'll be right."

"Tell me, anyway."

"It was probably my imagination, and I don't know what I'm talking about, really, since I'd never—" He swept his fingers through the rain-damp hair on his forehead. "Ach, maybe it's nothing."

"It's not nothing. Tell me."

"When we were together today, it was like—like we'd carved out a place in the universe for just the two of us."

My heart stopped. My voice came out a bare whisper. "A place where no one's ever been before."

Zachary's eyes lit up. "You felt it, too?" He pulled his knee onto the cushion between us, so that he faced me straight on. "Was it real?"

"It felt real. And I don't think—I mean, I'm not an expert, either, but I've never heard anyone say *that* happened. Especially not the first time."

He spread his hands as if illustrating one of the wonders of the universe—which he was. "The scientist in me hates to use this word, but—it was fuckin' mystical."

I laughed, both at his reluctance to use the *M* word and his rare burst of profanity.

He continued, "It was like I was taken somewhere else. Somewhere I belonged."

My lip trembled. Megan was right—Zachary had changed. The intensity in his eyes held me in place, not just here in the booth but by his side. How could I leave him to go back home? It scared me to need anyone so much. If our souls became inextricably tangled, would mine still be mine? Did I care?

Zachary leaned in, and I thought he was going to kiss me. Instead he pressed his cheek to mine and held it there. It felt more intimate than a kiss.

"What did you say to me before?" I asked him. "In bed. In Gaelic."

He sat back and looked away. "Oh. That. There's no exact translation."

"But roughly?"

Zachary rubbed his lips, as if to keep them closed. "Naw, you'll think it's too much."

"Not possible."

His gaze came at an angle, slightly guarded but full of hope. "It means 'soul mate.'"

His words made my world spin faster. We weren't the type to

believe in destiny or soul mates or anything that took away our choices. But sitting here, seeing the gazebo's glistening white lights dance in his eyes, I could believe in our magic.

"It's not too much," I said. "It's perfect. What were the words?"

"*Mo anam caraid*," he said slowly, pronouncing it *mo AN-am CAR-idge*.

I repeated it after him. "I'm glad it's something short. Can you write it down for me?" I pulled a felt-tip pen from my purse, then offered him the inside of my arm.

He spoke as he scratched out the letters in neat script along the palest part of my skin. "Dunno if there are words in any language to properly explain how . . . together I feel, now I'm with you again."

I stared at him, flustered by his unusual openness. "Together?"

"Like I was a pane of shattered glass, and you're the only glue that'll stick." Zachary began to draw the final word, *caraid*. "It's just started, this gluing, but it's started."

He put the cap back on the pen and held it out. When I grasped it, he didn't let go, but used it to pull me toward him into a lingering kiss.

"Here we are," the waitress said as she approached, shoes clomping the rough hardwood. We separated, attempting to look embarrassed. She gave us our pints, then took our meal orders, her eyes glinting with amusement.

The live music started then, a traditional band with fiddle, accordion, and a dynamic acoustic guitar. Zachary and I sat shoulder to shoulder and hand in hand, our heels tapping the floor.

I was thirsty, so I drank the ale quickly. It went straight to my head, turning my contentment to fatigue—and soul-crushing sadness.

It opened my ears and my heart to the fiddler's mournful strains as he played a lament for those who'd passed on.

My eyes burned, and my chest felt leaden. Guilt swamped me for thinking of Logan at a time like this.

Zachary put his arm around my shoulder and spoke low in my ear. "It reminds you of him."

I nodded, unable to speak.

"This was his music."

I swallowed. "But I'm with you."

"You can't fight memories. They come whether you look for them or not." He kept his eyes on the musicians. "You've never asked about my meeting Logan."

The name hung heavy in the air between us. "He only told me that you'd talked. No details."

"He said he was going to find you, then leave this world with just you there. It was good of him."

I waited for Zachary to say more, which after a moment, he did.

"He told me I was stupid, that if I really loved you, I should've tried harder to steal you away from him, and that I definitely shouldn't have gone to the prom with Becca. I told him he was one hundred percent right."

"Did he know how rare it is for you to admit you're wrong?"

"Ha. He asked if I knew about your father. I said aye, I was there when she found out. I said I'd die before I told anyone your secret." Zachary rubbed his chin and took a long sip of ale. "And then he apologized."

"For what?" I asked softly.

"For not letting you go when he should have."

My throat closed up as I wondered what would've happened if Logan had passed on right after dying, or even within a few weeks.

Would I have loved Zachary sooner? Would it have been too soon? Would we have broken up quickly because my heart hadn't mended yet? Would we be here right now?

"What else did he say?"

A sly smile graced Zachary's face. "He made me promise to do something for him."

"What?"

"It's a secret between us lads."

"Have you already done it?"

"No."

"Is it something to do with me?"

"A bit. Mostly him, though."

I wanted to ask Zachary what had happened next at the airport, about his capture and detainment. But he looked so serene, as if the peace inhabiting Logan on that last day had passed to him, a peace that returned at the mere memory of their conversation.

"I'm glad he came to you," I said, "and not just because it saved your life."

Zachary's gaze dropped to my left hand resting on my lap. He laid his own on top of it, aligning our wedding bands. "Last summer, there were times when I almost . . . in any case, I kept going because I couldn't let that happen to you again."

"Let what happen?"

He didn't look up. "Your heart broke when you lost Logan. If I didn't make it—not that I thought I meant as much to you as he had—"

"You did. You do."

"—and not that I don't think you're strong. But the thought of you crying over my . . ." He stopped short of the word "death" and shook his head forcefully. "No."

I folded my thumb tight over his. "Can you tell me what happened? Now that we're together?"

He lowered his chin, brushing his hair against my forehead. "I'm sorry," he whispered. "Someday, I promise, if everything works out the way I hope."

"What can I do to make that happen? Please tell me. I'll do anything."

"I can't ask it of you. Not yet." He took a deep breath, collecting himself, then sat back against the booth. "We're here now, let's enjoy that, a'right? It's all that matters."

I wished it were true. I wished that all that mattered was us, here. Together. Free.

Yet the damage done had become part of the fabric of Zachary's soul. There would be no forgetting or avoiding. Only a journey through.

But it was a journey he wouldn't travel alone. His soul's fabric was weaving itself with mine. I loved the frayed ends where it came unraveled, and I loved the strength at its firm, solid center.

I loved every thread.

Chapter Thirty-One

By the time we got back to our room at the castle (where no one had broken in and gone through our stuff), I was almost too tired to walk. I took out my contacts and collapsed into bed in a T-shirt and sweatpants. Hotness personified.

When Zachary slipped under the covers beside me, he said, "It's midnight plus one minute. Happy birthday."

"Hay burray," was my drowsy reply. Knowing touch would be more coherent than speech, I dug my fingers into his soft T-shirt and slid my feet against his flannel pajama pants.

He drew me close and kissed my forehead. *"Tha gaol agam ort."*

I recognized the Gaelic for "I love you" he'd taught me on one of our chats. I made my tongue wake up enough to say it back, managing not to mangle the pronunciation, *Ha gowl AKam orsht*. As the last syllable faded, so did I, fast asleep.

Jet lag and exhaustion had scrambled my brain-clock, so I woke up at four thirty a.m., even though that would've been my bedtime at home.

I lay there, listening to Zachary's deep, even, quiet breaths. Eventually I turned to watch him sleep, marveling at the smoothness of his brow, the stillness of his limbs, so different from the way Martin had described and the way I'd seen that night when Zachary had fallen asleep during our video chat.

Suddenly a violet light seeped through our translucent balcony curtains, casting a glow into the living room area.

I sat up in bed, excitement banishing exhaustion. This was the first ghost I'd seen in Ireland, thanks to Zachary's near-constant presence. By now it'd been hours since we'd kissed, so I'd returned to my normal, 100 percent post-Shifter state.

Maybe this ghost would know something about Newgrange. Maybe it'd be old enough to remember what'd happened during the Shine.

I slipped out of bed, grabbed my sweater, and hurried to the balcony door. The ghost had probably tried to come into the room itself and had been repelled by Zachary. From outside there was no direct view of the bed, so I parted the curtain in the middle to get a better look.

The ghost was a middle-aged man in a classic Irish cap, like the ones worn by the older guys in the pub. His trousers were a bit baggy, as was his tweed coat. He could've been from any time, in the distant or recent past.

I opened the door. "Hi."

He beamed and said something I couldn't understand.

"Uh, do you speak English?" I asked him.

He scowled and began to rant, gesturing wildly.

"Hang on." I closed the door, then ran to the bed and almost pounced on Zachary, but stopped myself in time.

Instead I crawled in next to him, snuggling close. "Zach, wake up."

"Can't. Sleeping."

I pressed my mouth to his in a full, deep kiss.

"Second thought, not sleeping." He rolled me atop his body and kissed me hard, one hand full of my hair and the other sneaking up underneath my shirt.

Though it tore my heart, I pulled away far enough to speak. "There's a Gaelic ghost on the balcony."

Zachary blinked hard. "Heh?"

"I think he speaks Gaelic. Obviously I don't, so this is your interview."

His hands dropped to the bed with twin thuds. "*That's* why you're kissing me? Taking my red so I can have a chat with a ghost?"

"Hurry." I hopped off the bed, pulling his arm. "Ask him about Newgrange, ask him how long he's been haunting this place, since before or after the Shift. Ask him anything."

"The dialect's different here." Zachary picked up his sweater from the back of the sofa, and the notepad and pen next to the room phone. He shuffled to the balcony doors, smoothing his pillow-tousled hair. "But I'll try."

I sat cross-legged on the bed, listening to Zachary's muffled foreign words through the door. At one point, he repeated the same phrase three times, slower with each pass. Either he had run up against a Scottish-Irish language barrier, or he couldn't believe his ears and had to confirm what the ghost was telling him.

Finally the violet glow disappeared. Zachary came back inside.

I bounced off the bed. "Anything interesting?"

"Aye." He wiped his feet on the woven rug, and I realized he hadn't put shoes on to go outside.

"You must be freezing." I handed him the green wool throw-blanket from the back of the chair. He took it from me, a dazed look on his face.

"Must be hard to get used to," I said. "Talking to ghosts?"

"Aura, that wasn't just any ghost." He moved stiffly to sit on the love seat. "It was Padraig Murphy."

I sat down hard on the ottoman across from him. "Brigit Murphy's son? The one my mom and dad said tried to raise the ancient gods on the day of the Shine?"

"That Padraig Murphy."

"How did he know where to find us? How did he even know who we were?"

"He said he had connections in the living world. Also, remember, my real name was on the original reservation for Ballyrock." He shook his head. "Stupid of me, but back in March I didn't know—"

"So what did Padraig want?" I grabbed for the notepad, but Zachary pulled it out of reach.

"Give me a moment tae think, lass." He switched on the lamp and squinted at his notes. I knocked my knees together in my impatience.

"Some of this could be wrong," he said. "His accent was brutal, and the Gaelic around here is so different from Scottish."

"But . . ."

"But he said a mistake was made. His mother did a ritual the morning of the Shine, trying to make the Tuatha Dé Danann—the ancient gods—rise again. They thought whoever was in the light at the moment of the solstice would give birth a year later to an incarnation of the day-god Óengus."

I gasped. "Just like we guessed! What'd he say about the mistake?"

"He said the ritual awoke an even older power within Newgrange."

"Older than the Tuatha Dé Danann?" I tried to remember who had supposedly lived in Ireland before those legendary folks. "More superheroes?"

"Not people. A gateway, between the living and the dead. A gateway that wasn't meant to be opened."

"Whoa. That makes it sound like since the Shine, more people are becoming ghosts." It fit with a theory we'd discussed after first reading my mother's journal: that the Shine opened up the world of the living to those who'd died suddenly. Then the Shift gave those wandering dead a better chance at peace by giving them people to talk to—all us post-Shifters.

"That wasn't the only mistake. The power from the solstice sunrise was supposed to go into only one person." He lowered the notepad into his lap. "But it split in two. It went into your mother and my father. Padraig saw it happen."

"He was there at the Shine, when they were filled with light? When Eowyn saw it?"

- 282 -

"He worked as a guide at Newgrange. It was his idea to have visitors walk through the light. Some guides still do it, some don't."

So Padraig Murphy had engineered the Shine, but instead of freeing the ancient gods, it had freed the dead—or at least some of them—in the form of ghosts.

"That's amazing!" I jumped to my feet, wishing I could tell the world what we'd just figured out. Except, I wasn't totally sure what that was. "Hang on. What exactly got split between your dad and my mom?"

Zachary paused, maybe translating in his head, and when he spoke, the words came slow. "Remember what Eowyn said about Newgrange being built for two purposes? To serve the dead, but also to separate them from the living."

"Right." I hopped on my toes. "Oh! If the Newgrange power split between your dad and my mom, then each of us has one, I don't know, manifestation of it? I help ghosts, and you scare them off."

"Usually."

"Did you tell Padraig we can trade powers when we kiss?"

"Of course not," Zachary said. "He seemed confused that we could both talk to him, but I distracted him with questions."

I paced behind the armchair, sliding my hand over its dark wooden frame. "So how do we know he's not making it up?"

"We don't. We only know that he believes it, because ghosts can't lie. There is a way to test it, though."

"How?"

"He said we need to go to the Dowth passage tomb for the solstice sunset. Not this afternoon, because the twenty-first is the one day during the year Dowth is open to the public. Tomorrow, when we can go alone."

"Cool." I'd wanted to go to Dowth, anyway. It was basically a mini Newgrange, but with two passages instead of one, and since it hadn't been restored, it looked the way Newgrange had for thousands of years. "If it's not open to the public, how do we get in?"

"Padraig says the gate's got just a padlock. Bolt cutters would do the job."

A thrill snaked up my spine at the thought of breaking into a historic monument. "Hey, the solstice is technically on the twenty-second, anyway, at like two a.m., so it'll be the right day. But I still don't understand *why* we need to go to Dowth."

Zachary hesitated, running his finger along the notepad's spiral spine. "I asked him to repeat himself, because I wanted to make sure. He said, if we both go to Dowth at solstice sunset, we could shut the gate between the living and the dead." He looked at me. "Aura, we could end the Shift."

Chapter Thirty-Two

Obviously, we didn't sleep the rest of the night. Instead, we built another fire and sat together on the love seat, sometimes speaking, sometimes silent, turning this mystery over in our minds.

Could we really end the Shift? we wondered. Did we even *want* to? My lifelong dream was to make the ghosts go away—until Logan had died, haunting me and the others he loved. As painful as that had been for all of us, it had given him a chance at peace and closure he otherwise wouldn't have had.

"But don't forget," Zachary said, "before the Shift, some people still became ghosts. And a few others could see them."

I couldn't forget that, not when my own father had haunted Aunt Gina, one of the few people who could see ghosts before the Shift (and who had lost the ability afterward).

"It would be like turning the world back to normal," I said. "But this *is* normal for me, for all post-Shifters."

"And how's that working out for ya?" His voice held a bitter edge.

I put my head on his shoulder, hoping it would comfort him. He'd probably suffered worse than any post-Shifter had. So far, at least.

"The DMP draft starts today," he pointed out. "Things are going to get really bad there in the States. Probably everywhere else, too."

"And we could stop it. Make it all go away." We'd be doing the world a huge favor by ending the Shift.

I checked the clock on the mantel: five thirty. Though sunrise wasn't until almost nine, we had to arrive at Newgrange by seven thirty, and we'd probably get lost on the way.

Time to get ready for the biggest day of our lives.

I stood, then froze as a new thought hit me. "Zach, what if Padraig Murphy isn't exactly right? What if it's not the sunset at Dowth we need to be at to stop the Shift? What if it's Newgrange at sunrise?"

Zachary rubbed the faint stubble on his chin. "Maybe. That is where it all started, with your mum and my dad." He gazed up at me. "Maybe it'll end there, too."

We didn't get lost on the way to Newgrange, and I decided to take this miracle as a sign that Zachary and I were meant to be there. (Even though it was his father's connections that got us VIP tickets, so we wouldn't have to go through the usual lottery.)

Like in an enchanted gateway, frost-speckled lanterns lit our way down the arched arbor connecting the parking lot to the visitor center.

Inside, the greeters gave us special solstice pins and offered us hot drinks while we waited for the bus that would take us to Newgrange itself. Zachary, of course, dragged me straight toward the visitor center exhibit, where I paced, overcome with excitement, while he absorbed facts he probably already knew.

I made a hasty trip to the ladies' room—too much hot cocoa plus nerves—and when I came out, what I saw stopped me in my tracks.

A middle-aged man was following Zachary, a man I remembered from my flight from Baltimore to Atlanta. He'd walked near me when I changed gates at the Atlanta airport, but then had taken a different international flight.

To Glasgow.

The man had mousy brown hair, rimless glasses, and the world's blandest face. Zero distinguishing features, which as Zachary had once told me, made him the perfect spy.

In the visitor center exhibit, he stood one display behind Zachary. Instead of the business suit he'd worn in the Atlanta airport, the Bland Man now wore a long-sleeved navy rugby shirt and khaki pants.

As he started to turn my way, I stepped into the gift shop. I stood by the jewelry stand, slowly rotating one of the spinning racks to examine the merchandise. For an excuse to look behind me in the mirror, I chose a pair of triple-spiral earrings and held them up to my ears.

Bland Man stood about twenty feet behind me, pretending to read a newspaper but glancing my way.

I put the earrings back and instead took the matching necklace to the cashier.

"Isn't it exciting?" she asked. "The sunrise?"

"Can't wait." I let my gaze wander as I fished in my purse for my wallet. Bland Man was in the same position, but now looking down the exhibit hall toward Zachary.

"With any luck, the clouds will lift just in time."

I grinned and held up a pair of crossed fingers, then wondered if that gesture meant the same in Ireland as it did in America. I was about to ask the cashier when Zachary came out of the hallway and spotted me.

He approached the counter with light steps. "That exhibit is so brilliant. I didn't think there was anything left to learn about Newgrange, but—oh, that's beautiful." He picked up the pendant on the leather loop. "A gift for your aunt?"

"It's for me. I probably should get her a souvenir, huh? Be right back," I told the cashier as I took the necklace and my change from her.

I led Zachary to the far wall near the picture frames. "There's a guy here who was on my flight from Baltimore to Atlanta."

"So?"

"So he didn't get on my Dublin flight. He went to Glasgow."

Understanding dawned on Zachary's face. "He went where he thought you'd be going."

"Where MI-X had booked Aura Salvatore a ticket. My Dublin flight was packed, so he couldn't change once he realized his mistake. He must've doubled back here once he got to Scotland."

"And you say he's in the building."

"He was behind you in the exhibit." I undid the clasp of my pendant, then handed it to Zachary and turned so he could put it on me and have an excuse to face the door.

"What's he look like?"

I lifted my hair and told Zachary what Bland Man was wearing. "He'd blend in anywhere."

"I see him." He fastened the clasp behind my neck but kept his hands beneath my hair, stalling. "The DMP and MI-X can't operate anywhere in the Republic, much less on Irish government property like this."

"He's also not wearing a pin for the solstice sunrise."

"Then he won't be able to follow us up to the monument."

I let my hair fall and adjusted the necklace around my throat. "But how did he even get into the visitor center without a ticket?"

"Let's find out." He led me from the gift shop.

Was he going to confront the guy? Whatever happened to secrecy and subterfuge?

We walked past the man, easing my fears, and continued on to the registration desk. The young lady behind it—Seana, according to her badge—beamed at him.

"Happy solstice!" she said.

"Cheers, and a fine one tae you, too, lass." Zachary laid on the Scottish accent harder than I'd heard him do since we'd arrived. "A bonnie morning, aye?"

"Aye," she breathed, then straightened her posture. "I mean, yes, it is. How can I help you?"

"I'm in a spot of bother." He leaned his elbows on the smooth black stone of the desk. "The man behind me to the left—no, don't look—he's been watching me, and I think he might've been a teacher of mine in primary school. It'd be pure awkward if I couldn't remember him, ye ken?"

Seana laughed. "I'm terrible putting names to faces, too. So embarrassing."

"Is there a wee chance he signed in? I noticed he's not got a pin wot the rest of us have."

"The visitor center here is free and open to everyone, not just the people going to the megalith." Her brow creased. "Although we don't open to the public until half past eight. I'll ask Mary Frances." She went to the other side of the desk and spoke in a low tone to an older, authoritative-looking woman, who peered past us at Bland Man.

Seana came back to us. "Sorry, we don't have his name and aren't sure how he sneaked in before operating hours."

Meanwhile, Mary Frances and a security guard were approaching the man. Zachary slipped his cell phone out of his jacket and pressed an icon on the screen that read "Simple Notepad." A camera function came up, one with loads more fancy options than the regular one.

The security guard spoke to Bland Man, who withdrew a black-leather folding wallet. He opened it to show the guard, who nodded, then curled his fingers to tell him to hand it over. Bland Man stepped back, shaking his head, then relented. The security guard brought the badge close to his face, then flipped it over to look at the casing.

"Got it." Zachary nudged my arm. "Let's go."

Though we still had ten minutes before meeting the bus to take us to Newgrange itself, we went out the door into the damp morning air.

The path led to a wooden bridge over the River Boyne, which was a couple of hundred feet wide. Zachary stopped halfway across the bridge, his back to the visitor center. I stood close to him while he flipped through the dozens of photos he'd taken in just a few seconds.

"Did MI-X give you that spy camera, too?" I asked him.

"I downloaded it from the app market. Anyone can get it." He glanced up at me once, then again, and this time his gaze stuck to mine.

"What's wrong?" I asked him.

"We're really here." He touched my face, then kissed me, with such aching tenderness I had to grip the bridge's railing to keep from toppling. "Sorry," he said when he pulled away. "Just having a moment."

"Not a problem." *Just my head spinning off my shoulders.*

"Ah, here we are." He pressed the phone screen repeatedly to zoom in on the image he'd found: the white interior of Bland Man's badge, displayed when the security guard had flipped it over to look at the outside.

I couldn't make out the agent's name, but the logo above it was brilliantly clear: NIGHTHAWK.

This guy was much more dangerous than a DMP agent. He was a superspy for the private security firm that SecuriLab had hired. The firm that might've been responsible for the crash of Flight 346. And unlike the DMP and MI-X, Nighthawk could go anywhere, even Ireland. They followed no laws.

Zachary drew himself up and looked back toward the visitor center. "Fucking hell."

On the bus ride, all twenty-two of us—the visitors, driver, and guide—were completely silent. The sky began to lighten as the bus rumbled down the narrow lane, so that when the trees cleared, we saw the grass-topped megalith mound, high on the hill.

Newgrange.

In the predawn light, its white quartz walls glowed an unearthly blue. My throat closed up with a wave of emotion.

Zachary leaned across me to see out the bus window, then sucked in a breath full of wonder. For once I didn't want to look at his face, or at anything but the megalith.

We held tight to each other's hands as they led us up the grassy slope toward the entrance. Dozens of spectators milled about, people who weren't lucky enough to go inside, but had come to be part of the festivities. Like my mom had done, until Zachary's dad had given her his extra ticket.

With that one act, Ian had changed all our lives. He'd made my life *possible*.

Our guide, Glenna, stopped us outside the entrance and explained what Newgrange was all about. Zachary and I stood beside the seven-foot-tall standing stone, placed directly in front of the entrance and aligned with the solstice sunrise. It was splotched with lichen and moss, which I found comforting. Even on a slab of dead rock, life was taking hold.

Like everyone else, we kept glancing eastward, past the road, past the fields of cows and sheep, past the steady silver River Boyne. We were all hoping the string of clouds along the horizon would dissipate in time for the sunrise.

Glenna clapped her hands. "Time to go inside, lucky ones."

We filed past the massive main kerbstone, etched with spirals and jagged lines, and approached the dark entrance door. I thought of the first time I'd seen it, in a photo my mother had taken nineteen years ago today. Sitting in Gina's closet two summers ago, I couldn't have imagined the journey I was beginning. Even now, I couldn't imagine where that journey would end.

We entered Newgrange at last.

Dim electric lights shone along the passageway. Zachary and I had to let go of each other so we could walk single file, then shuffle sideways. Even I had to duck below the wooden lintels supporting the ceiling. The passage curved to the right a little, then the left, then the right again. I remembered from my studies that this curvature gave the sunrise's beam of light a small path so that it would only enter on these few days.

We arrived at the chamber itself, tinier and yet more magnificent than I'd ever dared to dream. We were finally here.

"Welcome to Newgrange," Glenna said, then repeated it in Gaelic. "We've got about ten minutes until the sun enters the chamber, so I'll tell you a bit about some of the features here. First I need everyone to back up toward the walls to let the light shine through, with the shorter people in front."

Zachary stood behind me near the recess farthest from the entrance, the one with the triple spiral carved on one of its stones. I remembered we'd seen it on the replica at the Maryland Science Center back in April. My heart had broken that day with the pain of being near Zachary but not *with* him. Seeing it now, by his side, made my heart dance. When I looked back, Zachary's eyes were fixed on the spirals, too.

"The eastern recess over here has two stone basins instead of one," Glenna said. "Archaeologists believe that the smaller one was a birthing bowl."

"Women would have babies in here?" an English lady asked her. "In the same place where the bodies had been buried?"

"Yes, although probably not at the same time. Newgrange is a place where the living and the dead were side by side, spiritually at least. Quite like post-Shifters today. Newgrange's builders were acutely aware of the cycle of life."

"Did they do human sacrifices here?" asked a guy with a Brooklyn accent.

"No. We know the people who built Newgrange were peaceful. What a society values most, they bury with their dead. No weapons were found with the remains, only jewelry and household items."

I thought of Mickey slipping Logan's favorite guitar pick into the pocket of his blue burial suit.

"It's almost time now," Glenna said, "so I'm going to turn off the lights."

With a flick of a switch, the darkness was complete. I could barely breathe. Had my mother felt this way when she stood here waiting for the sunrise? Did she have any inkling of what her presence would bring forth?

Soon a great cry went up from outside. The sun had risen over the hills. Any moment now it would reach the roof-box, and then the passageway, and then the chamber.

Zachary slid his arm around my front as the passageway began to glow.

Then it suddenly dimmed. Everyone in the chamber groaned with disappointment. A cloud had stolen the sun.

"Just wait a moment," Glenna said. "There could be a break."

I clutched Zachary's arm with both hands, fearing I would pass out. But he felt as solid as the stone surrounding us.

All at once, a red-orange beam of light appeared, shooting into the chamber like a celestial laser. The tiny room echoed with gasps.

My mind blanked, suspended in that moment. I now understood, at my core, the meaning of the word "solstice": *sun standing still*. The whole world had stopped. Sound. Light. Movement. My heart. All stopped.

Zachary held me tight against him, his own breath uneven. The rare light exploding here in the dark chamber made me think, strangely or maybe not so strangely, of the two of us in bed. The ancients must have known how sacred every act of life and love could be, so they'd built Newgrange to honor this union of stone and sky.

Glenna spoke softly. "Right now, you are experiencing Newgrange the way our ancestors did five thousand years ago. If you'd like, you may step around the chamber clockwise and through the light itself. Beginning with you there by the door. Yes, the lady in the lovely pink coat."

The couple she pointed to stepped forward eagerly. We shuffled along the chamber wall, passing the eastern recess with the double basins.

All was silent except for soft sniffles and gasps. My own face was damp with tears, but I didn't wipe them away. Each drop felt like it carved a sacred river down my face. Each breath entering my lungs filled me with strength.

Ahead of us, an elderly man and woman holding hands moved forward out of the beam. Zachary and I angled our bodies sideways, his behind mine, then together, we stepped into the light.

For half a second, I gazed out toward the horizon, greeting the sunrise in its orange-gold glory.

Then a veil fell between me and the sun, turning it first bloodred, then black. Zachary gripped my shoulders. I drew in a breath to scream.

Out of the blackness emerged a new color.

Violet.

The sun had turned to ghost.

I stared, frozen, as Zachary whispered a soft word of Gaelic wonder.

The violet waves streamed toward us in a brain-blaring burst. Then it changed again, to that color I'd seen only four times before: the brilliant white-gold shine of a ghost passing on.

I blinked, and the beam returned to yellow-orange, a glorious but utterly normal sunrise.

Glenna cleared her throat. "If you please . . ."

Zachary and I moved as one, sidestepping out of the light. His face mirrored my shock.

No one else seemed to notice a change in the light. Their faces were painted in a deep bliss. While I felt that, too, it was swamped by one shattering hope, a hope that verged on certainty.

We had ended the Shift.

Chapter Thirty-Three

After months of wanting nothing more than to be inside Newgrange, I couldn't wait to get out.

Zachary and I emerged into the morning light, where the crowd outside was cheering for the solstice.

"Our bus leaves in thirty minutes!" Glenna announced. "Take your time, look around the monument and the satellite sites. I'm happy to answer any questions."

She definitely couldn't answer our question.

I tugged Zachary's hand, pulling him past intricately carved kerbstones that we should have been studying and admiring. We kept walking until we were completely alone, at the opposite side of the megalith.

Then I turned and grasped Zachary's forearms. "What. The. Hell."

"What did you see?" His eyes were wild with excitement. "The sun turn red, then black, then purple, then white?"

"Violet, not purple, but yeah. Then it was normal again."

"Could it have been a trick of the light? An afterimage?"

"A trick of the light?" I shook him. "Zach, the sun disappeared!"

I shut up as a family of three rounded the bend. They stopped at the kerbstone next to us, the most ornate of them all.

Zachary led me off the path, down the grassy hill. "What do you think it means?"

I tried to put the words in the right order to make some kind of sense. "The sun went through the light spectrum to red, then faded to nothingness. When it was black, it felt kinda like a shade."

"That's what shades feel like?"

"They feel worse. But then the sun turned violet again, like a ghost. And when it became golden-white, it felt like a soul leaving this world." My throat lumped. "I think it was the Shift passing on."

His eyes softened. "No more ghosts?"

"Maybe. I guess I'll find out soon."

"Only if you're away from me. And only if I don't kiss you for hours."

My heart sank. "Or you could look for them without me. I've given you my violet."

"No." Zachary held me at arm's length to look me in the eye. "You're the one who's spent your life seeing ghosts. You should be the one to *not* see them."

He was right. I hated the thought of not kissing him for however long it took his red to wear off me. But this was my journey first.

"It's been almost an hour since you kissed me on the bridge."

"Aye." His thumb traced my cheekbone. "D'ye think we could reset the clock right now, though?"

I heaved a sigh of mock reluctance. "If you insist." My arms encircled his waist, pulling him close. "But only because it's our birthday."

Zachary and I inhaled a huge breakfast at the Newgrange visitor center tea shop, then drove south to the Hill of Tara. Zachary insisted on going, despite the intermittent rain. I didn't mind. If we had to physically stay apart for hours, I wanted to keep myself occupied.

The guidebook's aerial shot of Tara showed impressive rings and mounds formed of earth and grass, and dotted with monuments. But from the ground, it kinda looked like, as I put it, "a big lumpy field."

Zachary threw me an exasperated glance as we walked through the center of the complex. "The most sacred site in all of Ireland, the burial ground of ancient kings, the legendary final resting place of a mysterious race of Stone Age beings—is a big lumpy field?"

"The view is pretty, now that the sun's coming out again." I watched him sputter over my irreverence before adding, "I'm kidding. It's definitely got charm."

"So it's a *charming* big lumpy field," he said.

"Exactly." We were heading along a ridge past the burial mound known as Cormac's House, but we weren't stopping to read the signs. Which wasn't like the information-hungry Zachary at all.

We reached the western end of the field, where there was a tree with a gnarled trunk split down the middle. It looked like a pair of trees had grown up beside each other and decided to entwine.

From nearly every low branch, amid the bright red podlike berries, hung a piece of cloth or ribbon. Many were faded and tattered from the sun and wind.

"What is this?" I asked Zachary.

"A hawthorn. A wishing tree. People hang things as gifts to the faeries and make a wish."

Now that we were closer, I could see a baby's pacifier dangling from a branch. A yellow sweatband was wound around another twig.

On impulse, I unclasped my new necklace with the three-spiral design. I looped it over a low branch, twisting the leather tie around the base of a clump of berries.

I wish Zachary could find a life of peace. With me. I touched my fingers to my lips, then the spirals.

On the far side of the tree, overlooking the wide, sun-speckled Boyne Valley, a child's stuffed animal hung by its feet. "Poor bunny." I tapped its pink plastic nose. "But I guess it's an honor to be put here, right? Better than going out in the trash or a yard sale."

Zachary didn't answer. I turned to see him tying something to a branch over his head. He tugged it, dropped his hand, then closed his eyes. His lips moved silently.

I didn't interrupt or look away. Zachary opened his eyes and saw me watching him.

"What is that?" I asked.

"Nothing. Let's go. It'll be dark soon and harder to see the road signs."

He strode down the hill back the way we came. I went to stand beneath the branch he'd just touched.

A bright blue shoelace flapped in the gathering breeze. Letters were written on one end, near the plastic tip. It was too high for me to grab without jumping, and I worried I'd break the branch if I yanked it down.

The breeze was twisting the shoelace so fast I couldn't read the letters on it. But I recognized that sky-blue color, and the skate shoes it had once matched.

At last the wind eased. The shoelace swayed faintly. I tilted my head to read the initials Zachary had written in black.

LPK.

He made me promise to do something for him.

I walked over the slopes of Tara, my chest aching, until I reached Zachary. He was waiting near a statue of a man with a tall pope-type hat. It seemed out of place here among entities and legends so much older than the Catholic Church.

Carved into the marble base were the words NAOMH PADRAIG. Saint Patrick, the one Logan had been middle-named after.

I looked out over the Hill of Tara and saw why Logan had wanted his ashes scattered here, and felt sad that his parents hadn't allowed it. Now, a form of his final wish had been granted—by his ex-rival, of all people.

"I love you," I told Zachary, and had never meant it more.

He gave a heavy sigh. "Don't say tha' now."

My heart thumped. "Why not?"

He turned to me, his mouth serious but his eyes alight. "Makes it even harder not to kiss you."

* * *

The rain had soaked through my shoes from the wet grass, so we went back to Ballyrock to change clothes and call our families before lunch.

As we mounted the last set of stairs to our fourth-floor room, Zachary put an arm in front of me and a finger to his lips. Then he beckoned me to follow him, moving softly.

Our door was closed, but the Do Not Disturb sign was missing from the knob, and the tiny piece of tape at the top was broken.

Zachary's eyes narrowed as he sidled up to the door. He listened for a moment, then opened it suddenly and silently.

Inside the room, a girl squeaked. "Oh my goodness! You scared me."

Everything was clean. The powder was off the floor, the sheets had been straightened. A girl our age, maybe even younger, was standing beside the bed, one hand holding a dust cloth and the other clamped over her heart.

"No one was supposed to come in here." Zachary stalked past the cleaning cart. "No one."

"I didn't know. They didn't tell me."

"We put the sign on the door." He looked at the knob. "Where is it?"

"It wasn't there, I swear." The girl looked like she was about to cry. "Please don't tell Mrs. McGuerin. I'll get sacked, and me ma's sick. I need the work. Please, sir." She clutched her hands together.

Zachary's shoulders lowered a fraction. "Was someone in the room when you arrived?"

"No. But I think—" She swallowed. "Someone was here before me."

I looked at Zachary, thinking of the Nighthawk agent. But he stayed calm and kept his gaze on her.

"Why do you say tha'?" he asked her, quietly but with an edge to his voice.

"There was baby powder by the chest of drawers. There were footprints in it." She brightened. "Maybe whoever came in took the Do Not Disturb sign, and that's why I didn't see it."

Zachary and I went to the dresser. He slid the left-hand top drawer open carefully, and I did the same on the right with my stuff.

"Maybe we should wait until she leaves before we go all 007," I suggested in a whisper.

"Good idea." He turned to her. "Thanks very much. That'll be all."

"You won't tell anyone?"

"Of course not," I said, digging in my pocket. "Here, take this as your tip." I gave her a five-euro note.

Her jaw dropped. "All of it?"

I stepped closer and lowered my voice. "Sorry if we scared you, um, what's your name?"

"Deirdre."

"Deirdre. Jack can be a little tense sometimes."

"Who?"

"Jack. My husband?" I angled my body slightly to indicate Zachary.

"Oh, of course." Deirdre pocketed the money and gave me a shy smile. "Thank you for your kindness. I hope you're enjoying your stay." The girl hurried out, avoiding Zachary's eyes.

The door closed behind her. He looked at me. "Five euros?"

"Is that too much?"

He drummed his fingers on the wooden dresser top. "Not if it keeps her away."

Zachary and I combed the room, but couldn't find anything out of place, other than what Deirdre had cleaned. Everything in the dresser was exactly how we'd left it.

"Could Deirdre be working for Nighthawk?" I asked him as we stood in front of the wardrobe, where our bags remained untouched.

"She barely looked sixteen. Why would an elite group of spies hire someone like her?"

"I don't know. But I'd feel better if there was only one group of bad guys after us."

"We should be so lucky." Zachary shut the wardrobe doors. "I'll start arranging things so we can go to lunch. After that, you should try searching for ghosts. It'll be long enough since we kissed." He looked at me with a longing that was more than physical. "I hope."

"Before lunch I need a hot shower. I'm all cold and damp."

"I'll be out here, then." He turned away quickly and spoke under his breath, "Thinking of you in the shower."

Chapter Thirty-Four

I n the shower, I thought about Zachary's reaction to Deirdre's mistake. For a few moments, I'd seen real rage and fear in his eyes, quickly masked by a studied self-control. His ordeal at 3A—whatever it was—no doubt made him sensitive to finding strangers in his personal space.

When I came out of the bathroom, Zachary was sitting on the bed, holding a strip of plastic packages up to the nightstand light.

"Reading your fortune in a pack of condoms?" I asked him.

"Aura, come look." His voice was serious. "Something's wrong."

I leaned close, holding back my hair so it wouldn't drip on him. "Is that a hole in the middle?"

"It's in about half of the packets, from a wee pin." He threw the condoms onto the nightstand. "It was that girl! She was standing by the bed when we came in, and while she was talking to us, she glanced over here. Only once, but I caught it. Also, I stepped on this." He held up an open safety pin.

The sight made me shiver. "That's the creepiest thing I've ever heard of. Why would Deirdre do that?"

"Dunno. Why would she want you to get pregnant?"

"But you would've noticed the hole, right?"

"Not in the dark. See, it's barely visible on the wrapper in the light. I wouldn't have known until it was too late."

"Holy crap." I sank onto the side of the bed, feeling dizzy at our close call. "Are we sure it was her? Maybe it was whoever was in the room before."

"There was no one here before. She lied about that."

"How do you know?"

"The Do Not Disturb sign was peeking out of her pocket. At first I thought she was just covering up her mistake so she wouldn't get sacked. But something bothered me about her. While you were in the shower, and I was trying not to think of you in the shower, I figured out what it was: She's Irish."

I nodded solemnly. "That is strange, considering we're in Ireland."

He shook his head. "These days, hotel cleaning people in the British Isles are mostly Eastern Europeans. Poles, Czechs, Romanians. It's an immigrant's job, like in America."

I thought about the other housekeeper we'd passed in the hallway. She'd been speaking on her cell phone in what sounded like a Slavic language. "So Deirdre doesn't really work here?"

"Aye, she works here. I saw her when we checked in, cleaning another room."

"Maybe she took the job just to get to us."

"Remember, our real names were on the original reservation I made back in March. So stupid of me."

I gasped. "Remember when I called you Jack? She looked confused, even though that's the name on the reservation now."

"Good point. Maybe she knows who we really are."

"So what do we do now? Do we have to leave? Is the place bugged?" I whispered.

"No, I checked again." He crossed his foot over his knee. "If she thinks we believed her story, then we should stay. We might learn more."

"We spy on the spy. I like that." I almost kissed him in appreciation of his wiliness, then remembered we had to stay apart.

"Besides," he said, "it's the holidays. Our chances of finding lodging anywhere in the country are less than nil."

I hated the feeling of violation and knowing that someone—even a crazy sixteen-year-old girl—knew who we were.

I looked at the condom box on the nightstand. "We're buying more of those, right?"

"Aye, first thing before lunch. And keep them secure."

"Why would someone want me to get pregnant?"

"No idea. If she's working for the DMP or Nighthawk, I can't see how that would fit their agenda."

"Unless—oh my God. You think they'd want to see what would happen? You're the Last, I'm the First. Your dad always said the DMP didn't want us together because they were afraid of what we might, um, make." My heart pounded harder. "Maybe they've changed their minds. Maybe they want to study us by studying our kid."

Zachary went utterly still. In the moment before he looked away, I saw a hurricane-size storm in his eyes. "They would," he said in a soft, cold voice.

"Zach?"

"Let's eat. I'm starving."

As we put the room back in order, dispensing the baby powder and mussing the covers just so, I considered the terrifying possibility we'd raised: Any child we'd have together would be scrutinized, examined, maybe even taken from us.

I'd never really thought about babies before. As a kid, I'd treated the dolls I'd played with like actors in a movie, not like my own offspring. But the idea of anyone harming a person Zachary and I loved drove me near blind with rage.

I would die before I let that happen.

The sun set while we were having a late lunch at a pub in the village of Slane. I excused myself before dessert and walked out onto the front porch. After what had happened this morning with the Nighthawk agent, I didn't want to stray far, but I had to get out of Zachary's sight.

Or at least, what I was looking for had to be out of his sight.

I walked to the nearest corner, ignoring the rain that dampened my hair. A few pedestrians were out, on their way to the jewelry shop across the street, where a sign advertised a Christmas sale on engagement rings.

My thumb shifted my own diamond back and forth, bumping my middle finger, then my pinkie. I'd gotten used to it so quickly. Maybe it was the travel, or spending the night with Zachary, or—well, *that*—which made me feel strangely grown up. I wondered what Megan would think, and had a sudden urge to call her. But I had to wait until later when she'd be with Gina at my house. MI-X had warned us about making calls to people whose phones might be tapped.

I couldn't go home without the answers I needed—not just about the Shine and the Shift, but about Flight 346 and the draft and what my government would do to me now that I'd turned eighteen.

But as I stood there in the rain, with no ghosts in sight, hope bloomed within me. If Zachary and I had undone the Shift this morning at Newgrange, most of my problems would disappear. My life would open up with infinite possibilities.

I headed back toward the pub, avoiding the large puddles. The storefronts' red and green holiday lights reflected in the water's shimmering surfaces.

I stopped short. Ahead of me, a round puddle next to a parking meter reflected a color that had nothing to do with Christmas.

Violet.

The young woman's ghost drifted between the parked cars, then crossed the road, ignoring the vehicles passing through her. She moved deliberately, maybe putting space between herself and the candy shop's red holiday lights.

Whatever had happened this morning at Newgrange had been mysterious and powerful. But it hadn't ended the Shift.

I entered the pub and climbed onto the barstool next to Zachary's. He gaped at my soaking hair and clothes.

"They have indoor plumbing here, aye?"

"I took a walk." I slumped to put my head onto my fist. "And saw a ghost."

"I'm sorry." He poured me a steaming cup of tea from a metal pot. "Maybe Padraig Murphy was right—it's Dowth we need to visit, at sunset tomorrow."

I pointed to the TV above the bar. "The weather guy said it's going to rain again."

"Maybe it won't matter whether the light hits us or not. Maybe it's our being there at the right time." He dug into his piece of chocolate cake. "After all, the sun goes where it goes regardless of clouds."

"I guess."

"Besides, Dowth means 'darkness.' So it makes sense that it would be the opposite of Newgrange. Talking of darkness, did you still want to try to turn a shade tonight at solstice?"

"Definitely."

"So no kissing you for hours before?"

I let out a whimper. "Sorry. Probably not after six p.m."

His knee nudged mine under the bar. "But now's good, aye?"

Before I could answer, he kissed me, letting the barest edge of his tongue graze my upper lip. Maybe it was the lingering taste of tea and chocolate, but the feel of his mouth on mine sent a shock of adrenaline out to the tips of my toes and fingers, and all parts in between.

Yes, I thought, *now is very good*.

The hearth held no fire, a draft whistled through the crack between the balcony doors, and our quilt was . . . somewhere. But winter couldn't touch me and Zachary. Our only shivers came from the touch of hands and mouths, our only shudders from the quakes within. And in that mystical place we dwelled in together—which we felt even more vividly than before—the air was anything but cold.

Afterward, we lay pressed together, our breath caught in the same slowing rhythm. I wanted to fall asleep just as I was, using him as a full body pillow beneath me. By the way he kept me snug against him, tracing lazy circles on the back of my shoulder blade, I didn't think he'd mind.

Finally Zachary whispered my name, his tongue barely tapping the *r*. Then he said, "I never want to leave this place as long as I live."

"You mean County Meath or this room?"

"This place." He spread his palm against my side. "Specifically."

I closed my eyes tighter. "Happy birthday." It was a statement, not a wish.

Zachary sucked in a breath. "Birthday! I have a present for you." He slid from beneath me, switched on the lamp, and opened the nightstand drawer. A small box wrapped in gold paper glimmered in the light.

My bliss turned to glee. "Thank you! Can I open yours last? Gina gave me something, too."

We washed up, got dressed, and met back in bed ten minutes later. The thought of opening my aunt's gift while naked totally squicked me out. After glancing at her card, I tore the blue paper off the gift.

The jewelry-type box looked suspiciously like the one she'd given me last year, which had held an obsidian necklace that drove Logan over the edge into shadedom. Had she regifted me that present?

I lifted the lid. It was a silver chain with a teardrop-shaped piece of clear quartz. Ghosts' favorite gem.

"Funny." I lifted the chain, examining the transparent stone. "Last year I had a ghost boyfriend and she got me obsidian. This year I have an anti-ghost boyfriend and she gets me clear quartz." I looked at Zachary. "She wants me to be a nun."

He laughed. "The stone doesn't bother me." He touched it. "See?"

"But you're not as red right now as you usually are."

"And you're not as violet as you usually are. Does the stone bother you?"

I laid it in my palm, letting the chain curl around it like a snake. "Nope."

"That's because we're alive." He folded my fingers over the gem. "Before all else, we're human."

I nodded as I put on the necklace, hoping he was right.

"My turn." He handed me his present. "It's not what it looks like. Well, it is, but not what you think it is. Except, it is."

"Ooo-kay." I took off the wrapping to find a square velvet jewelry box, just like the one my temporary engagement and wedding rings had come in. My heart thudded, then calmed. If Zachary were going to ask me to marry him for real, it wouldn't have slipped his mind, no matter how crazy the day got.

The box lid creaked open, revealing a silver Claddagh ring, hands holding a crowned heart. The classic Irish ring.

"I've always wanted one of these! How'd you know?"

"Look, there's an inscription." He pulled the ring out of the box and held it to the light. "I thought about having our initials done, but it seemed like a security risk. Then I had an idea."

I peered at the words. MO ANAM CARAID. Soul mate.

"Zach . . ." It perfectly fit my right middle finger. "It's beautiful, thank you. My gift for you isn't nearly as romantic."

"You've already given me the only thing I wanted."

I squinted at him. Did he mean my virginity? Because that was a little—

"Your trust." He ran his thumb over the Claddagh ring. "I know I broke it, on prom night. I still haven't forgiven myself."

"You've done plenty of penance." I slipped him a birthday card. "Your present's in here."

Zachary tore the envelope open with abandon. He pulled out the two pieces of paper and angled them to the light.

"What—what is this?"

"Vouchers. You trade them in for tickets once the game schedule's official. The match schedule, I mean."

"You—you're sending me to the U-20 World Cup final rounds? Next summer? In Milan?"

"Not sending you. Taking you." I fidgeted with my toes. "Hopefully by then I'll have saved money for our plane tickets."

He kept staring at me, seemingly unable to do anything else. "Will ye come with me, then?"

"That's the idea," I said slowly. "I thought it'd be cool to go to Italy together."

"You realize it's soccer-football, not American-football."

"Right. The college version of the World Cup. Are you okay? Did I—"

He tackled me, pinning me to the mattress and cutting off my words with a hard, joyful kiss. I realized that for Zachary, my gift to him was ten times as romantic as a ring.

"Aura, it's the best present anyone ever gave anyone. Sorry I was pure glaikit there for a moment. I couldnae believe it." His smile faded a little. "You hate my sort of football."

"Then teach me to love it." I drew my hand over his waistband. "When we go, will you wear your kilt to show national pride?"

Zachary laughed. "That's what this gift is about? Getting me into the kilt?"

"Getting you out of the kilt, actually. Why didn't you bring one with you on this trip?"

Comprehension dawned on his face. "Because I'm stupid. A kilt's like male lingerie to you American lasses, isn't it?"

"Pretty much. And you're not stupid, just innocent."

Zachary gasped. "Innocent? That sounds like a challenge."

"Are you up for it?"

"Completely." He sat up and started to remove his shirt.

The mini grandfather clock on the mantel chimed six. Reality time.

"Eight hours till solstice." I thumped my heel against the bed in aggravation. "We have to keep apart until after I call the shades."

Zachary tossed his shirt aside. "Earlier we only needed six hours."

"Six hours after *kissing*. We're totally mingled here."

"I know." He covered me with his body and pressed his mouth to the hollow of my throat. "I like us that way."

I wanted to melt into him, but forced myself to put my hand between us. "Zach, just this once."

"But you're on holiday. *We're* on holiday. And already spending too much of it at arm's length."

"After I fix the shades, we can—"

"After you fix the shades, you'll be heaving your guts out." His voice grew desperate. "The only bed you'll be warming is a hospital bed."

I pushed him away. "I have to try."

Zachary dropped to lie on his back beside me, bunching the quilt in his fist. "This is about *him*, isn't it? You care about shades not just because you're kind, but because you were in love with one."

He meant Logan, of course. My heart cracked to see his anger. "I loved him when he was a shade, but I wasn't *in* love with him."

"Love, *in* love—what's the difference?"

I kept forgetting that guys didn't grasp these nuances. "Loving someone means you care about them and want them to be happy. Being *in* love means you can't imagine living without them."

Zachary covered his face, dragging his fingertips over his brows. "Which is it, then, for us?"

He was really losing it if he didn't know the answer to that question.

"I'll always love Logan." I took one of Zachary's hands from his face and held it between my own. "And I'll always be *in* love with you."

He stared at the ceiling. "Do you want to know when I fell in love with you? When I knew I never wanted to leave your side?"

"When?" I imagined it to be some huge moment, like when I'd almost fallen off that cliff running from the DMP.

"That night under the stars, when you recited the Gettysburg Address with a Scottish accent."

"What?" I started to laugh. "You hadn't even kissed me yet."

"But I was about to. Before your aunt rang your cell phone and stopped me." He took a deep breath, let it out in a frustrated groan, then shifted to the other side of the bed. "If I could survive that, I can survive this."

I sat up, marveling at the rapid return of his composure. "Thanks."

He flopped back onto his pillow and gazed up at me with his arm across his forehead, looking positively irresistible. "Let's spend every birthday here."

"Okay."

"No matter where we are in the world, we'll come back to this room." He jabbed his finger against the mattress with a flourish. "To this bed."

"I'd like that," I said, making the understatement of the millennium.

He tucked his legs beneath the sheets. "Dunno about you, but I could use a wee nap before dinner."

"Me too." I slid under the covers.

Zachary rolled toward me, crooking his arm under his pillow. "If we ever want to work with ghosts together, we'll have to do this a lot."

"Stare at each other?"

"Stay apart for hours, even if we're in the same room."

I touched the soft, puffy quilt between us. "Beats video chats."

"Aye. And you know what the best part will be?" He placed his hand near mine, our fingertips an inch apart. "The end of each work-day, when we can put the ghosts aside."

Every tiny muscle inside me quivered. "Uh-huh."

"And be together. All over each other. In every way."

I closed my eyes, imagining. "I can't wait."

As soon as I said the word, a pang struck deep inside me. I had to go home, finish school, save up money. We *would* have to wait. But not forever.

When I opened my eyes again, Zachary was already asleep.

I wondered what he'd meant by "no matter where we are in the world." Did he mean together or apart?

My thumb stroked "Laura's" wedding band as I imagined our separate future lives: Zachary living in a house in the suburbs, married to a Scottish lady with red hair and freckles. Little kids playing tag through the kitchen, hiding behind Zachary's long legs. Him calling the smallest one a "cheeky monkey" and lifting her high over his head, face lighting up at the sound of her giggles.

The thought of him belonging to someone else sawed out a jagged hole in my chest.

What would I be doing? Teaching science at some university in America? Or at a high school? Scampering off to PTA meetings? Blech.

Separate, our lives seemed so mundane. Together, we could travel the world, have adventures, unravel mysteries beyond the Shift, in Egypt, Indonesia, Australia, Peru. Anywhere. Meld our minds and bodies, feed our hunger for answers and each other's touch. Carve out a shared destiny, not the one others had declared for us.

The future seemed so close. If I could reach out and grab it, I would guard it with my life.

Chapter Thirty-Five

U sing my red phone, I called Gina from the car to thank her for the birthday gift. In ten minutes, she told me she missed me approximately eleven hundred times.

Megan was at my house, as planned, so she could talk to me. In addition to a music download gift card, she'd made me two post-sex playlists, *Songs of Innocence* and *Songs of Experience*, after the William Blake poetry collections.

Songs of Innocence was romantic and earnest, to be heard after the first time I did it. The raunchier *Songs of Experience* was to be heard after the first time I loved it.

"Have you played the first one yet?" she asked. Code so that Gina wouldn't know what we were talking about.

"Last night." I gave Zachary a secretive glance, which he returned. He knew about the playlists.

"And the second one?"

I sighed. "A few hours ago."

She let out a yip. "I'm so happy for you. That you loved the second playlist," she added quickly.

"I loved it a lot. You know, that one was longer than I expected." I grinned, watching Zachary blush.

"Are we talking time-wise?" Megan said.

I replayed my words, and now I was the one blushing. "Yes. Well—yes." I covered my burning face while Zachary and Megan laughed at me. "I have to go die of embarrassment now."

Megan snorted. "You're being careful, right? With, you know, driving?"

Gina spoke in the background. "I am not stupid. I know what you girls are talking about."

Kill me now. "Yes, careful. Jeez, wait'll I tell you how careful we've had to be." I was carrying our new box of condoms in my purse—we didn't want them out of our presence for a minute.

"Can't wait," Megan said. "I miss you."

"I miss you, too." I looked at Zachary while I spoke. "But not enough to want to come home."

"Hang on," she said. "I'm going in the other room."

Zachary pulled into the parking lot of the restaurant where we were having our special birthday dinner. "I can go get a table if you want to talk to her alone."

I sent him a grateful smile as he left the car.

"Okay," Megan said, and I could tell her hand was cupped around the receiver. "You don't want to come home? Like, ever?"

"I totally see what my mom meant in her journal, about Ireland being magical. Why would anyone want to leave?"

"Things are still better here."

"Even with the draft?"

"I don't know. Aura, do what makes you happy, but do it for yourself. Don't do it for a guy."

"You know me better than that. Megan, I need to ask you something weird. When you and Mickey did it, did you feel like you were in another place?"

"You mean like fantasizing we were on the beach instead of the back of his car?"

"I don't mean fantasies. Somewhere totally different."

She paused. "I have no idea what you're talking about. But I'm sort of insanely jealous. You were, like, transported or something on just your second time?"

"The first time, too. It was cosmic. I know it sounds all New Agey, but that's the only word that fits."

"Aura, that's almost unbelievable. Except, I know you two, and I know about the power-mingling and the First and Last thing. I felt your connection the first time you met in the courtyard at school."

"You felt that?"

"Please. I wanted to give you guys bibs for your drool." She sighed. "Maybe you should stay there. You've found where you belong. Most people never get that lucky their whole lives."

The front door of the restaurant opened, and Zachary stepped out under the awning.

"I gotta go," I told Megan.

"Yes, you do," she said. "You absolutely do."

After dinner and a long night of live pub music, we drove to a secluded area near the coastal village of Clogherhead. When we stepped out of the car, I almost forgot what I'd come for.

"The sky!" I pointed to the crystal black expanse above us, then spied the North Star, Polaris, much higher than I'd ever seen it. "I forgot the stars would be in different places."

"Did you really?"

"No." I grinned at Zachary over the roof of the car. "That was one of the things I was looking forward to most. Does that make me horribly geeky?"

"You're asking the wrong person."

"Hey, have you ever seen the aurora borealis?"

He gazed at me. "Not with you."

My skin warmed at his implication: It wouldn't count until I was with him. Everything felt like that now—meteor showers, comets, even sunrises. They'd all be pale and dull if we were apart.

Zachary put his hands in his pockets as he surveyed our surroundings. "Are you sure you want to do this?"

"Positive. I can help these people. Besides, it might teach us more about the Shift. After what happened yesterday morning at Newgrange, obviously there's tons of stuff we don't know."

He gave his I-hate-that-she's-right-again sigh. "Just in case? I've mapped the route to the nearest hospital."

"Hospitals can't help shade sickness. It has to wear off."

"They could give you fluids."

"If my entire digestive system turns inside out, you mean?" I put a hand to my stomach, as it rolled with anticipation. "You should probably take cover now."

"Good luck." He pulled his sleeve down over his hand and reached for me over the car hood. I stretched forward and met his touch with my gloved hand, long enough to feel his warmth. Our eyes met, and in that moment under the north-shifted stars, I'd never felt more hope for our future.

Then he slipped into the backseat, where I covered him from head to toe with a thick black-and-purple blanket we'd bought at a local store. I double-checked that my change of clothes, nausea medicine, and case of bottled water were within easy reach. Who knew what state I'd be in after the shades had gone through me?

I walked toward the rocky shore, following the rumble of the Irish Sea. As I topped a small, sandy hill, a glimmer of violet appeared near the water.

The ghost of what looked like a young woman strolled along the beach, wearing a modest light-colored sundress that fell past her knees. She walked barefoot, swinging her arms in the carefree manner of a summer day.

As if sensing my presence, the woman turned and looked at me. Smiling, I raised my hand in a polite wave. She returned the gesture shyly, then moved on, her steps lighter than before.

My hope grew. If a ghost could stand to look at me, then I wasn't red at all. It was a relief to know that eight hours away from Zachary's touch was enough to return me to normal.

I pulled out the list of shades I'd gotten from the DMP website before I left. I'd been paranoid that someone would find the list on me, so I'd written them in code and then transcribed them when I got to Ireland.

It was time.

"Mary Pickering!" I yelled it to the sky. I shouted another name, then opened my mouth to call the third.

It was too late.

Like before, my head and stomach pitched as the screeching shades bore down on me, sounding like the sky ripping down the middle. Like before, blackness shrouded my vision as the shades enveloped me, bringing me to my knees.

But then, everything was different.

The dark energy roiled inside me in a maelstrom of misery, but this time, it didn't depart. It didn't stream out, leaving me a sick, empty shell.

It stayed.

On my knees, I stared at the inky, white-capped sea, wondering if I'd ever move again, stand again, breathe again.

But I must have kept breathing, though I felt as dead as the shades that dwelled within me now. I was caught in nothingness, lulled by the waves' uneven rhythm. I could stay here.

"Aura!"

Zachary's voice shattered the spell like a sledgehammer into a crystal ball. I covered my ears and screamed.

He called again, closer.

"No . . ." The pain punctured my ears, scrambling my brain. Now I *had* to move, had to get away.

I sprang to my feet and ran. When my boots met sand, I stumbled, but his voice rang out again, panicky. I threw my weight forward, hoping my feet would catch me. If I reached the water, I could put my head under to drown out his voice.

He grabbed me from behind, his fingers like hot pokers. I shrieked and struggled to get away, but he held fast.

"Aura, stop! What are you doing?"

I spiked my boot heel onto the top of Zachary's foot. He cried out, and his grip loosened enough for me to slip my arms out of my coat.

I kept running. Icy water splashed under my feet.

"I won't let you go!" He tackled me, dragging me into the cold sea. I punched and kicked, but he held on, wrapping me in my own coat so I couldn't get my arms up.

"Aura, Aura, Aura. It's me. It's Zachary. Aura, stay with me. Please."

The pain crescendoed, then exploded through my whole body.

Then at last, there was nothing but darkness.

Chapter Thirty-Six

I woke in the backseat, unable to move. The car was driving fast and jerky, and my head lolled around on my neck. I groaned at the ache it caused.

"Sorry," Zachary said. "I couldn't chance you hurting yourself, or—"

"Shut up!" Tears squeezed from my eyes, from the pain in my head and the hurt I knew I was causing him. I turned my face to the window so I couldn't see him.

"I don't understand," he whispered. "Just tell me what happened."

"The shades stuck. Inside me."

"Christ . . ."

"Don't talk! Please. It hurts."

I squirmed, trying to free my hands, then realized he'd put his jacket on me backward, wrapped the sleeves around me like in a strait-jacket, then somehow fastened them in the back.

He spoke softly. "We'll go back to the castle. I'll sleep on the balcony."

His words came as a relief. I needed to get out of his sight, but I didn't trust myself. I'd almost taken my own life at the beach just now. What if the shades made me take someone else's?

When we got to the castle, I staggered upstairs ahead of Zachary so I wouldn't have to see his face. Our room was empty and untouched.

I lay on the bed and curled into a ball, as every muscle knotted up in pain.

Zachary took something from the wardrobe and then the sofa. I knew he was sleeping on the balcony not just to be out of my sight, but to block my path in case I decided to throw myself off.

I loved him so much, even as the things inside me hated him. So much.

He opened the balcony doors, slipped outside without a word, then shut the doors behind him.

The relief was instant. My muscles untied themselves and relaxed into the mattress. After a few minutes, I could finally think straight.

The shades had entered me, and they'd gotten trapped. Why? I hadn't bothered the ghost woman on the beach, so I couldn't have been red from kissing Zachary hours earlier.

Zachary. The mere thought of him cast a shadow of pain over me. I tried to remember the happy times, but the shades had thrown a dark veil over my memory. I saw faint outlines of moments— sitting beneath the stars, kissing in the mountain river, making love in this bed.

What if I could never be around him again? And what would happen when I entered a BlackBoxed area—like the airplane, or *every bathroom in the United States*?

I had to get the shades out of me. But to do that, I had to know how they'd gotten stuck in the first place.

What was different between tonight and the September equinox? Besides the country and the company and the air temperature and about a hundred other factors.

Wait. Tonight was the *solstice*, not the equinox. Maybe there was a difference.

I slowly sat up, expecting nausea and dizziness. Oddly, I felt fine, unlike in September when I'd projectile barfed. I walked to the coffee table and picked up one of the research books Zachary had brought.

A half hour later I had scribbled a page of notes. The spring and fall equinoxes, in ancient beliefs, were about balance and movement. Near those dates, the sun's path through the sky—and the time of sunrise and sunset—changes most rapidly from day to day.

Solstice, on the other hand, literally means "sun standing still." For three days, it looks like the sun rises and sets in the same places. Before and after the summer solstice, the days seem long for weeks. Same with the darkness near the winter solstice.

So maybe the shades got stuck in me tonight because the solstice made things "stand still." Maybe in a few days, the effect would wear off, and the shades would leave me.

To go where? To hurt whom? And in the meantime, how could I be around Zachary during the precious little time we had left?

I summoned the courage to go to the balcony and push the curtain aside.

Zachary was curled up tight in the fetal position to keep warm, a line of sofa cushions under his body. The blanket covered him head to foot, so it didn't hurt me to look at him.

Not physically, at least. The sight of him huddled alone in the cold tore my heart in half.

I opened the door slowly, but he didn't move or speak. "Wiggle your foot if you're awake," I said.

A movement came from one end of the blanket. I set my notes, a pen, and a flashlight by the lump of his head. "Read this after I shut the door. Then write me back and knock when you're finished."

He nodded. At least, I thought he did.

I closed the door and realized what I'd just done. The shades were a powerful, painful presence, but they didn't control me. *I* wasn't a shade. I had a living body and soul, both of which were in tune with Zachary's. No way I'd let anything change that. I'd survive the shade invasion until I could figure out how to let them go.

A knock came at the balcony door. I opened it a crack, and the piece of paper slid through.

Maybe it is the solstice/equinox thing. Talking of which, are we still going to Dowth?

More than ever, I thought. We obviously hadn't ended the Shift by going to Newgrange, so Padraig Murphy's advice was our only lead. If we went to this place of "darkness" at sunset, maybe we could end the Shift. Which would get rid of ghosts *and* shades.

I wrote back:

Definitely. I'm not suicidal anymore, BTW. I think you can come in as long as you don't speak and I can't see you. Like if I'm on the bed and you're on the sofa.

I pushed the note through the opening. It came back ten seconds later:

1 minute.

I lay on the far side of the bed and drew the covers over myself.

The balcony door eased open. I forced myself to keep breathing as the pain writhed inside.

You don't control me. I control me.

The sofa creaked, and the pain faded to a dull ache. I peeled the quilt back far enough to tell that Zachary was concealed behind the back of the love seat.

I slept fitfully, half-conscious, dreaming I was trapped, tortured, my limbs twisted. Dreaming in red.

Was this what it had been like for Logan? All those months as a shade, had he felt this angry and restless? How did he survive without going mad? I would've given anything right then to speak to him, to ask him how he made it through.

I heard rustling, then something light hit my shoulder. I drew back the covers, cautiously, to find a paper airplane on the floor next to the bed.

I opened it to read:

It's seven a.m. I'll hide in the loo while you get dressed for breakfast. When you're done eating we'll switch, and I'll stay downstairs in the library until it's time to go to Dowth, around two. Okay?

"Okay."
I noticed the arrow at the bottom and flipped the paper airplane.

We will solve this together. Please don't let go. Promise me.

"I won't let go."
Another arrow led to a fold under the left wing.

Promise!

"I promise."
I followed the final arrow to the remaining wing.

I love you.

"I love you, too." I drew the blanket over my head and said, "Okay, go."

Zachary shot off the sofa and into the bathroom. When he'd shut the door, I got out of bed and dressed, numbly, not caring if my clothes matched. I brushed my hair at the vanity, then tried to use cover-up to hide the dark circles under my eyes.

Breakfast tasted like nothing. I made polite conversation with the B and B owner, who assumed Zachary was late getting up because he was hungover.

"Trust me." She touched my shoulder. "You're married to a Scotsman now, get used to it. And the brooding." She clucked her tongue, like my "wedding" had been my funeral.

Her words wormed into my mind. Zachary didn't drink much, but sometimes he felt beyond reach. Whether it was national temperament or a personality quirk, I'd have to accept it.

Whenever Logan and I had fought, he'd quickly switch to suck-up mode to try to stop me from being mad at him, even when I was at fault. All he cared about was harmony.

But Zachary was different. His feelings and desires were too complex for me to manipulate. With him—my equal in stubborn pride— nothing was guaranteed. Not harmony, not happiness, not peace. I was sure of nothing but his love.

I hoped it was enough.

Chapter Thirty-Seven

On the drive to Dowth, I huddled in the backseat, covered head to toe with a heavy blanket. Zachary cranked up the radio to mask the sound of his own breathing.

We made it to Dowth with fifteen minutes to spare before sunset. There was no parking lot, just a spot on the shoulder to pull over. No guards, no admissions desk, no welcome sign. Just a giant silent hill.

"Now I get why they call these places 'faerie mounds.'" I passed through a sheep gate into the green field surrounding the megalith. Just because Zachary couldn't talk back didn't mean I couldn't speak to him. No point in both of us being stuck writing notes.

When I heard the clank of the iron gate behind me signaling that Zachary was following, I stepped forward, pulling my hood forward against the light rain.

He passed me a note with a gloved hand. I felt a sharp pang as our fingers nearly brushed.

Walk clockwise around the mound.

I would've given him a skeptical look if I could've looked at him at all. Zachary wasn't normally superstitious, but it was clear that this place Dowth freaked him out as much as it did me. Unlike at Newgrange, which was polished and restored and crowded with tourists, here we were utterly alone with whatever ancient forces lay beneath the stone and grass. Druids? Gods? Faeries? Or something older and more powerful than anything that ever walked and talked, in myth or in reality?

We rounded the mound, dodging sheep poop and passing kerbstones half buried in the soil.

I reached the south entrance, the top of which only came up to my nose. "Looks like a hobbit hole." But instead of a cute wooden door, there was a rusty padlocked gate. "Is the iron meant to keep the faeries out?"

Scribbling came from behind me, then a crumpled note bounced at my feet.

To keep them in.

I shivered. This country was seriously messing with my scientific mind-set.

I checked the padlock, expecting Zachary would have to snap it off with the bolt cutters we'd bought yesterday. But it slipped from the gate, undone. *Huh.* Had it been left unlocked by yesterday's solstice celebrators?

I pulled my ponytail holder out of my hair and wrapped the elastic around the lock's peg so it wouldn't go into the hole, then slipped the lock into my coat pocket. This way we could secure the place when we left—and if someone came along, they couldn't lock us in.

The iron gate squealed in protest as I dragged it open. Then I switched on my flashlight and ducked inside.

The passage was short—I could already see the back of the chamber after just a few steps. My flashlight on the chamber's back wall revealed a breathtaking display of carved triangles, diamonds, and wavy lines. It almost felt more marvelous than Newgrange, because we were alone, not surrounded by tourists.

I stopped before the chamber's threshold. A six-foot-wide stone basin lay in the middle of the round room, taking up half the floor. I'd spent the day reading up on Dowth, and I knew that wasn't right.

"Isn't this basin supposed to be in the other chamber?" I crossed the threshold. "I wonder if—"

"Aura, no!"

"Augggh!" I raised my hands to my ears to block Zachary's voice, sending my flashlight beam careening over the wall.

Out of the darkness, something grabbed my arm, yanking me to the right. I yelped as the flashlight flew from my hand.

"Calm down, Aura. It's all right." The young Irish woman's voice was so soothing, I stopped struggling, confused. Were we supposed to meet someone here?

"Who are you—"

She slapped me hard. I staggered back, hitting the cold stone wall. Through my stunned haze, I heard Zachary's roar.

"Leave her alone! Don't you—" His voice was cut off in a punch, but it was enough to send a bolt of pain through my head, worse than any physical blow. I howled and covered my ears, barely hearing the clang of the bolt cutters against the floor.

"What's wrong with her?" said another girl's voice, this one oddly familiar.

"She's daft," the first girl answered. "Who cares?"

"Now, then," came a deep male voice by the door, also Irish. "Let's find out what other tricks you've got here. Bran, turn on the torch so I can see."

I opened my eyes as a second light clicked on. My own flashlight lay across the chamber, pointed at the far wall. Its reflected glow showed five hooded figures in dark gray robes. They must have been hiding in the chamber's closet-size recess when Zachary and I came in.

Two girls flanked me, each pressing one of my shoulders against the wall. One big guy restrained Zachary's arms while another rummaged through his jacket pockets. A shorter boy—Bran, I guessed—shone the flashlight in Zachary's eyes. A quick glance at Zachary was all the shades inside me could bear, but I could see that his face was bleeding and his posture slumped.

"What do we have here?" The deep-voiced boy flicked the button on Zachary's switchblade. "Looks useful."

The girl in front of me snapped, "Aidan, I swear ta God, you put one mark on him, I'll cut your throat."

Aidan put his hands up in mock surrender. "As the great Nuala commands it," he said sarcastically. He shut the switchblade and went to put it in his pocket, then seemed to realize he *had* no pockets in his Druid-type robe. "I'm keeping this, though. No one touches it—or any of my things—when we leave." He tossed the knife past me into the chamber's side recess, where it made a soft noise when it landed.

The sight of Zachary skewered my eyes, so I looked away, searching the chamber for a weapon. My flashlight? Its shaft was thick and heavy, but even if I could whack one person with it, I was hopelessly outnumbered.

Four iron stakes were drilled into the dirt surrounding the basin. They had small loops at the top, like closed hooks. Next to one of the iron stakes lay a pile of white nylon-plastic zip ties.

Dylan's words came back to me from the summer, before our "commando raid" on Area 3A.

If you ever get kidnapped, this'll come in handy.

Zachary groaned in protest, making my lungs seize. They were tearing off his jacket and shirt, sending the buttons bouncing across the stone floor.

"What are you doing?" I shouted. "Stop!"

"Colm, get his feet," Aidan said.

The two young men hoisted Zachary and dumped him faceup in the basin. The boy, Bran, picked up one of the zip ties and reached for Zachary's right wrist, ready to fasten him to one of the iron stakes.

You gotta be passive. Don't let them think you're a threat.

"Wait!" I stepped forward, presenting my hands in front of me, thumbs together, wrists flexed. "I'll do anything you want. Just please don't hurt him."

Colm snickered at me as he stood. "Oh, we're a clever one, aren't we? Guess what? I've seen that video." He spun me to face the wall, then dragged my hands behind me, crossing my wrists. "Now, Deirdre. The tie. Make it tight."

I screamed, long and hard. We were too far from a house for anyone to hear, but maybe someone was walking along the road.

Before I could draw another breath, a sweat-scented cloth was forced between my teeth. I shook my head and pushed at it with my tongue, but someone tied the cloth tight behind my head, pulling my hair. I focused on keeping my wrists flexed so the expanded muscles would make some slack in the zip tie. In my panic, it was the only strategy I could remember. I hoped it was enough.

"Aura, it's okay," Deirdre said. "We're not here to hurt you and Zachary."

It *was* the Deirdre who'd cleaned our room at the B and B. The one who maybe wanted me to get pregnant.

I wished they'd blocked my ears instead of my mouth. Behind me, Zachary sounded fully alert again as he struggled. He seemed to be trying not to speak, but his labored breathing alone was shattering my shade-infested body. I moaned as loud as I could to drown out the sound.

Deirdre let go of the zip tie. "There, it's done. I'll light the candles."

When she turned away, I let my wrists relax. There was room now to twist them. Because they were crossed and behind my back, it'd take some time and pain to slip my hands free of the binding.

"You asked what we're doing," Nuala said as she turned me to face the chamber. I looked away from the sight of the bare-chested

Zachary bound and gagged in the shallow basin, and instead focused on the pair of black pillar candles set at the base of the most beautiful wall-stone.

"We are ending the Shift," Nuala continued. "It started with the coming of the light to Newgrange nineteen years ago, and tonight it shall end with the darkening of the light in Dowth. The Children of the Sun's legacy lives on in us."

The boy who'd restrained me—Colm?—shook my shoulder. "What Nuala is trying to say is that we want to get rid of the ghosts, like the one that killed our da and nana. For the Shift to end, you and your boyfriend here have to die at sunset."

My mind blanked with terror.

"No!"

The protest wasn't mine, but Deirdre's.

"That's not what Nana Murphy wants," she said. "She wants us to do the fertility ritual so they'd have a child. The new day, remember? Aidan, you were the one who told me."

A cackle came from Aidan, now standing at Zachary's feet. "You still believe in all that Tuatha Dé Danann shite? There's no Dagda coming, and no Óengus. There never was such a thing, and no faeries, neither. The only thing there is, is ghosts, and we're gettin' rid of them now."

Zachary strained at his bonds, to no avail, but he remained silent behind his own gag—for my sake, no doubt.

I wriggled my wrists and pushed my right thumb toward my palm to make my hand as narrow as possible. My shoulders ached already, but the physical pain was nothing compared to the meltdown of the shades at Zachary's proximity.

Nuala withdrew a long knife from beneath her robe. Its curved blade glinted in the candlelight. "Bring her over here."

I cried out as Colm pushed me forward, toward Zachary. I wanted to shut my eyes, but had to keep aware of my surroundings.

"Don't do this," Deirdre pleaded. "It's not what Nana wants."

"It's what our da wants!" Nuala sneered at her sister. "You're just jealous because he visits me."

"'Visits'? Ha. More like 'torments.' I'm glad he doesn't haunt me that way. I'm glad it's not my fault he died."

Nuala brandished the knife. "Shut up, cow!"

The pieces assembled in my fear-drenched mind. Nuala must have been the one driving when Padraig Murphy was killed in the accident, the accident that happened because of a ghost.

"It's all right, Deirdre," said the youngest boy, who sounded maybe thirteen. "When they die, they'll be reborn in the Otherworld."

"That's right, Bran." Colm put his hand on my shoulder. "And if they die together here, they'll live together there. Happy ending."

"You don't believe that," Deirdre spat. "You're just trying to convince Bran it's okay to murder."

"There's no such thing as murder," Bran said. The words from such a youthful mouth chilled me. I shut my mind to the terror and focused on my hands again.

"Where is Da, anyway?" Bran asked. "He was supposed to be here for this. He was supposed to tell us what to do."

"We don't need him!" Nuala snapped. "We know the ritual, we know the chant, and it's time to start. There's five minutes until sunset. If he's not here by then, we kill them, anyway."

I knew why Padraig wasn't in the chamber—because Zachary was here. No ghost or shade could stand his presence.

"I can't do this!" Deirdre tore off her dark gray robe and fled the chamber down the passageway, leaving her four siblings behind.

"You think she'll tell?" Bran asked.

"She won't tell." Nuala sat on the edge of the basin. "Make the girl kneel."

Colm shoved me down near Zachary's head, atop his discarded clothes.

"Five minutes," said Aidan. "Time to clear our minds while Nuala prepares the first sacrifice." He lit his own candle with a lighter, then switched off his flashlight. "We call on the power of the oak. Give us your strength."

As the others lit their candles off his, then began to chant and sway, I flashed back to the first day I'd ever spent with Zachary. Eowyn had served us tea in mugs marked with letters of the old Irish alphabet, whose meanings went with the trees they matched. Logan had just died, so when I saw *quert*, the letter for apple and love, I nearly broke down. Zachary had traded me for his own, *duir*, the oak. The letter for strength.

My anger surged. *The strength of the oak is* mine, *you bastards. Zachary gave it to me when I had none of my own.*

By this point I'd turned one of my hands and tucked it inside the other. I pulled and twisted and felt my right hand slip halfway out. But even if I could get out of these bindings, then what? I couldn't overcome four people to escape—much less cut his ties. Though the shades made it hell to look at Zachary, I wouldn't leave without him.

Nuala's three brothers fixed their eyes on their own candles as she balanced the long knife on her fingertips, above Zachary's bare chest.

No . . .

I flexed my wrists again. The tie slipped another inch, just over the ridge of my thumb.

Nuala grasped the knife handle and made the first cut. Zachary let out a choked gasp, his eyes bulging wide with pain and shock.

I stared at the blood dribbling over his ribs and into the stone basin. The sight of it, and the sound of his voice, shot to the bottom of my soul—

—and stirred the shades.

The hum started low and angry, building in volume and power, throbbing inside my head. They wanted their freedom.

And I would give it to them.

Sticky with cold sweat, my hand caught in the tie. *Come on . . .*

Nuala cut Zachary again, on the left side of his chest. This time he made no sound, just chomped hard on the gag and shuddered all over. His eyes found mine and spoke all the pain he couldn't voice.

But it no longer hurt to look at him. Inside, the shades had separated from my soul. They were ready to leave. Ready to fight.

Yet if I released the shades, Zachary's presence would make them flee before they could stop our attackers. Unless I could somehow convince them to stay, at least long enough for me to free him and escape with our lives.

Logan's words, delivered through Dylan, came back to me now.

Shades can do whatever the fuck they want. Anything but become ghosts.

They. Can. Choose.

I closed my eyes, though I hated to break the connection with Zachary. I had to speak to the shades.

Malcolm and Mary, I've sheltered you for hours, given you a semblance of life. You've tasted food, drunk coffee, bathed in hot water again. Help me now.

They curled and hissed inside me, feeling nothing but fear of Zachary.

Please, I asked them. *If you help us get out of here alive, I promise in three months I'll call you again. I'll turn you back to ghosts.*

They were listening. I'd gotten their attention by offering the one thing all shades wanted and only a few had ever gained: hope.

When I let you go, attack everyone except me, okay? I had no idea whether shades could control or direct their toxic vibes, but if I felt even slightly less shade-sick than my attackers, I'd have an advantage.

Just as my right hand slipped free of the tie, I felt Mary and Malcolm's assent.

Nuala raised the knife. "Sunset has arrived." She wiped the knife on a red silk cloth, then placed the blade against Zachary's throat. "Time to die."

Now!

The shades came, shrieking like twin cyclones, relishing the darkness of this place and of the souls of our would-be murderers.

The post-Shifters screamed, dropping their candles and covering their ears. Nuala squealed loudest of all, her long knife clattering into the stone basin as one of the shades shot directly through her.

Fighting my own shade-sickness—milder than usual but still

powerful—I ripped off my gag, then retrieved the long knife.

"What the fuck?" Aidan yelled. He bent over his little brother, who was in a full-out shade-seizure. "Bran, what's happening?"

I paused for only a moment in my confusion, then sliced the binding around Zachary's right hand. My head was swimming from the shades, so I gave him the knife. He hacked at the binding on his left hand while I slipped off his gag. Without speaking, Zachary sat up to cut his legs free.

Colm crawled toward me, gagging and retching. He swiped a fist at me and missed. With no weapon, I backpedaled away, knocking over one of the black pillar candles. When Colm lurched forward again, I kicked out hard, smashing the sole of my boot into his nose. He collapsed facedown.

Beside me, Nuala vomited, moaning, and for a moment, I felt sorry—not for her, but for this ancient sacred site.

Aidan stepped out of the side recess, wielding Zachary's switch-blade. It gleamed in the light of the remaining candle. Despite the shades still whirling in the chamber, the young man's stance was completely steady.

"Did you think we were all children, ya stupid cow?" He pushed back his hood to reveal a face that was at least a year or two older than mine. A pre-Shifter.

My vision going in and out of focus, I looked at Zachary, who was still sawing away at his last binding. Aidan took a step toward him.

"No!" I reached for the closest objects, the pair of pillar candles. Afraid to lose our only light, I picked up the doused candle and hurled it at Aidan. It bounced harmlessly off his chest, but grabbed his attention.

Whimpering, I retreated against the wall so that he'd turn his back to Zachary.

"Maybe it's not too late to end the Shift." Aidan pounced, knocking me over and pinning my legs and arm to the floor. "Maybe we can kill you first."

I flailed my free hand. It hit the lit candle. I seized it and smashed the flame into Aidan's face, making him scream, and dropping us all into darkness.

But not total darkness. Dim light trickled in from the door. A shadow passed before it. Was Zachary running away?

Aidan shoved my chin up and set the blade to my throat. "No more pretty chants now. Just your blood on this stone."

Metal slammed his jaw, so hard I heard something pop. He sank to the side, groaning like a downed steer.

Zachary stood above me, wielding the bolt cutters he'd dropped at the chamber threshold. "Come on."

He helped me stumble past the basin, where his blood had formed a dark pool. On the way out, I grabbed his shirt and jacket, which I hoped still held our car keys.

We clambered over the writhing bodies and staggered down the passageway, following the light outside.

"The lock!" Zachary shouted. "Do you still have the lock?"

I pulled it from my pocket as we ran out into the rainy dusk. Zachary shoved the gate closed behind us.

"No!" Aidan leaped toward us down the passage.

I tried to hook the lock into the hole, but my hands were shaking from adrenaline and shade-sickness. It missed.

The gate shuddered with the full force of Aidan's charge, opening a few inches. Zachary roared and threw all his weight against it.

"Aura, hurry!" Face and chest bleeding, he planted his feet against the base of the rock wall for leverage. Aidan stepped back for another charge.

Fighting my vertigo, I felt for the hole in the dim light. The padlock slid through and snapped shut.

Aidan slammed into the gate. He made an incoherent grunt, holding his jaw.

Though Zachary's chest was still bleeding, he held me up and helped me stumble away. I whispered a silent thanks to the shades Mary and Malcolm and renewed my pledge to save their souls come March twenty-first.

As we drove off, and the place of darkness receded behind us, I sent out one last message, though its recipient probably couldn't hear me.

Thank you, Logan, wherever you are.

Chapter Thirty-Eight

We shot off down the country road, bouncing through potholes and veering into the oncoming lane at every turn.

I didn't tell Zachary to drive carefully. "Where are we going?"

"Out of this country. Now."

"Do you need a hospital?"

"I don't think so. They weren't deep cuts. I just want to leave." He winced as his arm moved to shift gears. "Clean me off while I drive?"

I sopped up the blood with his shirt, catching all but a few drops before they stained the seat of the car. The cuts were still bleeding, but slower than before.

"I'm guessing you released the shades, aye?" he said, hissing as I wiped too hard. "Why didn't they disappear, since I was there?"

"Because I asked them not to. Long story."

"Short story: You saved my life."

"And you saved mine." I started to shiver uncontrollably—remembering Aidan's red-eyed rage, and imagining the switchblade plunged hilt-deep in my gut.

I made myself talk, trying to joke, of all things. "I can't believe we almost got offed by a bunch of bampots."

"Aye." He nodded, maybe in approval at my Scottish slang. "Not what I was expecting."

I picked up his jacket from the floor, nudging aside the bolt cutters. "Do you want this on? It's cold out."

"No, it'll get bloody. I need a new shirt first."

"Maybe we should call the police," I said.

"Whoever finds those eejits will do it for us."

"And then what? Your blood is all over that place."

"I dunno, a'right?" His voice shook. "We almost just fuckin' died. I am *not* stopping this car."

Right. Escape. First things first. Good thing we had our wallets and passports so we didn't need to go back to the B and B. I even had a change of clothes in the trunk from last night's shade incident.

"What do we do once we get across the border to Northern Ireland?" I asked him. "Will we go to Glasgow?"

"Maybe. I dunno if it's safe at home." He shivered, his whole body jolting. "I dunno if anywhere is safe anymore."

I cranked up the car's heater, then leaned across the center console to rest my head against his shoulder. Partly to warm him, but mostly because I needed his touch. I could still smell the blood on his skin, and the bitter tang of fear in our sweat.

"I'll never forget Aidan, trying tae use my knife to hurt you." He released a low growl. "Nothing ever felt so good as smashing those bolt cutters into his face."

"You really whacked him. I think you broke his jaw."

"That was the idea. If I'd hit him that hard in the forehead I could've killed him. But I would've done it, if that's what it took."

Though the position was less than comfortable, I kept my head on his shoulder, unable to sit up straight if I'd wanted to. My strength was completely sapped.

Zachary brushed his fingertips under my chin, as if to confirm I was still there. "I wish I could believe in the Druids' Otherworld, where people go when they die here, where they can live another life."

"And then come back to this world when they die there, over and over again. It does sound comforting."

"Except for one thing." Zachary's fingers wound in my hair. "This is the only life I ever want."

Near the Northern Ireland border, the motorway became a smaller road, and the blacktop turned to a speckled macadam. I tensed, remembering tales of violence and mistrust, guards dismantling cars at the border to check for bombs.

As we went through a traffic circle, both our phones bleeped, making us jump. Simultaneous text messages.

I pulled out my phone. Was this a warning from MI-X? A threat from Nighthawk or the DMP—or worse, the Children of the Sun? Zachary thumbed his phone on, keeping an eye on the approaching traffic light.

WELCOME TO THE UNITED KINGDOM, said the message from my cell-phone carrier. DIAL +1 AND THE TEN DIGIT NUMBER TO CALL THE US. LOCAL CALLS DIAL +44 AND NUMBER.

I sighed with relief. "I thought entering Northern Ireland would be more dramatic. Guards and guns and big dogs."

"Not anymore. Just text messages." Zachary let out a soft curse. "But if we use our phones now, anyone tracing our lines will know we're in the UK."

"Someone like the DMP?"

He nodded. "Or Nighthawk."

"Gina will freak if I don't check in. She'll call your dad and have him send Scotland Yard out looking for us."

"Good luck to them, finding us." Zachary turned right on a road that would take us southeast, toward the Irish Sea.

"Isn't the airport in the other direction?" I asked him.

"Exactly."

Twenty minutes and three towns later, we stopped in Warrenpoint, an incredibly cute waterfront town on Carlingford Lough. The downtown was adorned with Christmas lights, and its festive atmosphere almost let me forget we were on the run.

Still bloody from his wounds, Zachary stayed in the car while I checked us into a hotel, wearing gloves to cover my own bloodstained hands. At the pharmacy across the street, I bought first aid supplies and a long-sleeved rugby shirt for Zachary—dark reddish brown so that his blood wouldn't show. I noticed a huge change in accent from the Dublin area, plus lots of the "hiya" I'd grown to love from Zachary.

In the cramped hotel bathroom, he held an ice pack to his bruised left eye and cheek while I cleansed his wounds, which had stopped bleeding.

After his tenth wince, he remarked, "Ever notice in the movies the hero gets shot or stabbed and doesn't complain, but when the beautiful girl is nursing his wounds, he can't stop flinching?"

"That's because of adrenaline, and Hollywood." My face warmed at his indirectly calling me "beautiful."

He lifted his arms and held still while I wound the bandage around his chest to cover the two cuts. I pressed the last piece of tape on his back, smoothing it against the material.

Zachary lowered his arms and looked over his shoulder at me. "Now that the shades are gone from inside you, d'ye think we could end this not-touching-each-other shite? It's frankly killing me, as sure as any knife."

As an answer, my fingers slid up, over the unbroken skin of his bare shoulder. Zachary turned and pulled me close, tensing with pain but uttering no sound. He ran his hands ran down my back, then up under my shirt. His palms pressed against my ribs, and I savored the feel of his once-forbidden skin. Nothing inside me shrieked, and nothing hurt. I was all me again. All his.

Zachary stood and tugged me out of the bathroom, toward the bed. The urgency of his grip made my pulse leap, and I wanted nothing more than to feel the weight of his body on mine.

But I stopped short, almost throwing him off balance. "Wait."

"Why? Are you all right?"

"Not really." I rubbed my upper arm. "I still feel wrong, after the shades. They're not in me anymore, but it kinda feels like they're, um, on me. Maybe if I take a shower—"

He released my hand. "Go."

"I'll be quick."

"I'll be waiting."

The hot water was just what I needed. Cascading over my scalp and shoulders, it chased away the last shadows of clamminess. I rested my palms against the sandy-tiled wall and let the flood caress the back of my neck, loosening the tension from the last twenty-four hours of—well, almost dying.

A knock came at the door.

"Yeah?" I heard the door open. "Forget something?"

"Aye." A sliver of curtain peeled back, enough to show one of Zachary's vibrant green eyes. "I forgot how hard it is to think of you in the shower."

I shifted back, the water now between us, blurring his image. "There's not much room in here."

"Aye." He stepped inside, putting half his body under the spray. The lower half.

I lifted my hands. "Your bandage'll get wet."

"Aye." He took my wrists and moved forward, pinning me against the hard, slick wall, arms above my head. Then he kissed me, settling himself fully under the stream of water that flowed from his skin onto mine, its path unbroken by air or space.

With my hands in his grasp and his name on my lips, I could believe that nothing—not even time itself—could tear us apart.

* * *

Later we fell asleep lying tight together, arms and legs entwined, making up for the hours apart, for everything that had almost been stolen from us.

So when Zachary began to stir in his sleep, I woke instantly.

"No!" He shuddered all over, then his legs jerked, his knee slamming my shin.

I hissed in pain and knew I'd have a bruise. "Zachary." I set my hand on his chest, then jerked it away when I felt his heart pounding, like it wanted to burst the bonds of bone and skin and bandage. In the clock radio's electric-blue glow, I saw his face covered in sweat, soaking the hair at his temples.

"Stop." I tried to keep the panic from my voice, but his arms were tightening like a boa constrictor. "You're hurting me."

"Don't go," he cried. "Come back!"

I pried one of his arms off me, enough to squirm over to slap on the bedside light.

He still didn't wake, just flailed, snarling. I ducked before his fist could connect with my face. It slammed the pillow.

"Zach, it's me." I grabbed his slick, goose-bumped arm. "It's Aura."

He stilled, then his eyes fluttered open.

"Aura." He half sat, jerking his head to scan the room. Then he sank back onto the bed with a wordless groan.

"It was just a dream," I told him, wondering if it was the same one he'd been having for months.

"Sorry." Zachary pulled a corner of the sheet to wipe the sweat from his face and neck. "The nightmares stopped the last few weeks, or I would've warned you." He drew his thumb over the edge of the fresh bandage on his chest. It had stayed in place, despite his thrashing.

"Can you tell me? Is it about last summer?"

He stared at the ceiling, breath heaving. "I can. But I'm not sure I *can*. If I have . . ."

"You do have the strength." I lay on my side facing him. "Let me help you. Start with the dream."

He was silent for several moments, then he swallowed hard. "The room's blank white. So quiet."

"Who else is there?"

"No one." He pressed his thumb and forefinger to his eyes, then pinched the bridge of his nose. "I'm alone."

"Are you afraid someone might come in?"

His whisper twisted. "I'm afraid no one will ever come in again."

My stomach grew heavy as my mind seized a terrible new possibility. I'd pictured him beaten, burned, half-drowned. All the things I'd heard about governments doing, especially to noncitizens.

But I'd never imagined . . . nothing.

"Zach, did they—leave you alone?" I couldn't say the word "isolation." I knew from Gina's civil rights cases that solitary confinement was the cruelest torture of all. It drove prisoners mad.

"Aye." Now both hands covered his face, trembling.

"How long?"

"Weeks."

My hands formed useless fists around my pillow. "Why would they do that?"

"After the witness ghost disappeared—the one who saw me with Logan—the DMP tested me, to see whether I could talk to ghosts."

I ached with guilt for inadvertently helping Tammi Teller pass on.

He continued. "There was a post-Shifter intern who told them how the test ghost screamed and cried when it couldn't get away from me. The DMP shipped me off to 3A that morning."

"And that's when they put you alone?"

"Aye. My room was comfortable enough. I had books." He drew his thumbs along the ridges of his eyebrows, wincing at the bruise on the left side. "No TV or video games or music, because of the wires, I suppose. And no mirror in the bathroom, or anything else that could be made sharp."

"What about food?"

"They'd slip it through a slot in the door. I'd wait for hours just to see the fingertips of the person delivering it. They wore white rubber gloves. I once tried to reach through to touch them, and they—" He rubbed the fingers of his right hand. "I never tried it again."

"Zach . . ." My tears started to flow. I took his hand and kissed his fingers, as if I could travel back in time and heal his pain.

His face contorted as he watched me. His other hand gripped the sheets so hard, his knuckles grew white. Then he turned his head away quickly and fixed his eyes on the wall. "I stopped eating. At first it was a *troscad*, a hunger strike to shame them, but then I just wasn't hungry. I was nothing."

"What do you mean, nothing?"

"I didn't feel real anymore. I didn't know who I was." His hand went slack in mine. "And when I did, I wished I'd been on that plane."

"Oh God, Zachary," I choked out.

He closed his eyes. "I would fantasize what it would've been like, to be snuffed out so quickly and mercifully."

"Don't say that."

Zachary tensed again. "You told me you wanted to hear."

"I do! I'm sorry." I clutched his fingers. "I want to know everything."

"Are ye certain? Because it'd be easier to stop." He dragged his nails over the bandages on his chest, like he wanted to rip out his own heart.

"No, please keep going. What made you decide to live?"

He turned his head toward me, and when he opened his eyes, they shone clear and wet. "You were the only real thing in that place. On the days when I felt so daft I couldn't remember my own name, I knew you were out there. I knew you existed, even if I didn't."

My chest felt like it was imploding. "I never forgot you."

"I knew that somehow, but listen: Thinking of you made me hungry." He wiped a tear from my cheek. "I thought, if I starved myself, you'd be so disappointed in me."

I wasn't sure if I should laugh or cry. "What were they doing all that time?"

"I never understood it. They would slip a wee black box under my door where the food came in. Then the slot would seal tight, and the lid of the box would pop off. I suppose it was controlled by a timer or a signal from another room."

My throat grew tight and cold, like I'd swallowed an ice cube. "How big were the boxes?"

He spread his hands about six inches apart, then two inches the other way. "They were empty. I thought perhaps they released an invisible gas, but I felt no different afterward."

I buried my face against his shoulder. "Zach, those boxes weren't empty." My fingers dug into the blanket. "They had ARGs in them."

He went completely still. "At-risk ghosts? Ghosts that were almost shades?"

"They collect them to protect us, and they're supposed to keep them at headquarters. But Nicola said they took some to 3A."

"And put them with me," he whispered. "They didn't take them away after. The boxes would be removed with nae lids on."

My breath trembled. "Because they can't put a shade in a box."

Zachary sat up straight. "All those boxes? The ghosts changed to shades because of me? Why?"

"There's something about you. It used to make Logan shady, remember? But he could always go somewhere else to escape. If your room was BlackBoxed, those ghosts couldn't leave unless they turned to shades."

"Christ, it must've been torture for them to be trapped with me." He looked at the window. "And all those shades are out there now in the world?"

"How many?" I asked, though I dreaded the answer.

He ran a hand through his sweat-damp hair. "Dozens."

"Dozens?" I thought of the few shades I'd been able to save in September. It would take a lifetime of equinoxes to make up for the shades the DMP had created while experimenting on Zachary.

I sat up. "But once they knew you could turn a ghost to a shade, why keep running the same experiment? Why would the DMP, of all people, want to make more shades?"

"How can you wonder that, after the way you saved our lives today?"

For a moment, my mind blanked. The details of the fight with the Children of the Sun at Dowth had blurred, as if it had happened days ago. All I could remember was pain and terror and Zachary's blood.

And the shades.

I put a hand to my mouth. "They want to use shades as weapons. They think if they can control them—or find someone who can—they can use them against post-Shifters." Dylan and I had talked about this the day he'd told me Logan said this was possible. "They want to use post-Shifters to hurt each other until we're all under their control."

"They had some of you working for them. I saw them before they put me in—in that room."

Interns. Nicola had bragged about their program and its coveted slots. Some of those post-Shifters must have worked at 3A.

"You sure there were dozens of boxes?" I asked him.

"Maybe more or less. I couldn't count when I couldn't remember one day from the next. The only day that was different was when the lawyer and the man from the British consulate came to visit. Before they came, someone shaved me and trimmed my nails." He touched his cheek. "It was heaven."

"Couldn't the consulate guy make them stop torturing you? What did your father say when he found out? What did MI-X say?"

Zachary looked down at his lap, bare shoulders hunched. "No one knows. Not my father, my mother, my psychiatrist. The DMP said if I told anyone, they'd get you, too."

I was suddenly as dizzy with fear as I'd been in the Dowth chamber. "They'd test me?"

"Aye. Or isolate you, to 'keep the world safe from freaks.'"

"But if they thought I was a danger, why didn't they just take me anyway?"

"Dunno. Because they treat their own citizens better? Or you were too high-profile because of Logan? Or maybe they were lying. I couldn't call their bluff with your freedom at stake." He took my shoulders. "Aura, I would've stayed there forever—I would've died—to keep you from that fate."

I clutched my pillow so hard my fingers cramped. I wouldn't have survived that kind of torture. He'd saved my life, and nearly lost his mind doing it.

"You must've been so scared."

"For you, aye, but not for myself. They were already doing the worst thing they ever could do to me. When you're in hell, there's nothing left to fear."

"What about now?" I drew the back of my fingers over his jaw. "Are you afraid now?"

His neck twitched, caught in the reflex of shaking his head. He wanted to say no. "I—I dunno. Sometimes." His lips barely moved as he uttered the last word.

"When?"

His gaze locked with mine, as if it was the only thing holding him up. "Every time you walk away, it feels like I'm dying."

His words split me open.

"I know it's wrong." He began to shake, the waves of hair over his brow trembling with the rest of him. "I shouldn't need you so much."

I thought of all the hours during the last two days when I wouldn't let him touch me, for the sake of ghosts and shades, and how he'd tried so hard to hold on to me yesterday.

Without knowing it, I'd made him relive his torture.

I whispered his name again, but this time in Gaelic. "Sgàire." The word felt tough and tragic in my mouth, sounding like *scar*. He had so many of those now, inside and out.

Zachary closed his eyes, turning his lips to the pulse at my wrist, his tongue brushing the beat of my life. Then he pulled me tight against him. His hand shook as it curved around my ribs.

"Wait," I said.

Panic flickered over his face as I pulled away slightly. My heart crumbled to see his expression, though I knew it would change in an instant.

"This time"—I gently pushed him to lie on his back—"let me."

I pulled back the covers, then drew down his boxers, all the way past his feet. Zachary sighed as I began to touch him everywhere, kiss him everywhere, showing how much I loved every inch of him, just as he'd done for me on the riverbank so many months ago. He swept my hair aside to watch, and the look on his face was pure wonder.

I reveled in the sounds of his pleasure, and the way he uttered my name at the height of it all, as if I were lifting him out of the hell that still scorched his soul.

As I lay beside him again, he turned his head to me. "You. You're magnificent."

"Oh." I didn't know what to say. "Thanks."

"Thank you." Zachary glanced down. "No' for that." He cocked a brow. "Well, aye, for that. But I mean, for before." His eyes met mine. "Thank you for letting me . . . speak."

My heart felt swollen. By telling me what had happened, he'd taken a huge step toward healing. But it was only the first step.

A bright thought occurred to me. "Now that I'm here in the UK, you can tell everyone. The DMP can't hurt us anymore."

"I thought of that." He shook his head. "But as soon as you set foot in the States again, they can grab you. If I report what happened to me, you can't go home."

My stomach sank. So this was my choice: stay here and help Zachary find peace, or go home and let the DMP get away with soul-murder. What about my family and friends? Gina? Grandmom? Megan? The Keeleys? Could I give them all up for Zachary?

It wasn't that simple, and it wasn't just about Zachary. It wasn't even about my own safety. It was about justice. It was about making the DMP live up to the ideals of the country that created it. This wasn't what America was about.

And if it was, I was better off without it. Before being an American, or a Baltimorean, or a Salvatore, I was a human being. There was no greater loyalty than that.

All these noble and moral thoughts ran through my mind, but the strongest force tugging at me was Zachary. I couldn't leave him without ripping my own soul in half.

I laid my head on the pillow next to him and wrapped my arms around his body, careful of the bandages. "I'll stay."

He let out a hard breath. "Aura, are you sure that's what you want?"

"I've never been so sure of anything." I pressed my forehead to his. "I promise you'll never be alone again."

Chapter Thirty-Nine

We caught a morning flight from Belfast to Glasgow, since returning to home base—for one of us, at least—still seemed like the logical next step. We were running out of cash, and Zachary was starting to worry about his parents worrying about us.

Once we were there, I'd call Gina and let her know I was safe. I dreaded telling her that I wouldn't be coming home. I knew she'd rather I stay here and be safe than go home and be detained by the DMP. But she'd be pissed I was missing Christmas with the family—like my mom did, nineteen years ago. I also knew she'd feel better if she could talk to Zachary's parents. Eighteen or not, I was still her little girl.

As we flew in, the late sunrise glowed pink against the distant snow-speckled mountains and rugged highlands. I could tell already that this was a wilder place than Ireland, than any place I'd ever been, and I had a feeling that in twenty-four hours, I would know Zachary far better than I did now.

Wispy snow fell as we took a cab through the city toward the northern end where the Moores lived, in the Maryhill section. On the way, I gaped out the window at the buildings' dark, brooding beauty, and sighed at the grand Victorian architecture. "You told me Glasgow was beautiful, but I figured you were biased."

"I am biased. It's not for everyone." He swept a light hand over the back of my shoulders, leaving the words *I hope it's for you* unspoken.

Zachary's neighborhood reminded me of my own Charles Village—rows of modest but well-kept homes, with lots of students, but possibly bordering on some dodgy areas where I wouldn't walk alone at night.

The cab pulled up in front of his house, which Zachary examined for a moment before paying the driver. "Wait a minute, would ya, mate? Might need you again."

We got out of the car and climbed the snow-dusted concrete stairs from the sidewalk to the house. "Why did you ask him to stick around?"

"Their car's here, but none of the lights are on. Mum and Dad should be up by now. If they've gone to the hospital, in an ambulance, we'll want to get there fast."

For some reason, I felt more nervous about seeing a very sick person than I ever did about seeing dead people.

Zachary opened the door quickly, revealing a foyer with a living room to the left. He motioned for me to stay behind him. I sent a nervous look back at the cab, then followed.

The living room was full of open, half-empty boxes of Christmas-tree lights and decorations. Which was odd—Fiona and Ian seemed like the type to clean up after themselves.

"Mum?" Zachary called. "Dad? Martin?"

No answer.

We moved past the stairs into the warm, spotless kitchen. Zachary passed his hand over the empty counter, tapping his fingers. Then he moved the microwave forward a few inches and looked behind it. Finally he peered inside the coffeemaker, in the compartment where the water goes.

"They didn't leave a note, even in our secret places."

"You weren't supposed to come home until tomorrow, though. Christmas Eve." The day I was supposed to fly back home, but wouldn't.

He nudged aside the curtain above the kitchen sink, taking a quick peek into the tiny backyard. "Nae footprints in the snow."

"There weren't any out front, either. So if they left, it was a while ago."

"They'd leave a note for Martin. He's at work, so we'll pop round to see him, see if they've rung."

"Can't we just call him from the house here?"

"We could." He smiled at me. "But this way we get a proper breakfast."

The cab driver let us out on the corner of a busy street near the Botanic Gardens, next to a huge stone church.

Zachary led me to a small courtyard beside the building and headed for the double doors.

"Martin works in a church?"

"Ha. No' hardly."

Inside, the place turned out to be a bar. There were a few pews, stained-glass windows, crosses, and even a choir box, but the rest was pure pub. I felt like Alice stepping from one part of Wonderland into another.

We pushed through the crowd of pre-Christmas revelers. Halfway down the bar, I saw Martin poised at the Guinness slow tap, joking with a customer.

He spied us, and his initial look of delight turned to confusion. He handed off the pint and hurried down to greet us at the end of the bar.

"A'right, mate!" They clasped fists across the counter, and Martin examined Zachary's black eye without comment. Then his gaze fell to my left hand. "Laura!"

"You can call her Aura," Zachary told him. "We don't need the cover, now we're back."

"I don't see youse takin' off the rings, though." The glimmer in his eye faded as he turned back to Zachary. "Dinnae panic, but your da's in hospital again."

Zachary cursed as he gripped the bar railing. "For what? When? Is he—"

"I said 'dinnae panic,' didn't I? It's only dehydration and fever, like last time. Your ma took him first thing this morning. She just rang and said they'll keep him a night or two, maybe have him home for Christmas."

"I hope so." Sighing, Zachary sat on the bar stool. "Visiting hours aren't till noon. Give me your phone so I can tell Mum we'll come then."

"You're family," Martin said. "You can visit now."

"Aura's not, and I won't leave her behind, so give me yer fuckin' phone."

"A'right, a'right." Martin handed him his cell, then tapped the bar in front of me. "Can I fetch ya a pint?"

It was barely eleven a.m. "Just a Coke, thanks." I watched Zachary's face as he put the phone to his ear.

"Voice mail," he said. "Mum must be in the room with him. Can't use her mobile there."

"Try the hospital and see if they'll put you through to his room."

"He'll be under a new false identity. I'll leave her a message to ring Martin with the name."

I went to the ladies' room, and when I came out, Zachary and Martin were deep in a serious conversation. Martin looked in my direction, and instead of smiling at me, his lips went straight and tight. He gave Zachary a nod of resignation, then a brotherly pat upside the head, a grasping gesture that Zachary returned.

"What's up?" I asked when I reached the bar. Martin had moved away to serve another customer, leaving behind a Coke for me and a neon-orange soda for Zachary.

"Martin said last night there were men in dark blue uniforms here looking for me."

"Oh my God, Nighthawk? What if they come back?"

"Don't worry—we've a plan. No' a sophisticated plan, but it's the best we can do short notice." He sipped his soda. "I think."

"Do you trust Martin?"

"With my life." He watched his friend ring up an order at the cash register. "Even with your life."

Martin signaled the other bartender. "Gonnae go outside." He mimed smoking a cigarette. As he passed us, he took his cell phone back from Zachary with what looked like a nod of understanding. The plan, no doubt. He disappeared through double wooden doors into what must have once been a church vestibule.

I fidgeted with the clear quartz pendant beneath my shirt, nervous at the thought of the Nighthawk agents searching for us. It hadn't even been twenty-four hours since our last brush with death. "We should call MI-X."

"I just did," Zachary said, but didn't look happy about it. "They'll be here at half past eleven."

I checked my watch. Twenty minutes.

"I should've called them the moment we crossed into Northern Ireland."

"Why didn't you?" I asked.

"Because I'm a coward. Because once they're here, I'll have to tell them everything. About the Children of the Sun, about Nighthawk."

"About last summer."

He kept his eyes down. "Aye."

"If you won't tell them, I will." I put my hand on his arm. "You need justice."

"I know! I know," he repeated softly. He scratched his ear, then straightened up and grabbed the laminated menu between the salt and pepper shakers. "But first I need a full Scottish breakfast."

"What's that?"

"Fried egg, baked beans, haggis, black pudding, white pudding, sausage." He handed me the menu. "You should try it. It'll give ya strength."

I needed some of that. "Black and white pudding, is that like chocolate and vanilla?"

Zachary was still laughing when Martin burst in.

"Upstairs," he said. "Now."

Zachary grabbed my hand, and we pushed through the crowd toward the back of the bar. A door marked PRIVATE led to a hallway with stairs and an elevator.

"It's the men from last night," Martin told me. "There's five of them this time. Two went around back to make sure youse don't escape." He handed Zachary a key. "Take her to the top. I'll stall them here until reinforcements arrive."

"Stall them how?" Zachary asked.

Martin shrugged. "Create a diversion. Maybe start a row."

"In a West End pub? Good luck with that." Zachary took my hand and helped me step over the chain that blocked off the staircase. Martin ran back into the bar, shouting something about Rangers.

I dashed up the stairs behind Zachary until we reached the third floor. He unlocked a door and ushered me into—*whoa*.

Morning sunlight streamed through stained-glass windows on either side of the . . . whatever this was. A cathedral? An auditorium? On my near left, at one end of the giant room, was a small stage flanked by two Gothic arches with thick red curtains.

"What's this place for?" I asked Zachary as he locked the door behind us.

"Parties, wedding receptions. The bride and groom sit up there." He pointed to the far end of the room, where a balcony with a table and two chairs overlooked the hall, about fifty feet up.

"For me it's been a bit of a sanctuary," he whispered. "Look up and see why."

I did and gasped. The ceiling held the richest blues I'd ever seen, paintings of dolphins and saints side by side. The zodiac constellations stretched on either side of the center length. At our end were pillars and more Gothic arches reaching toward the ceiling in sunset colors. Neatly painted letters ran along the underside of the crossbeams.

The nearest read, IF WE ARE TRUE TO EACH OTHER, THEN WE SHALL BE AS STARS. I took Zachary's hand, as if on cue.

Newgrange and Dowth had held an ancient, mystical magic, but this place made me believe that magic lived in modern times. It could still be birthed by the human mind.

"Now then, we'll need weapons." He strode past the stage and swept aside one of the red curtains. Cases of liquor were stacked in this small backstage area.

Zachary flipped the lid on two boxes of wine and pulled out a pair of bottles. "Red or white?"

"Uh, this isn't the time to drink."

"They're no' for drinkin', they're for bludgeonin'. Here, this one's lighter but'll do the job." He handed me the bottle of white wine, then hoisted one of the red bottles by the neck and took a small practice swing. "Good action on that."

"So now what?"

"Hopefully, MI-X arrives and ends the battle before it starts."

"What do we do if they don't come in time? What if Nighthawk comes through that door? Do we hide here and smash them over the head when they find us?"

Zachary turned to me. "I won't go back to 3A, and I'll die before I let them put you there."

I shook my head. "I mean specifically, what do we do if Nighthawk comes through that door? Hide here and smash them over the head when they find us?"

"I didn't say it was a sophisticated plan."

I parted the curtain to the main room. "We should hide in the balcony, where they can't surround us. They'll have to come up that little spiral staircase one at a time." I lifted the wine bottle. "Easy game of Whack-a-Mole."

Zachary thought for a moment. "You're a genius. Help me with these bottles."

We each lugged a case of wine to the bottom of the balcony's spiral stairway. They were too heavy for me to carry up the stairs quickly, so Zachary took mine and his in turn.

Then we waited. It was now 11:20. Only ten more minutes until MI-X were supposed to arrive. I hoped they were prompt.

"This building used to be a church, I take it?" I asked Zachary.

He nodded. "I don't care much for real churches, but this place feels, I dunno, sacred."

"I think there's a whole other side of you I've never seen."

He gave me a cryptic smile. "You will."

As I leaned over to kiss him, the door below burst open with a bang.

Zachary and I crouched on either side of the stairway opening, far enough back from the edge of the balcony that we couldn't be seen from the door. We waited, gripping the necks of our bottles, ready to fight off anyone who might come for us.

But no one did. Instead, an eerily calm voice rang out. "Come with us or your friend dies."

Chapter Forty

Zach, don't do it!" It was Martin, sounding like he was struggling. "Augh!"

"What the—" Zachary strode toward the edge of the balcony. I hurried behind him.

Five men in midnight-blue uniforms stood on the polished parquet floor. One of them held Martin in a tight grip, while another pointed a pistol at his head.

The Bland Man stood off to the side. "Mr. Moore and Ms. Salvatore." He extended his hand like he was inviting us to a garden party. "I am Agent Timian and I would prefer to avoid bloodshed, especially yours." His accent was a flat American one, maybe Midwest. "Please come with me."

"We're not going anywhere." Zachary dropped his wine bottle on one of the chairs. Before I could stop him, he climbed over the railing, using the table to steady himself. "If you hurt him, I'll jump." He dangled his legs over the edge of the balcony, and I wanted to scream.

Timian shrugged. "Go on then, jump."

"You're bluffing," Zachary said. "You need us alive."

Timian looked at his fellow agents, then back up at us. "I hate to break it to you, son, but—we only need her alive. Not you." He pulled out his own gun and pointed it at Zachary. "So be a good boy and come down from there."

"No!" I strode forward and clambered onto the balcony railing beside Zachary.

"Aura, what are you doing?" he whispered.

I kept my eyes on him instead of the distant wooden floor. I'd never been fond of heights, but I was even less fond of doing what Nighthawk wanted. "I'm not going anywhere, either."

"You're insane."

"You were insane first."

"Children!" Timian shouted. "Let's not be foolish." His words were scolding, but there was trepidation in his voice. He'd probably been ordered to take me alive no matter who else got hurt in the process.

Down the street, a church bell sounded the half hour. We'd done it. We only had to keep this standoff going a few more minutes, and then MI-X would—

The door crashed open again. I yelped in surprise and started to slip off the railing. Zachary lunged to push me to safety, losing his own balance. As I tumbled back over the table, I saw him disappear.

"Zach!" I leaped to my feet, legs tangling with a chair. Zachary had caught himself and was hanging on to the railing with both hands, while down below, five boys—including Martin, who had broken free—were fighting three of the Nighthawk agents.

I reached out for Zachary.

"I've got it," he said. "Guard the stairway. They're coming!"

I rushed to the back of the balcony just as one of the agents' heads appeared at the top of the stairs. I picked up a bottle, drew back, and smashed it atop his head. His skull crunched, and he slumped forward unconscious, twisting around as his hand caught the banister.

The agent lay faceup, his gun exposed. I unsnapped the holster and withdrew the weapon. To my right, Zachary was hoisting himself over the railing onto the balcony, blood from his knife wounds seeping through his shirt. Shouting his name, I slid the gun across the floor to him. Then I picked up another bottle to strike the next agent coming up the stairs.

Agent Timian. As I lifted the bottle, he delivered a bruising block to my arm, sending a shaft of pain up to my shoulder. The bottle flipped end over end, then fell to the floor, out of my reach.

As if in slow motion, I saw Timian pull his own weapon and point it at me.

"No . . ." Instinctively I put out my hands and backed away. I wanted to cover my face but couldn't take my eyes off the pistol barrel's pitch-black center.

"You touch her and I'll blow your fucking head off!"

I wheeled to see Zachary pointing the first agent's weapon at Timian. His hands shook, but his gaze was fierce and steady, as was his voice.

"Eight weeks of hell," Zachary snarled. "I'm never going back. You won't take me, and you won't take her, do you hear me?" His roar echoed throughout the hall. "If you move one inch closer to her, I will kill you."

Timian must have seen the crazy in Zachary's eyes. He lowered his gun and took a step away from me and toward Zachary. "Look, I understand how you—"

The world exploded in noise. I screamed and covered my ears. Timian stopped, his mouth opening and closing but forming no sound. Had I lost my hearing? Air seemed to come in warbling waves, pressing against my head.

Blood spurted from Timian's neck. He dropped to his knees, then his side.

Holy shit, Zachary shot him.

I turned to Zachary, expecting to see him holding the just-fired gun. But he was lying on his back, gasping, knees bent and heels scraping the floor.

Below his right collarbone, a new dark red spot blossomed like a rose. Blood.

Another *crack* came from the room downstairs, as Martin slammed a bat onto the outstretched arms of a rifle-wielding Nighthawk agent.

"Zach!" I ran to kneel at his side. "Can you hear me?"

His eyes were wild. "Aura, what happened? Why am I—"

"Shh, shh." I peeled off my cardigan and pressed it against his wound. "It's all right, it's all right. Just talk to me."

"He—I didn't—I didn't shoot him."

A young man bellowed below, "Someone call an ambulance! Two men have been shot!"

Zachary's gaze roamed the ceiling beyond me. "Two? Was I shot?"

"Yeah, but you're gonna be fine." I looked over my shoulder to see Timian staring at me. He mouthed the word *Help* as one scarlet-coated hand reached out.

Timian's blood pulsed slower. He was dying, apparently from the same bullet that had pierced Zachary's body, then continued its deadly flight.

Martin bounded up to us, stepping over the unconscious agent on the stairs. He saw Zachary.

"No!" He skidded to his knees beside us. "Listen to me, mate. You're not going anywhere."

Zachary's breathing was thick, and when he coughed, blood dribbled from his mouth. "Cold."

"That's right, ye're going into shock, but that's what'll save your life." Martin took off his shirt and wiped Zachary's face. "Boys, tear down one of those curtains and bring it here."

A familiar chilling voice spoke in the auditorium below. "I don't believe this. I can't even see my own body?"

Agent Timian.

I looked at the Nighthawk's still figure. "He's dead."

Zachary squeezed my hand. "Ghost?"

"Don't worry. He can't come up here, because of you."

"Keep him," he rasped. "He knows."

Knows what? I wondered. Then I realized what Zachary meant: Agent Timian could be a witness to everything Nighthawk had done in the name of protecting SecuriLab's profits. Maybe even Flight 346.

"Go," Zachary pleaded.

"I can't leave you."

"Not dying."

How do you know? I wanted to ask him.

"I'll stay wi' him," Martin said.

"Why the hell did you shoot him?" Timian railed below at his fellow agent. "I was standing directly behind. Where did Nighthawk recruit you from, Kindergarten Cops?"

I took a last lingering look at Zachary. "Don't go anywhere."

He swallowed and panted out one word, "Promise."

"Someone dim the lights," I called as I hurried down the stairs. A few seconds later, the auditorium went dark but for the soft Glaswegian morning drifting through the stained-glass windows.

And the violet glow of ex–Agent Timian.

"I can't believe I was killed by friendly fire." Ex-Timian jumped back as one of Zachary's friends ran toward the stairs, a red curtain bunched in his arms. The ghost shuddered at the near contact with the dreaded color, then focused on me again. "Do you know how many bodyguards I've killed to perform my duties? Back in '95, I took out a principal of the Cali drug cartel."

"Wow," I said. "I'd love to hear more about that." My tone was hollow and insincere. All I wanted was to be by Zachary's side, not pumping the ego of a dead commando.

He eyed me. "I'd better not. They might come after my family. It's best if I pass on before I say too much."

"No! We can talk about something else." I suddenly remembered I had more than my own voice to lull him. I reached under the collar of my shirt and pulled out the clear quartz necklace. "What was your favorite TV show?"

"Child, you are ridiculous, and I—" He stopped when he saw the stone around my neck. "Ah." The outlines of his violet form smoothed as he felt the gem's ghost-calming effects.

"Don't go," I whispered. "Please. Tell me how you followed me for so long."

Instead he frowned. "I've never been seen by a target, not until you."

"Is that why you disappeared after we saw you at Newgrange?"

He laughed. "I didn't disappear. I kept watching you."

Up on the balcony, Zachary made a choking noise, moaning. I started for the stairs, certain he was dying, then heard Martin say, "Dinnae worry yersel', mate. You only need one lung tae breathe."

I stopped and took a deep breath myself. Zachary was counting on me—the *world* was counting on me—to keep this ghost so he could give us the truth.

"If you were watching us," I asked ex-Timian, "why didn't you save us from those crazy Children of the Sun at Dowth?"

"All I knew was that you'd entered the megalith, not that anyone was waiting for you. When the girl ran out, I tracked her until she reached her car, then called two of my colleagues to follow her. Next thing I saw was you covered in blood. Then I lost you on the road— your boyfriend's a crazy driver, by the way—and decided to come straight to Glasgow. I figured you'd end up in Zachary's hometown, but I thought it'd be last night. You surprised me."

"Why were you following us, if not to kill us?"

"We wanted to ensure that you didn't enter the UK, where you'd both be out of reach if Zachary told anyone about his treatment at DMP hands."

"The DMP sent you?"

"No, they know nothing of our following you. But the agency has done so much for us and our client, keeping an eye on you was the least I could do." Ex-Timian stopped. "I should see if I can find my wife, have someone speak to her for me."

"Wait! If you show up as a ghost before she knows you're dead, it'll destroy her. Believe me, I know."

His chin tilted up. "Ah, yes, I read the report of your former boyfriend's death."

"It was horrible," I whispered. "Listen, there are lots of ways to find peace. Logan found it by doing the right thing. That might be your way, too."

"Maybe." Ex–Agent Timian wavered, his violet light shimmering. "Or maybe not."

Behind me a voice shouted, "MI-X! Nobody move."

"About fuckin' time," one of Zachary's friends said. "Zachary's up there bleedin' to death, and there's apparently a ghost here wot needs capturing," he added laconically, as if telling an exterminator where to find the cockroaches.

"Got it," said a female agent with an English accent.

A pure white light filled the dim room—an activated clear quartz summoner. The agent had a ghost-trapping box.

"No!" Ex-Timian windmilled his arms, trying to escape as his form slid toward the woman. Maybe it was old habit, but I felt a pang of sympathy as I watched him go.

In a few moments, a loud beep sounded, signaling that the ghost was in the box. As the noise faded, it was replaced by the siren of an ambulance.

I ran back up the stairs, where the agent whose head I'd bashed was now awake, though glassy-eyed. One of Zachary's friends, a hulking blond with a neck tattoo of a harp, was guarding him.

"Thanks," I said to the boy, who looked at least a year older than us.

"Nae bother. I'm Niall," he said, pronouncing it like *Neil*. "Downstairs is Roland, and Frankie's the fat one. The ugly one's Graham."

"Oh." As I moved toward Zachary, I glanced over the balcony edge to see which guys he was referring to.

"It's a trick," Martin muttered, wiping Zachary's brow. "They're all fat and ugly."

Two pairs of EMTs arrived with gurneys and med kits. I knelt next to Zachary.

"Get the ghost?" he whispered.

"We did. So now I can do this." I softly kissed his unbruised cheek. *"Mo anam caraid."*

He smiled up at me. "Always."

Chapter Forty-One

A week after his emergency surgery, Zachary was moved to a normal, non-intensive-care hospital room, where I could stay by his side for hours instead of staring at him through a window for a few minutes at a time.

The Nighthawk's bullet itself had gone through his shoulder and hadn't hit any vital organs. But the impact had collapsed his right lung and caused a ton of internal bleeding, not to mention cracked his collarbone.

I'd called Aunt Gina on the way to the hospital, and she'd boarded the first available flight to Glasgow, arriving Christmas morning. Ian himself was released from the hospital that day, so we shared a worried but thankful dinner together—just the four of us, since Martin had gone home for the holiday weekend.

On Monday, Simon arrived with his supervisor, Minerva Wolcott.

Ian had picked her as his successor because they'd worked together—as had their fathers and grandfathers—in the secret paranormal agency that preceded MI-X. She was as tough and wise as her Roman goddess namesake.

With Simon and Minerva came the secretary of the Department of Metaphysical Purity. To see me. And, surprisingly, not to kill me.

Between Zachary's revelations about his time in Area 3A, and ex–Agent Timian's statements about the role of Nighthawk and SecuriLab in the bombing of Flight 346, things were going to change.

The secretary outlined his plan to us.

It included major changes in the implementation of the DMP "selective service," which Congress might end up repealing anyway. Post-Shifters would still have to register and face heavy recruitment, but the penalties for avoiding the "draft" would be changed from prison and major fines to community service requirements. So if you objected to a job with the DMP, you could work off your "patriotic duty" (as Becca had called it) by volunteering at a soup kitchen or animal shelter, for example. Ghost-related charities would be worth double-time in meeting community service obligations. Not bad.

The DMP would end its "indefinite detainment" of at-risk ghosts, instead doing an annual review of each case, like a parole hearing. That way, some less dangerous ARGs could be set free to continue haunting—or better yet, to pass on.

Best of all, Area 3A would be shut down. I would've preferred that they let Zachary and me set fire to it ourselves, but it wasn't a perfect world.

Two days later, the secretary flew home, announced the changes, and promptly resigned. I might not have brought the DMP to its knees, but I'd made it sit in a corner until it could behave.

When I arrived at the hospital on New Year's Eve afternoon, Martin was already there—and so was Niall. Along with all the big-picture benefits of our showdown with Nighthawk, Zachary's friends were all friends again.

"Hiya, lass," the two of them said in unison as I walked in. Zachary's tired expression grew animated at the sight of the cookies in my hand.

"Where'd you find dark chocolate HobNobs?" He gazed up at me like I'd turned water into wine. "They're dead scarce around here these days."

"I heard there were some in a shop in Edinburgh, so I took the train."

Martin and Niall recoiled. "And how is Auld Reekie?" Niall asked.

I looked at Zachary for a translation. He rolled his eyes. "It's what Glaswegians call Edinburgh, because the distilleries used to make the city reek like burnt toast. But that was back when we were weans. It smells fine now."

"It did," I said. "Edinburgh's really pretty."

This time, even Zachary gagged.

"The only good thing ever came out of Edinburgh is the train to Glasgow." Martin snatched the cookies from me. "And now these biscuits."

"Hey! Those are for the patient." I grabbed for the packet, but Martin pulled it out of reach.

"And the patient's only got one hand. Just trying tae help." Martin slid his finger under the sealed plastic. "Possibly take a wee, one-biscuit fee for my trouble."

Zachary eyed his sling. "I'll be in this contraption a while. I'd better learn how to do a lot of things one-handed." At the sound of his friends' raucous snickers, he said, "Oh, shut up. Isn't it time for you lot to hit the pubs?"

"Past time." Martin stuffed a cookie in his mouth and handed the packet to Niall. "They've been open for hours."

Niall dropped the cookies into Zachary's lap (after taking one). "Sorry you'll miss your first Hogmanay, mate, but we'll raise a glass or thirteen for ya."

"Cheers." Zachary looked glum. Even though he wasn't a big drinker, I knew he wanted to celebrate this rowdiest of Scottish holidays with his friends. "We'll make up for it next time, right?"

I realized he was talking to me. "Right." I took his hand, warming at the thought of us together here next year, and the year after that, and so on.

"We'll be back to see ya when we've recovered," Niall said.

"If we recover." Martin patted Zachary's shoulder—the injured one, of course. "Oh, sorry." He saluted me. "Enjoy your one-handed visit."

On their way out the door, Zachary's friends chortled gleefully, like ten-year-old boys. One of them mentioned something about the "Prince of Wank."

"What did they call you?" I asked Zachary.

"Nothing. So, Edinburgh. It was lovely?"

I had a feeling I was treading on sensitive ground, like telling a Philadelphian about Pittsburgh. "It was all right. Glasgow's better."

"Good girl." He took a bite of cookie, then rolled up his eyes in ecstasy. "No, not a girl. A goddess."

I wanted to crawl into bed with him, but instead shifted my chair so I could sit and hold his hand. "Aunt Gina's flying back Sunday morning. Once she's gone I can stay here with you longer. I feel like I have to take her sightseeing and shopping to make up for scaring her so bad."

"When do classes start again at Ridgewood?" he asked without looking at me.

"Monday. I'll see if they'll let me take midterms long-distance. Maybe one of the teaching assistants at the college here can proctor my exams. Basically, watch me take the test and then sign a form that says I didn't cheat."

He traced my thumbnail with the pad of his finger. "And what if not?"

"Then I guess I'll drop out. I aced the SATs and sent in all my college applications. They never care what you do the last semester of your senior year."

Zachary frowned. "That's no' always true, and you know it."

"I don't care," I said softly.

"I do," he replied, even more softly. "Aura, you have to go home. Now that you're safe from the DMP. Go back with your aunt on Sunday."

"No."

"You have to finish school."

I gripped his hand. "But I promised I wouldn't leave you."

"No, you promised I'd never be alone again. And I'm not alone.

I've my friends, my parents." He sighed. "My psychiatrist."

"I know, but—"

"And I have you." He raised his gaze to meet mine. "Now that we've been together—and I don't mean in bed, though that's part of it—we'll never truly be apart again."

I hated and loved that he was right. It would be so hard to leave him, especially knowing all he'd suffered. Not to mention what *we'd* suffered.

But knowing for certain that we belonged together—a matter I'd lost all doubt about the moment I fell into his arms at the Dublin Airport—would turn our good-bye into a see-you-later. We'd always find our way back to each other.

Without letting go, I sat on the edge of the bed. "I promise I'll be back the second I graduate."

"I know you will. And I'll worry every hour. I'll wish you were by my side where I could watch over you and fight for you and kiss you, a lot." He touched the clear quartz stone at my throat, then drew his finger down, making my whole body tingle. "And other things."

I ached with need for his touch, and with the knowledge that I'd lose it again so soon. "I'll wish that, too." I leaned in for a lingering kiss. "Especially the other things."

As I pulled away, he looked to his right. His room wasn't private, but no patient occupied the bed by the door. Only the most serious cases remained in the hospital, since no one would undergo (or perform) elective surgery during the holidays.

Zachary gave me a wicked grin. "Close the curtain, aye?"

* * *

All my life, whenever I'd traveled to a cool place like Italy or New York City or California, a part of me thought, "Hmm, I could live here." But then as soon as I'd return to Baltimore and see the long, calm Chesapeake Bay to the east, or the green rolling hills and farmland to the west, I'd feel deep in my gut that Maryland was my home. I belonged here.

This time, flying across those familiar lands, I didn't get that feeling.

Not that I suddenly hated my hometown. Just the opposite—being away reminded me of all the things I loved about Baltimore. The food, the football, the weird and friendly people.

But it was no longer mine. I'd become dislodged, restless, homeless. I felt like a tourist. Every waking moment—and many of the sleeping ones—I felt a pull across the ocean, to Ireland's brilliant green fields and Glasgow's dark, brooding beauty.

It would be provoked by the stupidest things: like the first time I did laundry after I got back, seeing the shirt I'd worn the day I arrived in Ireland. Or when I ate the last of the packaged cookies I'd brought home (and had to hide so Gina wouldn't tell Grandmom).

But I had a job to do, and a story to tell.

Congress held public hearings on what SecuriLab had done in the name of promoting BlackBox. SecuriLab were the "other interests" Simon had referred to, and who Nicola had meant when she'd said someone else was "calling the shots." As the sole manufacturer of BlackBox, they were more powerful than either the US or UK governments. And as Simon had put it, they had "both our countries by the bollocks."

Hence, Flight 346. It was an inside job, but not by any government agency. Ex–Agent Timian's testimony led to the uncovering of a horrifying truth. A Nighthawk masquerading as a baggage handler had slipped the bomb into the suitcase of the British post-Shifter boy, turning him into an unwitting suicide bomber.

The bombing had two missions: ramp up people's fear of ghosts so they'd buy more BlackBox; and kill Ian Moore, who had pissed off the DMP and therefore SecuriLab—and therefore Nighthawk. I had a feeling their desire to eliminate Ian sprang from more than annoyance. Maybe he'd made these connections and had taken his discoveries back to the UK. Top secret spy maneuvers that even Zachary would never discover (not that he would want to).

Flight 346 also provided political will to get a DMP draft passed. Nicola had become a whistleblower, taking evidence to the media that the DMP had been secretly pushing for a draft long before Flight 346. *Now* the agency was on its knees.

In exchange for my testimony, Gina and her top-of-the-line criminal defense attorneys got me pardoned for obstruction of justice in speaking to ex–Tammi Teller, and the passing of information— none of which was illegally obtained—to foreign operatives.

In legal terminology, Aunt Gina saved my ass.

In exchange, I promised to quietly finish high school, stay out of trouble, and never, ever give her fuel for further heart attacks.

In late March—a few days after I turned the shades Malcolm and Mary back to ghosts—I received the e-mail I'd been waiting for.

Gina was still at the office, so I was able to tell Zachary first, just like I'd hoped.

He'd continued seeing his trauma counselor, now adding three new events to their conversations: his time in solitary confinement, his near death at the hands of the Children of the Sun, and his gunshot wound. He swore the nightmares came only once or twice a month now. I could tell from the absence of dark circles under his eyes that he was telling the truth.

But today on our video chat, his smile was strained. Something was wrong.

"Are you okay?" I asked him.

"Aye." He focused on my face. "You said in your text you had good news?"

This would definitely cheer him up. "I thought about forwarding you the e-mail, but I wanted to see your face." I held up the printed-out message from University of Glasgow admissions. "I got accepted! Woo!" I made the page dance in front of the camera.

His smile widened, then faded. "That's fantastic. You've got, what, six acceptances now?"

"Yeah, but this is the only one that matters, right?" I lowered the paper. "Zach, what's wrong? Is it your dad?" Ian's cancer was no closer to remission, but no closer to the final stage, either. Zachary had come to an uneasy acceptance of his father's approaching death, and simply appreciated the time they had left together.

"It's not him. I got something in the post today." He unfolded a white sheet of paper and held it up.

I squinted to see the bald-eagle logo of a US government agency. "The State Department? What do they want?"

He dropped his hands and the letter into his lap. "They say my restrictions have been dropped, since I didn't do anything wrong. I can apply for a student visa now."

The world itself seemed to shift. "You mean, you can come back here? For college? When?"

"As soon as an American university accepts me."

"Wow, it's not that late—you might still be able to apply for fall semester at some of the state schools." I stopped when I realized Zachary didn't seem happy about this development. And honestly, I was disappointed, too. "Don't you want to come here? I thought you liked it."

"I loved America. It's what I wanted for so long, to live there and to be with you. And now I can."

I noticed he used the past tense: *It's what I wanted.* Maybe he didn't want that anymore. Maybe going home made him realize that Scotland was where he belonged, at least for now. The opposite of the way I'd felt returning to America.

"What about your dad? And your mom, doesn't she need your help?"

The corners of his eyes drooped. "Aye, it would be hard, for all of us." He set his hands on the desk and met my gaze. "But Aura, I'll come if you ask."

I shook my head. "I can't ask you—"

"Don't answer now. Take the weekend, or longer, and decide what you want for yourself. Then we'll decide what we want for us."

Us. That entity we'd created, the one that craved a life of its own, the one that could only be nurtured by each of us equally. If Zachary or I—or both—put ourselves before the other, that Us would wither, until we were just another couple who met, fell in love, and grew apart.

We'd be ordinary. And after all we'd been through, all we'd overcome to stay together and alive, we were anything but ordinary.

"I'll think about it," I told him. "But there's something I need to know." I went to my dresser, opened my blue star-shaped keepsake box, and withdrew something that had lain there for almost exactly a year.

I sat before the computer again. "If you can apply for a student visa, you can get a tourist one, right? So you could come for a short visit?"

A slow smile spread across his face. "Aye, I could."

I unfurled the note he'd given me at dinner on our second date, the date that had ended in disaster. I held it up to the camera:

Want to go to the prom? (With me?)

Chapter Forty-Two

*S*olstice *is just a promise. But it's a promise kept. Light always returns. Unlike people.*

My mother was wrong. People do return. My dad did, if only for a while. Even though he hadn't promised.

And I returned to Zachary. Because I promised, and because I wanted to.

A week after graduation, on the summer solstice, it seemed like all my extended family came to Philadelphia International Airport to see me off to Scotland.

Megan and Dylan made the trip up from Baltimore. They were still recovering from Senior Week at Ocean City, where they'd finally admitted that they liked each other. Like, *like*-liked each other. They both swore it was going to be a summer fling and nothing more, that they would amicably break up the day she left for Cornell. I was skeptical.

At the security gate, Megan hugged me so hard I thought my eyeballs would pop out of my skull.

"When we visit in August," she said, "you better have your usual kick-ass summer tan. Scotland better not deprive you of your natural hotness."

Dylan gave me a less lung-crushing embrace, then handed me a manila envelope. "This is for you to read on the plane. Or at the snack bar at the gate, whatever."

I peeked inside the envelope, and the black spiral notebook I saw made my heart plummet.

Logan's *Fame Journal, Volume 1.* The thoughts he'd started writing the night before he died. Dylan had let me read it last May, right before we made out on his floor.

"Um, thanks?"

"I know, you're thinking, world's most inappropriate parting gift. But you haven't read all of it."

His words confused me, but that was nothing new.

Gina touched my shoulder. "Hon, you better go through security now." Her eyes were wet, and when she blinked, they overflowed. "I'm sorry." She wiped her face. "Was that the tenth or eleven thousandth tear I've cried over this?"

"Eleven millionth," I said, hugging her.

"I feel like I've barely started." She rocked me back and forth. "You know I am proud of you, right? You've been so brave. I'm even proud of you for leaving."

"Why?"

"Because you're never afraid to explore."

I hugged her tighter, holding back my confession that I *was* afraid. Afraid I'd get lost in a new city, afraid I'd fail all my classes, afraid I'd never learn to speak Scots. Afraid to look like an American idiot.

But not afraid enough to keep me from going.

"Thank you. I better hurry up and hug everyone else. There's a ton of them."

I went down the line, embracing cousins and aunts and uncles and in-laws, some I barely recognized. Grandmom tried to stuff more cookies into my carry-on.

With one final squeeze for Gina, I was off.

On the other side of the security gate, my dinner destination was obvious. Though Zachary had told me there was a Philly cheesesteak place in Glasgow's West End, I had to get one last experience of the real thing.

I settled into the food-court booth with my meal, then opened Logan's notebook.

There was a new entry, in Dylan's handwriting, from a year ago:

June 22

Hey, Aura. It's Logan. I know you probably wondered what the hell I've been doing these last two days since the concert. Friday night and Saturday I cruised around Dublin, then Disney World, then Ocean City.

Sunday, today, I went back to the room I died in. Kinda freaked out the girl

living there now. But she was nice enough
to call Dylan for me so we could hang
out for a few hours, and he could write
this down for me.

Anyway, before I find you and pass
on, I'm hoping to track down Bagpipes—I
mean, Zachary, ha!—at the airport. You'll
probably kiss him good-bye a disgusting
amount, so he'll be able to see me. I
want to ask him a favor: If he ever
gets to Ireland, with or without you, to
tie a bright blue shoelace, like the ones
from my Vans, on the faerie tree at
the Hill of Tara. (I wanted my ashes
scattered there, remember? But Mom
and Dad wouldn't let me.)

So if you see him do it, he probably
won't tell you why, and he won't tell you
the wish he's making while he does it. I'll
ask him to keep it between us guys.

Aw, screw it, maybe he can keep a
secret, but I can't. I'm gonna ask him
to wish this: "Let Aura find peace, but
not the boring, heavenly kind of peace
that I have now. Let her have the
crazy, burning peace that comes from
following her heart."

Or some less cheesy version of that.
Man, Oylan writes way too slow! Time
for me to go now and find That Guy, then
you. See you soon.
I love you,
Logan

I closed the notebook, first pressing the pages hard together, then pulling it close to my chest, my eyes squeezed shut.

"Thank you, Logan," I whispered, not caring if anyone saw me speaking to the air. "Nowhere you are could ever be boring."

Later, sitting at my flight's gate, I played "Yank or Brit" in my head, wondering how people would peg me in six months when Zachary and I flew back to the States for winter break.

Thick puffy rain clouds rolled in. I sighed, hoping our flight wouldn't be delayed by a storm or hit turbulence—not after I'd eaten that huge cheesesteak.

With the evening sun obscured, the terminal darkened enough to see a handful of ghosts wandering around. Across from me, a thirty-something mother of two watched her young son giggle and squeal at the antics of an unusually friendly ghost. I couldn't hear what the spirit was saying, but from her posture and tone of voice, during her life she'd been either a kindergarten teacher or a birthday-party clown.

As the ghost led the little boy in a clapping song, I looked at his baby sister sitting on their mom's lap. I expected her little face to fill with rapture. Infants generally love ghosts, until they're taught they're supposed to be afraid.

But the baby watched only her brother as he stomped and clapped in time to the ghost's tune. Then the little girl's gaze skimmed over the ghost and on to the passenger sitting across from her, an elderly woman in a bright pink polka-dotted dress.

The ghost moved closer to the baby and tried to get her attention, to no avail. She cooed at the Polka Dot Lady, who waved and smiled back.

Clearly perplexed, the ghost stood directly in front of the infant. "And what's your name, princess?"

The little boy giggled. "Her name's Angela, but she can't see you, silly!" He covered his mouth, then kicked up his left foot. "My shoe has a red light, like fire trucks!"

Baby Angela stared straight through the ghost.

"Oh my God." I shut my mouth and checked to see if anyone had heard.

"It's true," said a voice beside me. I turned to see a girl about my age. Her faded blue T-shirt had a white logo, INTERNATIONAL SCOTTISH DANCING COMPETITION, with last year's date.

"What's true?" I asked her.

"I work at a day care center in Upper Darby after school. They don't have BlackBox there except in the bathrooms, so ghosts come around all the time." She leaned closer. "None of the babies six months or younger can see ghosts. Isn't that wild?"

"Six months?" My face flushed, and I clasped my hands in my lap to hide their sudden trembling. It'd been six months since the winter solstice. Six months since Zachary and I had stood inside Newgrange and watched the sun turn red, black, violet, and white.

"It's totally bizarre," the girl said.

"Have you told anyone?"

She shook her head. "I only noticed last week. I was kinda afraid to tell anyone in case they thought I was insane."

"Why are you telling me?"

Her brow creased. "You're Aura, right? You stopped the draft?"

"Kinda." After the revelations I'd unearthed, Congress had repealed the DMP selective service program. I still couldn't get used to being recognized by random strangers, even though it happened only once every few weeks. "Not by myself."

She shrugged. "Whatever. I've been dying to tell someone, so it might as well be you."

The airline agent spoke into the microphone, calling the first zone to board the plane. The girl beside me picked up her bag.

"I'm in the last row, next to the bathroom. This is gonna suck so bad."

I felt like I should shake her hand or hug her. Instead I just said, "Good luck at this year's competition."

She looked down at her T-shirt, then up at me, pleased. "Thanks! Good luck with your boyfriend. I've seen pictures. He's made of hot."

"I know. I mean, thanks."

She laughed as she dragged her carry-on away, and I realized I hadn't even gotten her name.

I barely slept on the overnight flight, and not just because this time I was flying coach instead of first class. The dancer's words and the image of that oblivious baby and the frustrated ghost pinged around my brain.

We'd done it. Zachary and I had ended the Shift by being at Newgrange at winter solstice sunrise. We'd ended it the way his dad and my mom had started it nineteen years before.

We'd ended it not as we'd expected and hoped—by causing all the ghosts to suddenly disappear. But in a new way. No one born now would *ever* see ghosts, while the rest of us post-Shifters still would, probably for the rest of our lives.

Solstice magic had happened again. Our magic.

Because I am weird, I worried Zachary would greet me in Glasgow with a bouquet of red roses with no yellow. Of course I wanted him to love me now and forever with an insatiable, mind-blowing, sheet-melting passion, the way I loved him.

But I wanted to be his friend, too. Now and forever.

So when I saw him at the airport meeting point and he was holding a bouquet of red roses with one bright yellow rose at its center . . .

I knew I was home. For good.

"Aura." Zachary swept me into his arms, which felt stronger than ever. And when we kissed, I remembered every moment together—at the castle, at the Warrenpoint hotel. Even my prom night, when yeah, he wore the kilt.

He carefully set me on my feet, then took my suitcase handle. "I've arranged for a sunny day, but we should hurry. It'll be gone in an hour. Of course, it'll be back again another hour after that. And so on."

I laughed as I took the flowers, having heard of the famous four-seasons-in-one-day nature of Glaswegian weather. "At least it'll be light for more than twenty minutes now, right?"

"It's only light until about midnight." When I blanched, he kissed me again and said, "Don't worry, we've blackout curtains in our bedroom so ye can sleep."

Our bedroom. The words sent a tingle down my spine. As a foreign student I would've had to pay for room and board, so Zachary and I had decided to get our own apartment. It was close to school and only a five-minute bus ride to his house, so he could visit his parents every day and help his dad. When classes started in the fall, we'd be sharing the apartment with two other students, but for the summer, it was all ours.

I couldn't wait to get there.

"Can we pick up something to celebrate with?" I asked him as we went outside into the warm but delightfully non-oppressive summer air.

"What are we celebrating, besides the rest of our lives?"

I'd planned to wait until we were alone at home to tell him about the end of the Shift, of how we'd done the impossible once again. Of all the magic and mysteries that lay ahead of us, hiding in dark places in the earth and sky, even as we lived in the light.

But I couldn't wait. Not one more minute. I stopped and set the roses atop my carry-on.

Zachary's eyes danced with wonder and anticipation. "Well, what is it?"

I stepped into his arms, under the glow of the high northern sun. "I have good news."

Author's Note

After three years studying the astounding ancient megaliths of Ireland, I felt it important to keep the details of Newgrange, Dowth, and the Hill of Tara true to life, even when it was inconvenient. In the places I've changed the layout, such as the basin's being in the wrong chamber at Dowth, Aura notes it as such.

The legends of the Tuatha dé Danann are real, but as far as I know, no cult like the Children of the Sun exists. But it seems like it should.

The Glasgow church-turned-pub where Martin works is the Òran Mór, Scottish Gaelic for "big song" or "great melody of life." In reality it's exactly as described in the book (though memory may have failed me on a few very minor details). The upstairs auditorium isn't open to the public, but the pub itself is marvelous. If you go, do try the full Scottish breakfast, and tell Siobhan I said hi.

Acknowledgments

The story of *Shine* could've taken many different paths. Many thanks to my beta readers and critique partners for helping me find the right one: Rob Staeger, Cecilia Ready, Patrice Michelle, and Deborah Blake. Special thanks to authors Frankie Diane Mallis and Christine Johnson, who read multiple drafts and should be canonized for it; to Sya Bruce, who helped Zach and his friends become better Scots; to author Kate Milford, who came up with the MI-X motto; and to Melissa Hermann, who did my online fact-checking so I wouldn't get distracted for hours by the shiny Internetz.

Music is the perpetual savior of my sanity. In this book, Glasgow indie band Frightened Rabbit was there for me in the darkest moments, when I thought it would never work. Every day was better for their being a part of it. Cheers, lads.

Thanks to Clare Tuffy and Sharon Downey from Ireland's Office of Public Works, and especially our Newgrange guide, Sinead Morrison, for answering my rather odd what-if questions. Thanks to Fraser McFarlane, our splendid Glasgow tour guide, and his wife,

Heather Harris McFarlane. We *will* return for Kiltwalk 2013—see, it's here in writing!

Thanks to the fine folks at Simon Pulse for their tireless work and endless enthusiasm for the Shade trilogy: Bethany Buck, Mara Anastas, Jennifer Klonsky, Guillian Helm, Jessica Handelman, Russell Gordon, Katherine Devendorf, Anna McKean, Paul Crichton, Lucille Rettino, Carolyn Swerdloff, Dawn Ryan, Valerie Shea, Adam Smith, Kaitlin Severini, Christina Solazzo, and Lauren Forte; thank you to photographer Monica Stevenson for the beautiful new covers; plus a shout north of the border to Michelle Blackwell, and across the pond to Kathryn McKenna and Gail Hallett.

Mentioning my agent and editor in acknowledgments is a bit like signing a Christmas card to my mom. How do I say "AAAAHHHH I LOVE YOU SO MUCH! YOU ROCK!!1!!1! in a new and creative way? To Ginger Clark and Annette Pollert—there are no words to describe the support and caring you've shown in bringing *Shine* to its final form. Maybe next time I'll find the words.

And because I promised, but not *just* because I promised, millions of thanks to the readers who make up Team Kilt, especially founders Jennifer Strand and Amy Oelkers, who built and run the Shade series fan site KiltandKeeley.com; and "executive officer" Karen Alderman. These three wonderful ladies also read *Shine* in its last stage, when I was most paranoid about it.

So in no particular order, the magnificent Team Kilt ("NFF!"): Melissa Fonseca, Jennifer Duffey, Brooke "Team Logan's Empress" Goldetsky, Christie Taylor, Christine Danek, Tabitha Williams, Alicia Ester, Annette Stone, Susan Jakubowski, Anna Heinemann,

Jen Stewart, Melissa Garner Mitchell, Jessica Corra, Julie Jones, Jackie Burris, Tracy Hudson, Heather Burke, Nerissa Luna, Cyndi Martin, Cyndi Tefft, Deanne Dekle, Brittany Howard, Sandra Werbunat, Christy Bennett, Ashe Terry, Heather Elia, Pavlina, Kelly Lyman, Nicole Baldwin, Mel Boulrice, Courtney M. Heitman, Yiling Ni, Emily Pazienza, Kimberly Callegan, Julianna Helms, Deena Graves, Alyssa Anne, Ginger at GReads, Miri Epstein, Megan Kyser, Lindsey Redding, Somer, Tara Gonzalez, Ana L. Arroyave, Melissa Layton, Sarah Hardie, Jen Watson, Jena M. Freeth, Christy Khamphilay, Ashley Morrison, Dayna Pearce, Ida "TeamKilt's Crazymember" Bosita, Jaime Arnold, Kimberly Brasher, Brandi Gardner, Ashly Ferguson, Bailey Hewitt, Michele Blanchard, Kris Viers Armstead, Zeinab Zmurrod, Tabitha Qualls, Carli Bandeira, Lisa Sperry, Leilani Lopez, Becky Boyer, Lindsay Cox, Gabriella Turner, Christina Escalante, Meghan Raine, Heather Harris McFarlane, Fraser McFarlane, Michelle Molenderas Santiago, Mary Quiggle-Pickering, Megan Zaiser, Suzanne Rauch, Rachel Isom, Jessica Arb, Diana Chao, Johanna Reinberger, Raychelle Smith, Michelle Nadeau, Jessica Woodward, Bailey Purvis, Renee Combs, Ashley Lauren, Lucy D. Briand, Tara at Fiction Folio, Erin Stout, Cegluna, Kristin P. Jones, Heather Rosdol, Louisse Ang, Jessica Ware, Tori Reul, Stacey Canova, Amanda Wolfbauer, Panagiota Kalogeroudis, Ashley Nicole McKinsey, Patricia Mendoza, Aeriell Choquette, Tristan Bruce, JoAnne The Fairytale Nerd, Cassandra Pendino, Lisa Hoag, Daisy de Bruin, Scott Romanski, Jacinda and Jasmine at The Reading Housewives, Heidi Stegmann, Lynn Marie Spinks, Tamara Bašić,

Amy Stewart, Samantha Stoner, Bethany Larson, Christine Ko, Angela at Reading Angel, Edesa Y., Claire Wong, Melanie Stang, Marissa Odom, Lynsey Newton, Ariel Boeger, Barbara Walker, Samantha Heck, Shell Bryce, Jana Oliver, Jenn Martin, JoAnne Claudio, Kat Chamsay, Meredith from Mint Tea and a Good Book, Kelsey Jones, Rachel Clark, Nikki Oldenburg, Amy Pittel, Miss Jessica S., Frankie Diane Mallis, Shannon Condie, Sarah Mäkelä, Paola Martinez Parente, Jen Kovacs, Maria Laura Alvarez, Smash Attack, Nikki Ulmer, Lauren Goff, Wen Yan, Kendra McCormick, Janae Haygood, Laura Young, Michelle Coffey, Wendy Adams, Misty Evans, Artemis Gray, Paris Hansen, Bobby-Jo Boxall, Rachel Patrick, Jennifer Sanders, Kasey Hilyard, Suzanne Waligora, Tina Ljujic, Britney Wyatt, Beth Hickey, Jazmin Naomi Labrada, Lindsi Coleman, John F. Gardner, Sharon Mostyn, Lona Queen, Caroline Kimsey, Kara Lang Guminski, Casse Narome, Melissa Gibson, Grace Smith, Kailia Sage, and Kasey Paradis.

Last but not least, thanks to my family for their infinite understanding (at least I hope it's infinite) while these books take over my life. And most of all, thanks to my husband, Christian, for his love and patience, and for following my many whims around Ireland and Glasgow (different enough for you?).

About the Author

JERI SMITH-READY is an award-winning author who lives in Maryland with her husband, two cats, and the world's goofiest greyhound.

Like many of her characters, Jeri loves music, movies, and staying up very, very late. Visit her at jerismithready.com or follow her on Twitter at @jsmithready.